PRAISE

"With her trademark wit and warmth, Sheila Roberts delivers a story nestled inside a story, a novel of pure delight!"
—*Patti Callahan Henry,* New York Times **bestselling author of** The Secret Book of Flora Lea

"Perfectly composed, sweetly satisfying . . . Roberts deftly chronicles, with just the right mix of love and laughter, the search for happiness, artistic and romantic, by three generations of endearing women."
—*Kirkus Reviews* on *Mermaid Beach*

"A masterful blend of comedic timing with characters you believe in and want good things for . . . A wonderful summer read for anyone who wants to enjoy a well told story."
—*Midwest Book Review* on *Sand Dollar Lane*

"Small-town politics, meddling townsfolk, and gossip with a mean-girl vibe keep things upbeat in an irresistible story that will have readers wondering until the conclusion."
—*Library Journal* on *The Summer Retreat*

"The plot takes several unexpected twists and turns on its way to a delightful ending."
—*Fresh Fiction* on *Welcome to Moonlight Harbor*

Also by Sheila Roberts

STAND-ALONE NOVELS

The Merry Matchmaker

The Best Life Book Club

The Twelve Months of Christmas

Christmas from the Heart

One Charmed Christmas

A Little Christmas Spirit

The Road to Christmas

Three Christmas Wishes

MOONLIGHT HARBOR

Welcome to Moonlight Harbor

Winter at the Beach

The Summer Retreat

Beachside Beginnings

Sunset on Moonlight Beach

Sand Dollar Lane

Mermaid Beach

ICICLE FALLS

Christmas in Icicle Falls

Starting Over on Blackberry Lane

Home on Apple Blossom Road

Christmas on Candy Cane Lane

A Wedding on Primrose Street

The Lodge on Holly Road

The Tea Shop on Lavender Lane

The Cottage on Juniper Ridge

What She Wants (also published as *Romance on Mountain View Road*)

Merry Ex-Mas

Better Than Chocolate (also published as *Sweet Dreams on Center Street*)

The Man Next Door

SHEILA ROBERTS

/I/MIRA

MIRA

ISBN-13: 978-0-7783-6028-5

The Man Next Door

Copyright © 2025 by Roberts Ink LLC

All rights reserved. No part of this book may be used or reproduced in any manner whatsoever without written permission.

Without limiting the exclusive rights of any author, contributor or the publisher of this publication, any unauthorized use of this publication to train generative artificial intelligence (AI) technologies is expressly prohibited. Harlequin also exercises their rights under Article 4(3) of the Digital Single Market Directive 2019/790 and expressly reserves this publication from the text and data mining exception.

This is a work of fiction. Names, characters, places and incidents are either the product of the author's imagination or are used fictitiously. Any resemblance to actual persons, living or dead, businesses, companies, events or locales is entirely coincidental.

For questions and comments about the quality of this book, please contact us at CustomerService@Harlequin.com.

TM is a trademark of Harlequin Enterprises ULC.

MIRA
22 Adelaide St. West, 41st Floor
Toronto, Ontario M5H 4E3, Canada
MIRABooks.com

HarperCollins Publishers
Macken House, 39/40
Mayor Street Upper,
Dublin 1, D01 C9W8, Ireland
www.HarperCollins.com

Recycling programs for this product may not exist in your area.

Printed in U.S.A.

For Nancy

The Man Next Door

The House

THE HOUSE ON GLENWOOD AVENUE HAD taken on an air of darkness. Not simply because the last owners had painted its stucco exterior dark gray and trimmed it with black, although that hadn't helped. It was what had happened inside the house even before they moved in. A house that once leaked laughter and friendliness turned sullen and silent.

And sinister. Louise Hartman, who lived next door, had been the first to spot it. The single man rarely let his grandmother out, and he never let anyone in, no matter how many cookies they came with. He was the only unsociable person on the whole street. Louise had known early on that he was hiding secrets.

But there were things you couldn't hide from people who paid attention. And Louise paid attention. The curtains were always drawn, and the grandson rarely left the house. Neither did the old woman who had arrived with him, not even to care for the roses, which were starting to wither from lack of attention. Lawn service had been stopped and weeds were popping up everywhere. *Neglect!* cried the house. Often old cars with nefarious-looking drivers showed up after dark. Drug dealing, for sure, Louise thought. The place sent off keep-away vibes and the neighbors all did. Including Louise. A woman living alone had to be careful.

One day the old woman in the house next door got out. Louise had been checking her mail and saw the poor soul. She was a wraith, wearing dirty pajama bottoms and an equally dirty oversized T-shirt. Her hair hung in greasy, gray strands, and when Louise hurried over to say hello, she saw the woman had bruises on her arms. Yes, older people had thin skin, and they tended to bruise easily, but this woman had too many to have just bumped against a counter. When Louise asked about them, the woman had looked mildly puzzled for a moment, then replied that little Sammy was strong.

Louise had seen *little* Sammy. He was a mammoth. And obviously brutal. Louise had called the authorities, and it wasn't long before Sammy was no longer around, and neither was the old woman. According to the rumor mill, a relative had stepped in and moved her across the country and put the house up for sale.

Then had come the forty-something couple, who had decided a new look was in order and turned the house dark on the outside to unknowingly match what had happened on the inside. They both worked but still had time for an occasional chat by the mailbox. They had one daughter, married, about to give birth to the first grandchild. Louise had hoped they would bring back the happiness that had lived in the house when her daughter Zona was growing up and laughing children had run back and forth between the two homes.

But tragedy struck only a few months later. The wife died suddenly. Got sick, was all her husband would share. No one knew with what. The funeral was small and private, the wife cremated, and the man gone almost instantly. The house went on the market again, now under a miasma determined to cling to it. It huddled, waiting, like the neighbors, to see what would happen next. Potential buyers came and looked at it, but it remained empty.

That was hardly surprising. The place almost moaned, haunted by its past. Louise could feel . . . a presence hovering over there, peering over the property line, whenever she went up her own front walk.

Her daughter insisted she was imagining things. A house was just a house. It didn't have a life of its own. And no, Zona hadn't felt any creepy vibes since she'd moved in with Louise. Of course, Zona was dealing with so much in her own life she probably wouldn't recognize a creepy vibe even if it came up to her and rattled her bones.

Could a house absorb the emotions of the people who lived in it? Did bad vibes linger long after those people had moved out? Once infected, did that house become a magnet for more of the same?

Louise shivered as she watched the Realtor put a sold sign on the front lawn. Maybe the new owners would dispel the gloom. Maybe she would no longer pick up her pace every time she walked past the place.

But what if this unsettled feeling she was getting was a premonition?

1

LUCK HAD NOT BEEN A LADY to Zona Hartman's ex and now luck was really out to get Zona.

And here was her friend and real estate agent, Gracie, using the nasty L word. "It was a real stroke of luck that your buyer waived the inspection and came through with such a high bid. And cash. It really sped up the process," she enthused as they sampled the champagne she'd ordered for them.

Luck. A certain word that rhymed with it came to mind.
Don't say it.
Zona didn't. She may have lost everything she owned, but she still had her dignity. Instead, she set down her glass and scowled. "Let's not use that word."

June was brand-new and it was a beautiful sunny day, like most days in Southern California. Gracie was treating Zona to lunch at Luca Bella, a high-end restaurant in Glendora, not far from Azusa where Zona lived.

Correction: had lived. Someone else would be living in Zona's four-bedroom Spanish revival home in Rosedale with its view of the mountains and the city lights, the outdoor barbecue and the orange tree in the backyard, and the large kitchen she'd planned on updating with new appliances but now never would.

Someone else was also driving the Tesla Gary had bought for her. That had been replaced with a fifteen-year-old Toyota.

Gracie blushed.

Way to go. Make your friend who sold your house feel bad. What had happened to Zona wasn't Gracie's fault.

"I sound like a bitter ingrate. Sorry," Zona said.

"No, I'm sorry. That was thoughtless of me."

"But you're right. I'm glad I got such a good offer and that the deal went through so fast. I need to be grateful for that. I just wish I was able to keep some of the money."

"Gary is an overflowing septic tank of a human," Gracie said, frowning.

"Yes, he is."

He didn't look like one. Gary looked like the quintessential nice guy, complete with a broad smile that reached all the way to those baby blue eyes that he hid behind glasses with trendy frames. Those glasses gave the illusion that he was smart. It turned out he wasn't as smart as she'd once thought.

"And he didn't deserve you."

"No, he didn't."

He had started out as a wonderful husband. So encouraging, so fun, so sweet, so good at handling their money. He was a solid businessman, dedicated husband and father. In those early years there was money growing in the bank accounts. They discussed what they wanted to spend that money on and they enjoyed spending it. Those dollars were always where they were supposed to be.

Until he'd taken a sledgehammer to both their finances and her trust.

"At least you're out of debt now," said Gracie.

Thanks to the sky-high value of California real estate. Although when you had a second mortgage on your house and debt coming out of your ears, you didn't exactly walk away from a sale with a profit. Zona may have been out of debt technically speaking, but she owed her daughter big-time thanks to the mess Gary had created. And Zona was completely broke.

"I appreciate you helping me get through this," she said.

Gracie had been a good friend, providing a listening ear and therapeutic doses of chocolate on a regular basis as Zona processed her husband's financial infidelity, cried through their divorce, and tried to be strong as the house she'd pretty much raised her daughter in went up for sale. Gracie's life was like a Jane Austen novel, with everything turning out as it should. Good husband, two great kids, successful real estate career. Jane would have approved.

Zona's life, on the other hand, had been more Dickens than Austen. It was the best of times, it was the worst of times. One of the best being when she'd met her first husband, Luke. When she'd had her daughter Bree. Then came the worst when she found out Luke had been cheating on her while she was pregnant. Then came divorce number one and the struggles of being a single parent. More worst times when her gift shop went under. But then came . . . the best: Gary, the solid businessman who wined and dined her, who loved her daughter. They bought their dream house, Zona got a secure job with the department of licensing, issuing drivers licenses—boring but steady work. Double income, dinners out. Yep, best of times. Then halfway down the yellow brick road, Gary developed this problem. Which eventually turned into epic disaster. And now it was the worst of times again.

Zona was divorced and flat broke. Nothing in savings, the nest egg broken and scrambled, Bree's money for nursing school gone. And Zona's share of the profits from the house sale would all go to pay off the last few stones from the mountain of debt that Gary's gambling addiction and financial infidelity had built. His debts had become her debts. Community property was a rip.

"Sometimes I still can't believe this happened," she said. "Gary seemed so solid. I thought we were solid. I thought our life was solid."

Gracie shrugged. "Some people hide who they really are.

Or they have, I don't know, a little crack in their foundation, and with time, if they don't do anything, the crack gets bigger."

"Gary was definitely cracked," Zona said.

It made her grind her teeth every time she thought about what had happened to them. If only she'd caught those early warning signs that Gary's gambling hobby was becoming an addiction. But she hadn't. He'd hidden it, like pornography.

Then came the day she went to make a deposit to the savings set aside for Bree's nursing school and discovered it had been drained. And that was only the beginning.

"I was going to put it back," Gary had insisted as if he actually had a plan, as if he could be trusted ever again.

"I swear, if I could have gotten away with it—" Zona began.

"Aack! Don't finish that sentence," said Gracie. "I know where you're going."

Zona frowned. "I'm just fantasizing here."

Anyway, murder was too good for Gary. He should have to suffer. Work on a chain gang in the blazing sun with no water to drink. Nobody did chain gangs anymore. Too cruel. But how cruel was it to ruin your family's finances and your marriage? To steal your stepdaughter's future?

"Stick to romance novel fantasizing," Gracie advised.

"That's probably what got me in trouble in the first place," Zona muttered. "I'm never reading another romance novel again, and there's nothing com about rom."

Gracie shrugged. "Don't blame fiction. Your problem was with real life. Your mom brainwashed you. She had you convinced that every man was like your dad."

"Yours is," Zona pointed out.

"I got lucky."

"Aaargh, that word again."

"Sorry," said Gracie, and tucked a strand of blond hair behind her ear.

Thanks to her new budget, Zona's once blond 'do had gone

from trendy shadow roots to desperate for sunlight. Total disaster. Like her life.

She frowned at the salad remaining on her plate. "How could I have been so oblivious to what was going on?" It wasn't the first time she'd asked it. Probably wouldn't be the last. It was a song on constant replay.

"Because at first it was too small to take any notice of. Like when something's going wrong with your insides, but you can't see it until your intestines explode."

That effectively killed whatever appetite Zona had left. She shoved away her plate.

"And you trusted him," said Gracie.

"He'd been trustworthy. Once. Before . . ." Her hand fisted, strangling her napkin. "All those times he needed to take extra money from savings for the business. Needed to stock new appliances in the store or get new office equipment. Had to cover for a supplier. Instead, he was covering for himself." Discovering his raid on the college money opened a financial Pandora's box filled with credit card advances and payday loans. He'd even used up the line of credit on the house, which had been reserved for that upcoming kitchen remodel that never happened.

If she'd only known what lay ahead, she wouldn't have signed off on that HELOC when he'd first suggested it. "We probably won't even use it," he'd said when she worried about adding that to the second mortgage they'd taken out three years earlier to expand the business. "But better safe than sorry." She wound up unsafe and very sorry.

"Gambling is like any addiction. It takes over and you end up doing things you would never have done if you weren't hooked," said Gracie.

"That last huge withdrawal. I didn't know until it was too late." Zona sighed. She would have sobbed, but she was too emotionally exhausted.

"I know. But you're rid of him now. You can make a new start."

"Back to square one," Zona said bitterly, examining her chipped nail polish.

She was lousy at giving herself manicures. But she'd have to get better. Visits to the nail salon were now a thing of the past.

She'd had money in her account after the house sale for about two breaths and now, two years after discovering Gary's betrayal, all she had left after two marriages was her dishes, her clothes, and her "new" Toyota with a hundred and fifty thousand miles on it. And her Wolfgang Puck pots and pans, ghosts left from better times. She'd sold her furniture. All except Grandma's brass bed, which had been in the guest room. Which maybe someday she'd use if she ever in her lifetime could afford a house again. She didn't need the California king she and Gary had slept in anymore. She had no one to share it with. All she had was plenty of nothing thanks to Gary. The human septic tank.

"At least you've got a roof over your head," Gracie pointed out.

"Who moves in with her mom at forty-two?"

"Someone who needs to get money back in her bank account. You'll be okay. It's a place to live, and you've still got a job."

And she had her freedom. Gary would probably keep circling the drain, but he wouldn't be taking her any further down with him.

"It could be worse," Gracie finished. "It can always be worse."

"Don't even say that," said Zona.

"Nothing more is going to happen," Gracie assured her.

And then the building began to shake.

LOUISE WAS CHATTING online with one of the men who would be going on her singles cruise when she felt the movement under her. At first, she thought she felt unbalanced because of an oncoming migraine. Or was she having a stroke?

But then she knew, it was the earth under her that was unbalanced. This was why her fur baby, Darling, had been whining all morning. And here she'd thought he just wanted more attention. Darling's doggy senses had picked up on the quake long before Louise had become aware of it.

With a squeak, she pushed her chair away from her kitchen table. "Run, Darling," she cried, and raced into the hallway with her dog by her side. The unsteady floor beneath her shifted and jiggled like a county fair fun house, making it a challenge to keep her balance. It was a good thing she did yoga.

She slid to her bottom, pressed herself against a wall, and hugged Darling, who whimpered and licked her face. People were always saying you should hide under a desk or table, but the idea of her kitchen table collapsing on top of her freaked her out.

She heard a crash coming from the living room, a sure sign that her fancy glass lamp had fallen over. "Oh, Lord, don't let me die," she prayed as Darling whined. "I'm wearing my old underwear."

Another moment and the shaking settled down and she let out her breath. Darling gave another doggy whimper.

"It's okay," she assured him. "We're fine." Just another day in paradise.

Louise hadn't always been a California girl. She'd gotten married and become an import from Central Florida's Lake County. That was years ago, but she'd never gotten used to earthquakes. They were so . . . unsettling. Things had never gotten too unsettled in Glendora, but reading about the damage those quakes did to other parts of the state, the lives they claimed, had embedded fear at the back of her brain.

Harold, when he was alive, used to remind her often that there was no such thing as a safe place to live. Something or someone would get you anywhere. She supposed he was right.

She waited for the aftershock. It came a few minutes later as only a slight jiggle, like a giant somewhere was simply turning over in bed. It looked like it hadn't been a big enough quake for anything more, for which she was thankful.

"We're okay now," she assured her dog and herself, and Darling barked his agreement and licked her face again.

She texted both her daughter and her granddaughter to make sure nothing had fallen on them.

OK no worries, Bree texted.

I'm fine, texted Zona a minute later. You okay?

Yes but bring home wine, Louise texted back.

They would need more Gewürztraminer by dinner because Louise intended to drink what was left in that bottle in the fridge ASAP.

She had just finished vacuuming up the last tiny shards of her broken lamp when her doorbell rang. She wasn't surprised to find Martin Zuckerman on her doorstep. "I came over to see if you were okay," he said, attempting to pet Darling, who was excited to see him, jumping on him and trying to lick him. Darling had a lot of poodle in him and he could almost jump high enough to reach Martin's face.

Martin had moved in two houses down four years earlier. They'd met at a neighborhood garage sale and, both bookworms, had bonded over a selection of books, on sale for fifty cents each. He'd been single for years and was sixty-nine now, one year older than Louise. But, unlike Louise, who considered herself still in her prime—no aches, no pains, only a little overweight but in almost all the right places, and no gray hair (visible, anyway)—Martin looked his age. He was tall and had a nice smile, but he had a belly that refused to be corralled by a belt. He was getting jowly, and his hair was quickly sneaking off his head. Not exactly the stuff dreams were made of.

Not that Louise was a snob when it came to a man's looks, but she did have dreams. She was going to find herself a stud muffin to skip into her golden years with. Maybe she'd find him on her upcoming Hawaii cruise. She had prospects.

Still, even though Martin wasn't the most handsome man in town, he had to be one of the kindest, and she enjoyed his friendship. He was always happy to share his latest mystery novel find or help her with her tax returns. Martin was a retired accountant, and he knew his stuff.

"Come on in, I'm about to finish off the wine. Would you care to join me?"

"It's a little early for me," he said as he stepped inside.

"Well, it's not for me, not after that shaking. It's five o'clock somewhere and it's earthquake o'clock right here. I've been here over forty years, but I swear, I'll never get used to them," Louise said as she led the way into the kitchen, her dog beside her.

"I've lived in California all my life and I'm still here. I bet we'll both survive another forty years," Martin assured her.

Considering Martin's current physical condition, she wasn't sure he'd make it another twenty. If they were in a serious relationship, she'd be whipping him into shape in a hurry.

He picked her laptop off the floor where it had fallen, then settled at the table.

"I hope my laptop didn't get broken," she said, and opened it to check. She was relieved to see that it was still working.

"Were you starting your mystery novel?"

"No." She closed the laptop.

He frowned. "Oh, you're getting ready for your singles cruise?"

The scorn in his voice irritated her. She'd mentioned the cruise when she first signed up and suggested he come along, too, and he'd pooh-poohed it. He was still pooh-poohing.

"I'm already meeting some nice people," she said. She dumped some shelled pistachios in a bowl and set them in front of him and he dug in without hesitation. Then she gave

Darling a doggy treat so he wouldn't feel left out. After surviving that unnerving shakeup, everyone deserved a treat.

"I'm sure you have, but you have to be careful, Louise," Martin cautioned. "You're too trusting. Remember that con artist Bree saved you from at Christmas?"

"Anyone could have been taken in by him," Louise insisted. She poured the last of the wine into a glass and took a healthy slug. First the earthquake and now Martin the doomsayer. And her day had been going so well.

He shook his head. "An American working in Turkey, all ready to come home and meet you until someone broke into his truck and stole all his tools, and he just needed a little loan until he could sort things out?"

In hindsight, Louise could clearly see how the creep had slowly wooed her, feeding her lies like a little piggy being fattened for a trip to the slaughterhouse.

"I'd already come to the conclusion that it was a scam," she said. Or at least had been getting suspicious. So there. "And I didn't send him anything," she added.

"I remember you were considering it."

"I was not," she insisted. "And a singles cruise isn't the same as an online scam."

"It could be," he insisted right back. "There could be all kinds of fakers on that ship. People lie."

She thought of her daughter's ex-husband. "Yes, they do."

Had Gary been a liar when Zona first met him? Or had his gambling addiction hatched the behavior?

Poor Zona. She was so pretty, with her father's green eyes and that perfect figure and a bottom that still had plenty of curve (unlike Louise, whose caboose was starting to slide off the track). She was kind and hardworking and she deserved much better real estate in Love Land than she'd been allotted. She needed a good man, one like Harold had been.

Louise was keeping her eyes peeled for one, and she thought

she may have found one in her new neighbor to the left. Thank God, Louise's earlier premonition about the new owner of the house next door had proved wrong. Alec James was tall and sandy-haired with deep-set hazel eyes. He was muscly, with a strong jaw and a neck like a bull. She'd seen the *Better Builders* logo on the side of his truck. Obviously a nice, solid man with a nice, solid job. Hopefully a nice, solid bank account. Zona didn't need any more insecurity in the finance department.

Louise had stopped to say hello when she was walking Darling only a couple of days earlier. He hadn't been very talkative, but then it was hard to carry on a conversation when you were holding one end of a leather sofa. And the man helping him had sported a jovial smile. That had been a good sign, because everyone knew that happy people hung out with other happy people.

They'd only gotten as far as a quick name exchange and a "Welcome to the neighborhood," as he and his friend walked the couch from the moving van up the walkway to his front door, and that had been it. But she'd had a good feeling about him. He was going to bring good vibes to the house and their street.

Sadly, the man had moved in on a Friday, and Zona had missed meeting him. But Louise was sure it wouldn't be long before they had their own meet-cute.

Maybe it was serendipity that Zona would be living with Louise while she got her feet back under her. The man next door could prove to be the perfect man for her. The third try, as the saying went, was the charm. It was about time Zona started living a charmed life.

Yes, Louise had a good feeling about this. And she had a good feeling about her cruise, too.

Unless . . . was that earthquake some sort of harbinger of things to come?

No, of course not.

2

FEN CLARKE SHOWED UP AT THE Starbucks where Zona's daughter Bree was working just as she was about to end her shift. Fen had a habit of doing that.

"Guess who's here again," said her work buddy and roomie Gaylyn.

"I saw," she said. She'd also seen Gaylyn flirting with him.

Who could blame her? Fen was a legitimate hottie, ultra cute with shoulder-length hair as blond as Bree's and a tanned six-pack. He was easygoing and solid, and he had a nice family. Unlike Bree, he was already halfway through college.

Sometimes she wondered why she'd broken up with him. Then she'd remember. He'd been getting too serious, and they'd been too young.

Yet, here he was, back in her life again. And he looked good. But they were still so young. This wouldn't end in something permanent, and they would both wind up hurt. It was stupid to hang out with him. And yet she was doing exactly that.

"Hey, if you don't want him, I'll take him. That man's got aura," said Gaylyn.

Gaylyn was a man pig. She wanted every man she met. And with her glossy dark hair and perky boobs, she usually got every man she met. And then got tired and dumped the poor fool. Even though Bree was never going to let things get serious with Fen, she sure wasn't going to let him get gobbled up and spat out by Gaylyn.

"He's not your type," she said.

"Cute is my type," Gaylyn insisted. "Anyway, I'm bored with being alone."

"You've been alone for what, two weeks?"

Gaylyn shrugged.

"That's the trouble with people," Bree informed her. "They rush into relationships and then when everything blows up, they're miserable."

Who did that remind her of? Her mother had changed her last name three times already—once with each marriage and now she was back to her original one. Bree Knox wasn't going to do any name swapping ever. Yeah, Knox was her dad's last name, a lifetime reminder that most people never really lived up to their promises. But it was a cool one, so she was keeping it. And she was keeping her dad. Sort of. She hung out with him once in a while, even though he had a whole new family that he claimed was keeping him too broke to help her much with tuition. At least he'd paid child support when Bree was growing up. That was something.

She was sure glad Gary had never gotten around to adopting her. The last thing she wanted was any reminder of that loser.

"I didn't mean to hurt you or your mother," he'd said tearfully after she'd confronted him about depleting the savings that had been set aside for her college tuition.

"Gee, I'd hate to think what you could do if you ever meant to," she'd shot back. Of course, he'd looked at her like she'd stabbed him in the heart with a steak knife. That had really made her mad. "And to think my mom thought you were so great. *I* thought you were so great. But really, you're as ungreat as a human being could be."

That had been the last conversation they ever had.

"You're scarred. You need therapy," Gaylyn informed her.

"Why do I need therapy? That's just talking to someone. I have you for that."

Gaylyn rolled her eyes. "Yeah, but you never listen to me."

"Truth." Bree had concluded that, of all the people in her life, the best person to listen to was herself. And the multitude of women on social media who testified that they were much better off alone than with a man. That many women couldn't be wrong.

Fen was waiting for her at the order counter. "Hi, coffee queen," he greeted her.

"Hey there. Did Gaylyn take your order?"

"I was waiting for you," he said with his thousand-watt smile.

"What can I get you?" she asked.

"Caramel frappe, Grande," he said, and she scanned his phone. "You want to hit the beach? I got your favorite drink in a thermos in the Jeep."

It had been a typical busy barista day with a nonstop flow of customers. Flopping on a blanket on the beach with a big thermos of lemonade mixed with 7-Up sounded great. They'd surf, play beach volleyball, and chill.

Santa Monica would be the beach of choice. On the weekends it was so packed with both tourists and locals you could barely find a square foot to park your butt, but this being a Tuesday, the beach wouldn't be as crowded.

Bree didn't have a problem with having people around them. The last thing she wanted was to find a nice, deserted stretch of sand like Escondido, which lay farther up the coast. She didn't need Fen getting inspired by any romantic settings.

He'd resurfaced in her life a few weeks earlier, wandering into the coffee shop and discovering her working there. They'd broken up early in their senior year of high school but had vowed to at least remain friends, promised to keep in touch after graduation, and then he'd gone off to Pomona and she'd gone nowhere. Now he was already half done with school, back for the summer and throwing out get-together vibes.

There would be no getting together. Not with Fen, not with anyone. She'd applied to the nursing program at Citrus College and been accepted, but instead of college she'd wound up taking a Life 201 course from her mother. She'd come away with a graduate degree in mistrust. No way was she ever getting serious with a man, not even Fen. Sharing a bed when inspiration hit? Maybe. Sharing a bank account? Never.

Anyway, she didn't have time for romance. She had to stack up cash, so she could go to nursing school.

"Don't worry about school. We've got the money saved for you," Mom had assured her during her junior year in high school.

Then, in spring of her senior year, right after she'd gotten her welcome letter from the college, it was "Sit down, sweetie. I have something to tell you." This was followed by another "I have something to tell you," which wound up with divorce and saying goodbye to their house.

And now here she was. Instead of learning how to give people shots, she was making espresso shots. So wrong.

But she'd get her life back on track. And at least sharing an apartment with Gaylyn and Gaylyn's bestie, Monique, was saving her a ton of rent money. She could have stayed with Gram and Mom and saved even more, piled up college money faster, but, much as she loved them both, that would have made her feel like she was back in high school. She preferred to be adulting.

Poor Mom. No adulting for her. That had to suck, moving back in with your mom when you were old. Pathetic. And all because of Gary. One man had managed to mess up both their lives. Mom should have seen what a loser he was. If she'd just kept tabs on their finances instead of trusting a man to take care of things, she would have figured out what was going on long before their world fell apart.

But the sun was out, and the beach was calling. She wasn't going to waste a perfectly good afternoon thinking about what her mom should have done and what her stepfather had done. He was history, blocked from her phone, and maybe, eventually, blocked from her memory.

It was hard to block out the good memories though—trips to Disneyland, Sunday afternoons playing Monopoly (Gary always lost. That should have given him a clue that he shouldn't gamble), teaching her how to play poker. She would never pick up a deck of cards again.

And she would never talk to Gary again.

"Let's do it," she said to Fen. The beach, that was.

"I'm gone," she said to Gaylyn after she'd finished up.

"Guess you don't need a ride home."

"Nope. We're going to the beach."

"Whoa, we just had a quake, girl."

"It's over. We'll be fine."

"I guess," Gaylyn said dubiously.

Bree wasn't worried. After she and her mom had survived what Gary had done to them? Bring on the tidal wave.

ZONA HAD RETURNED to work after her unsettling lunch and the day had fallen back into the usual routine that came with being a licensing service rep. (Translation: worker bee at the department of licensing.) No more earthquakes. She administered half a dozen written tests and had to deny renewing an octogenarian's driver's license when he failed the eye test.

"I was driving before you were born," he informed her.

"I'm sorry, sir, but I can't renew your license when you can't see where you're driving," she said.

"This is not right," he informed her. "The government has

too much control over our lives. I'm writing my congressman. And then I'll be back."

Just like the Terminator. What to say to all that? "I hope the rest of your day goes better."

"It won't," he snarled. "And neither will the rest of my life." He turned and wobbled off, leaning heavily on his cane.

The woman who had come in with him, probably a daughter, mouthed, "Thank you," before following him out.

Zona couldn't help feeling sorry for the man. Aging was hard enough, but to give up driving had to be right up there near the top of the yuck list. To give that up was to sacrifice your independence.

She took a deep breath and let it out slowly as she waited for the next person in the crowd seated in the room to come up to her. It was on days like this that she didn't like her job.

But it paid the bills.

It would pay them a lot better now that she was on her own and wasn't dragging around the financial ball and chain that was Gary.

Renewing a driver's license was much more pleasant than refusing one. The woman smiled at Zona when they were finished. "Have a good day."

"Thank you," Zona said, and thought, *One day at a time*. Then she remembered the earthquake and the usual unsettling feeling that had accompanied that moment when everything under her had shaken. She almost allowed herself a crazy-woman laugh. How symbolic that had been of her life. Maybe her motto should be *One earthquake at a time*.

After work, she stopped by the store to purchase the wine Louise had requested, along with some chocolate chips. Louise may have wanted wine, but Zona needed a sugar fix, and she hadn't had chocolate chip cookies in ages.

She hadn't had much of anything other than dark chocolate

and coffee and soup, which was easy to make, thanks to a sinking appetite. All the foods she loved—pizza, Pad Thai, even fruit salads—had turned to ash in her mouth when she tried to eat them. The divorce diet. It had taken off twenty pounds, ten of which her worried mother insisted she didn't need to lose.

But the cookie craving was a sign that Zona's taste buds were slowly coming back to life. Louise had a Mrs. Fields knock-off recipe, and she was already anticipating how one of those cookies would taste, warm from the oven. With milk. Cookies and milk.

Good grief, she was so reverting to childhood. Living with Mom, cookies and milk—what next, a curfew? *Snort.* No need for one of those. Zona no longer had a life.

She parked her new used car in the driveway—between Louise's car and Zona's boxes and the mattress and bed frame stacked against the wall in the garage there was no room for Zona's car—grabbed her grocery bag and got out. Her mother's modern Spanish-style home with its arched windows and covered front porch beckoned her like the proverbial port in a storm. Which was exactly what it had become.

She couldn't help but notice that the new neighbor her mother had mentioned had just pulled his truck into his driveway. That was where it stopped. His garage was probably full of boxes, too.

She half raised her hand to wave hello to him as he got out and then realized he wouldn't see her. That was just as well. The better to ogle that broad-shouldered, Jack Reacher body, though she had learned the hard way that male bodies, no matter how sturdy they looked, always housed trouble.

He was marching up his front walk, busy talking on his cell phone. More like growling, really.

She understood the growling into the phone thing. She'd done her share of that with Gary. Who was making this chunk of hunk growl?

Who cared? She had enough problems on her own plate. She didn't need to be looking over at anyone else's.

"Good. You're home," Louise greeted her when she walked into the kitchen.

Her mother looked none the worse for wear, not a strand out of place on her carefully dyed California-blond bobbed hair. If there'd been any crying and carrying on, there was no sign of it as the black eyeliner and mascara that Louise favored were still intact. Wearing a stylish sleeveless top and hip-hugging jeans, Louise Hartman looked like the kind of social influencer who would inspire seniors and garner insults from younger women insisting she dress her age and give up those jeans and that cute little top.

"You're only as old as you think you are," she liked to say. Which kept her firmly in her forties right along with Zona—instead of her sixties. And that was fine with Zona. Louise had had her share of earthquakes, but she'd never let them keep her down. She was Zona's hero.

"I've got dinner almost ready," she said from where she stood at the counter, tossing sprouts into a large red Fiestaware bowl. "Asian chicken salad and leftover muffins from yesterday."

"Sounds great," said Zona. "And I got chocolate chips for cookies."

"Cookies. That sounds like a good idea. Maybe we can take some to our new neighbor," Louise suggested.

Zona knew an ulterior motive when she heard one. "Mom, I don't need to start getting friendly with the next-door neighbor."

"He doesn't appear to be married. And he is gorgeous."

That he was. The man was a hormone fire-starter. But Zona didn't need her hormones catching fire. In fact, her hormones needed to be put on ice. Permanently.

"He may be gorgeous, but I don't want to share my cookies."

"It's been two years since your divorce. The dust has finally settled. You could move on," said Louise.

"From the frying pan into the fire? Mom, I've got my hands full trying to get financially healthy. I don't need to add relationship angst to that."

"I bet he's doing okay financially," said Louise.

"Betting is what got me into this mess. And anyway, with my track record, no one would be betting on me." Ugh.

Louise shrugged. "You don't want to stay single forever. And you know what they say. The third time's the charm."

"*They* say a lot of things. And you know what else *they* say? Fool me once, shame on you. Fool me twice, shame on me. I'm done being duped. Anyway, I'm not sure he's in the market. He was on the phone with somebody when he got out of his truck just now, and that somebody was getting an earful."

"Well, there you go. What he needs is a good woman."

"You don't really want to see me getting together with someone after what happened with Gary, do you?"

"I want to see you getting together with someone who will erase what happened with Gary from your heart," Louise said. "There are still good men out there. Like your father was."

"Yes, and there are unicorns living in Echo Park," said Zona.

"I wonder what would have happened if your father and I had stayed in Florida," Louise mused later as she helped Zona with the cookies. "Your life might have turned out so different if you'd grown up there."

"Dad might not have had a job," Zona suggested. Her father had done well working in California as an urban planner.

"You wouldn't have met Luke," Louise said.

"Or had Bree."

"There's proof that something good can come out of anything." Louise brightened. "So, who knows what good will come out of all of this?"

"Maybe I'll write a memoir and become famous?"

They both laughed at that. Even though she liked to read, Zona was not a writer.

What was she? Good with kids. (She'd always wished she and Gary had been able to have a couple. Now that failure looked like a blessing in disguise.) Maybe she should have become a teacher. Although she'd never been very good at helping Bree with her homework. She searched around her mind and, as she had before, she didn't find any spectacular talent that made her special. She liked to hike, she liked to read. She enjoyed being in the kitchen, but she wasn't clever enough to make it on any TV cooking competition. She could sing, but she didn't have the voice of a superstar. She was just an ordinary woman, one who had a lovely, smart, and very bitter daughter.

Bree. What a mess Gary had made in her head. Like Zona, Bree had loved him. He'd spent more time with Bree when she was growing up than her real dad ever had. It made his betrayal all the worse.

There it was again, another verse of the lame song, playing in Zona's brain. She had to stop that. She needed to focus on the future.

She'd found Angel Ram, a finance guru who had an entertaining and informative money management podcast, and had checked out her latest book from the library. She was taking Angel's words to heart. "Debt is an ugly beast. Throw that beast off you. Get going and get working!" Angel liked to say. "Your past is not your future. Change your attitude now. Change your habits now. Tomorrow will thank you."

Angel Ram was right. Zona had bucked that beast off her and she was rebuilding. Her tomorrows would be better. She would make sure of it. After all, she had chocolate.

She scooped up four cookies from the cooling rack, put them on a plate, and set the plate on the kitchen table. Then she got out the milk.

"Cookies and milk," Louise said happily as Zona poured them each a glass. "That always brings back such happy memories of my childhood."

"Mine, too," Zona said and smiled at her.

Louise lifted her glass. "Here's to better times ahead and making better memories."

"I'll drink to that," said Zona, and the ground under the house gave a little quiver.

Darling whimpered and Louise said weakly, "Oh, I don't like the timing of that."

Zona grabbed a cookie. "It's only an aftershock, Mom. Not a cosmic warning."

Right? Right.

3

ZONA HAD LEFT WORK AND WAS at Stater Brothers grocery store in the candy aisle, hovering over the Dove chocolates, when Gracie called to see how she was doing. The cookies were long gone, and Zona needed chocolate. That was how she was doing.

"Chocolate emergency?" Gracie teased.

"Every day is a chocolate emergency."

"So, what's the latest?"

Zona sighed. "Nothing, really. Mom is pushing me to move on with my life and find the last good man left on earth."

"Oh? And where is he?"

"Next door. She's already met our new neighbor."

Gracie laughed. "Lucky you. Is he hot?"

"He's a regular jalapeño, but it wouldn't matter if he was on fire. I'm not looking to get involved with anyone," Zona said, and picked up a bag of dark chocolate bites. They were only a temporary fix, she knew that. She needed . . . something. Therapy, probably. Or, as Angel Ram would say, a plan.

"I wasn't looking either, until Bradley came along," said Gracie.

The Ken to Gracie's Barbie. Zona told herself not to be jealous.

She frowned at the bag in her hand. She'd already splurged on the cookies. She put the bag back and walked away.

"Just so you know, I put the bag back," she said.

"You have my permission to eat as much chocolate as you want," Gracie said, making Zona smile.

"I need a more lasting fix. I'll get there," Zona added, talking more to herself than her friend.

"You will," Gracie said.

"Yes, I will," Zona said.

She walked out of the store and into the late-afternoon sunshine. The sun's rays felt good on her shoulders. Maybe she'd go home, get out of her work clothes, and take a nice, brisk walk on Big Dalton Canyon Trail. It was hot out but not horribly so, and she could use the solitude to . . . feel sorry for herself.

Stop that. No feeling sorry. You'll be fine.

"Maybe I need a side hustle. A job waiting tables somewhere. Minimum wage is pretty good these days. Plus, there's tips."

"Seriously?"

"Why not? I did it in college."

"Yeah, when you were young. You'd probably be the oldest one at the restaurant, and you'll end up with varicose veins."

Okay, so Zona wasn't twenty, but she wasn't that old at forty-two. Forty was the new . . . what? Twenty? Thirty? "My veins will be fine."

"What about your pride?"

"I can keep my pride and still work."

Which, considering her financial state, she would be doing until she was ninety. It was a good thing the women in her family lived a long time. Her grandma had made it to eighty-nine.

"But come on, waiting tables?"

"What else am I going to do on the weekends?"

"Go out with the hot neighbor," Gracie teased. "Seriously, don't rush into any side hustle just yet. Give yourself a minute to breathe. You know your mother is practically doing cartwheels over having you with her. So let her enjoy your company."

"Some company I am," Zona grumbled. "Anyway, I'm definitely not going to go after her hot new neighbor. Being in a relationship is like trying to win a three-legged race. I've already been tied to two men who just ended up dragging me down." Zona sighed. "I'm running alone from now on. At least I know on my own I'll be able to finish the race."

"Sometimes you can fall running on your own. That's when it's nice to have someone to help you get back up."

"I've got plenty of people helping me up," Zona said. "Thanks for being there for me, bestie."

"Always," said Gracie. "And I'm going to start thinking of ways you can make some extra money without trashing your veins."

Zona chuckled. "Go for it."

Louise wasn't any more impressed with Zona's side hustle idea than Gracie had been. "Why kill yourself?" she argued when Zona shared her idea over dinner. "You'll already be saving the equivalent of a house payment every month living here. That should help."

"It will more than help, but, honestly, Mom, it doesn't feel right sponging off you."

"Since when is keeping me company sponging?" her mother retorted.

"You might want your house to yourself at some point."

"Like if I meet a stud on my cruise and bring him home with me? If that happens, you'll be in the downstairs bedroom instead of upstairs," Louise said with a wink and a grin.

The cruise. Louise's floating gold mine of potential Mr. Louises. When it came to men for her mother, Zona had been thinking more along the lines of her nice neighbor, Martin. She could understand Louise's loneliness after losing her husband. Zona's dad had been as good-natured as he was good-looking, and he'd adored Louise. They'd been a shining testimonial for happily-ever-after, and his death nearly six years ago had left a big hole in her life. In all of theirs. But the ways Louise was trying to fill hers lately made Zona nervous.

"You be careful on that cruise," she said. "I don't want you falling for some loser with a gambling habit. Or a drinking problem. Or any other kind of problem," she added, covering her bases.

"I know a good man when I see one," said Louise. Her smile faded. "I probably shouldn't be taking this cruise. It's more money I could give you for Bree's school when she starts."

"You're already helping us enough. And it's time you had some fun. Have you decided what clothes you're taking?"

"Almost. Come upstairs and help me make my final decision."

Louise's large suitcase and carry-on wouldn't hold half of the mountain of clothes on her bed. A pile of shoes formed the foothills below.

"Mom, seriously? The cruise is sixteen days, not sixteen months."

"I want to look nice," Louise said.

"You always look nice. And, honestly, you can mix and match and nobody will notice."

"Someone might," Louise insisted. "I haven't traveled in years. I want to do this right."

Less would be doing it right. "It's Hawaii. You probably don't need that many shoes," Zona said.

Louise looked at the five pairs on the floor. "I guess I don't have to take all of these."

"You're probably good to go with the sandals and the Skechers."

"No, I'll need something for formal night."

"So, three pairs?" Zona suggested.

Louise began pointing to her footwear. "Eeny-meeny-miny-moe, one of you has got to go."

More than one. "How about the tennis shoes for starters?"

"I might want to play pickleball. The ship does have a court."

"You tried pickleball and didn't like it," Zona reminded her.

"I might want to try it again."

In the end, no shoe was left behind, although two pairs of jeans and three sweaters were. With a bulging suitcase and a carry-on that looked ready to explode, plus a purse the size of Texas, Louise was prepared.

"You need that many clothes for Hawaii?" Bree commented when she joined Zona and Louise for dinner the night before Louise was ready to leave. "I'd just take my bikini, flip-flops, and shorts."

Zona hid her smile and refrained from saying anything about their previous conversation.

"You could rock a bikini and shorts all day. Me, not so much," said Louise. "Anyway, I can't go on a cruise looking dumpy."

"You could never look dumpy, Gram," Bree assured her.

It was true. Louise looked great. She had some wrinkles, of course, and complained bitterly about the crepey skin starting to show on her arms, but she had a lot fewer wrinkles than most of her friends who had been sun worshipers and were now paying for it with lizard skin. Her hair was a carefully curated blond and she had big blue eyes, a cute, small nose (which she'd given to Zona), and full lips (thanks to a certain doctor in Los Angeles).

"I know I'm not going to look like I did when I was your age," Louise said to Bree. "Or even when I was fifty. But I still want to look the best I can. I think everyone should do that. How you take care of yourself says a lot about what you think about yourself," she added.

What did Zona's hair and scruffy nails say about what she thought of herself? She stifled a sigh.

"And the best-looking women attract the best men," Louise continued.

"There is no such thing as a best man," muttered Zona. *Way to go, scar your daughter for life with your bad attitude.*

Too late. She was already scarred thanks to the bad behavior of the men her mother had chosen.

"There are still good ones out there," Louise insisted.

"Yeah, right," scoffed Bree.

"I'm serious. Your grandfather was a good man."

"Part of the patriarchy," argued Bree, and stuffed a big bite of enchilada in her mouth.

"Oh, for heaven's sake," Louise said in disgust.

Bree shrugged.

"I know it looks like everyone these days is cheating or lying," Louise began.

Or gambling.

"But they're not. There are still normal people out there who just want to enjoy backyard barbecues and softball games on a Sunday afternoon and a good movie on a Friday night. Take our new neighbor."

"No, let's not be taking the new neighbor anywhere," said Zona. Though *taking him* was exactly where her dreams had been headed the night after she'd caught a glimpse of him.

"Neighbor?" asked Bree, raising both eyebrows at her mother.

"Don't ask," said Zona.

"He just moved in. No ring on that left hand," Louise reported.

"That doesn't mean anything, Gram. He could still be with someone."

"True," Louise allowed, "but I haven't seen anyone."

"Well, there you go. That proves it," said Zona.

Louise frowned and pointed a finger at her. "Don't be smart."

"I haven't been, and that's my problem," Zona retorted. "I have enough to deal with, Mom. I don't need anything more on my plate."

"Meeting a neighbor isn't putting something on your plate. It's just being friendly," Louise argued. "And you can never have enough friends."

"Sure, you can," said Zona.

"Give up, Gram. Mom's not interested," said Bree, then added, "Thank God."

"I don't have time for a relationship, anyway," said Zona.

Louise held up a hand. "I know, I know. You have to make money."

"I do," Zona said, and looked apologetically at her daughter.

Bree frowned, and Zona could see the traces of bitterness in it. But then she shrugged and said, "I'll come up with the money for nursing school."

"*We* will come up with the money for nursing school," Zona corrected her. "I'm going to replace every penny Gary took."

"And don't forget, I'm going to help you with that, too," Louise said.

It all felt like a small drop in a very big bucket. Even with the pittance Luke was contributing they had a long way to go. Zona was determined to get there though. She didn't need her daughter saddled with student loans.

"And who knows?" Louise continued. "Once I sell my book . . ."

Bree politely bit down on her lip and didn't snicker.

Zona didn't either, but she wasn't able to resist saying, "The Agatha Grafton mystery novel that you haven't started yet?" Okay, probably just as bad as laughing.

Louise raised her chin. "I'm still collecting ideas."

"I think you should collect some more ideas for names," said Zona.

"Agatha Grafton is perfect," Louise insisted.

"I don't think Agatha Christie or Sue Grafton would have approved," Zona said.

"Well, I'm not using either one of their names exclusively for my pen name, so I don't see what the problem is."

"You might when their estates sue you," said Zona.

It was a moot point. Louise was never going to write that novel anyway. It was simply something she liked to talk about. Like learning to play the piano. The keyboard she'd bought at a garage sale two years earlier was still in the upstairs guest bedroom covered with fabric scraps from the quilt she was working on.

"It's okay, Gram. Take your time," Bree said.

Louise smiled approvingly at her. "These things do take time."

"You've read enough mystery novels," said Zona. "You ought to be able to write one in your sleep."

"That's the problem. Everything's been done," said Louise.

"Nothing new under the sun?" Zona teased.

"I'll come up with something eventually. There's always something in the news. You wouldn't believe what I saw on *Deathline* the other night."

Bree made a face. "Am I gonna want dessert after this?"

"Probably not," said Zona.

"Everyone thought this man was so nice," Louise began.

"That proves my point," Zona interrupted her.

"Yeah, Gram. You've got to be careful. And you'd better be careful on this cruise, too. There are sweetheart scammers everywhere."

"I'm aware of that," Louise said stiffly, and Zona and Bree exchanged concerned looks.

"YOU SHOULDN'T LET Gram go on this cruise," Bree said to Zona later when it was just the two of them, standing out by Bree's car. The new Bree, always bossy.

"She's an adult. She can do what she wants. Anyway, she'll

be careful. Almost getting taken in by that scam artist opened her eyes."

"That was scary."

"It was," Zona agreed. "It's sad that there are so many creeps out there."

"You would know, Mom," Bree sniped, then muttered, "Sorry."

Every once in a while, the bitterness spilled over like acid, and it always burned. "You're right. I'm a walking cautionary tale," Zona said.

"Which is why I'm never getting married," Bree said forcefully. "I'm not even going to live with a man."

That again. It wasn't the first time Bree had made her declaration. She had serious trust issues thanks to Zona.

She sighed. "Your grandmother was right about one thing. There are still good people in the world. Not every man is a creep or a tool." If she said it often enough, she might come to believe it.

"Enough of them are. Not worth the gamble," said Bree, making her mother cringe. "Sorry. I shouldn't use that word."

"It fits," Zona said.

"And the neighbor. You're not—"

Zona cut her off. "Don't worry. I'm not interested."

"Good. Don't even think about it, Mom. We don't need any more man crap in our lives."

Zona wished she could think of something, anything to say that would chip off the hard shell that had grown over her daughter's heart. She couldn't. She had a shell of her own to deal with. So, she settled for hugging Bree and telling her she loved her. It was what her mother had always told her.

Ha! Look how well that had worked. Sometimes love wasn't enough to protect people from their own stupidity.

4

"**YOU AND DARLING HOLD DOWN THE** fort while I'm gone," Louise said to Zona after Zona had unloaded her suitcases on the cruise ship's dock at the San Pedro port early on Sunday afternoon.

"We will," Zona assured her.

Darling had been left behind. He'd stationed himself on the couch so he could watch out the living room window, and they'd heard him howling as they backed down the driveway. Darling, who was still a puppy, was going to have a tough couple of weeks without his dog mom around to pamper him and with Zona gone at work during the day. Well, it was a dog's life.

Yeah, and what a rough one. Meals, treats, his own personal trainer who took him for walks and kept him fit. No worries about replacing lost savings. Just eat, sleep, and romp. Boy, did that sound like a good life.

Zona shoved away the thought and turned over Louise's suitcases to the porter who was organizing them. Suitcases were everywhere. Excited travelers everywhere. She couldn't help but marvel at the fine-tuned system the cruise line had for moving so much luggage and so many people.

"While you're keeping an eye on things, you might want to keep an eye on the new neighbor," Louise added. The woman never gave up.

"You have fun," Zona said, keeping the focus where it belonged, and hugged her.

"I intend to," she said.

Louise was dressed for fun, wearing her favorite floral painted Skechers accented with a silver ankle bracelet she'd ordered online along with a flared skirt and a pink top with a matching sweater. She'd had her hair cut in a layered bob and she looked ten years younger than her actual age. She'd probably have at least three men trailing her all over the ship by the end of their first sea day. She was already looking over a well-dressed middle-aged man in jeans and a crisp white shirt rolled up at the elbows and loafers with no socks.

Poor Martin. It was obvious he was smitten with Louise, and even though she spent so much time with him they could have been married, she had her sights set on bigger game with bigger muscles. Sweet as he was, Martin didn't stand a chance.

He'd come over shortly after Bree's visit to wish Louise bon voyage and had left looking downright discouraged after listening to her talk about the people she'd already met online and all the excursions she'd signed up for.

"Sixteen days of gourmet meals, sun and sand, fabulous shows and beautiful coral reefs. You should have come," Louise had told him.

Yes, you should have, Zona had thought.

It still surprised her that he hadn't. Maybe the idea of being on a boat with other men competing for Louise's attention intimidated him.

"I guess I should have," he'd said. "But then, why go to Hawaii? We already have plenty of sun here."

"But we don't have luaus and Tahitian dancers, and people greeting us with leis. We don't have sea turtles or the Pearl Harbor Memorial. You would have enjoyed that."

"I already saw it." Then he'd added, "I hope you don't get coronavirus," probably in a last-ditch attempt to discourage her from going.

Louise did not discourage easily. "I'll be fine," she'd said with a flick of her hand. "I've packed Imodium. This is going to be so much fun."

That was when Martin had decided it was time to head back home.

Zona wished he was going with her mother. At least then someone would have been around to make sure she didn't do anything crazy. With the frame of mind she'd been in the last year, that was not outside the realm of possibility, although it seemed to Zona her mother should have learned something watching her daughter's love train wrecks.

"No weddings at sea," Zona said sternly as her mother settled her purse over her shoulder, and Louise laughed.

As if Zona was kidding. She wasn't.

"No weddings at sea," Louise promised. "But maybe some hanky-panky."

Zona just shook her head.

"Don't you worry about me. I'll be great," Louise assured her. "And don't be worrying about money while I'm gone. You've got a place to stay, you've got a job. You're doing fine."

For someone who can't afford to retire before ninety.

"Meanwhile, be nice to our new neighbor. You never know," Louise finished. Then she gave her daughter one more kiss and practically skipped off.

A feeling Zona hadn't had in a long time came back to visit. It was that same feeling she'd experienced when Bree was little and Zona had dropped her off at school on her first day. Worry combined with a wish that she didn't have to let her mother out of her sight.

She shook her head over her silliness. Louise was a grown woman, and, despite a couple of near romantic misses, she was a smart one. She'd learned from her latest near mistake. She'd be okay.

It was more than Zona could say about herself.

Don't think like that, she scolded herself as she drove away.

You'll get through this. So what if you're back at the starting block? You're still in the race.

She just had to keep pushing forward. And she would, darn it all. She was not going to end up a loser.

On her way home she stopped at her favorite discount grocery store in Azusa and purchased enough produce to take her through the week, then left, pleased with the money she'd saved. She had her Angel Ram finance book to read, plus a bestseller she'd found at the library, and a movie, an Audrey Hepburn–Cary Grant classic. That would be her exciting night. Audrey, Cary, Zona, and a bowl of popcorn. Maybe library movies and home-popped popcorn would be the rest of her life.

But that beat the adventures of the first half of her life, which had been filled with fights and sleepless nights and upset stomachs. The only drama she wanted now was what she found on the small screen.

Which meant no love life, because you couldn't have love without drama. At least Zona couldn't. Sigh.

As she turned into her driveway, she noticed her new neighbor was home. His lawn was freshly mowed and he was getting ready to put away his lawn mower. He wore board shorts and was shirtless. The man had perfect pecs and a six-pack. And yes, those biceps were lovely as well. Even though she wasn't interested she couldn't help but appreciate a beautifully sculpted body.

She gave him a wave and he smiled and waved back. And she told her eyes they'd looked enough and had other things to do. She opened her trunk and fished out her grocery bag, which she'd foolishly stuffed too full, and managed to tip out half its contents. Out spilled a bag of apples, a head of lettuce, and a red onion that went rolling away.

She frowned. Now some of her apples would be bruised. She set the bag down and bent to grab the apples and lettuce.

And suddenly there was her neighbor, scooping up the onion. "Can't go wrong with a red onion," he said with another smile as he handed it over. He had a killer smile.

"Thanks," she said. Then her mind went blank. *Quick! Fill in the blank.* "Welcome to the neighborhood," she said. Not very creative, but oh, well.

"Thanks," he said.

"I'm Zona Hartman. I think you already met my mom," she added. *Who wanted me to bring you cookies. Do you like cookies? Don't say that. No cookies! No more men!*

"Alec James," he said. "Looks like this is turning out to be a friendly neighborhood. Condos, you don't always get to know your neighbors. I wasn't sure about buying a house, but this one was a steal. Looks like it was a good investment."

"Well, we are friendly."

Don't even think about it. Friendly leads to trouble.

Okay, it was time to get inside before she did something foolish like invite him to join her and Cary and Audrey for the evening. "I guess I'd better let you get back to your lawn mower," she said.

"And I'd better let you get busy with your onion."

She nodded. "If you need a lawn service, I can recommend a good one."

"Nah. I'm not big on having strangers around. Anyway, it's not much to mow. Thanks, though."

"No problem," she said. "Have a good one."

"You, too," he said, and returned to his own property.

She stuffed the onion back in with the other produce, took a firm grip on her bag, and went inside the house.

Darling was thrilled to see her, jumping on her and nearly tipping the produce out again.

"I know, you've been abandoned for forever," she said. "I'll give you a treat and then we'll put on your doggy Crocs and go for a quick walk."

After Mr. Temptation was back inside his house and out of sight. Out of sight, out of mind, right?

Half an hour later they were out the door and on their way.

It looked like her neighbor had plans for the evening because here came a red PT Cruiser pulling into his driveway and parking next to his truck. A thirty-something woman with long, curly red hair popped out of it, grabbed a designer overnight bag, and skipped to the front door. She wore white shorts with a black T-shirt half tucked in them, showing off great legs and fit arms.

A moment later, Alec James, Louise's candidate for Zona's perfect man, came to the door.

"Surprise, I'm here," caroled the woman, loud enough for Zona to hear, and stepped inside.

Zona hadn't heard what he said in response, but considering how cute his visitor was, it had to be something welcoming. So much for Louise's theory that the man was available. Zona had known all along he wasn't. Good-looking men were always taken. And if they weren't, there was something seriously wrong with them.

Who needed a man, anyway? Zona had Darling.

Martin had kindly offered to check on Darling and take him for a midmorning walk in Louise and Zona's absence, which helped, but Darling was young enough to want to move constantly and Zona knew they would be doing early morning and evening walks in addition to what Martin had offered. In an ideal world, Zona would leave Darling in the backyard, with plenty of water, but she wasn't sure how well that would work. Would the heat be too much for him? Would he bark and howl and make all the neighbors mad? Zona wouldn't be able to be as attentive as her mother, and Darling was a little on the needy side.

Zona preferred cats. They knew how to entertain themselves without chewing up sofa pillows. So far, Darling, part poodle, part who knew what else, and entirely spoiled, had shredded two of Louise's.

When Zona was a child, the family had only had one dog. Poor Buster had gotten hit by a car, and she still remembered how confused and then crushed she'd been when she came home from school and learned that Buster had crossed the rainbow bridge. He'd been her dog in name only. He'd really been Louise's baby, and Louise had gone into mourning after losing him. That had been the end of owning dogs. They'd switched to cats. Inside cats. Zona had gotten her own cat when Bree was in grade school. But Pitty-Paws died a year ago and Zona had decided she was done with pets. Losing an animal on top of everything else awful happening in her life had been the cherry on top of the poop cupcake.

Louise, on the other hand, had decided she needed companionship. With Dad not around to raise objections and remind her about Buster, she'd gone to the local animal shelter a few months earlier and fallen in love. So now Darling was a part of their lives.

It smelled like someone nearby was barbecuing as they made their way back down their street. Was that someone Alec James? He was probably grilling steaks, drinking an IPA beer. Maybe his guest was putting together a salad to go with what was on the grill.

Who cared what the neighbors were doing? Zona had a life of her own. Her book and Cary and Audrey were waiting.

THE SHIP'S LIDO deck was buzzing with happy people and the band was playing "Sea Cruise" for the throng enjoying the sail-away party. One of the happiest buzzing people at that party was Louise, who was enjoying her second piña colada. This was the life. Why had she waited so long to do something fun?

"Cruises and piña coladas just go together, don't they?" she said to her fellow cruisers, George Winston and Wayne Champagne. ("Yep, darlin', that's my real name.")

She'd already met George online. He was short and stocky with a baby beer belly. He owned a tire franchise, and, like Louise, he was widowed. They'd enjoyed several online chats. Like Louise, he loved a good mystery and had said more than once how much he was looking forward to talking books with her. He had plenty of time to read now that he was retired, and homes in both California and Idaho to read in. George was not hurting for money. Not that Louise needed a fortune. Harold had left enough so that she could be comfortable, and she had enough extra to help a little with her granddaughter's schooling. What she wanted was a man who had a wealth of smiles and good humor, and who loved dogs. George had checked a lot of the boxes.

But George paled in comparison to newcomer Wayne, who was a tall, fit Texan with gray hair and a face like George Clooney. And a Southern drawl. And he could dish out enough flattery to swell a woman's head and keep it swelled for the whole cruise. He was pumping Louise's up pretty fast, for sure.

He smiled at her from across the table where the three of them were sitting not far from the table tennis action. "Piña coladas and a beautiful woman."

He raised his glass to Louise, and she could feel George, next to her, frowning. Louise hadn't dated since college, certainly hadn't flirted since she'd been married or enjoyed this kind of flattery. Her deceased husband had been a good and kind man, but never much for flattery. Sucking so much up now was almost more intoxicating than her drink.

A fifty-something woman with long black hair and brown eyes slid into the one remaining empty seat at their table, which was next to Wayne, smiled at everyone, and asked in a throaty voice, "Is this seat taken?"

"No, join us," said Wayne, and the woman smiled at him.

Louise could tell the woman was plumper than her, but the black sundress hid the thickening waist, and its low-cut neckline accentuated a hefty serving of boobage. She had eyelash extensions and was wearing lipstick as red as Louise's. She'd overloaded on the perfume.

Louise sneezed.

"Bless you," said George, but he was looking at the newcomer.

He was also sucking in his stomach. Why did men do that? It was impossible to hold back a beer belly forever. And why was he tummy tightening for this woman? She wasn't all that great.

"I'm Ursula," the woman said. She had a slight accent, which Louise couldn't help envying. There was something so sexy about a foreign accent.

Okay, maybe the woman was all that great.

"Well, now, where are ya from, Ursula?" Wayne asked after they'd all introduced themselves.

"I'm from Germany."

"An import," Wayne said, and grinned.

Louise forced herself not to frown. "You came all the way from Germany to do a Hawaiian island cruise?"

"Why not?" the woman retorted. "Anyway, I live in Washington now. I'm divorced," she added.

"I'm sorry," said Louise. And in a way she was. Divorce was hard on the heart. She'd seen just how hard close up and had ached for her daughter both times she'd gone through it.

Ursula shrugged. "He was verbally abusive. I was glad to be done with him."

"Now, I'm really sorry," Louise said. "I had a wonderful husband." Harold may not have majored in flattery, but he had been loyal and kind, the bedrock she'd lived her life on.

"You were lucky," Ursula informed her.

"I was," Louise agreed. "He was one of a kind. But I think

there are still a lot of good men out there," she amended, sharing her smile with both George and Wayne.

"Hear, hear," said Wayne, and grinned at Ursula.

And Ursula smiled back. The woman was almost licking her over-plumped lips. She gave her hair a little shake, making it dance like waves. The hair hula.

But Louise was not threatened. Really.

Okay, maybe a little. She'd been enjoying being the center of attention at this table, feeling like the queen bee of the cruise. Ursula was after her throne. And her drones. Well, that wasn't happening. Younger women didn't have a monopoly on sexy. People who looked at older women like they were all washed up and their lives were over needed glasses. Louise had lots of life left in her, and she was feeling pretty sexy herself in her cute little skirt and pink top.

The band started playing "YMCA." Party time!

"Oh, let's go dance to this, everyone," she said, jumping up.

Wayne laughed and got up. So did George, and they followed her into the dancing throng. Ursula was in the process of ordering a drink and wouldn't be joining them. Gee, what a shame.

Louise threw herself into the song and movements, grinning alternately at the men on either side of her. The band should have been playing "It's Raining Men" because it certainly was. She was sure she was going to find romance on this boat. Let the Ursulas onboard beware. They had competition. Hehe.

After "YMCA," the band started in on the "Cupid Shuffle." Louise knew the dance to this one. She'd done it at line dancing at the senior center and she had the moves.

She was happily displaying them when Ursula arrived and sandwiched herself in between Louise and Wayne. So rude. Well, Louise could dance circles around the woman. So what if Louise was older? Age was just a state of mind. And she was of a mind to outdance this middle-aged import.

Oh, yes, moving in that little quarter turn, she showed off her hip action big-time. How fun was this! And shuffling to the right and the left, she still had the moves for that, too. She'd probably pay for showing off later when her bursitis kicked in, but a nice massage would take care of that, so she kept right on showing off. The early-evening sun was still on hand and the sky was blue. She felt thirty again, joyful and in love with life.

Until her dancing went as south as the ship was heading.

Whether it was that second drink or gremlins that caused her to stumble, who knew. But stumble she did, pitching forward and knocking poor George off-kilter in the process. He at least stayed upright and tried to catch her, but she was beyond catching. She fell over a nearby deck chair and landed on her leg in a way no leg should ever be landed on.

She wasn't sure what was worse, the sudden excruciating pain or her embarrassment. *Old lady goes down doing the "Cupid Shuffle."* She was sure people had their phones out and were recording the whole mortifying fall.

One of the staff rushed up to her, right along with George and Wayne, and all three helped her up. She'd sprained an ankle a couple of different times, but this wasn't her ankle, and it was the worst sprain she'd ever had. She couldn't put weight on her leg without crying out in pain.

"I think I sprained something," she said.

"I think you did worse than that," said Wayne, pointing to the bit of bone poking out.

That was the last thing Louise heard before little bells started ringing in her ears and the world went black.

5

ZONA HAD FINISHED PARTYING WITH CARY and Audrey and had settled in bed with *Fix Your Finances*, when the call came in.

"I'm at the hospital," Louise informed her.

Zona sat up so suddenly the book went flying. "The hospital? What? Where?"

"I'm at Little Company of Mary in San Pedro," Louise clarified.

"What happened? Did you have a heart attack?" *Please, God, don't let it be that.*

"No," Louise said irritably.

She didn't exactly sound feeble, so not at death's door. That was good.

"What did happen? You should be on your way to Hawaii."

Louise sniffed. "I know I should. I fell. I broke my leg," she added, her voice teary. "They took me right off the ship and carted me here to the emergency room and I've been here forever."

"I'm so sorry, Mom."

"That makes two of us. They're putting this temporary cast on me and then, after the swelling goes down, I have to get a bigger and uglier one. It looks like I'm going to be stuck in it for the whole summer. I can't believe this is happening," Louise added miserably. "Anyway, I'm going to need a ride home sooner than I thought. Can you come and get me?"

"Of course. I'm on my way."

"Thanks, darling," Louise said.

Louise was normally a cheerful woman. At the moment, she sounded like she'd been drained of all happiness. *The bad luck vampire strikes again.*

Zona did a quick mental search for some words of comfort. All she could come up with was "It'll be okay, Mom."

"It will," Louise said, resigned. "It could have been worse. I could have broken my back, fallen overboard, drowned in the pool. I need chocolate," she finished. It was followed by a tiny sob.

"I'm on it. Be there soon," Zona promised.

She texted Bree.

Gram broke her leg.

What???

She's in the hospital in San Pedro. I'm going to get her now.

Coming with don't leave, came the reply.

Zona didn't turn down the offer. Having Bree along for moral support for both her mother and herself sounded like a good idea. She quickly ran to Stater Brothers grocery store and picked up a bag of Godiva dark caramel chocolates for Louise. Chocolates were small consolation for missing a cruise and spending the summer in a cast, but they were better than nothing.

By the time she got back to the house, Bree was there and waiting in her car. She joined Zona in hers and off they went.

"How did Gram break her leg?" Bree asked.

"She fell. That's all I know."

"You don't even know how she fell?"

"No. All I know is instead of being on the cruise ship she's in the emergency room in a cast."

"Oof. Poor Gram. She was so excited about her cruise."

There was nothing to add to that, so Zona kept quiet.

An hour later they were standing next to Louise's emergency room bed, keeping her company while she waited for someone to come discharge her. The diagnosis: tibial plateau and condylar fracture. Complicated terms for stuck in a cast. It would be sponge baths—doctor's preference—and then an even more cumbersome cast and shower assists with proper precautions. Help with meals during the day. Help with dressing? Possibly. How were they going to manage with Zona working?

"I have to pick up crutches on the way out," Louise said. "My consolation prize," she added bitterly.

"I'm sorry, Gram," said Bree.

Louise sighed heavily. "I was sure having fun. Till I wasn't."

"So, what happened?" Zona asked.

"I tripped," Louise said with a frown.

"Slippery floors? You could sue the cruise line," offered Bree.

Louise shook her head. "I didn't slip on anything. We were doing the Cupid Shuffle, and I tripped and fell over a deck chair."

Bree began to laugh, and Zona gave her a motherly glare. "Sorry," she said. "It's just so weird. Like something out of a movie."

"Oh, it was a movie moment all right," Louise said bitterly. "I'm probably all over social media by now, the star of my own comedy. Except it wasn't funny," she finished, her voice wobbly.

Zona saw the tears in her mother's eyes and hurt for her. She took Louise's hand. "I'm so sorry this happened, Mom."

"It's what I get for showing off," Louise said. Then she added with a half smile, "I had the moves."

"I bet you did," said Zona.

The smile fell away. "But look at me now. Here I am stuck in a cast. How am I going to do anything?" She laid her head back on the pillow and shut her eyes. "I feel old."

Zona and Bree exchanged looks. This wasn't the Louise they knew and loved. She never cried, rarely complained. Even when Zona's father had died Louise had worked hard to keep a positive attitude, being thankful for the years she and her husband had enjoyed together, thankful that he was no longer in pain.

It was as if the real Louise had escaped and left this sad shell of a woman behind.

Keeping her spirits up was going to be a challenge. Louise was not one to sit around. There would be no line dancing for her, no garage sale bargain hunting, no walking Darling around the neighborhood and visiting with the neighbors. She wouldn't be cooking or cleaning in the near future, either.

"Don't worry. We'll get you back to feeling young," Zona assured her mother.

Louise sighed again, and a tear trickled down her cheek. "You're already dealing with so much and now you've got me to deal with as well."

"We'll be fine," Zona said even as she wondered yet again how she was going to take care of her mother and keep working.

She wasn't going to, that was the bottom line. She'd have to get in some help.

"We can hire someone to help," Louise said as if reading her mind. "I'm sure my Medicare will cover it. If not, my other insurance will."

Zona hoped Louise was right. She didn't have the money to pay someone.

She pulled the bag of chocolates out of her purse. "We brought you sustenance."

Louise smiled for the first time since they'd arrived. "Every cloud has a silver lining."

Zona hadn't found hers, but she kept her mouth shut.

Eventually, Louise was released, and issued crutches, and between Zona, Bree, and the orderly who had wheeled Louise out of the hospital, they got her into Zona's car.

"I guess I won't be driving anytime soon. It would have to be my right leg," Louise said miserably.

"I'm not sure you would have been driving even if you broke your left leg," Zona said. "That cast is a monster, and I don't see how you could get in and out of the car." It had been hard enough getting her into the passenger seat of Zona's compact.

Louise said nothing to that, just shut her eyes and leaned her head back against the seat's headrest.

Zona sneaked a peek in her direction. Louise's humor and energy were the magic show that hid her age. She was the bubbly counterpart to the Great and Terrible Oz from *The Wizard of Oz*. *Pay no attention to the woman behind the curtain.* But exhaustion and discouragement had pulled aside the curtain, forcing Zona to look. Her mother was growing old. Not ancient, but old enough for a daughter reality check. She wouldn't have Louise forever.

It was a chilling thought. Her mother had always been her biggest fan, bragging to everyone and anyone when Zona got the role of Miriam the Librarian in her high school's musical production of *The Music Man*, framing Zona's college degree, assuring her that her Bachelor of Arts degree was just the beginning of great things.

It hadn't been. Zona hadn't done anything great. Had never climbed the corporate ladder to the top. Never became a singing sensation, never written the bestselling novel Louise had predicted she'd write, and she'd failed at business. And marriage. Twice. You couldn't forget that.

Louise had been there to catch her. "This is not your fault. You're better off without him and better times lie ahead," Louise had said after things blew up with Luke. Then, when the better times became the worst of times and Gary ruined their life together and ruined Zona's credit, Louise again said, "You're better off without him and better times lie ahead." She'd opened her arms and her home. She was always there, helping Zona move toward those better times, Zona's own personal safety net, and Zona couldn't imagine life without her.

Yet at some point every daughter had to learn to work without a net. And at some point, that daughter became the net for her mother. That was where they were, for the moment, anyway.

The good news was, Louise had broken her leg and not her neck. Or a hip. She'd recover. Get back her spunk. And she wasn't that old. They would have lots of years together. Zona needed to remember that and stay out of negative territory.

If she weren't so tired and miserable, Louise would have shared one of her favorite sayings, "Things have a way of working out."

Zona said it for her.

Louise opened one eye and glared at her.

"Who knows? The universe might have been saving you from falling overboard or something," put in Bree from the back seat.

"The universe does not care about humans," Louise snapped. "The universe just exists. Honestly, where do people get these ridiculous ideas?"

"Whatever," Bree said, ending the philosophical discussion. "The point is Mom's right."

Mark this moment on the calendar. Heaven knew, Zona hadn't been right about much of anything when Bree was a teenager. She couldn't help smiling.

She turned to the pop classics music station, hoping it would cheer Louise up. Gloria Gaynor came on, singing, "I Will Survive."

"You guys should make that your theme song," said Bree.

"Yes, we should," said Zona.

Louise just grunted.

Next came "Footloose." Oops.

"Can we turn that off?" Louise snapped.

"Sure," said Zona, and they drove the rest of the way home in silence.

Back at the house, Darling was excited to see Mommy and about knocked Louise off balance, which made Zona's heart stop.

"No. Down, Darling," she commanded as she helped her mother to the couch, Bree following behind with Louise's purse and the one sandal that was no longer a fit thanks to the cast.

"Can I get you something to drink?" Zona offered.

"Yes, a piña colada. Oh, that's right. I'm not on the boat anymore," Louise grumbled. Then sighed. "You know what, I think you probably should just get me to bed."

Zona thought of all the stairs between Louise and her bedroom and envisioned her mother losing her balance, falling down them, and breaking her other leg. Or an arm. Or her neck.

"Mom, I'm thinking maybe we'd better move you to the downstairs guest bedroom for a while," she said.

This inspired another sigh. "I think you're right," Louise said, grabbing for her crutches.

"Want me to get your nightgown?" Bree offered as Zona hurried to help Louise struggle back up.

"Thanks, honey," Louise said. "Look in the top drawer of my dresser."

"Got it," said Bree, and headed up the stairs.

"This is darned inconvenient," Louise grumbled as Zona followed her to the downstairs bedroom.

"I'm really sorry, Mom," said Zona.

"Oh, well. Hawaii will still be there once I get out of this stupid cast."

"There you go," said Zona.

"Maybe I'd better go potty before I settle in," Louise decided, and turned around and headed for the downstairs bathroom.

"Okay," Zona said, and started to follow her.

"I can manage on my own," Louise said firmly.

Her mother had one leg that looked like an ironing board. How was she going to manage? But, "Okay."

Louise limped off down the hall. Thank God that bathroom had a walk-in shower in it. A tub was going to be out of the question for a long time.

Bree was back down with the nightgown and found Zona hovering in the hall. "Where's Gram?" she asked.

"In the bathroom," Zona said.

Bree nodded and moved on to the bedroom.

A moment later, Louise called, "Zona!"

Zona hurried into the bathroom and found her mother struggling to get up again. "This is really inconvenient," Louise said between gritted teeth.

"At least you can move," Zona said, trying to help her look on the bright side. "Imagine how miserable you'd be if you'd broken both legs."

"I don't want to. I'm already miserable enough," Louise snapped.

"It won't last forever," Zona said, parroting what her mother had told her about her financial situation.

Ten minutes later Louise was settled in her bed, a glass of water on her nightstand, and Zona and Bree were back in the living room.

"She's not going to be able to stay by herself," Bree said.

"I know," said Zona.

"How are you gonna manage this, Mom?"

"I'll take the rest of this week off, then I'll have to get her set up with some in-home care during the day."

"I can help in the afternoons," Bree offered.

"Just come visit her once in a while. That will keep her spirits up. I can handle the rest," said Zona. So much for getting that evening job as a waitress that she'd been considering. She'd have to come up with something else, something more flexible. Burglary, perhaps. She could do that while Louise was asleep. Haha.

"Gram's gonna go nuts," Bree predicted.

"At least she has a good view of the new neighbor's house from the guest bedroom. She can spy on him. And watch her true crime shows."

Bree grinned. "And work on her mystery novel."

"There's an idea. How about doing me a favor and picking her up a fancy notebook to write in after you're done with your shift tomorrow? It might help take her mind off her troubles."

"Good idea. I'll get her some colored pens, too."

"Great. Wait a minute." Zona hurried to her purse and pulled out her wallet, fishing out the twenty-dollar bill she'd been hoarding.

"Keep it, Mom. I've got this."

"No, take it," Zona insisted, shoving it at her. "Call it bad Mom tax." She'd half hoped her daughter would say, "You're a great mom."

She didn't. But she did say, "No way. Save it and buy yourself some chocolate. God knows you're gonna need it by the time you're done getting Gram set up." She gave Zona a quick kiss on the cheek, then went to the door where Darling had been whining and scratching.

"Oh, crud. Poor Darling. He's probably dying to go out. I'll get his leash," said Zona just as Bree opened the door.

"No, Darling," Bree said, trying to push him away from the opening with her leg.

Darling was too good an escape artist to be stopped by a leg as slender as Bree's. Off he dashed into the night.

"Oh, for crying out loud. Grab him, will you?" said Zona, and hurried to fetch his leash from where Louise kept it hanging on the coat closet doorknob.

DARLING WAS HAPPILY already on the new neighbor's driveway, pooping. No wonder he'd been whining.

Dog poop. Ick. Bree was willing to help with Gram, but no way was she picking up poop. Anyway, Mom would be out in a minute to pick it up. Poor Mom.

"Come on, Darling. Let's get you back inside," she said, and herded Darling back toward the house.

Her mother was on the porch when they got there. "Darling pooped on the neighbor's driveway," Bree informed her.

"I'll get it," Zona said just as Gram swore and called out, "Zona, I knocked over my stupid water glass."

"Want me to stay?" Bree offered. It was late and she had to be up before the birds, but so what? She didn't need that much sleep.

"No, go on home," Mom said as Darling raced off to the guest bedroom to check on Gram. "Thanks for helping."

"Anything for Gram," Bree said.

Her mother looked exhausted. "You gonna be okay?" Bree asked.

"Of course," Mom said. "We'll be fine."

Things have a way of working out, Gram always said. If you asked Bree, nothing was working out for any of them.

6

BY THE TIME ZONA HAD FINISHED dealing with the spilled water and her mother's frustration, she felt like she'd been chained and dragged by wild horses over a rocky mountain trail. Sleep. She needed sleep. And sleep she did, the dreamless dead sleep of a woman whose life roller-coaster ride had taken one final turn too many and who wanted off.

Come morning she was back on the roller coaster, calling in to work and leaving a message for her supervisor explaining her need for the week off. Then giving Louise a pain pill and helping her to the bathroom.

And speaking of bathroom, Darling needed to go out. Zona had a poop pick-up bag in hand and Darling leashed up and ready to go when she opened the door to hear a raised male voice coming her way from the new neighbor's house.

"Shit!" said the voice. It wasn't a shout, but it was loud enough for her to hear.

Darling was prancing and whining next to her, but she pulled him close and peeked out the front door. There stood the new neighbor next to his truck. He was dressed in work boots, jeans, and a T-shirt that showed off those beautifully sculpted pecs and arms. Ready for work. Ready to start the day.

Until encountering the present Darling had left the night before. Which Zona had completely forgotten about.

If only Darling had at least done his doggy business on the

man's lawn, he wouldn't have stepped in it. Or seen it. He certainly should have seen it there on the driveway. The phone in his hand was a big clue as to why he hadn't. He'd probably been texting on his way to his truck. Not expecting to encounter a mess from a dog he didn't own on his driveway.

He inspected the bottom of his boot, then lifted his head and looked her direction. His scowl felt like a laser beam shooting right at her and she ducked behind the door and quietly shut it. *Way to foster good relations with the neighbor.*

"We'll walk later," she said to Darling, and escorted him out the back door into the backyard for his bathroom break.

Darling bounded out and got busy marking his territory. He'd be fine out there for a little while, she decided, and went back to check on her mother.

As she went, she wondered if there was a way she could try to blame the poo present Darling had left next door on some mysterious dog from some other house. Probably not, since Darling was the only one living on their street.

She'd have to go over later and apologize. But first she had her mother to deal with.

She found Louise perched on the edge of her bed, leaning on her crutches and scowling. Her hair looked like a rat's nest.

"Just shoot me now," she grumbled.

"I'm sorry, Mom," Zona said. Her poor mother.

"Oh, don't listen to me. I'm just grumpy," said Louise.

"You have every right to be," Zona assured her.

"In some ways, yes. But it really could be worse. I didn't break my nose. Or my neck. I'm still alive." She looked sadly up at Zona. "I'm sorry I've tipped your life upside down."

Zona couldn't help but laugh. "My life was already upside down, and I did a pretty good job of tilting yours when I moved in."

"Nonsense. I'm happy to have you. And I'm grateful you're here. I'm just sorry I'm adding to your troubles."

"I guess we're equally sorry," Zona said, and managed a smile. "We'll get through this, and we'll be fine. Now, which would you like first, a sponge bath or breakfast?"

"Breakfast," Louise said. "But first, the potty. My big, exciting life."

Yeah, they were both living the life.

Zona had just assembled ingredients for an omelet when she heard the stump-stumping of Louise's crutches. She looked so different from how she'd looked when Zona had dropped her off for her big adventure. Maybe Zona's bad luck was rubbing off on her mother.

"Are you going to have an omelet, too?" Louise asked. "I have a feeling you're going to need your energy."

What Zona would have liked was a big, fat Cinnabon cinnamon roll. Pricey treats were now a thing of the past.

"Yes," Zona said. "And toast." Toast with jam. It wasn't the same as a cinnamon roll, but it would have to do. Maybe she'd attempt to make cinnamon rolls while she was home.

"Toast," Louise said, and sighed. "I should be eating fancy pastries and fresh pineapple."

"Who knows? You could have ended up with some stomach bug on the ship and been eating nothing but dry toast," Zona said, trying to spin the situation.

Louise wasn't having it. She scowled at her daughter.

Okay, so much for that. Zona shut her mouth and concentrated on serving breakfast.

"That was delicious," Louise told her after she'd finished. "But then you always were an excellent cook."

"It's hard to mess up an omelet," said Zona, and took the last bite of hers.

Thanks to Zona stocking up, they'd had an onion in the fridge as well as green bell peppers and tomatoes. Zona would have loved to add some fresh thyme, but she'd had to part with her garden when she'd parted with her house. Someone else was now enjoying her herbs and would be harvesting her tomatoes and zucchini. At least she had access to Meyer lemons and oranges from Louise's tree when they were in season. Maybe someday she'd have a house again, with fruit trees in the backyard.

When she was ninety. She frowned at her empty plate and picked it up, along with Louise's, taking them to the dishwasher. "Let's see if we can get you all dressed and gorgeous."

"With my new fashion statement," Louise said sourly.

Yep, they were both having fun.

Helping her mother with a sponge bath felt awkward, but they managed.

"I guess if I want to wash my hair I'll be stuck using the kitchen sink," Louise said with a sigh.

"Or dry shampoo?"

"Yuck."

"It won't be long before you can shower," Zona said, hoping to encourage her. The idea of getting her in and out of the shower and keeping her from falling once the permanent cast was on made her nervous. "I'm ordering a shower chair today," she added. A visual sign that this phase of Louise's misery would soon come to an end.

"Ugh. Those are for old people," Louise muttered.

"And for people who've broken a leg," said Zona.

Once Louise was dressed, Zona settled her on the couch with a second cup of coffee and the TV remote and slipped off to the kitchen to settle at the table with a second coffee of her own and see about getting some help. It appeared that, indeed, Louise would be able to afford someone to come in and hang out with her during the day, assist her with showers and make sure she didn't starve. Things were looking up.

Until Zona's first three calls to agencies that provided such help proved fruitless. It seemed everyone in Southern California needed in-home care.

After she'd refilled Louise's coffee cup a third time and failed on her fourth attempt to find someone, she called Gracie to vent.

"Poor Louise," said Gracie.

"Poor both of us," Zona amended. "I don't think my mom's cut out to be an invalid and I'm sure I'm not cut out to be a nurse."

"I might know somebody," Gracie said thoughtfully. "My Aunt Gilda does that kind of thing. She quit the agency she was working for a couple of months back, but maybe she'd be willing to help you guys. She's a nurse, but she got burned out on hospital work during COVID."

"Why'd she quit the agency?" Zona asked.

"She claimed they were sending her to take care of creepy old guys who kept hitting on her."

"Really?"

"Did I mention that Aunt Gilda is a legend in her own mind?"

"So, we could have a legend helping us out?"

"That you could."

"Give me her number."

Five minutes later Zona had left a message on Aunt Gilda's phone and was working on making lunch.

Louise claimed she wasn't hungry, so maybe she ate the grilled Gouda cheese and apple sandwich Zona made her just to be polite. After that it was another trip to the bathroom.

"Now I wish I'd done my pelvic floor exercises," Louise muttered as they made their way to the living room when she'd finished.

"I'm glad to see your sense of humor is returning," Zona said.

"Who said I'm joking?" Louise retorted. She studied Zona. "How are you doing with all of this?"

"I'm fine," Zona said. "I've got a call in for someone to come help you next week when I'm back at work."

Louise did not look pleased. "A stranger helping me bathe and dress? I'm sure not looking forward to that. Wait. Is he young and handsome?"

"See? Your sense of humor is returning."

"You keep saying that. Tell me about this person."

"He is a she and she's not young. It's Gracie's aunt."

Louise sighed. "Maybe I won't need help once I get a shower chair."

So far Louise wasn't doing all that well with maneuvering herself onto chairs. She half fell onto the couch with a grunt. *Yes, leave this woman home alone. Great idea.*

"I don't want you stuck here all by yourself when I'm working," Zona said firmly, and her mother frowned and looked out the window. The frown turned to surprise. "Oh, my gosh, Darling," she said, sounding panicked.

Zona had been so busy with her mother she'd forgotten all about the dog. "He's in the backyard." Wasn't he?

Louise leaned toward the window and squinted, shook her head vehemently. "Zona, he's loose!"

Zona looked out the window. Sure enough, there went Darling, trotting down the sidewalk. His second escape in twenty-four hours. Great.

"Don't worry, Mom. I'll go fetch him," Zona said, and started for the door.

"Hurry, before he gets run over," Louise said, panicked.

Zona rushed out the front door and reached the porch in time to see Darling trotting toward Martin's house, probably in hopes of finding a treat, since Martin spoiled him nearly as much as Louise.

"Darling!" Zona called, racing down the front walk.

Darling ignored her. He had places to go, people to see.

"Treat," she called. "Come get a treat!" She should have thought to grab a dog biscuit out of the cupboard.

Darling obviously didn't trust her to come through. He kept right on moving.

"Darling! Come here!" Zona commanded, running after him.

Of course, he didn't come. He'd spotted his friend Martin, out checking his mailbox.

Martin petted him and began looking around for Zona. At the sight of her, he waved. Then he gave Darling a good rub behind the ears, keeping him in place.

Darling's tail was still wagging like a metronome when Zona reached them. "Thanks for holding him here," she said. "I had him in the backyard, but he escaped."

Martin nodded. "Ah, our boy is a digger, is he?"

"I guess so," said Zona. She knelt to pet Darling, who was busy trying to lick Martin's hand. "You are a bad dog," she informed him.

Darling knew women loved bad boys, so he merely barked and licked her face.

"He's a good boy. He just wanted to come say hi," said Martin the softie. He looked at Zona, puzzled. "You're not at work."

"We've had a development," Zona said. "I should have called you earlier, but it's been crazy."

His brows pulled together. "What's going on?"

"Mom's back home."

"Back home?"

"She fell on the boat before they were even out to sea."

Martin's eyes instantly doubled in size. "Oh, no. How badly is she hurt?"

"Broken leg. She's in a cast and she's not happy."

He frowned and shook his head. "I can imagine. I'm sorry. I know how much she was looking forward to that cruise."

"She's going to be stuck in a cast all summer," Zona said. "I hope I've found someone to come in and help her when I'm at work."

"I could do that," Martin said.

"With showers," Zona clarified, and he blushed. "But she could really use some cheering up if you're interested in dropping by."

"Of course," he said. "How about I pick up something from Panda Express and bring you ladies dinner tonight?"

"That would be wonderful," said Zona.

"Great. I'll be over at six."

Zona thanked him, then took Darling by the collar and led him home. "You are not to do this again. You scared Mom half to death. And I will find where you got out and patch it, so don't think of pulling that stunt again."

Darling seemed to have gotten the message, since he whined.

"It's okay. You just can't be doing this stuff. I've got my hands full right now."

Back inside the house, Darling raced to Louise and buried his face in her lap, looking up at her soulfully and wagging his tail.

"What were you doing out there?" Louise scolded him as she rubbed his head.

"Looking for Martin. Who is, by the way, bringing us dinner tonight," said Zona.

"So, I guess you told him what happened," Louise said, sounding none too happy.

"I didn't give him details, and he was properly sympathetic."

Louise sighed. "I feel stupid."

"You shouldn't. Accidents happen."

"Ones like that only happen to foolish women who are showing off," Louise said, shaking her head.

"Accidents can happen anytime, anywhere," said Zona. She smiled at Louise. "I bet you were rocking your moves."

Louise smiled back. "I was." She lost the smile. "Until I made a fool of myself. Now I'm the talk of the boat."

"Only for a minute. People move on."

"Including George and Wayne. I probably won't hear from either of them. They'll both find some cute forty-year-old and probably be engaged by the time the ship docks in Maui."

"You don't know that."

"I do," said Louise. "Neither one has contacted me to see how I'm doing."

"They don't sound like keepers then."

"Somebody's keeping them. Probably Ursula," Louise grumbled.

"Ursula?"

"Never mind," Louise said with a flick of her hand. "Do you fancy an iced tea?"

Zona got the message. "That's a great idea. I'll make a pitcher."

By the time they'd finished their drinks, Bree had arrived with writing supplies and a Starbucks blended drink.

"Oh, sweetie, that was so thoughtful," cooed Louise.

"Mom and I figured you might get inspired and start your book. Maybe you can write a thriller about a woman who gets murdered on a cruise."

Louise frowned at that. "I'd hoped to do some research on the cruise."

Research into available men. Zona kept the remark to herself. Instead, she said, "You never know where you might find inspiration. Maybe something right here at home will inspire you."

"Yes, I can write about a woman who breaks her leg and falls in the shower and drowns," Louise muttered. Then, catching herself being cranky, added, "Never mind me. I think I need a pain pill. And a nap." She grabbed her crutches and struggled to get up. Both Zona and Bree rushed to help her. "I can do it," she said irritably, then fell back on the couch and swore.

"You'll get the hang of those crutches," Zona said. "You just have to get your sea legs." Oops. She pretended not to see her mother's scowl as she helped Louise to her feet.

"Poor Gram," said Bree once Louise was medicated and resting in the bedroom.

"Poor both of us," said Zona.

"I can stay with Gram if you want to go out," Bree offered.

And what? thought Zona. *Go shopping? Ha!* Like that would be happening anytime in the future. The temperature had climbed, and it was too hot to go for a hike or even a walk. Her biggest excitement would come in the evening when temperatures dropped and she took Darling out.

"I'm fine," she said to Bree.

"You don't look fine," Bree countered.

Zona was pretty sure she hadn't looked fine in a long time. She shrugged.

"I'm sorry your life sucks," said Bree.

"So does yours, thanks to me."

Bree didn't correct her. Instead, she said, "At least I got to go to the beach."

"You went to the beach? Who'd you go with?"

Bree suddenly looked wary. "Just a friend."

"Fen?" guessed Zona.

"Like I said."

"I don't blame you for being cautious," Zona began.

"It's more than cautious. Never going where you've been, Mom."

"I'm sorry I scarred you."

"I'm not scarred. I'm smart. I learned from watching what happened to you."

"Not all men are like Dad and Gary. You know that." Didn't she?

"Yeah, but you can't tell the difference because they all walk around with masks."

"Even Fen and his family?"

"They're okay, but people change. Men change. Anyway, we're fine just hanging out."

"There might come a time when you want to do more than hang out," Zona suggested.

"No way. Marriage is a trap designed by men."

Zona sighed inwardly. It was hard to see her daughter so cynical at such a young age. "Your grandpa was a good man."

"He never let Gram have a dog."

That was all Bree remembered of her grandpa? Really? How about when they'd made birdhouses together when she was a kid? Or the times he'd taken them all out for burgers and shakes at The Habit?

"Gram wasn't ready for another dog after losing Buster," Zona explained.

"Until after Grandpa died." Bree held up a hand before Zona could say anything. "I know. He was a nice man."

"And he left your grandma well taken care of financially, which ought to prove to you that not all men leave their families messed up."

"There's more than one way to mess up a family," said Bree.

Husband fail number one. "I know your dad hasn't always been the best."

That provoked a disgusted snort.

Luke had gotten busy with his hot young girlfriend and, other than a few random outings, had ignored his daughter, leaving Zona to have full custody. He'd paid child support, mostly on time, but other than that and giving her presents on birthdays and at Christmas, he'd opted out of being part of Bree's young life. He'd tried to make up for it later, when she was a teenager, but by then she'd built a wall between them he couldn't scale, no matter how many times he'd offered to take her to Disneyland . . . with his second family.

Bree shook her head. "If Dad comes through with any money for nursing school, I'll keel over from shock."

"He will," said Zona. They both knew it would be a pittance though.

"You sure can pick 'em, Mom."

The words stung and it was a welcome relief when Zona's phone rang. Caller ID showed it to be Gilda Radovich. "It's the nurse I called for your grandma," Zona said, and took the call.

"This is Gilda Radovich, calling you back," said the woman.

"I'm really glad to hear from you and I'm hoping you can help me," Zona said.

"What do you need?" asked Gilda, making no promises.

"My mother broke her leg and is in a cast and I need someone to hang out with her during the day when I'm at work."

"No housecleaning," Gilda said firmly.

"No, just helping with bathroom duties and making lunch. Mom's pretty easy, and she's very nice." When she wasn't feeling grumpy. "We really could use some help," Zona added.

"I'm not doing much home care these days. I'm semi-retired," said Gilda. "It has to be a special case."

But she had called. "This is pretty light duty," Zona pushed. "Mostly hanging out watching true crime shows. Maybe playing some cards."

"True crime shows? Does she watch *Deathline*?"

Well, well. A kindred soul for Louise. "Mom would like to be a mystery writer. She says that show is good research."

"A writer." Now Gilda sounded almost in awe.

"Could you maybe come over later this afternoon and meet us?" Zona asked.

There was a moment's silence, but it was followed by a firm, "Give me your address."

Oh, yes, it looked like Zona had found the perfect nurse for her mother.

7

"SO YOU FOUND SOMEBODY?" BREE ASKED.

"I'm hoping so. She's coming over later to meet your grandma."

"I think I'll come back," said Bree. "That way I can be sure you haven't hired a serial killer to take care of Gram."

Zona ignored the snark. "She'd probably be thrilled if I did," she said, and Bree snickered.

They'd moved their conversation away from the ugly past. Good. Now, all Zona had to worry about was her mother.

LOUISE WAS AWAKE and back on the couch, Bree keeping her company when the potential caregiver arrived for her interview at four. Louise was not looking thrilled.

"I really think I could manage on my own while you're at work," she said right before Gilda arrived. Neither her daughter nor her granddaughter believed her. Zona didn't think Louise even believed herself.

"Remember, it was your idea," Zona reminded her.

"I was in the hospital, on drugs. I've changed my mind."

The doorbell rang. "Too late. You may as well meet her."

Gilda Radovich looked like a LEGO woman come to life. Her body was short and square and so was her face, and her straight, dark hair was cut in a no-nonsense chin-length bob. She had hefty arms and looked like she could wrestle an alligator to the ground. She would have no trouble getting Louise in and out of the shower. Or helping her up if—heaven forbid!—she fell.

"I'm Gilda," she announced when Zona opened the door, Darling at her side, wagging a greeting. Gilda accompanied this with a smile that looked... Yes, even her squared-off lips made Zona think of LEGO. She was a walking social media filter.

"Thanks for coming," Zona said. "We really could use some help."

"Nobody calls me unless they do," Gilda said as she stepped inside.

The minute she did, Darling, the welcoming committee, felt it important to jump on her and give her some doggy love.

"Down, dog," Gilda commanded, trying to block Darling with a raised knee.

Gilda's knee couldn't reach high enough and Darling didn't discourage easily. He barked and tried again, determined to brace his paws on her chest.

"Down!" Gilda cried. "This dog is going to knock me over."

Zona doubted that. It would be easier to knock over a truck. "Bree, can you take Darling away," she called.

"He's high-spirited," Louise said from the couch as Bree came over to grab the dog's collar.

"Don't put him outside," Zona was quick to say as Bree led him away.

"I'll put him in Gram's room," Bree said, and hurried Darling off.

"Sorry about that," Zona said to Gilda as she led the woman into the living room.

"Dogs and children, they all love me," Gilda said with a shake of the head as Darling's whines followed them. "I don't know why."

The Man Next Door

"Do you have a dog?" asked Louise.

"Oh, no. No time," Gilda said. "Dogs are too messy. Believe me, I've spent enough time changing adult diapers. The last thing I want to do is have to pick up a dog's poop." She plopped onto the couch opposite Louise, who was half frowning. "I'm Gilda."

"I'm Louise and I really don't need help," Louise informed her.

"Probably not much," Gilda agreed. She turned to Bree, who was coming back into the living room. "Who are you?"

"This is my granddaughter, Bree," Louise answered for her.

"You look strong enough to help your grandma," Gilda observed.

"I can," Bree said, and sat down on another chair. "When I'm not working," she added.

"Bree is going to go to nursing school," Louise bragged.

Gilda nodded approvingly. "Good career choice. If you don't let yourself get burned out. All that being on your feet. Make sure you always wear support stockings. And never forget, doctors aren't gods, even though they think they are. Oh, and never marry one. My friend Gail married a doctor, and he has made her life miserable ever since." Gilda shook her head over her friend's foolishness. "That man is a control freak. Their children are grown, but she still won't leave him. He keeps telling her she'd never make it without him. Disgusting. I never trusted the man. I'm good at reading people."

And talking about them.

Bree looked at Zona and raised her eyebrows. *Who is this woman?*

Zona shrugged. *She's available, that's who she is.*

Gilda pointed to Louise's cast. "How'd you break your leg?"

"I fell. I was on a cruise."

"That's too bad," said Gilda. "Travel can be dangerous.

You never know when disaster's going to strike. My cousin took a trip to London, and when she was waiting for the train to Croydon, she fell off the platform."

"Was she hurt?" Louise asked, wide-eyed.

"Oh, yes. Broke her neck and died."

Louise gasped. "That's horrible. Did someone push her?"

"We'll never know," Gilda said. "Of course, you don't have to go far from home to get hurt. One old fool of a man I was called in to care for got on his grandson's hover board at Christmas. Fell off and broke his hip. Let me tell you, after a certain age, you break a hip and it's the beginning of the end."

This was cheery stuff. "Mom's doing fine," Zona said.

"I can tell, you've got spirit," Gilda said to Louise. "And you're still young so you'll be up and around in no time," she added, and Louise preened. "You know, I'm not doing much of this anymore, but after talking to your daughter I had to meet you," Gilda continued.

Louise raised her eyebrows. "Oh?" she prompted and looked at Zona.

"You're a writer, right?"

"Well, I want to be," said Louise. "I haven't written anything yet."

"I love mysteries," said Gilda. "I could give you ideas. I had one woman . . . I'm sure her husband was trying to kill her."

Louise leaned forward. "No."

"Oh, yes," Gilda said with an emphatic nod. "He had her on this strict vegan diet because, according to him, he was worried she was going to gain weight while she was recovering from foot surgery. But it wasn't a balanced diet, and she wasn't getting enough calories to keep a bird alive. I tried to tell him, but he wouldn't listen. He wouldn't even let her have the dark chocolate I brought her. She was wasting away, looked like a skeleton. Let me tell you, I kept my eye on him."

"Is she okay?" asked Louise.

"Thank God, yes," Gilda said, then added, "For the moment. I still go by and visit once in a while, just to check on her. She still doesn't look very good if you ask me. Too gaunt. I don't trust that man."

"You never know about people," said Louise. "When a person dies mysteriously, it always turns out the murderer was somebody no one suspected. Unless money is involved. Then you know right off the spouse was behind it," she added.

"You sure do," Gilda agreed. "Did you watch the *Deathline* episode about the honeymoon killer?"

"Oh, my gosh, yes," said Louise, and the two began dissecting the story of the supposedly distraught husband who had wound up making sure his new wife met with an accidental death after heavily insuring her.

Yep. Gilda would be staying.

"Hopefully, we don't have any killers around here," Zona said, bringing them back to the reason they'd called Gilda. "Gilda, what do you think? Can you help us out?"

"As long as you don't need me to stay the night. I don't do graveyard shifts."

"We don't really need you at all," Louise said, then added, "But I wouldn't mind some company."

"May I show you around?" Zona offered.

Gilda nodded. "Yes, I want to see how your bathroom is set up." She eyed Louise's cast. "Doing sponge baths for now?"

"Yes, until the swelling goes down and after that I get an even clunkier cast," Louise said sourly. "Then at least I'll be able to shower."

"That'll be a pain in the patootie," predicted Gilda, the little ray of sunshine.

"We have a shower chair arriving tomorrow," Zona said. "And I've ordered rails for the toilet."

"Excellent," Gilda approved. "I'll get you through this.

Don't you worry," she assured Louise. "Let's check out the living environment," she said to Zona.

"And while you're at it, honey, get Gilda some of that lavender lemonade you made," Louise said.

It looked like Gilda was not only staying, but she was also going to become part of the family.

An hour later all had been arranged. Gilda would be stepping in when Zona was at work, helping Louise with her personal needs and making lunch. And, at the rate they were bonding, probably staying for dinner. But not, she was quick to inform Zona, taking the dog for walks.

Both she and Bree left just as Martin arrived with dinner. Soon they'd need traffic lanes. Louise was not going to be bored during her recuperation.

"Why don't you keep Mom company while I get this plated," Zona said to him as she took the giant bag of food.

"Happy to. Look at you, you poor thing," he said to Louise as Zona went to the kitchen to dish up. What her mother was missing out on in fun was being more than made up for in sympathy and attention.

Zona set things up on the dining room table, and they all settled in to eat with Darling looking longingly on.

"Not for you, baby," Louise said to him. "Zona will get you a dog biscuit."

Zona had been about to dig into her chow mein, but she went to the kitchen and fetched a treat for Darling. She should have remembered to put on her Fitbit. Heaven knew she was certainly getting her steps in, and it would have been interesting to see how many.

She'd settled back at the table when they heard the rumble of Alec James's diesel truck and saw it pull up into his driveway. "Looks like our new neighbor is home," said Louise. "Have you met him, Martin? I haven't had a chance to say more than hello."

"He seems like a nice enough man," Martin said, and reached for an egg roll.

"I think he's single," said Louise.

"I've seen a woman over there who drives a red PT Cruiser, so don't start making plans," Zona told Louise. "Anyway, I'm not looking for anyone," she added. Just as a reminder to her mother. Okay, and herself, too.

"I know," Louise said with a shrug. "But that's when you often find the love of your life, when you're not looking. Sometimes that person can be right under your nose. Right, Martin?"

"Right," Martin agreed. The smile he gave Louise was all hearts and kisses. Funny how blind her mother was when it came to what was right under *her* nose.

Zona cleared the table and left them to visit while she cleaned up. She could still hear them out there talking after she'd finished. There was never a lull in conversation between those two.

Louise laughed at something he said. They didn't need her company so she went out to the backyard to see if she could find where Darling had gotten out.

There it was, a nice deep hole beneath a section of the fence between them and their new neighbor. Ugh.

Well, it was a first offense. And one hole did not a doggy felon make. She fetched a shovel from the toolshed and got to work filling it in. She was halfway through when she heard a female squeal of disgust coming from next door, followed by a male voice demanding to know what the matter was.

"Dog poop," wailed the female voice. Oh, no. A second deposit from Darling.

Zona heard the male voice swear. She felt her cheeks heating and was glad no one could see her. Her face probably looked lobster red. She would have to go over later and explain about Darling getting loose. Once she'd filled Alec James in on what was going on with her mother, he'd understand. Hopefully.

She patted down the dirt she'd replaced, returned the shovel to the shed, and then came in and washed up. Louise and Martin were still chatting, so it seemed the perfect time to go next door and apologize.

Darling was immediately dancing at her side, ready to go with her. "I'll take you out in a little bit," she promised, "but I don't think you'll be welcomed where I'm going."

He whined as she gave him a gentle shove away from the front door and then slipped out.

Some of the day's heat had drifted away, leaving behind a pleasant warmth, and the gardenias from the bush in her mother's front yard were sending out their perfume. She could hear children's shouts and laughter coming from a few houses down, a sure sign that the grade schoolers who lived there were enjoying the pool in their backyard. Her neighborhood could have been a movie set, all calm and tranquil: Mayberry, the California version.

Except as she approached her neighbor's front door, doggy-do bag in hand to show she intended to clean up both messes, it didn't sound like Mayberry. She could hear raised voices inside through the front door, though she couldn't make out the words. She leaned in closer and heard what sounded like a cupboard slam. And was that something breaking? What was going on in there? The living room drapes were closed so she couldn't see. Should she ring the doorbell and find out?

She pressed her ear to the door, but words were still muffled. Suddenly, she heard a shriek. It made her jump a step back. The rumble of an angry male voice pushed her another step away.

This was obviously not a good time to come calling. She backed off the porch, half afraid the front door would fly open, and her neighbor would come out and demand to know what she was doing on his property.

She had a good reason for being on his property, looking like an eavesdropper. The little bag was proof of that.

But she could apologize for Darling's bad behavior another time. She hurried over to the scene of Darling's crimes and scooped up the mess sitting on the walk as best she could. Next, she stopped at the yard, where Darling had also left a present, and got that, too. Then she speed-walked back to her own property, her heart beating fast for no good reason, and got rid of the evidence.

Back in her mother's house, everything was calm. Martin and Louise were still talking, demonstrating how civilized people behaved.

Although Louise was looking drawn and tired.

"How are you doing, Mom?" Zona asked.

"I'm starting to hurt," Louise confessed.

"You need to stay ahead of the pain," Martin cautioned, and she nodded. He stood. "I'd better scram and let you relax."

Louise didn't encourage him to stay, a sure sign that she was, indeed, done for the day.

Zona walked him to the door. "Thanks for everything," she said.

"Anything for your mother," he replied. "I'll be happy to stop by and look in on her while you're at work. And walk Darling."

"You're a good friend, Martin," Zona said.

He wanted to be more, she knew it, and he probably knew that she knew it. But he left that unspoken. Instead, he said, "Call if you need anything."

"We will," she promised.

She stood for a moment, watching him go down the front walk. He was so easygoing, so caring, so . . . unimpressive. Her own father had been handsome and fit. Louise had always been a little too proud of his looks, and she would probably never settle for less in a partner. It was too bad, really, but the heart wanted what the heart wanted.

Zona frowned. What a stupid expression. Hearts never

wanted what was good for them. She was sure never letting hers have its way ever again.

She looked over to Alec James's house. The red PT Cruiser was still parked out front. She strained to listen for sounds of arguing but heard nothing. Of course, she wouldn't. She was too far away.

"None of your business," she told herself.

Then remembered her mother's conversation with Gilda about murdering spouses. "Oh, stop," she muttered, and shut the door.

Louise was already up on her crutches. "I'm pooped."

"I bet you are. Let's get you in bed and get another pain pill in you."

"Let's get you to bed," Louise repeated bitterly. "I feel like I'm five."

"Just please don't act like it," Zona said. "No pouting."

"I wouldn't dream of it."

"You know, this isn't going to be so bad," Zona said as she and Darling accompanied Louise to her bedroom to change. "Martin's going to spoil you rotten and you and Gilda are going to have fun talking about murderers."

Louise did half smile at that. "Yes, I think we are. I'm not sure she and Darling are going to become friends though."

"Darling has enough friends," said Zona, and Louise chuckled. Then she sobered. "Did you see how he got out?"

"Yes, he dug under the fence. I've filled in the hole."

"Good. We don't want him getting loose again."

"Our new neighbor sure doesn't. Darling left a present over there and he stepped in it this morning."

"He did? How do you know?"

"I was about to go out and heard his reaction."

"It could have been some other dog."

"Could have, but I doubt it."

"Should you go over and apologize?"

"I tried while you and Martin were visiting, but it wasn't a good time."

"Oh?"

"I told you he's got someone. She drives a red PT Cruiser. They were fighting. I went to the door to explain about Darling getting loose and I could hear them inside, screaming at each other."

"Oh, dear. You're right. It wasn't a good time," Louise said. "I hate it when men yell. Your father never yelled."

Neither had either of Zona's husbands. She'd always been the one doing the yelling, though she didn't mention that to her mother.

"I'll catch up with him at some point," she said.

"But keep your distance when you do. It sounds like he's got a temper."

"So now you're saying our neighbor is dangerous."

"Probably not. But maybe it's just as well he's with someone. You don't need a man with a short fuse. They can become abusive, and you've already put up with enough."

She sure had. Alec James was a fine-looking specimen, but good-looking men were a little like walnuts. The shell might look fine, but that didn't mean you wouldn't find something rotten inside once you broke it open. Anyway, she was done with men and done with love. Both had brought her enough pain to last a lifetime.

She helped Louise settle in for the night, then got Darling's leash and took him for a walk. The red PT Cruiser was still parked in the driveway next door, so things must have settled down between Alec James and that woman. Either that or he'd barked her into submission, and she was currently huddled in a corner, whimpering.

"Oh, stop," Zona told herself.

She was living in a normal boring neighborhood. Scenarios like the ones that played out on true crime programs were few and far between. People fought all the time and even yelled, then made up. For all she knew, her neighbors were over there having make-up sex at that very moment.

But their interaction had sounded so . . . intense.

She'd done some intense arguing herself. Yelling didn't mean a thing.

Why was it so quiet over there now?

8

THE NEXT MORNING ZONA WAS HAULING in a huge box left by Amazon on her porch when Darling made his third great escape, leaping over the obstacle. She tried to catch him but only fell over it, landing with an "Oof," like a track runner who'd missed the hurdle.

"Darling!" she called, scrambling to her feet. "Come here!" Darling kept going. "Treat! Come get a treat," she added hopefully. He'd heard that word enough. He should have known what it meant.

Apparently, he didn't, since he kept going. Or he'd lost either his hearing or his appetite. Or the lure of freedom to rove all over the neighborhood outweighed doggy house arrest, no matter what was being served.

Louise picked that moment to come swinging out of her room on her crutches. "What's happened?" she demanded as Zona carried the box back inside.

"I was bringing this in and Darling got loose," Zona said. "Don't worry, I'll go get him," she hurried to add. "I'll just put on some shorts and grab my shoes." No way was she running around the neighborhood in her sleep tee.

The words were barely out of her mouth when a male voice asked, "This is your dog, right?"

She stood up to see Alec James on her doorstep, holding onto Darling's collar. Darling was whining and straining to get free.

Her neighbor was dressed for work in a pec-hugging gray T-shirt and jeans and boots, freshly shaved and frowning.

Zona found herself feeling self-conscious over her sloppy nightwear and messy hair, which looked like bats had used it for a playground. She was almost as embarrassed over how she was coming across as a neighbor.

She took hold of Darling's collar and scooted him inside the house, then stepped out to join her surprise visitor on the porch, shutting the door after her. "He's my mother's dog," she began. Underlying message, *Don't blame me.* "I'm afraid he got out when I was trying to bring in a package," she continued, hoping her morning breath wasn't making its way to her neighbor's nose. Even if she wasn't interested, she still had her pride.

"I found him taking a dump in my yard," Alec James said, sounding more put-upon and long-suffering than angry.

"I did see that Darling had left a mess on your property and I came over last night to clean it up and apologize." *And tried to eavesdrop.*

Zona the nosy neighbor. She could feel her cheeks heating. "But I think you had company," she hurried on. "I did my best to pick it up."

"It doesn't pick up well once it's flattened by a shoe," he informed her.

It put a sizzle on her face. "Sorry," she said.

The frown downgraded to a frustrated lip clamp. "Never mind." He switched gears and offered the same killer smile she'd seen when they first met. "Sorry I came across as a tool just now. I'm dealing with some shit." Judging from the yelling she'd heard, he wasn't dealing very well.

"Sorry you stepped in some," she said, smiling back.

"Shit happens, huh?" he joked.

"It sure does," she agreed. "We're deep in it over here."

"I guess there's always enough to go around," he said. "Well, have a good one."

"You, too," she said.

She watched as he went down her front walk. It was hard to picture this man in a yelling rage. What to make of their new neighbor?

Nothing, she told herself firmly.

"You were out there a long time," Louise called from the couch when Zona came back inside. "What was that all about?"

Zona joined her on the couch. Darling came over and laid his head on her lap as if to say he was sorry, and she rubbed behind his ears. "Our new neighbor was trying to be nice about Darling pooping on his property."

"I hope he wasn't mad."

"A little irritated. I can't blame him. It was a second offense. Third, actually."

"Oh, dear," said Louise.

"At least he was cool about it. Nice, actually. Way different than what I heard last night when I went over to clean up the mess and apologize."

Still, even someone nice was bound to yell if pushed hard enough. What had pushed Alec James?

"People often hide who they really are under a veneer of politeness," said Louise.

Zona had seen two sides of Alec James. Was the nice side just a veneer?

Okay, that was enough analyzing the neighbor. She had things to do.

"Never mind him," she said. "Let's get you ready for the day. Then I'll take Darling for a walk. After that I'll get your shower chair assembled so it will be ready for when we need it," she said, pointing at the large Amazon box.

"There goes your day," Louise said, shaking her head. She scooted forward, leaning on her crutches, bracing to stand, and Zona moved to help her up. "I'm making so much work for you," she said sadly.

"I made enough work for you when I was growing up," pointed out Zona.

Louise had lost a baby when Zona was a toddler and had turned into a helicopter parent. Zona in turn had eventually bolted for freedom every chance she got, just like Darling, sneaking out to unsanctioned teen parties, trying weed, sneaking into bars, keeping Louise running for the hair salon to hide a growing crop of gray hairs.

And now here she was, a needy adult, back home after her latest slide sideways. Nothing her mother could require would ever be too much.

"I loved every minute of it," Louise assured her as they made their way to the bedroom. "And I love having you here with me. I just wish it was under happier circumstances. For both of us."

"I guess even if circumstances can't be happy, we can. Right?"

Louise smiled at her. "Yes, we can."

Zona smiled, too. She wasn't even remotely happy about what had landed her in her current situation, putting her back at the proverbial square one, and she felt sorry that her mother had missed out on her big adventure. But she was happy that they had each other and enjoyed a good relationship. They had food in the pantry, a lovely house to live in, and good friends. It was more than many people had.

After she helped Louise get dressed and gave her a smoothie and a pain pill, she got herself showered and dressed and then took Darling out for a walk.

Alec James's truck was gone, but the red PT Cruiser was still parked in the driveway, and she could hear the music of Nigerian rapper Olamide, one of Bree's favorites, drifting out from inside the house. Which meant it was cranked up high. The pretty redhead in there was already in party mode. Obviously, nothing horrible had happened next door.

Zona found herself wondering if the woman worked. She was pretty enough to be a model. Maybe she was. Or maybe she was in between jobs. Or maybe Alec James had said, "You don't need to work, baby. I'll take care of you."

Thinking of the raised voices she'd heard, Zona thought of the controlling husbands in the true crime shows her mother watched. Maybe he was like them. Maybe he had his woman convinced she needed him and would be nothing without him. There were men like that out there. Thank God Zona had at least avoided that kind of loser.

Still, he didn't seem like the type. She shared her theory when she got back home and she and Louise were in the living room, drinking coffee, Zona in a chair, Louise on the couch, with Darling lying on the floor next to her. Yep, sure done analyzing the neighbor.

"With all the yelling you heard, it's certainly possible," said Louise. "If he hurt her, he probably apologized later, promised it would never happen again. He'll come home with flowers or jewelry."

"Yuck," said Zona. "Of course, we're just speculating here," she added, reeling in her imagination.

"But still, whatever's going on over there doesn't sound good." Louise shook her head. "I'd hoped he might be someone you could get interested in."

"I've come to the conclusion there's no one for me," Zona said. There was a sad thought. But this was the hand she'd been dealt, and she'd have to play it.

No, no, no! No gambling metaphors.

"I'm sure that's not true," Louise insisted. "You'll find someone wonderful eventually. But it won't be this man. He could have the woman with him brainwashed. The Svengali effect."

"Who the heck is that?"

Louise looked at Zona in surprise. "How is it you've never heard of Svengali?"

"You never read me any bedtime stories about him?" Zona cracked.

"He was a fictional controlling monster. There are plenty of men out there like that. Men who are charming and seem normal, but they overpower and manipulate. Sounds like our neighbor, doesn't it? It just goes to show, you can't trust a man with two first names."

"Oh, that's the problem," Zona teased. "So, I guess our new neighbor isn't going to turn out to be my perfect man after all?"

Louise gave a one-shouldered shrug. "It looks like I was wrong. And it's a good thing you never took him any cookies."

"Yes, he might have lured me into his house and Svengalied me."

Louise didn't laugh. "Like I said earlier, people can be good at hiding who they are. Take that man in LA, the one who murdered his wife and chopped her up and stuck her in the freezer. Everyone thought he was so nice."

"I don't think our neighbor is planning to chop up his girlfriend and stick her in the freezer."

"Who knows? Let's not be getting neighborly with him."

"No worries there," said Zona. She already had two love strikes against her. She wasn't about to go for a third.

"I'M GETTING SQUIRMY," Louise complained. "I hate all this sitting around."

"Maybe you need to start writing your book, Gram," suggested Bree, who'd stopped by to visit. "Have you started working on it yet?" The book Louise kept talking about writing but kept postponing.

"I'm not in a good place right now," she said.

"But isn't that a good thing? You probably have all kinds of negativity swirling around in you that will make a great murder mystery," Bree said.

"There's nothing swirling here. We are a hotbed of boredom," Louise complained.

"Spy on the neighbor," Bree joked. "You might get inspired."

"Oh, there's a good idea. Everyone should spy on their neighbor," Zona said in disgust. She'd already come a little too close for comfort to doing that herself.

"People spy on each other all the time," said Bree.

"Yeah? Who's spying on you?" Zona retorted.

"You. You're always wanting to know what's going on with me and Fen. Which is nothing, by the way."

"Well, that's boring," said Louise.

"You've got the neighbor. You don't need me," Bree joked.

AND I'M ABOUT as exciting as a slug, Bree thought on Friday afternoon as she let herself into her shared apartment. No one was there when she arrived and that was mildly depressing. She should have gone to the mall with Gaylyn and Monique. Not that she would have bought anything. Recreational spending was so far gone it wasn't even in the rearview mirror. Well, except for Mrs. Fields. She'd have splurged on a cookie.

Bree hated living in a social void. Which was what her weekend was going to be if she didn't make some plans. She needed to come up with something fun to do.

Fen. He'd be up for a good time. Just as friends, of course. He knew the rules.

She texted him.

Hey what U doing 2nite

Wedding rehearsal Need a date Sat Want 2 come

Weddings. When she was little, she'd thought weddings were better than Disneyland—the bride in her gorgeous gown, the music, the beautiful cake, and the big party where she never got to stay long because her mom was always informing her that she was tired and it was time for bed. After running around the reception and trying to imitate the grown-ups dancing, she usually was tired by the time Mom took her home. She'd been eight when Mom married Gary and had been her mom's flower girl. Mom had let her help choose the wedding colors and decide on the cake. Gary had danced with her and told her she looked like a princess. She'd felt like a princess in her fancy dress. It had all seemed so perfect, especially when her own dad wasn't much in the picture.

But then as she'd moved through grade school and middle school, she'd started seeing the wedding fairy tales go bad all around her, her friends' parents splitting up, the fighting and having to get shuttled back and forth between houses. One of her friends' dads had cheated just like Bree's dad had done, another's dad was balking at paying child support and the mom was mad and telling everyone about it. Happily-ever-after gone sour. She told herself it wouldn't ever happen in her family. Dad was a mess, but Gary was solid. He loved her mom and her. They were golden.

And then they weren't. And it was just Mom and her, reeling from the shock of having their lives turned upside down.

Weddings were a joke.

No thanx, she texted back. Byeee

She'd find something to do. She'd text Gaylyn and meet up with her and Monique. Then Saturday she'd talk Gaylyn into going to Lost Worlds with her. She'd play laser tag and find some cute snack of a guy to hang out with. Much smarter than going to a wedding and drinking the happily-ever-after Kool-Aid.

A stupid thought stole into her mind. What if there really was such a thing as happily-ever-after, like what Auntie Gracie had? What if you could get it right?

It was a big what-if, and she'd seen the dark side of playing that game. She would have to be insane to follow in her mother's shaky footsteps and rush into love. She hoped Mom had learned her lesson. The last thing they needed was for Mom to drag them into another mess.

In the end, she wound up hanging out with Monique that evening, binge-watching episodes of *Love Is Blind*. Gaylyn had plans. Of course she did. How was it that Gaylyn always managed to find the guys who didn't want commitment?

What was Fen doing? Had he met some cute bridesmaid and fallen for her? Had they gone out for drinks after all the rehearsal stuff?

Oh, who cared!

9

LOUISE ALREADY HAD CABIN FEVER. "Let's hit some garage sales tomorrow," she said to Zona.

The last thing Zona wanted to do was visit a collection of lovely homes in Glendora and pick over the owners' castoffs like a buzzard. She was sure it would remind her of having to sell most of her own possessions to right her sinking financial ship. And what if Louise fell?

"I don't know, Mom. It's going to be hard for you to get in and out of my car with that cast on, and your car isn't any bigger."

"We'll get Martin to take us. It'll be fun."

"Let's get Martin to take *you*," Zona corrected her.

"I know you haven't done much of this," said Louise.

Not since she'd been a kid and Louise had taken her along on what she'd called treasure hunts. Louise had given her a few dollars to spend, and she'd been happy to come away with children's books and toys. But once she became a teenager such nonsense was behind her, and during her years of false security with Gary she'd had everything she needed and enough money to buy anything she wanted.

Her mother could certainly afford to buy anything she wanted from a store or online. Not that she needed anything.

"But it can be fun," Louise continued. "It's all about the thrill of the hunt. One woman's junk is another woman's treasure. You might even find something you could resell online and make some money."

Make some money. Those were the magic words.

Except, as the saying went, you had to spend money to make money. And Zona had a whole ten dollars in her wallet at the moment. Not much of an investment. Still, if it would make her mother happy.

"All right," she said, "but only if Martin will drive us in his car."

Martin's Hyundai was a sedan. It was roomier than Zona's car and it rode low enough to the ground that they wouldn't have much of a problem getting Louise in and out of it. Zona didn't think her mother realized how taxing her proposed adventure was going to be, but even if she got out for an hour, it would probably do her good. As long as she managed to stay upright.

The call was made, and Martin happily signed on for chauffeur duty, promising to come get them at eight the next morning.

"Eight," Zona groaned, thinking of how long it would take to get her mother ready and fed. "Don't garage sales usually start at nine?"

"We'll have to go to the ATM first," said Louise.

"And we have to leave at eight for that? It will take all of ten minutes to go to the ATM."

"People always get to garage sales before they start. I don't want anyone scooping us."

"Oh, by all means, let's be rude, too," Zona said.

"Sellers won't mind if we're a few minutes early, believe me, especially if they see I'm on crutches."

"Playing the sympathy card," Zona murmured.

"Why not? Anyway, the early bird catches the worm," Louise informed her. "I've looked, and there are a lot of worms available starting at nine, so we need to get going right away."

"We don't want to miss out on any worms," Zona teased.

Looking for worms. How humiliating. Maybe it wouldn't have been under different circumstances, if Zona had money and was simply out for fun. After all, half of America was into garage sales. Considering her lack of money, this felt more like desperation, and she said as much.

"There's nothing desperate about finding a bargain," Louise insisted. "It's no different than shopping a sale at a department store or online, except someone else already tested out what you're buying. Trust me. You'll get addicted."

There was another word Zona didn't like. It reminded her of Gary and what he'd done to himself and to their family.

"That won't be me," she said.

"I'll remind you that you said that." Louise so loved having the last word.

OFF THEY WENT on Saturday morning, Louise excited to hunt for treasures, Zona half wishing she was a kid again, clueless about money and excited to find a My Little Pony or a book.

"Thanks for doing this with us," Louise said to Martin once they had her settled in the front passenger seat.

"I'm always happy to spend time with you. You know that," he said to her. "Your mother and I met at a garage sale," he told Zona.

"I remember," Zona said. Probably the best garage-sale treasure her mother had ever found.

And Louise took his devotion way too much for granted. Zona wondered if her mother even realized how very woven into the fabric of her life Martin had become. Would she see him in a new light if he lost some weight? Started going to the gym? Louise couldn't be that shallow.

Or maybe she could. Dad had been a hard act to follow. He'd prided himself on being in shape and had sneered at men who didn't do the same. Maybe Louise had become a sneerer by association.

Zona knew better than to focus on the outside wrapping. Look at the two men she'd chosen. Both were proof that what was on the outside could be nothing more than false advertising, hiding something faulty beneath. Their neighbor was another example. If ever there was a woman magnet, it was him. But who knew what was hiding behind that charming smile?

"You never know where you're going to find your next best friend," Louise was saying.

"Or more," added Martin.

Louise pretended not to hear. It looked like Martin was doomed to be forever kept on the friendship shelf.

After stocking up on cash, they were off to their first stop, an estate sale where Louise was delighted to find a set of pink Depression glass sherbet bowls. Louise needed more dishes like Disney needed more princesses, but it didn't stop her from scooping them up.

"Twelve dollars for that set," she crowed as they returned to Martin's car, Zona carrying the newspaper-wrapped dishes in a small cardboard box along with the salt and pepper shakers shaped like roosters that Louise had fallen in love with. "I'm going to use those sherbet dishes next time I have Susan and Carol over for lunch."

"They were a find," agreed Martin, who had scored an old video player.

The two of them were having fun on their own. They didn't need Zona. She said as much as she and Louise made their slow progress down a driveway past other treasure hunters to their next destination, a garage bursting with tables full of housewares, while Martin parked the car farther down the street past the crowd of vehicles.

"Of course we do," Louise said. "Anyway, I really think

before the morning is over you might find some things that you can sell and make a little money."

"Yes, with my whopping ten dollars," scoffed Zona.

"I have money."

"Which I want you to spend on yourself."

"Don't be silly. I don't need anything. You know that. Ooh, look. Purses!" Louise swung herself over to a rack where a large collection of purses hung.

You couldn't not look at purses. Zona followed her.

A patchwork leather one caught Zona's eye. She took it down and inspected it. Twenty dollars, huh? Coach. Hmm. It was in excellent condition.

"That looks like it escaped from the seventies," said Louise.

"It's Coach," said Zona.

Louise took it and inspected it. "That could be worth something. Get your phone out and check," she whispered.

Zona pulled her phone out of her back pants pocket and did a quick check on eBay. A similar purse had sold for twice that amount. She turned the phone so Louise could see the screen.

"Get it," said Louise.

"Loan me ten? I'll pay you back," Zona promised. Providing she really could sell that purse. Then she'd make a profit of a whole . . . ten dollars? Or less minus the selling fee. Was this worth the effort?

It was, she decided. She could possibly make more on the purse, and if she found other things to sell, the small profits would snowball into larger profits.

"Done," said Louise. "And you will not pay me back. Don't be ridiculous."

They found more than a purse that morning. Zona scored a turquoise-and-silver beaded belt that, after a quick bit of research, she realized she could sell for a nice profit.

She also found a Harley-Davidson Barbie doll. Very Cool

Barbie. "I might have to keep you for inspiration," Zona murmured.

In the end, she didn't. She wound up giving the doll to a little girl who had seen it in Zona's hand and fallen in love.

"She must want to come live with you," Zona said, and handed the doll over.

"Thank you," the mother gushed.

"Your kindness will be rewarded," Louise predicted.

It was at the next garage sale, where Zona scored yet another purse she suspected would sell for more than what she paid and a pair of reindeer-shaped candleholders that Louise said were Fitz and Floyd, and a vintage Oscar the Grouch Sesame Street cookie jar.

"There's your reward. Those candleholders will go for a high price if you wait and put them up for sale in November," she assured Zona. "I think you've had a profitable morning."

The bonus was Martin taking them to lunch after their final stop. But at lunch, Louise was looking exhausted and in need of a pain pill. "I'm ready to flop on the couch," she announced.

"We shouldn't have kept you out so long," Martin said, looking at her in concern.

"Oh, yeah, we twisted her arm," Zona cracked.

"It was fun," Louise said. "I'm very happy with my finds."

"So am I. Thanks for the help, Mom," Zona said, and smiled at her.

"It's going to be fun watching what happens when you put those up for sale," said Louise.

Yes, it was.

Martin dropped them off and as soon as Zona had Louise settled on the couch with her cell phone, the TV remote, and a glass of ice water and the extra-strength Tylenol she had switched to taking, she let Darling out into the backyard for a romp and a potty break. Supervising him to make sure he didn't dig. A few games of fetch and his tongue was lolling and she was ready to get inside and start learning the art of selling online.

Selling online, she decided, wasn't as snap-your-fingers easy as she'd heard. There was work involved. Staging her items and taking pictures, figuring out shipping, double-checking prices, writing descriptions, and posting the items. It took her the whole afternoon.

But so what? What else did she have to do on a Saturday? Nothing. Probably nothing for the rest of her life, except continuing to dig out of the deep money pit she was in.

She reminded herself that even though her money troubles had seemed to come on her overnight, they hadn't. They'd been stealthily sneaking up on her over time. Getting free from them would take time as well. A lot of it.

"You can do this," she told herself. "You're not dead yet."

Then she thought of the scene in the Monty Python movie with the plague victim who refused to die and she started to laugh. It was more hysterical than happy, but it was the first laughter that had escaped her mouth in over a year. Maybe that was progress.

By the time she was done, her mother had enjoyed streaming half of her favorite true crime show, had a nap, and was in the process of talking on her phone with one of her neighborhood friends. "Come on over, and bring Susan, too," she said. "We're not doing anything tonight."

It was true, but it was depressing to hear. Once upon a time on a Saturday night Zona would have been going out to dinner and a movie with Gary or catching a show at a local comedy club. Now it was home with Mom, doing nothing. But that beat what she'd been doing only a few months earlier—crying, pacing the floor, worrying, mourning the safe, happy life she'd once thought she had.

So, Carol and Susan, Louise's two besties, came over, insisting on bringing dinner—Carol's curried coconut shrimp paired with Susan's Thai beef salad. They also brought lemon bars for dessert and white wine to wash it all down.

The friends were shown Louise's garage sale scores and raved over Zona's finds. "Take the belt down. I'll give you a hundred for it right now," said Susan. She was tall and slender, with long chestnut hair (not colored, she always insisted). She would look great in the belt.

"Done," said Zona.

"Ka-ching," said Louise and winked at Zona.

Martin stopped by to check on Louise and was invited to join the party, and the group wound up streaming the movie classic *Rear Window*.

"That's still a good movie," Carol said as the ending credits rolled.

"But a little preposterous," said Susan.

"Not really," Louise said, and proceeded to tell them all about the murdering husband in nearby Los Angeles who'd made the news after cutting his wife to bits.

"Gross," Carol said, wrinkling her nose.

"Everyone has a dark side," Louise said, making Martin frown.

Zona laughed. "Yeah, Mom? What's yours?"

"I don't share chocolate," Louise said, and everyone laughed. "Not to tell tales on myself," she continued, "but there was a certain sea witch on my cruise who I might have wanted to shove into the pool."

"At least you didn't say overboard. You had me worried for a minute there," Susan said.

"Still, it wasn't a very nice thought," said Louise.

"I've had a few like that about my sister-in-law," Carol said.

"My old boss," added Susan.

"But I'm sure none of you ever contemplated murdering them," said Martin. "You ladies are all too nice."

"I may have contemplated a few fatal ends for both Luke

and Gary," Zona admitted. "But I never would have acted on them," she was quick to add.

"All it takes is a person being pushed one step too far and they can snap," Louise said. "Not you, of course," she said to Zona.

"Not me," Zona agreed, then added, "Maybe," and they all laughed.

But later, after everyone was gone and Louise was in bed and Zona had returned from walking Darling and was sitting on the back patio with a cup of mint tea, she couldn't help wondering if there was some truth in what her mother had said. What did it take to push a person over the edge?

She thought again about the screaming she'd heard next door. Alec James was a strong man, a man who worked with his hands. If he got angry enough, if he gave a woman a violent shove . . .

The night was still warm, but she shivered. Time to go inside.

Come morning, with the sun shining and the neighborhood quiet, she had to shake her head over her out-of-control imagination. What percentage of the population ever committed murder like this latest man in the headlines?

She did a little phone research while walking Darling. One obscure article she found claimed that the average person could walk past up to thirty-nine murderers in one lifetime. Yikes! Another short blurb popped up informing her that one in ten thousand Americans were guilty of having killed someone. It wasn't exactly in-depth research, but that statistic felt less terrifying than the one telling her how many murderers she was bound to walk by.

When she and Darling returned, she saw that while the truck was still in the driveway next door, the red PT Cruiser was gone. Maybe its owner had decided she was in an unhealthy relationship and had left for good.

Alec James was coming out of his house. Just an average guy. Well, more like above average, the way he filled out his T-shirt and those jeans.

She called good morning and held up the full little blue poop bag. *See? I am a responsible dog owner.*

He gave her a friendly smile and a thumbs-up. It felt . . . weird.

Were there two Alec Jameses, the one he showed to the world and the one he kept hidden behind closed doors?

"Oh, stop," she told herself in disgust. She had enough going on in her life and she needed to quit giving headspace to the man next door.

10

"YOU SHOULD HAVE COME WITH ME," Fen said when he picked up Bree for a Sunday afternoon of beach volleyball.

"Yeah, I haven't read a fairy tale in a while," she said as they drove off down the street in his Wrangler.

"Hey, fairy tales can be fun."

"Well, yeah, 'cause you stop with the glass slipper. Nobody ever tells you about what happens when the king takes a mistress."

"Not every man cheats," Fen argued.

"Enough do."

"Love how you lump us all together," he grumbled.

She shrugged. "It's what I've seen."

"In your life, in your one corner of the world. It's like judging an entire city by one sketchy neighborhood. Not logical."

"It's logical to protect yourself," Bree argued.

"Yeah, from bad guys. But we're not all bad, Bree. Look at my family. My parents have been married for thirty-three years and they're still best friends."

"They're the exception, not the rule."

"So, I guess, bottom line is, you have to make up your mind whether you're gonna be the exception or the rule. I already know which one I'm gonna be."

You say that now, but you can't guarantee how you'll act in five or ten years.

It would have been rude to let that thought loose. Fen was a good guy. But he was as human as the next, just as human as Gary, who'd wound up ruining their family.

"Nobody makes wedding vows expecting to break them," she pointed out.

"Nobody gets up in the morning expecting to be in a car crash or get cancer. Life's full of risk, Bree. You can't hide from it all."

No, but you could make sure you had your armor in place. "I'm not hiding from anything," she insisted.

"Okay, if you say so," he said.

"Can we drop the subject?" she snapped.

"Fine with me. Like my dad always says, just because you want someone to open a locked door it doesn't mean they will."

"Whatever that means."

"I think you know. But hey, done talking about it. What did you get up to this weekend?"

Here was another less than desirable topic. She'd done . . . nothing. Her Saturday had been as lackluster as her Friday. Bree had called a couple other friends, looking for someone to hang out with but had struck out. It seemed all her friends were either deep into serious relationships or starting them. She'd liked to have gone clubbing with Gaylyn, but Gaylyn's plans with her two-second love didn't include a third wheel. Monique had also had plans, with her family.

Bree hadn't been in a family mood, so she'd binge-watched the *Jack Ryan* series with John Krasinski, who she was sure was the nicest actor on the planet and who she would have loved to have had for a dad.

"I just hung out," she said vaguely, and hoped Fen didn't ask for more details.

"Well, you missed a great band and awesome food," he said.

"There are lots of great bands in LA."

He nodded. "Truth."

And that was the end of all conversation. He turned up the music and kept it going until they got to the beach.

Once there, it was all about surfing and playing two-on-two pickup volleyball games. The beach was populated with smooth-chested men in board shorts and girls with long hair, showing off perfect bodies in bikinis. Bree, herself, was aware of a couple of guys checking her out—who were there with girlfriends, the skeezoids! Well, that was the beach. Everyone checked out everyone.

Had her dad's cheating on Mom started with just checking someone out? Neither one of her parents had said much about what happened. It was obvious neither of them wanted to think about it. Her dad's favorite line was "It didn't work out." Her mom's was "We got married too young." That was the deal with Dad, but she'd been older when she married Gary. That time should have worked. It hadn't. Two love fails, two broken hearts. Mom insisted she wouldn't go for a third try. She'd better not.

A woman with a serious butt hanging out of a thong bikini walked by as they were taking a pop break on their beach blankets and Fen sneaked a look. But he quickly moved his eyes another direction. As if he knew Bree was watching him.

"Too late, I saw you looking," she teased. Except it was more of an accusation than a tease.

"Hey, tell me you're not looking when a fine set of pecs and a six-pack walks by on full display."

He had a point. "You're right."

"Nothing wrong with looking. Nothing wrong with moving past looking and getting to know someone, either. Or maybe even falling for someone."

Here they went again. She rolled her eyes.

"Or committing to a life together, to having each other's back."

"Or just staying friends all your life."

"Friends with bennies?"

She smiled. "I like bennies."

He smiled back. "Me, too." Then he sobered. "But I want more than just friends with bennies. I want a whole life with a partner. Kids someday."

She nodded, acknowledging both his words and the fact that things wouldn't work out for them the second time around any more than they had the first time. They wanted different things.

As if sensing the conversation taking a downward turn, he got up. "Come on. Let's get back in the game."

MONDAY MORNING IT was time for Zona to return to work. Louise hated to see her go. It had felt a little like a party having her daughter home for several days in a row. Except for the pain and the itch of the cast, and the frustration of swinging herself around the house and having a hard time doing things. The cumbersome cast made things she'd taken for granted difficult.

She'd caught a glimpse of the mysterious woman who appeared to be living with Alec James from the dining room window. The woman was certainly pretty. She looked younger than him by maybe ten years. Which meant she was younger than Zona. So their brute of a neighbor liked younger women he could bully and control. Zona didn't need that in her life.

Maybe this other woman didn't either, though. Louise should keep an eye on the neighbors. If the woman was in danger, someone needed to step in.

She was back in her bed after a bathroom run and Zona had just returned from taking Darling on a quick walk when Gilda arrived to take over. Zona opened Louise's bedroom door and announced, "Gilda's here. I'm just going to show her what we've got in the fridge, then I'll be going."

Left with Gilda the caregiver like she was a little kid with a babysitter. It was so embarrassing. Louise nodded and tried to smile. She could hear voices as the two women walked down the hall toward the kitchen, could hear Darling's excited barks. She supposed voices were better than silence.

What was everyone doing on the cruise? Had all the singles paired off? Were people enjoying drinking champagne and watching sunsets? Dancing till all hours? She knew she shouldn't be dwelling on what she was missing. It would only make her grumpy. But too late. She'd dwelled, and now she was grumpy.

Zona returned with Gilda behind her. "I'm on my way. I hope you two have fun," she said, and kissed Louise on the cheek.

Be a good girl. Louise frowned.

Zona hurried past Gilda and then was gone, leaving Gilda leaning against the doorpost, a canvas bag over her shoulder. Darling came and parked next to her.

"You look unhappy," Gilda observed.

"I am," Louise said. "I feel like a little kid who's been left with the babysitter."

"You're not going to throw a tantrum, are you?" Gilda asked, deadpan. "I hate it when patients throw tantrums."

Louise chuckled at that. "No, I'm not. And do they?"

"You'd be surprised," Gilda said with a knowing nod.

"Part of me would like to," Louise confessed. "Except I can't jump up and down or throw myself on the floor, so what's the point?" She sighed. "I should have been in the Hawaiian Islands by now. Who falls over a deck chair and breaks her leg? So pathetic."

"Is that what happened?"

"Sadly, yes. I got a little off-kilter."

"That stinks," Gilda said. "But things do happen for a reason. Sometimes even bad things."

"I can't see any reason for this," Louise said. "But oh, well. As the saying goes, it is what it is."

"Yeah, it is," Gilda agreed. "You want to freshen up before breakfast?"

"I can't shower yet," Louise reminded her. Which was a good thing. She'd met this woman all of once. The idea of getting so personal with her did not appeal. Even taking a sponge bath held a certain ick factor.

"Good, because I never shower on a first date," Gilda quipped. She pulled out a pack of body wipes from her bag and set them on the bed. "This will probably be enough for today. I'll be back to help you get your pants on," she said and left.

Louise smiled and got busy.

Later, as they sat at the kitchen table, eating the egg casserole Zona had made the night before and chatting, Louise quickly realized that Gilda could become more than a part-time nurse. They could become friends.

Gilda proved it when, after Louise finally settled on the couch and they got talking about favorite novels, she pulled out her favorite mystery novel by an author Louise hadn't yet discovered. "I brought this in case you want some bedtime reading."

"That was so sweet of you," said Louise, her fingers itching to get her hands on it.

"This has so many twists and turns in it you won't know which way you're going. And some of the people seem so nice, but oh, my, they are anything but."

Louise nodded knowingly. "Just like in real life."

"Absolutely," Gilda agreed. "We had a neighbor when I was growing up. Everyone thought he was the kindest man. He was single. Always had treats for the kids."

Louise knew exactly where she was going. "Oh, no."

Gilda nodded. "Oh, yes. My mother, God rest her soul, caught on to him, thank God. He'd lured the little boy across the street over to his house and was talking him into skinny-dipping in his pool. Mom heard them out there and went marching right over and that was the end of him. You can't trust single men," she finished with a shake of her head.

"Some you can," said Louise, thinking of Martin. "Not every man is a pervert."

Gilda shook her head. "A man living alone? It's not natural. At least for men our age."

"Unless the man's a widower," Louise argued.

"Ha! Those are usually the ones rushing to get married. Heaven knows I've had a couple propose to me. After a certain point in life, they either want a nurse or a purse. I already get paid to be a nurse and I'm not going to be anyone's purse."

"Well, my neighbor Martin is the nicest man you'd ever want to meet," Louise said.

Gilda looked speculatively at her. "Oh?"

"There's nothing between us," Louise hurried to say. "We're just good friends."

Gilda gave a knowing nod. "That's how it starts."

The doorbell rang. "Company. You are popular," Gilda said.

"It's probably Martin, checking on me," Louise said as Gilda went to answer the door.

Sure enough, like an actor who'd been waiting in the wings for his cue, Martin entered the room.

"I came by to see how you're feeling," he said to Louise. He held up a box of doughnuts. "Thought you might like a treat."

"Thank you. I'd love a treat," Louise said, and made the introductions. "Would you like some iced tea?" she offered after she'd finished, then felt foolish. She wouldn't be fetching the tea. She was turning Gilda into a servant. "Oh, Gilda, sorry to ask you."

"No problem," Gilda said, and disappeared, Darling following her, probably hoping for a dog treat.

While she was gone, Martin set the box of doughnuts on the coffee table. "How's your leg today?"

"It's still attached," Louise said. "I guess that's something to be thankful for."

Gilda returned with two glasses and then left. And didn't return.

Louise couldn't have her newfound friend feeling left out. "Gilda, come join us," she called.

"I got things to do out here," Gilda called back from the kitchen.

No, she didn't. The only thing she had to do was help Louise, and Louise didn't need help at the moment.

"Maybe she wants to give us some privacy," Martin suggested.

"We don't need privacy," Louise said. "Will you go bring her back?"

Martin didn't frown at her request, but he didn't smile, either. And when he said, "Okay," he sounded resigned. It was a little out of character for him, especially when he'd been more than happy to settle in and enjoy the fun the night before.

A moment later he was back with Gilda in tow.

"Now, let's sample those doughnuts," said Louise.

And so the three of them sat together eating doughnuts, drinking iced tea, and visiting. Actually, it was mostly Louise and Gilda visiting with Martin nodding agreement when called for. He wound up staying for lunch.

As they ate, the subject of Louise's book came up. "Have you started it yet?" Martin asked.

"I'm still mulling over ideas," Louise said. "But so far nothing comes to mind."

"Base it on something in real life, like the freezer husband," Gilda advised.

"Freezer husband?" Martin repeated, his eyebrows flying up.

"The man in Los Angeles who killed his wife, then cut her up and stuck her in the freezer," Louise clarified. "The one I told you about the other night. Remember?"

"Yes, and I can see why I forgot it," he said.

"You could write about something like that," Gilda said. "You know, the man who looked so nice, who nobody suspected. I love characters like that. I read a Dean Koontz book years ago. Oh, my gosh! It started with this happy couple in the woods hiking. They found an old ranger tower and climbed up it. One minute they're talking about how high up it is and the next—boom!—he pushes her off."

Martin frowned. "That sounds preposterous."

"This from the man who loves Jack Reacher," Louise teased.

"You never know about people," Gilda said. "Pressure builds and builds and then, what seems like out of the blue, they snap. But it's never really out of the blue. Write about someone like that."

"A man on a cruise," Louise said thoughtfully. "He's there with his wife and he suddenly snaps."

"What about the woman? Maybe she snaps," Martin suggested.

"Not as believable. Men are much more violent," said Gilda. "Everyone knows that." Martin didn't look convinced, so she continued, "All the best serial killers are men."

Martin scratched his chin. "Well."

"You all have too much testosterone," Gilda informed him.

"I don't," Martin insisted, then looked like he regretted saying that.

Louise giggled. "We know what you mean. I'm not sure I want to write something really grisly."

"So don't have him cut her up," said Gilda.

"Inspiration will come," Martin assured Louise.

Who knew? Maybe from the goings-on next door.

By the time they'd finished brainstorming, Louise was pooped and ready to spread out on her bed, so Martin took his leave and leashed up Darling for a walk.

"Let me know if you need anything," he said to Louise before going out the door.

"Just company, and thank you for giving me yours," she said, which made him smile.

"That man is crazy for you," Gilda told her after he and Darling had left.

"Really, we're only good friends."

"One of you is. One of you is hoping for more. I think he'd have been perfectly happy if I'd stayed in the kitchen all day and he'd had you to himself."

"No, Martin's not like that. Anyway, I don't think of him that way. He's so . . . mild-mannered."

"So was Clark Kent until he turned into Superman," said Gilda, which made Louise laugh.

Martin was not the Superman type. She thought again of the sexy Texan she was missing hanging out with on that cruise. What possible silver lining was there to breaking her leg and having to leave the ship? She certainly couldn't think of any.

Oh, well. It was what it was.

Gilda helped Louise settle on her bed to relax. "Want me to pull the curtains?" she offered.

"No, I like the light coming in," said Louise. She also rather liked keeping an eye on the new neighbor's house. It paid to be vigilant. She'd learned that thanks to past inhabitants.

At the moment, everything looked normal. The sun was shining, the grass was mowed. The pool in the backyard was probably sparkling in the sunlight.

Gilda's words were glued into her mind. *You never know about people. Pressure builds and builds and then, what seems like out of the blue, they snap.*

What kind of pressure was building in the house of Alec James? What was going on between him and the redhead?

Louise picked up the book Gilda had loaned her from her nightstand, ready to read. The book was fiction. Next door was real life. It would be silly to mix the two. She needed to ignore her neighbors. She opened the book.

Then put it down as she heard a car door shut. She could see that the red PT Cruiser was back, and the young woman was walking up the front walk, carrying several shopping bags from different department stores in the mall over in West Covina. She certainly didn't appear to be suffering.

And she was still in one piece. *So, nothing to see here, folks.* Time to read and forget about the neighbors.

You never know about people.

Louise opened her book again. For the moment, all was well next door, but it couldn't hurt to keep an eye on things.

11

ZONA ARRIVED HOME FROM WORK TO find Louise and Gilda settled in the living room with iced tea and popcorn, streaming an old episode of *Deathline*. Future besties.

"You home already?" Louise greeted Zona.

"The workday is over," Zona said.

"That means my workday is over," said Gilda, rising from her chair.

"Stay and watch the end of the show," Louise urged.

"I have to walk Darling, so I'd love it if you'd stay a little longer," Zona said to her.

"It's almost over anyway. You don't want to leave now," Louise added.

"All right. Just a few more minutes," Gilda agreed. She sat back down and dug into what was left of her popcorn.

"Thank you for sending Gilda our way. She and Mom are sisters from another mister," Zona told Gracie when she called to chat while she was walking Darling.

"I'm glad it's working out," Gracie said. "That takes a load of worry off you."

True. And she'd been lugging a large enough load for the last couple of years.

"What's the latest with the neighbor?" asked Gracie. "Any more neighborly chats?"

"Not since he brought Darling back from pooping on his property."

"There's a conversation starter."

"It wasn't much of one. He's got someone anyway. Although it doesn't look like they get along," Zona added.

"Were you over there eavesdropping?" teased Gracie.

"Actually, I was over there to apologize for Darling and wound up hearing a major fight. Obviously, I decided it wasn't a good time."

"Is she still there?" Gracie asked.

"She left, but it looks like she returned, so I guess they made up. Anyway, who wants a man who yells?"

"Someone who yells back?"

"There was plenty of that going on. I can't judge though. I did my share of yelling at Gary. And Luke."

"Who both deserved it. Too bad about this guy though," Gracie said. "That whole boy-next-door thing could have been fun."

"Fun and men have not exactly gone hand in hand in my life," Zona said.

"I know. But don't give up."

"Too late."

"Don't talk like that. You have half your life left. You don't want to live it alone."

"Alone is emotionally and financially safer," said Zona as she and Darling rounded a corner and started down a new block.

Mr. Eggerton was out watering his lawn and waved at her. She said goodbye to Gracie and stopped to chat about his roses. He was such an innocuous old guy. Why couldn't a nice little Mr. Eggerton live next door to them? Why did they have to end up with trouble in blue jeans?

She and Darling were just coming back up their front walk when the truck with the Better Builders logo pulled into his driveway next to the red PT Cruiser. She was determined to keep her distance, but that didn't mean she couldn't be polite.

She started to give him a friendly wave, but Alec James was not looking her direction. She noted the clenched jaw and the fast stride as he walked to his front door. The man was in no mood to be friendly. He yanked open the door and disappeared inside, slamming it after him.

Something had put Alec James in a foul mood and he probably wasn't calling, "Honey, I'm home." Poor Miss PT Cruiser, having to deal with such a mercurial temperament. It made the man look like a modern-day Jekyll and Hyde.

Now she could be narrating a *Deathline* episode, for crying out loud. *There was something about him, we knew it. It practically buzzed like a downed power line.*

There was more to that buzz than anger. She felt the current when she looked at him. The man reeked of pheromones. It was a good thing she was done with men.

Even if she wasn't, she wouldn't want to start anything with this one. No one in her right mind reached out and touched a downed power line.

Miss PT Cruiser, the fool, could have him and whatever baggage he brought with him. Zona had dealt with enough baggage to last a lifetime.

An image of Luke, explaining that he couldn't help falling for another woman, telling her he needed someone who understood him, floated into her mind like a ghost from the past. It put other ghosts on parade. She saw herself trying to explain to Bree that Daddy wasn't going to be living with them anymore. Saw her daughter crying.

The parade continued, showing Gary hurrying into another room to take a *business* call. Him calling her from the store to say he'd be home late. "Trouble with the books. I've got to straighten things out here." There'd been trouble with the books all right. On those nights he'd come home late, smelling like smoke. His new accountant smoked. Right. It turned out that so did his poker buddies. Gary had been a cheater, just like

Luke. The only difference was that Gary had cheated on Zona with Lady Luck instead of a flesh-and-blood woman.

More images drifted past. Her daughter's shocked expression when she delivered the news that the college money was gone. Her sitting in the divorce lawyer's office, stoical and numb. Finally, there she was leaving what she'd thought would be her forever home.

She was practically growling as she let herself back in the house.

Stop already, she told herself. She had a home, and even though her savings were gone she still had her job. And she had good people left in her life, people who would always be there for her and not betray her. So what if her love life was dead and buried. She was finally safe, and safety trumped love any day. And her daughter was right, not scarred.

Once inside, Zona dug out a frozen pizza and put together a tossed salad with the last of the greens and the half tomato left in the fridge. It would be time to go to the grocery store the next day.

"Stay and have pizza," Louise urged Gilda.

"I should get home," Gilda said. "See you tomorrow bright and early. We'll get you all spiffed up. Then I've got the DVD for *The Woman in the Window*. I'll bring it."

"Sounds good," Louise said with a smile.

"It looks like you two are getting along great," Zona observed after she returned from seeing Gilda out.

"I like her," said Louise.

Her mother was smiling. That made Zona smile.

They ate their pizza, filling each other in on their days. Zona's had been uneventful.

"Not much went on here, either," said Louise. "Except Martin came over and brought doughnuts."

"You don't deserve him," Zona teased.

"Of course I do. I'm a good friend. I'd be doing the same for him if he was laid up."

"You know what I mean," Zona said.

"I'm afraid the spark isn't there."

"Sparks can blind you," Zona said. She'd had plenty of sparks when she met both Luke and Gary and look where they'd gotten her.

"I had a happy marriage with your father. He was a wonderful man—fun and loving and so handsome. Why should I settle for less after that?"

Good point. "I guess you shouldn't. But I'm not sure I'd label Martin as less."

Louise shrugged. "He's a little too mellow for my tastes. I need a man with some male energy."

Zona thought of their next-door neighbor. He was not lacking in male energy. But she was willing to bet all that male energy drew a lot from the poor woman staying with him. What had happened to make him come home so angry? Shouldn't a man be glad to come home after a hard day's work? The way he'd stormed into his house, he had to be taking out his anger on her. Why didn't she leave? Couldn't she see behind the façade?

Ha! Just like Zona had? When it came to love, people could be so stupid.

Thank God she was done being stupid.

After dinner, Louise started reading her murder mystery and Zona pulled out her ancient laptop and checked the bids on her items. Holy moly! Bidders were going berserk over the purse she'd listed and three people were watching and waiting. The bidding on the vintage cookie jar she'd found was hot and heavy and that was up to fifty dollars. At the rate the bidding was going, Zona was going to make a tidy profit. Maybe she would be visiting some more garage sales.

Her smile faded. Garage sale season wouldn't last forever. What would she do for a side hustle when that died down? Having her mother home with a broken leg complicated matters. There had to be something though. She'd think of something.

LOUISE WAS READY to face the day, maybe even ready to think about that mystery she wanted to write. She sat stretched out on the couch with her cup of coffee and the notebook Bree had brought her, Gilda sitting in a nearby armchair with the half-finished blanket she was crocheting.

"I think I definitely want to have the murder take place on a cruise ship," Louise said, "but now that I'm not cruising I have no way to do my research."

"I've been on a cruise. I can help you with some of the details. Just don't push the person overboard. That's so cliché."

"How do I write something that isn't cliché?" Louise bemoaned. "Everything's been done."

"True. But there's always a new way to tell an old story. One thing we know. Money is a powerful motivator, and if someone is married, it's almost always the spouse who bumps the poor schlub off for their money," Gilda said.

"So, a man and woman go on a cruise to celebrate their . . . tenth anniversary. Maybe he has gambling debts she doesn't know about," Louise continued, thinking of Zona. It would be very satisfying to make her daughter's ex the bad guy in a novel. Let him get arrested. Or have fate take a hand just when he thought he'd succeeded. He could accidentally fall overboard. Or fall off his surfboard and knock himself unconscious, then get eaten by sharks. Maybe he should just get caught and the detective who got him would look exactly like Zona.

"An anniversary, I like that," Gilda said with a nod.

"Of course, he would look like a loving husband."

"But have her heavily insured."

"How can he murder her though?"

"He could slip something in her food," Gilda suggested.

"That would be hard to do in front of a whole table full of diners," Louise said, and thought of all the lovely dinners she was missing.

"I don't know. That huge buffet area on the Lido deck goes on forever. He could slip something into her food and never get caught. Who would know where she got the poison or from who? It's a zoo in the dining area at lunch."

"Hmm, not a bad idea," said Louise.

"People get food poisoning all the time on cruises," Gilda continued. "You probably had a lucky escape. You could have gotten Norovirus."

Louise frowned. "I'm not sure a broken leg is a lucky escape."

"We'll never know." Gilda studied her. "You're looking tired. How about some lunch? Then you can lie down on the couch and I'll put on the movie."

"That sounds like a good idea," said Louise.

"Want a turkey sandwich? You've got sandwich meat and lettuce in the fridge."

"That will be great," said Louise.

Gilda put her crocheting back in its bag and went to the kitchen, Darling trotting along after her, ready to supervise, and Louise relocated to the dining table to think of possible names for her murderer. She supposed using the name Gary would be a bad idea. Gary could take it in his head to sue her for libel or something. What about Luke? Same issue. What if she named the killer Lucas? Gary Lucas? Garfield Lucas?

The sound of a car pulling into the driveway next door distracted her. There was Alec James's houseguest, unloading several bags of merchandise. More shopping. The woman certainly loved spending money. Was she spending hers or his?

Her thoughts were interrupted by a strangled squawk coming from the kitchen, followed by the sound of a plate breaking and the firm command, "Move, dog."

Gilda was not a dog lover, and Darling wasn't exactly winning her over. He did love to hang around in the kitchen and had a habit of getting underfoot when Louise was working.

"Here, Darling," she called.

Darling didn't come. Maybe Gilda had given him a treat and he was busy with that.

"Everything okay out there?" she called.

"It is now," Gilda called back.

Five minutes later she appeared, bringing two plates. She set one in front of Louise. "There you go. We had some breakage, but I'll pay to replace it."

"Thank you," Louise said. "I'm guessing that wasn't your fault though. Was Darling making a nuisance of himself?"

Gilda frowned. "I tripped over him. He shouldn't be in the kitchen when you're working," she added firmly. "You could fall and break a hip."

"He's usually much better behaved," Louise fibbed, which inspired a disbelieving raised eyebrow. "Is he still in the kitchen?"

"No, I put him in the backyard. He was scratching at the door to go out."

"He probably needed a potty break. We should bring him in."

"Let's wait until we're done eating," Gilda said. "He'll be fine out there for a few minutes, won't he?"

"He should be, but I don't want him out for long. It's too hot. Plus, he's liable to dig holes."

Gilda made a face. "Dogs," she said in disgust.

"Darling is a sweetie," Louise insisted and frowned at her.

Which made Gilda backpedal. "He's a nice dog. But if he's a hole digger, you'll never break him of that. My brother's dog was a hole digger."

"How did they break him of it?" asked Louise.

"They didn't. They gave him away."

"That's sad. Poor dog."

"Poor dog? What about my brother? Always having to fill in holes. I don't know how many flowers that dog killed."

"If I have to choose between my flowers and my dog, the dog wins," Louise said. "We probably should bring him in."

"All right," Gilda said and went off to the kitchen. Louise could hear her out there calling in Darling. Then she was calling the dog again. "Darling?"

That wasn't a come-here call. That was a where-have-you-gone call. Louise's sandwich began to roll around in her stomach.

Gilda returned. No Darling by her side.

"Where's Darling?" Louise asked, even though she already knew the answer.

Gilda was frowning. "He's escaped. Dug a hole."

"Oh, no," Louise said miserably.

"Now, don't you worry. I'll find him," Gilda said, and made for the front door.

Forty minutes later, she'd returned, sweaty, frustrated, and alone.

"Where could he have gone?" Louise fretted.

"I don't know. I've been up and down every street within a two-block radius calling him."

"Maybe he went to see Martin," Louise said, and grabbed her phone.

The call went to Martin's voice mail.

"Where does Martin live? I'll go to his house," Gilda offered.

"Just two houses down," said Louise. The minute the words were out of her mouth she realized that if Darling had gone to find Martin, Gilda would have seen the dog. She shook her head. "He's not there. You would have seen him. I hope he's not hurt."

Gilda's eyebrows pinched together. "I'll go look again," she said. "This time I'll take my car."

"Who knows how far he's gotten," Louise fretted.

"I'm sorry, Louise. I'll find him. I promise," Gilda said earnestly. "He can't have gone that far."

A dog didn't have to go too far to get hurt or lost. Louise bit her lip and nodded.

Gilda's second search didn't prove any more helpful. "Where could he have gone?" she moaned.

Please, not to doggy heaven.

12

ZONA WALKED THROUGH THE FRONT DOOR to find two very upset women waiting for her. Louise was on the couch, unharmed but teary-eyed, and Gilda was right there at the door, looking as if the world had ended. If she'd been a Samurai, she'd have fallen on her sword.

Panic rained down on Zona, sending her blood pressure skyrocketing. "What happened?"

"Darling is lost," Louise wailed.

"It's all my fault," Gilda said. "I'm so sorry. I put him out in the backyard and the little stinker dug a hole under the fence and escaped."

Zona groaned.

"I'm sorry," Gilda said again. "You can fire me and I'll understand."

"I'm not going to fire you," Zona said. "You couldn't know."

"Your mother tried to tell me. I only put him out while we were having our lunch. I was tripping over him in the kitchen. It couldn't have been more than ten minutes."

Houdini dog had probably accomplished his escape in five. "It's okay," Zona said. "I'll go look for him."

She opened the door to begin her search and found Alec James standing there, holding a whimpering Darling by the collar. Again.

Startled, she yelped and backed up a step. "I didn't expect to find someone on my porch."

Before she could thank him, he said, "I didn't expect to be here. Again." The downturned lips and cold eyes told her he was in no mood to be as tolerant as he'd been the last time he'd returned Darling. Alec James revealing the man behind the friendly mask.

"He got loose," Zona said. Nothing like stating the obvious. "I was gone and . . ."

Gilda stepped forward. "It's my fault. I left him out back."

Alec James replied with something that sounded like a cross between a sigh and growl and handed Darling over. "Take your damn dog."

Louise joined them, leaning on her crutches. "We've been looking all afternoon." She was smiling gratefully, as if their neighbor had done a good deed. As if she'd forgotten that he was not a nice man.

"Next time, just look on my front lawn," Alec James said. Not graciously. "He'll be there, taking a dump. And you'd better hope I don't find him," he said to Zona, making her heart give a nervous skip.

"Well," huffed Gilda.

Louise lost her look of gratitude and glared at him.

Zona stepped outside and shut the door behind her, determined to defuse his anger. "Obviously, your patience is at an end, but we're really trying over here." Why was she bothering? He was in no mood to be reasonable.

He sigh-growled again. Looked heavenward. Praying for patience? That would definitely require an act of God.

Then he spoke. Tersely. "You can get a fence barrier on Amazon. That will keep him in and keep us all happy."

"I'll order one tonight," Zona promised. Tersely.

"Good." He gave her a curt nod and then marched back down her driveway.

"That is a mean man," Gilda announced when Zona came back inside and joined Louise and Gilda in the living room.

"He's got issues," Zona decided as she toed out of her shoes. She slumped onto an easy chair and stretched out her legs. The day was over, and the dog was back, and all she wanted was to sit like a lump for the rest of the evening.

"I'm glad you got your dog back," Gilda continued. "I'm really sorry I left him out." She looked apologetically at Louise.

"It's okay. Don't feel bad. Darling is back and all is good," Louise told her.

"I tried to call him."

"He doesn't always come when you do," said Zona.

"You should take him to obedience school," Gilda advised.

Right. In her spare time. Zona would get right on that.

"I'll take him once my cast is off," Louise vowed. "Right now I'm just glad he's okay."

"He probably hadn't gone far," Zona said.

Darling had settled himself right next to Louise. As if he knew they were talking about him, he laid his head on her lap and looked up at her.

"I wish our new neighbor hadn't been the one to find him. I don't like to be in his debt," Louise said.

Debt. Zona tried not to cringe at the word.

"Of all the people to end up with as a neighbor," Louise finished with a frown.

"He is an awful man. You should put him in your book," said Gilda before raising her eyebrows with a new thought. "Never mind. He might come after you."

"I doubt that," said Zona, acting as the voice of reason.

"You never know," said Gilda. "When I was growing up, we had a neighbor who fed our other neighbor's dog ground hamburger with glass in it, all because the dog kept pooping on his lawn. No one could prove it, so he got away with murder."

Zona shuddered. Gilda was a ghoul. "Our neighbor wouldn't poison Darling." He was too straightforward. He'd simply kick the poor dog.

"Men are beasts," Gilda said, shaking her head.

"He must be rich," said Louise.

"If he was rich, he'd be living in Bel Air or Beverly Hills," said Zona.

"Maybe he wants to be near his work," Gilda hypothesized.

"Not every millionaire flaunts his money," Louise insisted. "He's got some and I'm sure that's why that young woman is with him. Earlier today I saw her hauling in a bunch of shopping bags. That's the second spending spree she's been on."

The sound of a key in the door signaled that Bree was stopping in for a visit. Darling bounded over to her, tail wagging, and jumped on her, and she gave his ears a rub.

"Am I in time for dinner?" she asked.

"Haven't even started it," said Zona.

And she had no desire to. But, of course, what you wanted to do and what you had to do rarely matched up.

"Good, 'cause I ordered pizza. It should be here in ten minutes," Bree said, and went to kiss her grandma.

A pizza repeat sounded fine to Zona. She smiled at Bree. "Bless you. You get the good daughter award."

"And the good granddaughter award," added Louise. "But you shouldn't have splurged."

"It's okay. I made good tips today and I had a Groupon. How are you doing, Gram?" Bree asked, perching on the other end of the couch.

"Better," Louise said. "Although we had some adventures today. Gilda let Darling out and he dug a hole in the backyard and escaped."

One more thing Zona would be taking care of after ordering that fence barrier.

"Only for a few minutes," Gilda said in her own defense. "I need to be going."

"Darling, what is your problem?" Bree said to the dog as Gilda scrammed.

"He probably gets bored," said Zona.

"Get Gilda to walk him," Bree suggested.

"She told us right from the start that wasn't in her job description," Zona said.

Bree didn't say anything, but the look on her face showed what she thought about a health care worker who wasn't willing to double as a dog walker. "I can come over a couple times a week and walk him after work," she offered.

"No, you have enough to do," Louise said, letting her off the hook. "Martin's helping. I just think Darling gets bored."

"I could take him to the beach with me," Bree suggested.

"Not the beach," Louise said quickly. "He might run away, and once of that was enough. Poor Gilda must have spent an hour looking for him."

"How'd you find him?" Bree asked.

"We didn't. Our neighbor did," said Zona.

"We were just talking about him. He is not a nice man," said Louise. "It's a shame. I'd had such high hopes when he first moved here."

"You were wasting those hopes on me," said Zona.

"Thank God," Bree said heartily.

Louise sighed. "I'm so sorry Cupid's been cruel to you, Zona."

Zona shrugged. "It's in the past. We're moving forward now." She was dropping as much money as she could into the savings account she'd set up for Bree's school. "I'm sorry your plans got delayed," she said to Bree for probably the hundredth time. "And I'm sorry you're having to work so hard."

Bree nodded. "I'll get there."

"*We'll* get there," Zona corrected her.

"You're both working hard," said Louise. "But there's more to life than work. You need some kind of social life. And you shouldn't give up on love. You know what they say, Zona. The third try's the charm."

Bree looked horrified. "No more tries, Mom. You're a magnet for losers."

Sad but true.

"Your mother has a right to be happy," Louise said sternly.

"I'm happy," said Zona. Sort of. Most of the time. She spotted their DoorDash delivery person coming up the walk. "Looks like dinner's here."

They moved on to dinner, Louise showing off her skill with her crutches as they went to the dining table.

"You're getting pretty good with those, Gram," Bree observed.

"Nothing to it," said Louise. She handed over her crutches to Zona, who propped them against the wall, and then lowered herself into her chair with a groan she tried to hide.

"Nothing to it, huh?" teased Bree.

"Clomping around with this thing does tend to wear me out," Louise admitted.

"By end of summer you'll be up and dancing," Zona assured her.

"I'm ready," said Louise.

Although by the time they were done eating, the only thing she was ready for was bed. Bree took off and Zona helped her mother get settled in with the latest mystery she was reading.

"I'm sorry you're having to deal with this," she said to Zona.

"You're the one who's having to deal with it," Zona replied, and kissed her cheek. "But you're strong. You'll get through it."

Louise smiled. "Yes, I will. Now, you go relax. You've had a long day."

And it was going to be longer. Zona ordered a fence barrier online, then went out back and filled in Darling's latest hole. The faint sound of raised voices drifted over to her from next door.

She remembered the angry set of the man's jaw when she'd seen him storming into his house. What was he doing to that woman? Who knew? Who wanted to know? Not Zona. She wanted to stay as far away as possible from the man next door.

Finished with her hole repair, she took Darling for a walk. Then she came home, showered, and fell into bed. She picked up the book from her nightstand, a World War II tale about a woman spy who was smart and tough and invincible. Oh, to have any of those traits. So far, she'd been stupid, wimpy, and vulnerable. Well, no more of that.

"The only way you beat back the darkness is to get up and rise above it," claimed the novel's heroine as she spoke to her terrified younger sister. *"Don't you dare give up. And don't you dare trust anyone but yourself."*

Those words hadn't simply been written for a fictional little sister. They were for Zona. She was putting her life back together. She was done being stupid and she was done being wimpy and she was done being vulnerable. And she was certainly done trusting anyone made up of muscle and testosterone.

"AND TO THINK I thought that man was nice when I first met him," Louise lamented the next day as Gilda set out her breakfast. She was usually so good at reading people. She'd sure misread Alec James. "Of course, what can you tell from someone just saying hello, right?"

"Men like that put up a false front," Gilda said. "They can seem real nice until you cross them. Then look out."

"There's something off about this one." You couldn't trust a man who didn't like dogs. "And the poor woman with him. Zona's heard raised voices over there. I'm afraid he could be violent."

"So much goes on behind closed doors," Gilda said knowingly. "Everything can look so normal and yet once you shut the door it's all darkness and evil. You saw the *Deathline* episode about the man whose wife fell off a cliff when they were hiking, didn't you? He kept claiming it was an accident. Everyone said they were the perfect couple until all these little things started coming out. Like the woman's girlfriend who said he'd hit on her at a party once. He claimed he'd just had too much to drink."

"Right," scoffed Louise.

"And then the neighbor saw him clear on the other side of the city having lunch with another woman. It's always about money or lust."

"Or rage," added Louise.

"You'd better keep an eye on your neighbor," Gilda advised.

"I intend to, believe me," Louise said heartily. "We could be living next to a potential murderer. Like in *Rear Window*."

"Or *The Woman in the Window*," said Gilda.

"A good reminder to be watchful," Louise said. "Truth is stranger than fiction."

They were discussing how Louise could keep a watchful eye on her neighbor when Martin showed up, bearing a gift for Louise.

"I thought you might like this latest book by Karin Slaughter," he said, as he settled in at the table with the two women.

"Thank you, Martin. That is so kind of you," Louise said.

"It might give you ideas for your novel," he suggested.

"I'm always open to ideas. I'm going to set it on a cruise," Louise told him.

"A cruise, huh?" he said thoughtfully.

Louise frowned. "I'd hoped to do some research while I was on the boat."

Martin shied away from following her down that conversational path. "What's going to happen? Is someone going to get thrown overboard?" he asked.

"Poisoned," said Gilda.

Martin nodded thoughtfully. "Poisoned on a cruise. That could work."

"It could. I just have to figure out everything else. I need inspiration."

"I bet you'll find it next door," Gilda predicted.

Martin raised a questioning eyebrow. "Next door?"

"Alec James," Louise clarified. "There's something not right over there."

Her words made Martin frown. "What on earth makes you think that?"

"He's got suppressed violence," Louise said. "He was downright ugly to us. And made a veiled threat to harm Darling."

Martin's brows pulled together in disbelief. "When was that?"

"Yesterday," said Louise. "Darling got loose."

"That was my fault," Gilda added.

"I'm afraid he might have left a little something on Alec's lawn again," Louise admitted.

"That can make people upset," Martin said in Alec James's defense.

"That man's thermostat is set to anger all the time. You can tell," Louise insisted.

"I agree," said Gilda.

"We hardly know him. Let's not jump to conclusions," Martin cautioned.

Jumping? It only took a baby step to conclude that Alec James was not a nice man. Who knew what he was capable of?

"He bears watching," she said.

And she was.

13

ZONA CAME HOME FROM WORK THE same time as Alec James. Neighborly people called a friendly hello to each other from their driveways when that happened, but she didn't want to be neighborly.

He did though. "Did you find a fence barrier?" he called.

"I did," she replied, her voice frosty.

"Good." It wasn't said in the warmest of voices, but she could have cut him some slack and decided he wasn't as bad as she and her mother were making him out to be if he hadn't added, "Now I won't have to kick him off my lawn."

Seriously? This is how he chose to respond? "Anyone ever tell you that you have a sick way of expressing yourself?"

"No, but thanks for pointing that out," he responded.

Did she see a glimmer of a smile? She must have because there came that tingle she'd felt when she first talked with him. It was completely misplaced. *Stop it!* she scolded herself. *No tingles.*

He told her to have a nice night, then disappeared into his house, and that left her scowling as she walked into hers.

Louise and Gilda were sitting at the dining room table, playing cards. "Hi, dear. How was your day?" Louise greeted her.

"Fine, until I talked to our neighbor," Zona replied.

"That is a bad man," Gilda said as Zona came over to give Louise a kiss.

"Anyone who doesn't like dogs is not to be trusted," added Louise. "You shouldn't be talking to him."

"We're watching him," Gilda added.

"Watching him?" What on earth did that mean? "Like spying on him?"

"No, just . . . keeping an eye out. There could be big trouble over there at some point," Louise explained.

"There already is, but it's none of our business," Zona said firmly.

"Gin," said Gilda, laying down her cards.

Louise groaned. "There's no point in even writing down the score. You smoked me."

"I just got good cards," Gilda said, gathering them up. That done, she stood and said, "I'll be going now. I hope you two have a good night."

It looked like they would. Louise was in a good mood, and so was Zona when she checked the items she had for sale on eBay and saw how well they were doing.

"We should hit some more garage sales," Louise said.

"For sure," Zona agreed. "The faster I can bring in money the better I'll feel."

"Honey, you're not in a race."

"In a way I am. I only have so many earning years left."

"I know. You're *so* old," Louise scoffed. "Like I said, you need to budget in some fun."

"Okay, how about this for fun? Let's eat out on the patio," Zona suggested. Her mother was spending too much time holed up inside.

They dined al fresco on the back patio, eating a chicken curry salad Zona had thrown together and drinking chai iced tea. It was hot but not uncomfortably so. Darling was happily sitting at Louise's feet, gnawing on his chew toy. All was calm and quiet.

Until the angry voices started. "Get in here," commanded Alec James.

Darling stopped his gnawing and looked up.

"No!" shouted the now familiar female voice, and Darling growled.

"I'm done screwing around with you," he snarled. "Get in here. Now!"

The fierceness of his words made the hairs on Zona's neck rise.

It put Darling on his feet. He raced over to the fence and began to bark.

"This isn't good," said Louise, her voice low.

There was an understatement. Zona could feel her pulse rate going up.

"I don't want to talk to you," the woman wailed.

And Darling howled in sympathy.

"You'd better."

"We need to call the police," whispered Louise.

Should they? Zona wanted to. But, "All we're hearing is raised voices. We don't know what's going on over there."

"I know what goes on in that type of situation. One minute people are yelling, the next someone is getting hurt," Louise said and reached for her phone, which was sitting on the table.

As if on cue, the neighbors went silent.

"I don't hear anything over there now," said Zona. "We can't just call the police because we heard people arguing. My gosh, Mom, if my neighbors had called the police every time they'd heard Gary and me arguing, we'd have had a squad car pulling up at our house every night. And I'd have been mortified."

Louise hesitated. Frowned. "But we can't simply turn a deaf ear."

Her mother was right. What could they do?

"Maybe I could just go over and ask if everything is all right," said Zona.

"I don't want you approaching that man," Louise said firmly.

"I could stop by with some . . ." What? She hadn't baked anything since her chocolate chip cookie therapy.

They heard a car starting.

"Go see who's leaving," Louise urged.

Zona went around the side of the house and peered over the fence. There went the PT Cruiser. Her pulse settled back down. She returned to the patio. "It's okay. She's gone."

"Good. At least we know she's all right."

Maybe Zona should still go over there. "I think I'll make some snickerdoodles," she decided. "Then I'll stop by and casually ask if everything is okay."

And Alec James would certainly buy her concern after their latest encounters. This was a stupid idea.

"But don't take them over if that man's by himself," Louise cautioned. "It's not safe."

"I don't think he's going to pull me in off the front porch," Zona said.

She got to work baking cookies, but by the time she had the first cookie sheet out of the oven she was feeling hesitant. What possible excuse could she have for showing up at the neighbor's door now that all was calm?

Olive branch, she decided, and put them on a paper plate.

Her heart was pounding when she walked across her lawn to his. The PT Cruiser was still gone. For all she knew, the pretty redhead had left for good. The only way she'd find out would be to ask. A scene from *Rear Window* flashed through her mind, Grace Kelly snooping in the killer's apartment.

"Ridiculous," she muttered. Her mother's overactive imagination was turning viral and grabbing ahold of her, too.

She rang the doorbell. Nobody answered. She waited for what felt like an excruciatingly long time, but was probably only a few seconds, before telling herself to go home.

She had turned to leave when the door opened. Alec James stood in the doorway in dark jeans and a snug-fitting T-shirt, five-o'clock shadow shading his chin. And there was the power line buzz.

She gulped and held out the plate. "I think we've gotten off on the wrong foot."

He took it and raised an eyebrow. "Yeah?"

"Time to bury the hatchet?" Why on earth had she said that? Her face flamed.

He sighed heavily, then gave her a half smile and the buzz got stronger. "It should probably be me bringing you something. Sorry I was a jerk the other day. I've been under a lot of pressure."

Like a volcano about to erupt? Her nerves began to start tap-dancing as she geared up to ask about the screaming she'd heard earlier.

"Did that fence barrier come?"

"Not yet."

"I'll help you with it if you want," he offered. "It's the least I can do after the way I acted."

It threw her and she had to remind herself that she hadn't come over for a neighborly chat. She was supposed to be finding out what was going on in the troubled house of Alec James.

"That's okay. I can handle it," she said.

Now what? She couldn't exactly say, *By the way, what's going on over here?*

Inspiration hit. "Feel free to share those," she said, pointing to the plate.

The half smile went away. "With who?"

"With . . . anyone. I thought I'd seen another car out front, but maybe I was wrong." She was on the verge of babbling, and she knew she was blushing. She could feel the heat of it on her cheeks. She finished with a lame, "Good night," then bolted off, running back across his lawn and half tripping over a sprinkler head from his in-ground sprinkler system.

"You okay?" he called.

"I'm fine," she called back and raced for her front door.

Louise was seated at the kitchen table, finishing up the two sample cookies Zona had given her. "Well? What happened?"

"He apologized for being a jerk and offered to help me with the fence barrier. And I almost tripped and he called and asked if I was okay. He seemed . . . normal." And that was unnerving.

But not half as unnerving as what she'd overheard.

"Putting up a false front," Louise said, shaking her head. "What did he say about the woman?"

"Nothing." Zona returned to the bowl of cookie dough and began dropping the last spoonfuls of it onto a cookie sheet.

"You should have asked him if everything was all right over there," Louise said.

Zona sighed. "I guess I should have, but . . ." Her sentence trailed off as she tried to figure out what the but was. "I felt stupid," she concluded. "Two people had a fight and we overheard and that's probably all there is to it."

She put the cookies in the oven and joined her mother at the kitchen table. "I feel like a snoop."

"Better to be a snoop than do nothing and have someone end up getting hurt," Louise said.

Zona sighed. There was that.

"I WOULD HAVE called the cops," Gilda said the next day as she helped Louise into her pants.

Zona did have a point. "If people called the police every time they heard a couple yelling at each other, there'd be no one left to control traffic or arrest criminals. Still, what's going on next door makes me nervous."

"It pays to be watchful," said Gilda. "Who knows how much hurt this man is capable of?"

The red PT Cruiser was gone for most of the day, which gave Louise hope that the woman had fled, but she eventually returned, laden with bulging department store bags.

"He's bought her loyalty," said Gilda as the two women watched out the window in the dining room where they sat playing cards.

"The poor little fool," said Louise.

AFTER A DELAY of several days, the fence barrier finally arrived and Zona was in the backyard, sweating as she struggled to install it. Darling was doing his best to get in the way and Louise was watching the whole procedure from a patio chair when they heard the raised voices from next door again.

Darling perked up his ears and ran along the fence, barking.

He wasn't the only one with ears on the alert. Zona stopped her digging and moved along the fence to get closer to the source of the commotion.

"Get in the house," Alec James commanded.

"No!" shouted the redhead's voice, and Darling barked encouragement.

"Darling, stop," Zona hissed. How could she hear what was going on next door with Darling making a racket right next to her?

Darling let out another bark and she tapped his nose and whispered, "Shhh." He sat down with a whine.

"The whole world needs to know what you are," cried the woman on the other side of the fence. "Come any closer and I'll drop this in the pool."

Drop what? Evidence of something? What was going on over there?

14

ZONA TURNED AND LOOKED QUESTIONINGLY AT Louise, who looked back, baffled and concerned.

"Get. In. Here," snarled Alec James over on his side of the fence.

"I won't! And see how you like it when something you need gets taken away."

"Don't even think about it. Get inside. Now!"

"Stop! You're hurting me," squealed the woman, which started Darling barking again and racing to put his front paws up on the fence to see what was going on.

He wasn't the only one. Zona was trying to find a spot between the boards where she could see. She jumped a couple of times, trying to see over the fence. She caught a one-second glimpse of the couple at the edge of the pool, the woman pulling to get away from him and him glaring at her as he tugged on her arm.

"What's going on over there?" Zona called sharply.

The couple next door was too busy to reply.

Suddenly Alec James roared, "You bitch." Zona could hear the woman laughing hysterically. This was followed by a big splash. Was he drowning her?

Zona stooped with her eye to a tiny hole in the fence. Darling joined her and she nudged him away and squinted through the sliver of space. She could see Alec James climbing out of the pool, dripping water. Was that a phone he was holding in his hand?

So, Ms. PT Cruiser had pushed him in. If the arguing hadn't been so violent, Zona would have laughed, but this was no laughing matter. His expression was fierce. *If looks could kill.* Suddenly she truly understood the meaning of that expression.

Where was the woman? Zona moved down the fence as quietly as she could and looked through another slit and saw her standing on the patio, hugging herself and biting her lip. Alec James appeared next to her, dripping wet and furious. He grabbed her arm and started dragging her in the direction of the house.

"Let me go! I hate you," she cried and tried to pull back, but he kept moving her forward. Darling began barking again, rising up on his hind legs and scratching at the fence.

The pair moved out of Zona's line of vision. She tried to look through the next space between the boards, but Darling was in the way.

The noise evaporated to the faintest muffled voices through the sliding glass doors. Zona turned and looked at Louise. What to do?

"This time we should call the police," Louise said.

"And tell them what? He yelled at her, and she pushed him in the pool?"

"Probably in self-defense."

Zona joined her at the patio table.

"Something bad is happening over there. He could be beating her even as we're sitting here," Louise fretted.

The woman was back outside again, crying. Zona moved along the fence, trying to find a place she could peek out to get a good glimpse of the poor victim. "Are you okay over there?" she called. "Do you need help?"

"He's a monster," the woman wailed.

Zona finally saw her. She was crumpled onto a patio chair, her face buried in her hands as she cried.

"Let us help you," Zona called.

The woman shook her head and ran back into the house. Yikes! Right back into the lion's den.

"We really need to call the police," Louise insisted.

Next door a big engine sprang to life. Alec James's truck.

"I'm going over there," Zona said.

"No, it's too dangerous," her mother protested.

"He just left. I'll be fine. I'll get her and bring her here," Zona said, and went out the backyard gate.

The truck was gone from the driveway, but the red PT Cruiser remained parked in its usual spot. What was that woman still doing inside the house? This was her chance. She needed to get away. Zona crossed his lawn and hurried to the front door, all the while wondering what she could say.

Her heart was thudding as she rang the doorbell. What if Alec James came back while she was there?

The woman didn't come to the door. Zona rang the doorbell again and then knocked. Still, the woman remained inside. Afraid to answer?

"Please, let us help you," Zona called. Could the woman even hear her? Maybe she was off in a bedroom, crying. Or packing.

Zona rang the doorbell again and pounded on the door but still got no results. Unsure what else she could do, she gave up and went back home.

She reentered the backyard and Darling bounded over to greet her, jumping up and putting dirty paws on her chest. "Down, Darling," she commanded, taking a step back. Darling barked happily and jumped again, and she gave him a gentle shove back onto all fours.

"What happened?" Louise asked as Zona joined her at the patio table.

"He's gone, but she wouldn't come to the door."

"Too embarrassed," Louise surmised.

"Probably," Zona said, and sighed. There were way too many rotten men in the world.

"There must be something we can do to help that woman," said Louise.

"When someone's determined to stay in a relationship, there's not much you can do to help her until she's ready to leave."

What was the deal with this woman? Was she so in love with Alec James that she couldn't let go? What was keeping her there?

What kept any woman in an unhealthy relationship? The hope that things would change? Fear of repercussions if she left?

Zona was still mulling that over when she heard their neighbor's truck pull back into the driveway sometime after midnight. She went to her bedroom window and saw him walking back to his front door. He didn't seem as angry, but what would happen once he was inside?

She wished she'd never taken over cookies. He didn't deserve them. Maybe she needed to bake another batch laced with crushed sleeping pills so she could get that poor deluded woman out of the house and to a shelter.

THE TROUBLE NEXT door was escalating and Louise was now on high alert.

"Things are not right over there," she told Martin when he stopped in the next afternoon to see if she needed anything from the store. "Alec James and that woman had a terrible fight last night. I'm sure he hit her."

Martin's brows pulled together. "What makes you think that?"

"Because of all the commotion. Plus, Zona went over later,

and the woman wouldn't come to the door. Her car is still sitting outside, but we haven't caught a glimpse of her all day."

"She could be embarrassed that you'd heard them fighting," said Martin.

Honestly, Martin was so naive. "Embarrassed about a black eye, more likely," Louise argued.

Martin was not swayed. "Louise, people fight all the time. Sometimes they even raise their voices."

"This wasn't your average argument," she insisted. "Zona and I both heard. It was scary. She even pushed him in the pool."

"Who, Zona?" Martin asked.

Louise frowned at him. "No, the woman."

"Violence always escalates," said Gilda, who had returned with a glass of Zona's homemade raspberry lemonade for him.

"If this woman was able to push him in the pool, she's probably perfectly capable of taking care of herself." He sampled the drink. "This is good. What all has it got in it?"

If he thought he was going to change the subject that easily, he was very much mistaken. "I'm sure he hit her once he got out," Louise said. "Maybe you could go over there and talk to him."

Martin's brows furrowed. "And say what? Are you beating your girlfriend?"

"Just feel things out."

He shook his head. "Louise, unless you know someone is being hurt, what goes on between two people is nobody's business. I've talked to the man a couple of times. He seems like a nice guy. And this woman clearly doesn't want your help."

"Looks can be deceiving," Gilda said as she settled in with her crocheting.

"I really think you should stay out of the man's business. Which is exactly what I'm going to do." Martin finished his drink and stood. "Are you sure there's nothing you need?"

"I need you to go talk to Alec James."

"I meant from the store."

Louise frowned. "Nothing. Zona shopped the other day."

"All right. I'll be going then. You ladies have a nice afternoon."

"Wimp," Louise muttered as he went out the door. "I need to find out more about what's going on over there," she said to Gilda.

"How are you going to do that?" Gilda asked. "Martin does have a point. You can't go over and ask your neighbor what's going on with his girlfriend."

"No, but I can at least let him know that I'm watching him. Maybe when he comes home from work I'll be out checking my mail. I can certainly make it to the mailbox. Let's watch for his truck. He sometimes beats Zona home, and if he does, I'm going to be ready to have a little talk with him."

COME FOUR THIRTY in the afternoon the two women were seated at the dining room table, watching out the window. "As soon as we see his truck coming up the street, I'll go out," said Louise.

"Don't you hurry with those crutches," Gilda cautioned. "I don't want you falling and breaking a hip on my watch."

"I'll be careful. Oh, wait. Here he comes now. He's early. Hand me my crutches!"

Gilda obliged and hurried to open the front door, then grabbed Darling's collar so he wouldn't make a break for it.

Louise swung her way over and out the door, then carefully made her way off the porch. She managed to arrive at her mailbox just as he was getting out of his truck.

"Hello, there," she called as if she hadn't heard the commotion of the night before.

He gave her a nod, then walked to the back of his truck and fetched his toolbox.

"How are you settling in?" she called.

"Okay," he called back. Not warmly.

Louise swung her way a little closer to his yard. "It looks like you've got some company staying with you."

"Just someone who needs a place to stay for a while," he said, his voice cooling a few more degrees. He had his toolbox and was starting toward the house.

"We heard some commotion over there last night," Louise called.

That stopped him in his tracks. Had his face gone pale? He was so suntanned it was hard to tell.

"Is your friend all right?" she asked.

"She's fine. I hope your leg heals soon," he added, then picked up his pace.

"If you need anything," she called after him.

He pretended not to hear and went inside.

"Well, he's on notice now," she said to Gilda when she got back into her own house.

"You be on your guard. Remember what happened in *Rear Window* once the killer knew they were onto him."

A shiver needled its way up Louise's spine. Maybe it wasn't such a good thing that Alec James was now on notice.

Really, though, what could he do to her? She had locks on her doors. She had people coming and going all the time.

But her kitchen door had a glass window, the kind burglars and crazed killers easily broke. She shivered again as a vision of a beefy arm reaching through a jagged hole in the glass to unlock the door swam into her mind.

Now she was being silly. Alec James was an angry brute, but his anger wasn't directed at her or Zona. Darling was another matter. But the fence problem was solved and the only person he had left to be cruel to was that poor deluded woman who was with him.

Why did she stay? Details from *Deathline* episodes ran

through Louise's head. Was he bribing her to stay with spending sprees? Or . . . had he threatened to find her and kill her if she left him?

Oh, now there she was back to making her new neighbor a murderer. Martin was probably right. She needed to mind her own business.

But when Zona went to shut her bedroom blinds after she was in bed that night she said, "Leave them open."

"You won't sleep," Zona protested.

"I'll sleep fine, and I like the moonlight coming in."

"It's not a full moon," pointed out Zona.

"I'll enjoy it anyway," said Louise, and didn't add, "I'll enjoy keeping an eye on the neighbors, too." That would have made her sound like a voyeur.

Which she wasn't. She was simply being vigilant. So there.

Zona said her good-night, then left Louise to enjoy her book.

Louise awakened a little after eleven when the book fell on her face. She was putting it on her nightstand when she heard, "I hate you!" coming from next door. Easy to guess who that was. Elementary, my dear Watson. It was the poor, foolish woman staying with Alec James.

Louise struggled to roll onto her side with her encased leg, leaned over, and peered out through the sheers. Craning her neck just so, she could see the form of a woman running from the house. The woman got into her car, started it, and raced away.

Good. Maybe she'd finally come to her senses.

Except she hadn't taken anything with her, not even a purse. No suitcase, no box of personal items, none of the goodies from her shopping sprees. Would she be back with a policeman accompanying her to get her things?

"SHE MUST HAVE been terrified not to even take her purse," Louise finished the next morning after she'd filled Zona in on what she'd seen.

"Just because you didn't see one doesn't mean she wasn't carrying one," Zona said. "You couldn't exactly get a full view from your bedroom window. Maybe next time we should prop you up in a chair right next to it. That way you'd have a better view of everything going on over there."

Louise scowled. "Very funny."

"I thought so. Seriously, Mom. We can't let ourselves get sucked into our neighbor's dysfunctional life. I've offered help and the woman refused it. And now she's gone, hopefully for good. Let's let go of this."

"What if she comes back?"

"If she needs help, we'll help her." Zona changed the subject. "There's not much exciting for breakfast this morning. I'll make puff pastry when I get home tonight."

"You don't have to go to all that trouble," Louise said.

"I want to. I've been craving some."

Louise's phone buzzed with a text from Bree. Want company later today?

"Looks like you'll get more than one taker. Bree wants to come over," said Louise.

"She probably wants to hear what you've got written on your book."

"I haven't written anything yet," Louise protested.

"I guess you'd better get cracking."

"You girls are getting rather pushy," Louise grumbled. Did they think she could simply turn a spigot in her brain and the creative juices would start pouring out?

"We're not being pushy. We're motivating you."

So was what was going on next door. No. That wasn't accurate. What was going on next door was just plain scaring her. She hoped the poor woman had truly left for good.

"I DON'T KNOW where to begin on this story," Louise said later to Gilda after they'd settled at the kitchen table with cereal.

"Sure, you do. You've read enough mysteries. You start by showing us the murder victim and the potential killers. Let's get you all set up after you're dressed. I'll be quiet as a mouse so you can work."

Quiet didn't help. Louise sat for half an hour and stared at the doodled-on first page in the notebook her granddaughter had bought her. Then she grabbed her phone and checked Facebook to see what was going on there. Then she called her friend Carol and checked on her. Gilda said nothing, but she raised a judging eyebrow after Louise ended the call.

"I have writer's block," Louise informed her.

"Okay, let's talk about your woman. The wife who gets poisoned, right?"

"Right."

"Maybe she should be . . . older. Desperate for love."

"All older women aren't desperate for love," Louise protested.

"Heaven knows I'm not," Gilda said. "But this is fiction. This woman can't stand being alone. Her first husband died suddenly. He was the love of her life and she was lonely. That's how she got into this mess in the first place. She married a man who was a smooth talker, but he doesn't really love her. He only married her for her money, but she can't see it."

"Love is blind," said Louise and began writing. "I'll start with showing him bringing her breakfast in bed, looking like the world's most considerate husband. And he's surprising her with a cruise. To Hawaii."

Like the one she should have been taking. But there was no sense crying over spilled piña coladas. She kept scribbling. Yes, the juices were flowing now and she was on a roll.

When Bree came over later with hamburgers from In-N-Out, Louise had two pages to read to her.

"I wish our mother wasn't taking this cruise. I have a bad feeling about it." Emily Dickinson said to her brother.

"Emily Dickinson. Isn't she a famous poet?" Bree interrupted.
"It's a nice name," Louise insisted, and read on.

"It's their five-year anniversary. Just what she needs after being sick," said the brother.

Louise interrupted her reading to explain, "Marion's husband has already been slowly poisoning her so we're setting things up for later."
Bree nodded. "I like that."

"Poor Mother," Emily said. "She's had one thing after another wrong with her ever since she and Gerard married. He's been awfully patient."

"While he sets her up to die," Gilda put in, and smiled as she worked her crochet hook.
Louise's narrative continued, explaining how lonely poor Marion, the future victim, had been before Gerard came into her life. She'd been unwell off and on ever since they married, and worried at one point that he was cheating on her. But this grand gesture proved he was still as in love with her as ever.
"This is good stuff, Gram," said Bree when Louise had finished.
"Gilda's been helping me," said Louise. "She suggested the poisoning idea." And most of the best lines. Hmm. Maybe Gilda should be writing this book.
"You two should become a team, like Christina Lauren," Bree said.
"Oh, no. I'm no writer," said Gilda.

But after Bree left, Louise said, "Bree might be right. You're the one who came up with all the good ideas for my book."

"But you're the one who wrote them down."

"More like taking dictation," said Louise.

"All I did was help free up your creative juices," Gilda said, refusing to take credit for anything. "But let me tell you, I've seen a lot of crazy things in my life. I could probably write a dozen books if I had a mind. It's shocking what people are capable of."

That was all it took to launch her into another story of the shady life of a doctor she'd once worked with. "And everyone thought he was a saint," she finished. "I tell you, you never know."

"So true," said Louise. The man next door was proof of that.

"THAT WOMAN NEXT door still hasn't returned," Louise reported later when she sat at the kitchen table, slicing avocados into the salad bowl while Zona stood at the stove, finishing up quesadillas.

"Good," said Zona. "I've had enough of them both."

It was true. She had. The bad vibes from the house next door had been making it hard to settle into the stress-free routine she was trying to create. The things she'd heard, coupled with her mother's speculations, kept bouncing back into her head.

Before she got into bed later, she found herself looking down on the house next door from her upstairs window. A woman fleeing in the middle of the night spoke volumes. Even though it had turned quiet over there it felt like the calm before the storm, like something dark was crouching, just waiting to pounce. Those thoughts were enough to make her shudder.

And the fact that she was standing at her bedroom window

looking down at nothing was enough to make her shake her head in disgust.

She had better things to do than spy on the neighbor, for crying out loud. She wasn't going to waste any more brain energy on the man next door. He and his girlfriend had fought and yelled a lot and now she was gone. That was it. That was all.

15

LOUISE LET OUT A SCREECH AS the man on her TV screen suddenly appeared out of the shadows on his neighbor's back patio. "Oh, my gosh, don't let him in," she said to the woman.

Of course, fictional people never listened to you. The woman invited him in.

"What do you know about what I do for a living?" he asked.

"Never mind that. Ask him what he does in his off hours," Louise commanded, and Martin, who was keeping her company, chuckled.

"She can't die, Lou. She's the main character."

"You can't be sure with these modern movies," Louise said.

Martin helped himself to more of the Parmesan popcorn Zona had made for them before she'd disappeared into her bedroom. "I'm sure," he said.

She looked suspiciously at him. "Have you already seen this?"

"Maybe."

The man on the screen took a pair of thin surgical gloves out of the back pocket of his jeans. It wasn't looking good for their heroine.

But their heroine just happened to have her handy-dandy pink Taser, and she was ready for him.

"I knew all along who you were," she told him as he writhed on her kitchen floor.

"Good," Louise said, happy to see that this story was turning out exactly as it should. Maybe she needed to look online for a Taser. You never knew when you might need one. A pink one.

The ending credits were rolling when Zona wandered into the living room and helped herself to the few kernels of popcorn left in the bowl. "How was the movie?" she asked.

"Chilling," Louise replied. "And proof that you never really know about the people who live around you."

Zona's smile flat-lined. "You never really know about the people you live with, either."

Martin turned the subject into more pleasant avenues, asking Zona, "How did your latest eBay items do?"

That put a smile back on Zona's face. "Excellent. In fact, I'm going to reward myself and take the night off. I'm meeting Gracie at Mariposa."

"Good. I'm glad you're getting out. You deserve to have a little fun," said Louise.

"I won't be late," Zona said. Looking at Martin. As if Louise needed a babysitter every second of the day.

"Stay out as long as you want," she said to her daughter. Then to Martin, "And you don't need to feel like you have to stick around here all night."

"Are you trying to get rid of me?" he teased.

"Of course not. But I am perfectly fine on my own," Louise said, looking pointedly at Zona.

There were times when mothers needed to be allowed the last word, and Zona obviously sensed this was one of them. "All right. I'll see you later."

"Have fun," Louise said.

Darling had assumed he'd be going, too. "Not you," Zona said. "We'll go out after I get back."

Walking around so late at night with a dog who would

probably lick an attacker rather than bite him? Louise didn't like the sound of that. She was definitely going to buy a Taser for her daughter.

"Do you want me to leave?" Martin asked after the front door had closed.

"No, of course not. I'm wide awake. That dark chocolate we had earlier plus my late afternoon iced coffee have taken effect and I feel like an owl."

"Well, night owl. We could play some cards."

"An excellent idea," Louise approved. "But first, would you mind doing me a favor?"

"Name it," he said.

"Would you take Darling for a walk? I really don't like the idea of Zona being out late at night all by herself."

He nodded. "I understand. Happy to."

Darling was happy that he was happy, jumping with excitement as Martin took his leash from where it hung on the coat closet doorknob.

"Be back in a few," Martin said. "Lock the door after me."

Louise swung herself over to the door and locked it. She texted Zona that Martin was walking Darling and there was no need to hurry home. Then she got the cards from the kitchen junk drawer, put them in her sweater pocket along with a pen and a folded piece of paper, and set everything out on the kitchen table. There. She wasn't totally helpless.

But if they wanted anything to drink, Martin would have to fetch the glasses. Sigh.

She frowned. She wasn't helpless, but she wasn't independent, either. She couldn't take her own dog for a walk. She couldn't trust herself with a pitcher of lemonade or a cup of tea. This was not how her summer should have been going.

By the time Martin and Darling returned from their walk, she had a list of complaints waiting to be shared.

"I know. It's no fun hobbling around," he said. "But come

September it will be off. Meanwhile, you're finding time to write your novel."

Finding time and making progress were two different things. She hadn't written a word since those first two pages. Maybe Louise was meant to be a reader rather than a writer. Maybe she should become an influencer and talk about books instead.

"You know, I thought it would be so much fun to write a book, but I had no idea it was so hard."

Martin shrugged. "Most things turn out to be harder than we think."

"Like getting a glass of lemonade," she complained.

"That's what you've got me for," he said with a smile.

"You are a good friend. Thank you," she said.

He bit off a corner of that smile and went to fetch the pitcher of lemonade from the refrigerator.

"I'll make this up to you when I'm walking again," she said.

"I'm not keeping score." He returned to the kitchen table with the pitcher, then fetched their glasses.

"I know. But I am. I hate being a pain in the neck."

"No one thinks that, especially not me. Louise, you must know how much I care for you."

She knew. She'd hoped he wouldn't ever bring it up. "I do. And I care for you, too, but only in a platonic way."

She saw the disappointment on his face. He hid it by concentrating on filling their glasses. "Feelings can deepen, you know," he said in an attempt to keep hope alive.

"Yes, they can," she agreed, then felt compelled to add, "Martin, you must know how much I appreciate you." Offering a thirsty a man a thimble of water.

"I'm not sexy. I get it."

He wasn't. He was sweet and fun and a good friend. But Martin had never done anything to make her heart beat any faster. Being with him was like having an emotional pacemaker—her emotions stayed steady, boringly steady, and never spiked. She appreciated his friendship, enjoyed doing things with him. That was as far as it went.

She'd hate to lose what they had. "Martin, you are a wonderful man. Are you okay if we stay as we are? I don't want to lose your friendship."

"You know you'll never lose that," he said. He returned the pitcher to the refrigerator. "Of course, a lovely woman like you isn't going to settle. You'll want a Sam Elliott or a Kevin Costner."

That was hard to deny, but she had no intention of hurting his feelings. "I don't think you have to worry because neither of them has called. And last I heard neither one has a twin. Come on, let's play gin."

He nodded, managed a smile, and they got busy with their cards.

IT WAS KARAOKE time at the Mariposa Bar and Grill in Covina, and Zona and Gracie sat eating chips and salsa and drinking Millionaire Martinis. ("Thinking positive about the future," Gracie had said when she'd ordered them.)

"You have to be insane to get up there and make a fool of yourself," Zona said as a woman sang an off-key version of "I Will Always Love You."

"Or drunk. Either way, it's always entertaining. Bradley and I love coming here," said Gracie.

"Is he feeling left out?"

"A little." Gracie smiled, took a sip of her drink. "He knows he'll get rewarded later."

Zona experienced a twinge of jealousy. She wouldn't mind enjoying some rewards herself.

Have another chip.

"Hey, things are bound to get better," Gracie said, sensing her discontent.

"No way to go but up," Zona said, and took a slurp of her drink.

"Your mom's doing good."

"Yep, she is." There was always something to be grateful for. "And Gilda's working out. She and Mom do a great job of feeding each other's appetite for murder and mayhem."

"Aunt Gilda does have the stories to tell."

"And Mom eats them up." Zona gave her glass a thoughtful twirl. "I guess that's okay. It keeps her from being bored. I just wish she'd quit focusing on our neighbor."

"Things have calmed down now, right?"

"Yes, thank God. Hopefully, they'll stay that way." The less they had to do with the neighbor the better.

THREE GAMES AND a little more chocolate later Louise was wide awake and ready to play another round of cards, but Martin was yawning.

"You should have had more chocolate," she told him.

"I guess I should have." He reached for the cards.

She pulled them away. "You need to go home and get some sleep."

"I'm fine," he said.

"Martin, I'm all right on my own. Truly."

He looked dubious.

"I am capable of putting myself to bed." She said it firmly to make sure he got the message.

"Okay, if you're sure. But if you need anything, all you have to do is call."

She patted the sweater pocket where she kept her cell phone. "I know."

He gave up insisting on watching over her and she walked him to the door. "I'm glad you could come over," she said.

"I'm always glad to spend time with you," he said. "Garage sales tomorrow?"

"Absolutely."

"I'll be over at eight thirty."

"We'll be ready," Louise said.

Of course, Zona would go with them. Her daughter was obsessed with making money. Louise had been surprised that Zona had gone out at all. She was glad she had though. Her daughter was going hard and pushing hard, and she looked exhausted. A time out had been exactly what she needed.

Life was such a mixture of sweet and sour, she thought as she made her way to the bathroom. One minute you were biting into a Tootsie Pop, the next you'd lost a filling and were on your way to the dentist. Or you'd broken a leg. Lost a husband. Lost all your savings.

But they were strong women. They could handle both the good and the bad. Her cast would eventually come off and she'd be back line dancing. Zona would slowly right her financial ship. Bree . . . Louise sighed. Bree would hopefully be able to break through the hard shell she'd formed around herself and realize that while you couldn't trust everyone there were still a few someones left in the world that you could.

She left a note for Zona that they were on for garage sales in the morning if Zona was interested. Then she went to bed and settled in, Darling jumping on the foot of the bed and making himself at home.

He'd take off later. Zona hadn't let him sleep with Louise when she first came home for fear he would somehow plop on her injured leg or trip her if she tried to get up in the night. Darling had switched allegiance and started following Zona upstairs to bed. But when she wasn't around, he remembered who his mommy really was. Once Zona returned, he'd forget again so Louise left the door halfway open so he could go be her shadow. She liked leaving it halfway open so she could easily get out, too. When nature called, it was best to make it as simple as possible to answer that call.

She picked up the novel Martin had loaned her and started reading. It was hard to put down and she was wide awake. She'd probably finish the book before she finally fell asleep.

Zona returned home a little before midnight to find her still reading. "You're still up? That book must really be good."

"It is. Plus I think I had too much chocolate. It won't stop me from getting up to go garage-saling tomorrow though. You probably aren't going to want to go after getting home this late."

"It's not that late. I'll be ready," Zona assured her.

She kissed Louise good-night, called to Darling, who jumped off the bed to join her, then went upstairs.

Louise decided she'd better try to go to sleep if she wanted to have enough energy to treasure hunt. One more visit to the bathroom first, then maybe she'd make it through the night.

Oh, the things you take for granted, she thought after she'd struggled on and off the toilet and was swinging herself back to her bed. How did people who had to cope with physical handicaps keep a positive attitude? It couldn't be easy.

She was about to get back in bed when she thought she saw movement next door. What was going on over there at this time of night? She hurriedly swung over to the window and got the curtains parted just in time to catch sight of Alec James striding to his truck.

He carried a pink overnight bag and several shopping bags. And what looked like a purse, a small one, the kind younger women favored. Louise couldn't be sure in the weak light of the streetlight, but judging from the bow on it, she suspected it was a designer purse. He threw everything in the truck cab and then got in and backed out of the driveway. Where was he going with the woman's things? Where was the woman?

Louise's first thoughts ran toward Hitchcock's *Rear Window*. "Don't be silly," she scolded herself. And yet . . . who sneaked out late at night getting rid of another person's personal items? And the purse.

No woman in her right mind ran off and left her purse behind. Especially a designer purse. Something was dreadfully wrong over there.

"IT'S PROOF. THAT man is up to something," Louise told Zona the next morning as they hurried their way through Zona's homemade waffles.

"No, it's proof she's gone for good and we can stop worrying. He probably wanted to get rid of her stuff," Zona said.

"So late at night? Don't you find that a little suspicious?"

Maybe it was time to put Louise on a strict reading diet. Romance novels only. And no more *Deathline*. Nothing but Hallmark happiness for her and Gilda.

"No, I find it a relief," said Zona. "The woman got smart and got out of there."

"But why didn't she take her things? And why leave in the dead of night?"

Her words gave Zona's nerves a jangle. "There will probably turn out to be some simple answer," she said to both her mother and herself, and forked the last bite of waffle into her mouth.

"Yeah, he murdered her. Plain and simple."

Zona swallowed hard. It had been horrifying enough thinking their neighbor might be capable of hurting someone.

She settled her nerves with a firm dose of reality. "With CCTV, DNA, and nosy neighbors, do you know how hard it is to actually get away with murder?"

"Does *he* know?"

The doorbell rang, signaling Martin's arrival. "You need to let go of this idea," Zona said, and rose to go let him in.

"What if it's true?" Louise called after her.

"What are the odds?" Zona called back, then cringed. She hated when she slipped and used gambling terms. It triggered all kinds of unhealthy emotions.

She ditched the surfacing bitterness and replaced her frown with a smile for Martin. "Come on in. We'll be ready to go in a minute."

He nodded and stepped inside just as Louise was coming out from the kitchen, Darling escorting her. "I just need to brush my teeth," she told him.

"While you're doing that, I'll take Darling for a quick walk," Zona said. She'd have time. In addition to brushing her teeth, Louise would also be making good use of the bathroom and checking to be sure her makeup was perfect.

Zona grabbed a doggy-do bag, snapped on Darling's leash, and let him race her down the sidewalk past Alec James's house. His truck was in the driveway, and all was quiet. It hardly looked like the scene of a crime. But if a crime had taken place, would it have taken place in that house or somewhere else? Like one of the trails in the foothills?

Oh, good grief, she was turning into her mother.

Darling was a good boy, and Zona was a good pet owner, picking up after him. By the time they returned to the house, Louise was ready to go.

"Quite a few garage sales today," said Martin after they were all in his car. "Did you see there were a couple in San Dimas? Those might be good."

"Oh, yes," said Louise. "Good hunting for Zona," she added.

Looking for treasures sure beat indulging in morbid speculation about the man next door. "This garage sale hunting has turned out to be a brilliant idea," Zona said from the back seat.

"I'm full of good ideas," Louise quipped, and Zona could hear the smile in her voice.

"Yes, you are," Zona agreed. Well, she was full of ideas. And most of them were good, anyway.

Their treasure hunting yielded some charming Christmas ornaments, including one with a Boston terrier that Zona was sure would get fought over when she finally posted it. She was equally pleased with the women's brand-name bicycle shorts and top that she found, which were in mint condition.

"My teenage daughter wanted to get into cycling," explained the woman selling them. "But she said the seat hurt her butt. She's into running now. We'll see how long that lasts."

"Next year we might find all kinds of running shoes," Louise joked as they left.

Zona supposed the next year she would still be selling garage sale finds online. And doing who knew what else.

At their last stop Louise and Martin were drawn to two boxes of books marked at a dollar each.

"A steal," Louise crowed as Martin showed her a vintage gothic novel.

Zona, too, was drawn to the bargains and started looking through the second box. One book in particular practically jumped into her hands. She picked it up and read the title: *The Psychology of Dangerous People.*

She showed it to Louise. "This might be good research for your book."

"Maybe," said Louise, but she didn't sound all that interested.

"I'll get it for you," said Zona.

"We can both read it," said Louise.

They were done faster than anticipated and it was only midmorning when they arrived back home, Zona laden down with her goodies and Martin following her up the walk with the pile of clothes and mystery novels Louise had found.

Alec James was outside, wearing board shorts and a faded T-shirt, mowing his front lawn. Looking like a regular guy, a non-screaming, non-violent, nice, hot guy. A sheen of sweat made his arms glisten.

Zona told her awakening hormones to go back to sleep and averted her eyes. She was not ever going to allow herself to get interested in their neighbor. He wasn't a murderer, she was sure of that. But he was verbally abusive. Scarily different from the charmer she'd first met.

She was halfway up the front walk when she realized her mother wasn't with her. A little flutter of *oh, no* in her chest told her to look to her right. Sure enough, there was Louise, swinging on over to talk to their neighbor. Zona gave the house key to Martin and sent him on to deposit her mother's purchases, then hurried over to make sure Louise didn't say anything that could upset the man.

He had turned off his lawn mower and Louise was talking. Double *oh, no*. The hurrying turned into bolting.

"We haven't seen your company lately," Louise was saying.

Alec James wasn't smiling. Zona's heart turned to lead and dropped down to her stomach.

"She left," he said.

"Rather suddenly." Louise sounded like an amateur sleuth, trying to grill a suspect.

"She found another place to stay," he said shortly.

Zona stepped up before Louise could say anything more to antagonize him. "Come on, Mom," she said, "Martin's waiting."

"Have a good day," Louise said to their neighbor.

He nodded—still no smile—and started his lawn mower back up.

"What were you thinking?" Zona demanded as they walked up their own front walk. She cast a look in Alec James's direction, half expecting to see him standing by the running lawn mower, glowering at them.

He was walking the opposite direction, but she was sure he was glowering.

"That man has something to hide," Louise insisted.

"Don't go looking," Zona said. Her mother needed to rein in her runaway imagination.

So did Zona. She made the mistake that night of leafing through the book she'd bought at the garage sale. One paragraph in particular caught her attention.

> We're taught from a young age to believe the best about people. The problem with this is that it makes us unwilling to see the worst. A charming smile may hide a narcissistic personality or violent tendencies.

Zona slammed the book shut. She would not be reading any more of this, and she wasn't letting her mother anywhere near it.

But what if Alec James was hiding . . . something?

16

THE SWELLING IN LOUISE'S LEG HAD gone down and her temporary cast was swapped out for a sturdier, all-encasing one, which allowed her to finally shower with the proper precautions. Even though that brought its own challenges, she'd been happy to abandon washing her hair in the sink and was counting the weeks until her leg would be completely free.

June was on its way out. The temperature was rising into the high eighties and ice cream sales were up. Flags and buntings were starting to appear on houses, proof that the Fourth of July was peeking around the corner. "We need to have a party," she announced to Zona.

Of course they did. Louise could never let a holiday pass without throwing a party, and she had no intention of letting a little thing like a cast on her leg stop her. When Zona was growing up, she'd made enough potato salad and three-bean salad to feed an army and had put Zona's dad to work on the grill, serving up hamburgers and hot dogs. There was always a water balloon toss or three-legged race for the kids and enough ice cream to clog every artery in Glendora.

The first year after her husband died, Louise hadn't been able to bring herself to entertain, but by the next year she had decided enough was enough and had thrown a big open house bash for the entire neighborhood. She had toned things down since then, but not much.

This party would be work and Louise wouldn't be able to

do much of it, but Zona didn't mind picking up the slack. It was the least she could do for her mother. She, herself, wasn't in a party mood, but maybe that was when you most needed to gather with friends.

"Don't worry, we won't make a big thing of it," Louise promised. "Gilda can take me shopping and we'll pick up a couple of rotisserie chickens, some salads in a bag, and garlic French bread and call it good. And maybe some ice cream bars," she added. "And makings for a fruit salad. Watermelon. Pop. Chips. Candy for the kids." Yep, Louise was on a roll.

"What kids?" asked Zona.

"You're going to invite Gracie and her family, aren't you?"

"I guess I am," said Zona. "Although they might have plans."

"Oh, I'm sure they'll be going to watch fireworks somewhere," Louise said. "But that all happens later. We can do this in the afternoon. I do wish we'd put in a pool when we first bought this house. It would have been so much fun to have a pool party." She frowned. "The Livingstons always used to let us use their pool."

The Livingstons had been good neighbors. As a child, Zona had spent a lot of time next door, playing in that pool with Lotus Livingston and her sister, Ginger. And tolerating their pesky little brother. The Livingston kids had grown up and scattered across the country, and the last Zona had seen of Lotus was when she'd come back to help her mother get the house ready to sell before moving Mrs. Livingston to live with her in Texas.

"I hope your mom will become good friends with whoever buys the place," she'd said to Zona. "It's always been a happy house."

It hadn't been a happy house since the Livingstons moved, and it still wasn't.

Zona pulled her mind back to the topic of party prep.

"What makes you think Gilda's going to want to go shopping with you?"

"She's getting invited to the party. Of course she'll want to help," Louise reasoned. "Maybe we'll get Martin to go with us. He can carry the heavier items." Martin the pack mule.

And so, by the third of July Gilda, Martin, and Louise had stocked up on party food and decorations, and Zona came home from work to find both women seated at the kitchen table, cutting up fruit and dropping it into one of Louise's giant Tupperware bowls.

"That's a lot of fruit," Zona said, and kissed her mother's cheek.

"It's a lot of hungry stomachs. Gracie's two boys could probably single-handedly down this entire bowl."

Two teenage boys were the equivalent of locusts for sure, but Zona was willing to bet they'd spend more time working their way through the meat, the chips, and the vat of potato salad Louise had purchased.

They proved her right the following day, inhaling almost everything. Not as much of the fruit salad, but leftovers would work great in smoothies. Bree had called dibs on the bag of Cheetos and was existing on that. Darling was enjoying the party, scrounging tidbits of chicken wherever and whenever possible. Louise's friend Carol was the biggest soft touch, and he only left her side when the boys began to play on the old Slip 'N Slide Zona and Bree had brought out.

"This is the life," said Martin as he enjoyed a second bottle of beer.

"We should have put in a pool," said Louise, watching as Bree joined the boys.

"I don't hear anyone complaining," said Zona as her daughter made a running leap for the wet strip of plastic.

"I'm surprised nobody's in the pool next door," said Louise's other friend Susan.

It was certainly hot enough. Even under the shade of the pergola it was toasty, and everyone was consuming the various beverages like camels stocking up for a long journey.

"Nobody's doing anything over there now," said Louise. "Somebody has gone missing," she added, and Zona made a face at her.

Carol leaned forward. "Yeah?"

"The woman moved out," Zona said. "That's all."

"She left all her things behind, including a designer purse," Louise said. "I saw him ditching them in the middle of the night. No woman leaves behind a designer purse."

"You know what that means. *Rear Window*," said Gilda, and Carol's big baby blues got bigger.

Alec James's truck was parked in his driveway. Who knew if he was out on his back patio, drinking a beer or getting ready for a swim? Thank God the boys and Darling were all noisily enjoying themselves. Their laughter and barking masked the conversation taking place in the land of the nosy.

"Anyone want ice cream?" Zona asked, hoping to distract them. "I made no-churn cherry chocolate chip last night."

The topic of food turned the conversation, and the Hitchcock obsession with life gone wrong was abandoned. Soon even the food was abandoned and then the Slip 'N Slide, and Darling vanished around the corner of the house to flop in the shade. The younger generation started playing Cards Against Humanity and the adults chatted idly. Afternoon edged toward evening. Finally early evening began to bleed into the day, slowly stealing its light.

Gracie's husband suggested they get moving and get a spot for the fireworks show in nearby Monrovia and they were sent on their way with a bag of chips.

Bree had another party to attend, and she was next to leave, and that left Zona and the sixty-pluses to sit around and wait to watch the fireworks on TV.

"You should be out partying," Carol said to her.

"I am partying," Zona said.

"I mean with your own kind. Not us oldies," Carol said.

Louise frowned at her. "Watch who you're calling old. You're only as old as you act."

"Which puts us at fifty," Susan said with a grin.

"I was in bed with a book by ten when I was fifty," said Carol.

"Old soul," joked Susan.

"There's nothing wrong with going to bed with a good book," Zona argued. Every forty-two-year-old woman went to bed with a book on personal finance, right?

"At your age, you should be in bed with something more than a book," Susan scolded her. "And doing more than reading."

Was it Zona's imagination or was Martin blushing?

"What do you think, Martin?" asked Carol.

Yes, he was definitely blushing.

"I think Zona has plenty of time to figure out the rest of her life," he said. "Did you say there's more of that special ice cream you made left, Zona?"

"There is."

"Stay where you are. I'll get it," he said, and made his escape.

"You embarrassed him," Louise said to her friend.

"He was probably embarrassed because of what he was thinking, and I don't think it was about Zona in bed with someone," Susan said to Louise. "That man is crazy about you. When are you going to come to your senses and appreciate him?"

"I'll be happy to appreciate him," said Carol.

"He's your own personal knight in shining armor," Susan continued.

"Martin is a dear, but I'm afraid he'd hardly qualify as a knight," Louise said, lowering her voice.

"I think he qualifies just fine," said Carol. "It stinks that the only woman he can see is you."

"I'm very seeable," Louise joked.

Martin came back out with his second bowl of ice cream just as a whiz and a pop sounded from somewhere in the neighborhood. "Sounds like things are about to get lively."

"Afraid so," said Carol. "How people manage to get their hands on illegal fireworks and set them off where they shouldn't is a mystery to me."

"The police can't be everywhere," said Susan.

"I just hope nobody sets the foothills on fire," Carol said. She stood. "I should get home. Poor Socks is probably cowering under my bed already."

Susan stood, too. "This holiday is hard on animals." She stacked some plates. "I'll load these for you, Louise."

"Just leave them. I'll get to them later," said Louise.

"Many hands make light work," said Carol, and she took the bowl with the fruit salad.

"I'll help with cleanup, then I'm going home," said Gilda, and grabbed some disposable cups.

Ten minutes later the kitchen had been cleaned and everyone but Martin had left.

"I'd better bring Darling in," said Zona.

"Good idea," said Louise as she and Martin went to the living room to pick out a movie to watch to pass the time.

A little tickle of unease accompanied Zona back outside. Darling hadn't been underfoot trotting in and out as people brought in the leftovers.

Playing with the boys had probably worn him out. That was it. She'd find him sacked next to the house.

"Darling," she called.

No Darling came trotting around the house to greet her. She heard no answering bark. He had to be flopped somewhere, recovering from his busy afternoon of play. Who was she kidding? Darling always wanted to be in the thick of things and never walked away from an opportunity to beg food.

"Darling!" she called again, panic taking over.

Zona hurried around the corner of the house. He had to be there, please be there.

He wasn't. *Nooo.*

There were no holes, which meant he had to have taken escape to new levels and managed to scale the fence. Or . . . Who cared what the *or* was. He was gone.

She ran out to the front yard. "Darling!" She got to the sidewalk and stopped, looking each direction. All she saw was cars parked at curbs and a neighbor's watering system going off and a sky giving up more of its light.

Nooo.

BREE WAS IN Santa Monica with Fen at the house of one of his college friends. The revelers were fueling up before moving on to watch the fireworks display at nearby Corsair Field. The beer and soft drinks were disappearing down thirsty throats and everyone had already made a huge dent in the mountain of chip bags sitting on one of the counters in the outdoor kitchen. The aroma of grilling hot dogs and veggie burgers filled the hot summer air. How could it not? The houses were packed in close together and probably everyone in the neighborhood was grilling something. The house where Fen had taken Bree to party wasn't on the beach, but it was only steps away, and it was worth a small fortune. One Bree would probably never have.

"Money isn't everything," Gram liked to say. No, but it sure helped when that bill for tuition came due. It paid the rent. Or the house payment . . . unless your stepfather put the family so deep in debt the house had to be sold.

She stood at a table loaded with bowls of potato salad, seven-layer dip, baked beans, and half a dozen different desserts and watched Fen pulling out two bottles of root beer from one of the coolers. His friend, whose parents owned the house, was standing next to him and said something to Fen, making him laugh. He had such an easy laugh.

Of course he did. His whole life was easy. Always had been.

Oh, great. Now she was going to be jealous of Fen? She frowned.

"He is so hot," said Uma, a woman Bree had only met an hour earlier.

"Jimmy?" asked Bree.

"Jimmy," the woman scoffed. "He's my cousin and he has the IQ of a peanut. I meant your man. Lucky you."

"He's not really my man. We're friends," Bree explained as Fen started making his way toward her, smiling.

"Yeah? Friends don't look at friends the way he looks at you. But hey, if you don't want him . . ."

Did she? She liked Fen. A lot. She could easily love him, but then what would happen? Great as Fen was, was he worth taking a chance on?

"Go for it," she said.

"I think I will. He seems nice."

"He is," Bree confirmed.

"That should be a change. I just broke up with the world's biggest loser."

No, Bree's stepdad was the world's biggest loser. Nobody could be bigger than him.

Fen reached the table as they finished loading their plates. Bree made the introductions. "Fen, this is Uma." *She's looking.*

Uma cocked her head, letting her sheet of straight blond hair drop to the side, and smiled at Fen. "Hi."

Bree frowned.

"Hi," he said. "Great party, huh?"

"Oh, yeah," she agreed. "Jimmy has some awesome friends."

Fen didn't appear to have picked up on the fact that she was flirting with him. "Yeah, he does." He turned his attention to Bree. "Where do you want to sit?"

Uma frowned. "Told you," she said to Bree.

"Told you what?" Fen asked as they settled at one end of the outdoor table.

A couple of little boys raced past, shooting each other with squirt guns. "Nothing," Bree said, watching them. "You know she's into you, don't you?"

He shrugged. "Not looking." He smiled at Bree, and it made her heart turn over. "There's only one person I'm really interested in."

"I don't know why you're wasting your time," she said.

"Since when is hanging out with you a waste of time," he countered.

"Since never," she joked.

"Exactly." He wasn't joking.

She decided she needed a cookie.

By the time she'd gotten one for both her and Fen, two of his friends had joined him. Good. That spared them from getting into dangerous conversational territory and the time passed comfortably.

"We should get going," someone said eventually, and the party moved on to its next destination, leaving behind nothing but crumbs and a recycle can filled with cans and bottles.

Fen drove and conversation on the way stayed light. He ignored a text coming in from his uncle, who owned the nursery where Fen worked. His job mainly consisted of lugging around large bags of soil and fertilizer, which anyone with eyes could see wasn't hurting his pecs or biceps. But he also had to ring up sales, and sometimes deal with irritable people.

"He probably wants me to work tomorrow even though I'm not scheduled," said Fen.

"You should. I bet Orange Tree Lady has told all her friends about you. They'll be coming in wanting you to come over and prune their roses."

Fen made a face. Orange Tree Lady had come in earlier in the week, sure she'd been sold a defective tree and had lugged the poor dying thing back to the nursery as evidence. She'd not only wanted a refund. She'd also wanted Fen to come back to her house and give her advice on where to plant its replacement.

"She'd had it for three months," he said. "If it was so defective, why didn't she bring it back right away? And how am I supposed to know where to plant a tree?"

"You are working at a nursery," Bree said. "Anyway, she probably wanted more from you than to plant a tree."

He made a face. "Gross."

She laughed. "Well, you are a pretty hot gardener."

"I'm not a gardener," he said with a frown. The frown grew into a smile. "I'm hot, huh?"

"You know you've got aura," she retorted.

His smile got bigger.

"Don't be reading anything into that," she said tersely, and the smile shrank. "Moving on," she said, and switched them to talking about the cool house his friend had.

"I wouldn't mind having a place like that," he said.

"You'll be able to afford it once you're a superstar financial planner."

"Being with a finance expert sounds like a safe bet to me," he said.

"There's no such thing as a safe bet," she muttered.

He pretended not to hear.

Later, as they sat on camp chairs, watching the fireworks burst and rain down colors from an inky sky, he scooted his closer to her and said, "Remember the fireworks I took you to when we were going together?"

She did. A big pop produced a fountain of gold that lit the

sky. Her heart mimicked it as she remembered a steamy collection of kisses they'd shared later that night. Clothes had almost been shed. Almost.

She forced herself not to look at him. If she did, they'd be right back reenacting that other night on the Fourth of July and her willpower would be in the toilet.

"I love you, Bree," he said. "I never stopped thinking about you after we broke up. I know you're going to pull away again, I can feel it coming. And the crappy thing is, I still won't be able to stop thinking about you." He tried to take her hand. She pulled it away.

"Can't we just be friends?" she protested. Now she had to look at him, but she wished she hadn't. She hated seeing the disappointment in his eyes.

"Can't we think about being more than that someday? I'll wait for you forever is there's any chance we can."

"You know what my life's been like. You know about my dad and my stepdad. I don't want to turn into my mom."

"Your mom's pretty nice. I can think of worse things to turn into," he said.

"You know what I mean."

"Other people's mistakes don't have to be yours. And I'm not a mistake."

She wanted to throw her arms around his neck and say, "No, you're not, and I love you." But she forced herself to sit there like a boulder. She did love him. Sadly, she didn't love him enough to trust him with her future. She bit her lip and trained her gaze on the fireworks above them.

He didn't say anything more after that. In fact, he didn't talk at all as he drove her back to her apartment. She looked at his stony expression and felt sick.

Finally, when they were a block away, she couldn't stand it anymore. "I wish you'd say something."

"What's left to say?"

"That you want to be my friend."

He sighed. "I do, but I want more, Bree. I mean, yeah, it's better than nothing, but sometimes better than nothing isn't enough."

The sick feeling grew worse. "What are you saying?"

"I'm saying . . ." He bit down on his lip, shook his head. "I don't know what I'm saying. I guess I need to accept that we can't go any further. I'll have to get used to the idea of not being with you, not being able to touch you, make plans for a future with you, talk about where we'd like to live and how many kids we want, 'cause none of that's going to happen. There's no future for us, Bree. You won't let there be."

He pulled his Jeep into the guest parking space nearest her upstairs shared apartment and turned to look at her. "I'm sorry. I hate this, but we're done. I thought I could, but I can't keep doing this. It's killing me."

She felt the same misery she saw on his face. This was all wrong.

He got out, walked around the Jeep, and opened the passenger door.

"This is crazy," she protested.

"No. Come on. You know the definition of crazy. It's doing the same thing over and over and expecting different results. That's all I'd be doing. I can't do that, Bree. I wish I could, but what's the point of it?"

"The point is, we care about each other."

He shook his head again. "You don't care enough. I wish you did, but you don't."

He was right, of course. She cared more about protecting her heart than she did wounding his. His words poured sorrow and shame over her. She didn't want to hurt him. But she also didn't want to wind up hurt herself. She stood there, her brain on fire, trying to think of something to say that would keep him bound to her but getting nothing in return. She couldn't. It wouldn't be fair to him.

He walked back around the Jeep and got behind the wheel. She stepped away and watched with tears filling her eyes as he drove off.

17

BOTH ZONA AND MARTIN HAD DRIVEN all over the neighborhood and beyond looking for Darling. Neither one found him.

"He's probably hiding somewhere," Martin said to Louise when they returned. "I'm sure he'll come back."

Louise nodded stoically.

"Let's watch that movie," he suggested. "It will take your mind off your worries."

"Oh, Martin, I don't think I could enjoy the movie now."

He nodded. "I guess not. Try not to worry though."

"I'll try," she said.

"I'm sorry, Mom. I should have kept a closer eye on him," Zona said after Martin had left.

"It's not your fault," Louise said. "You've done everything you can to keep him in. Now I wish I'd given him something to sedate him," she said miserably.

"He got out long before you would have," Zona said.

It didn't appear to make her mother feel any better. It didn't make her feel any better, either.

"Text me a picture of Darling and I'll make posters to put up first thing tomorrow," she said.

Louise managed a wobbly smile. "What did I ever do to deserve such a good daughter?"

"Other than being the best mother in the world? I don't know," Zona said back, and that brought a slightly sturdier smile to her mother's face.

"I realize that a lost dog isn't exactly on par with a divorce or lost savings. Or a lost husband," Louise began.

"But we all love our pets," Zona said. "He's a sweet dog and he's your fur baby."

"I do hate to think of anything bad happening to him," said Louise.

"Nothing will," Zona said, and hoped she was right.

THE NEXT MORNING was a Saturday, but instead of prowling garage sales, Zona was hanging lost dog posters with Darling's black furry face on them.

She'd hung posters far and wide and was duct-taping the last one to a streetlight pole on Louise's street when Alec James's truck pulled up next to her. "Your dog's missing," he guessed.

This was the last man on the planet she wanted to talk to about their missing dog. Or anything. They were going to ignore Alec James and keep their distance.

"Yes," she replied curtly, and turned to leave.

"Get in. I'll help you look for him."

Yes, grab ahold of that buzzing power line. "I can look for him on my own."

"You can look better if someone else is driving," he pointed out. "Come on, get in. Let me help you." His tone of voice was polite. Civilized. Kind? No, that was going too far.

Go riding around in such tight quarters with this man? Bad idea.

"I won't bite," he said. "Come on, get in."

It was broad daylight. What could he do to her?

Her mother would suggest all kinds of grisly possibilities.

He leaned across the seat and opened the cab door.

Polite woman syndrome won out and she got in.

Politeness kills, cried her nerves.

Broad daylight. We're fine, she told them.

"Fireworks scared him?" Alec James guessed as they pulled away from the curb.

"Yes."

"You should have sedated him."

Unrequested advice a day late. "My mom didn't want to."

"It doesn't really hurt them."

"Oh, so you're a vet in your spare time?" She sounded snotty. What was she doing talking snotty to Alec James? The last thing she wanted to do was antagonize a man with a temper like his.

He frowned and shut up. The silence in that small, enclosed space made her feel like fire ants were crawling under her skin. What was she doing riding around with him?

He was the first to break it. "Okay, was that what's called mansplaining?"

Don't make him mad. "Maybe a little. Man starting to 'splain."

"Don't mean to," he said as they slowly turned a corner. "You're probably not going to believe this, but I'm not a dog hater. And I wouldn't ever kick your dog. I've never kicked a dog in my whole life. And I've had two of my own. You really need to train him though."

"You did notice my mother's cast, right?" The response escaped before her common sense could catch it.

He frowned. "Of course I did. But you're there."

"Barely. Right now, I'm working two jobs."

"Yeah? Where?"

"I work at the department of licensing."

"Where you stand in line until you die," he cracked.

They were understaffed and overworked. She didn't laugh. "Doesn't sound like a very fun job. What's your other one?"

"Garage sales." Okay, that sounded ridiculous. And why did she have to justify her lack of time to train Darling to this man? More to the point, why was she in this truck with him?

His lips lifted in a smile. "Garage sales are a job, huh?"

"They are when you're looking for things to sell."

"How come you've got to work two jobs?"

No way was she sharing her personal problems. "Why does anyone work two jobs?"

They rounded another corner. "To pay for stuff they shouldn't have bought in the first place," he said, his voice hardening.

She felt the shift away from friendly, but she couldn't let that go. "You know, there's usually more to people's lives than you see on the surface."

"Might be a good thing for you and your mom to remember."

Was that a scold or a threat? The fire ants were scrambling, and the truck cab was closing in on Zona.

"Just drop me off here," she said. "I'll have better luck finding Darling if I'm on foot." *And feel safer.*

"Yeah, right," he scoffed.

Her imagination shot into overdrive and she suddenly wondered if he was going to let her out.

"You might want to call the animal shelter. Maybe someone's found him and turned him in. Is he chipped?"

Now he was all kindness and concern again. How many personalities did this guy have? "Yes," she said, her hand on the door handle.

"Good." He pulled to the curb and stopped the truck. "Good luck," he said as she opened the door.

"Thanks." She slid out, shut it, and stepped away. Then started walking fast down the street.

She was still feeling jittery as he drove off. And a little concerned for her own mental state. Alec James gave her the creeps and yet she was attracted to him. Only a fool would be attracted to someone who gave her the creeps.

Well, she'd already proved twice that she was a fool so no surprise.

She called the animal shelter as she walked back to the house. Darling had not been a guest there. Zona ended the call with a sigh. If only she had some good news to give her mother.

Louise had been sitting at the dining room table drinking coffee with Martin when Zona walked in. Her mother's hopeful expression suffered a quick death on seeing Zona by herself with no Darling in tow.

"I'm sorry, Mom," she said.

"He's gone for good," Louise said sadly.

"We don't know that," Martin said. "It's only been a few hours."

"He should have come back by now," Louise said.

"Dogs like to wander," said Martin. "Sometimes it takes them a while to wander back. What about calling the shelter?"

"I just did," Zona said.

"Maybe we should drive around and look for him," said Louise.

"I just did," Zona said.

Louise's brows pulled together. "I never saw your car leave the driveway."

"I was with Alec James." *I had a lapse in sanity.*

Louise looked at her daughter, bug-eyed. "You were in his truck? What were you thinking?"

Zona shrugged like it was no big deal. "He saw me putting up posters and offered to help." *And then he dared me to get in his truck.* She decided not to share further. Her mother would for sure have something to say about her daughter's sanity.

"I find that hard to believe," Louise said with a frown.

"I don't. He seems like a nice guy," said Martin.

"Martin, he's mean. And rude. We've seen enough and heard enough to know exactly what kind of man he is. And you shouldn't be riding around in his truck with him," Louise scolded Zona. "I don't want that man snaring you in his net."

"Trust me, he won't," said Zona.

"We have enough to worry about with Darling missing without you getting in trucks with horrible men," Louise continued.

"We'll find Darling," Zona said, shifting the spotlight off herself.

"Yes, don't worry," said Martin.

"Why do people say that?" Louise grumbled. "It never stops you from worrying."

Martin cleared his throat, checked his watch. "I need to get going. Got Annie and the girls coming over this afternoon. I'll keep my eyes open for Darling though."

"And I'll look again after lunch," Zona promised.

Martin left to go to the store in preparation for a visit from his daughter and her children, and Louise decided to enlist Bree's help in the search for Darling. Zona got busy making lunch.

She'd just finished making a shrimp salad when Bree showed up.

"Did you see any sign of Darling?" Louise asked.

"Sorry, Gram, I looked. I drove all down Sierra Madre and almost up to Big Dalton Canyon Trail and no sign of him."

Louise sighed heavily.

"Don't worry, Gram. Don't you remember *Homeward Bound*? Of course he'll come back."

Bree spoke with such confidence. Zona hoped her daughter was right.

"Thank you for helping," Louise said. "I guess we'll just have to wait and see if he returns. Meanwhile, stay and have lunch with us. How was your Fourth of July party?" she asked once they were settled at the kitchen table.

Bree shrugged. "It was okay."

"Only okay?" asked Zona, passing her the salad bowl.

Bree's mouth drooped. "Fen and I are totally finished. He doesn't even want to be friends."

"Doesn't want to be friends? Why on earth not?" Louise wanted to know.

"Because he wants more," Bree said with a scowl.

"That's understandable if he's in love with you," said Louise.

"Yeah, well, I've seen how well love works out." Bree stabbed a shrimp with her fork and stuck it in her mouth.

Zona said nothing. She was too busy feeling guilty. If only she could have saved Bree's money. All her daughter had now was that chip on her shoulder and Zona had no idea how to dislodge it.

"I guess it's all for the best then," Louise said, opting for diplomacy.

Bree shoved away her plate. "Why can't he be happy being friends?"

"Because he wants more out of life. He wants more out of you," Louise said reasonably. "That's the thing about love. You come together as both best friends and lovers and teammates. You build a life together. You raise children. You help each other over the hard bumps along the way."

"Yeah, like Dad and Gary did for Mom?" Bree said, her voice dripping sarcasm.

"Things didn't work out for me. That doesn't mean they won't work out for you," Zona said. "Look at Auntie Gracie. She's happy. Look at your Gram."

"I was very happy," Louise said. "Your grandpa was the best and I miss him every day."

"If you miss him so much, why were you taking a singles cruise?" Bree argued.

"Because I miss him every day. I had something special and my heart wants to feel that again. Growing old alone is no fun."

"You're not alone. You've got us," Bree told her.

Louise's smile didn't reach her eyes. "I know. And I'm grateful for both of you. But you each have your lives to lead, and

I can't be inserting myself in the middle of them every time I feel lonely."

"But you have lots of friends," pointed out Bree.

"True. So do you, dear one. So why are you looking so glum?"

Bree bit down on a corner of her lip.

"It sounds like he loves you," Louise persisted.

"Love. Right," Bree scoffed. "I don't think it says much about Fen if his love is so wimpy he can't stick around. He should give me more time."

"How much time?" asked Louise.

Bree scowled. "I don't know. But he should understand, and he doesn't."

"Understand what?" Louise persisted. "That you're afraid?"

"I'm not afraid. I'm smart. I'm not going to screw up like Mom did."

"I'm not psychic," Zona snapped.

"What a thing to say!" Louise scolded. "You think your mother should have been able to see into the future?"

Bree's face flushed. "Sorry."

"Even the most loyal man will eventually lose hope," said Louise. "And really, would you want to stick with someone who didn't want to stick with you?" she added reasonably.

"I just want to be friends," Bree grumbled.

"Well, we can't always have what we want," said Louise, clearly out of patience.

"Thanks, Gram," Bree said and frowned. She stood. "I need to get going."

"Busy social life waiting?" Louise baited.

"Mom," Zona warned.

"It's okay. She knows I love her. You'll always be my favorite grandchild," she told Bree.

Bree let out a snort. "I'm your only grandchild."

"Still my favorite."

It was a good note to leave on, which was what Bree did. She promised to stay on the lookout for Darling, then kissed both her grandmother and her mother on the cheek—no smile for either of them—and then was gone.

"That girl," Louise said with a shake of the head. "What are we going to do with her?"

Keep loving her, of course.

"I hate that she's so fearful," Zona said.

"One thing I'm confident about. There will come a point when she lets go of that fear. It will take the right person and the right circumstance is all. She's young. Give her time to figure things out."

Zona sighed. "I wish I'd chosen better men."

"You chose with a trusting heart. There's no shame in that. And there's no point staring at the past. What's important is what you're doing right here in the present."

Like not being able to find her mother's dog. Honestly, she couldn't seem to do anything right. Zona blinked back tears.

"Sweetie, I think you're exhausted. You need a nap," Louise said gently.

"No, I need to go look for Darling. And then I need to close out my bids on eBay."

"You've done enough. I'll make some calls. You go do your eBay thing and then relax."

Relaxing was nowhere in Zona's future. "I will," she lied.

While Louise called around the neighborhood, Zona got busy with her second job, packing up items she'd sold so they'd be ready to take to the post office. She'd made a small amount of money that week, but not as much as she'd hoped. There was the writing on the wall, and it said it was time for Zona to step up her game.

She spent an hour poking around online, looking for potential lucrative side hustles. After an hour, she found something she thought she could make work. Her car was far from new, but she kept it clean. If she became a rideshare driver, she could set her own work hours and still be available whenever her mother needed her. And if she only worked weekends, well, Louise had enough friends to keep her company on a Friday and Saturday night. If not one of them, Gilda could be persuaded to come hang out with her. It might just work, and at least Zona wouldn't get varicose veins from being on her feet waiting tables. Instead, she'd probably get a big butt from all that sitting.

Oh, well. *Into every life a little fat must fall*, she told herself.

After some research, she decided to go with a new rideshare company called HopIn. *Hop into more money as a driver for us!* She was ready for that. She was smiling by the time she finished filling out the very long application form, glad that she was being proactive. Once she'd passed the company's security check, she would be good to go. She could still find items to sell online, but this side hustle would keep her earning money during the fall and winter months after garage sale season ended.

"Who knows? You might meet a millionaire," Louise's friend Carol said when she came over to cheer up Louise and Zona shared her possible new job.

"Or get strangled," Louise said, frowning. "I'd rather you found a waitress job."

"This way I won't get varicose veins," quipped Zona.

"I don't like it," Louise said.

When it came right down to it, neither did Zona. She'd much prefer to spend her weekends relaxing in front of the TV with her mother or reading a good book, but a girl couldn't always have what she preferred. This was the way it had to be until she could replenish her daughter's college fund.

It was going to be easier than restoring Bree's faith in men.

BREE'S SNOTTY JAB at her mother was camped out in her brain, roasting her conscience like a marshmallow.

But what she'd said was true. Mom had been stupid and naive. She'd screwed up, gotten screwed over, and then so had Bree.

She was the one depositing money in that account for years, whispered Bree's conscience. *Even Gary had contributed.*

Yeah, and then drained it all, and Mom had let him. Why was Gram taking Mom's side?

Her conscience spoke more loudly. *You love your mom.*

Of course she did. But she needed a break from her. And Gram.

No, you need to apologize.

"Oh, shut up," she told her conscience, and smothered it. Then she went back to staring at the movie she was streaming and not watching.

"I DON'T LIKE the idea of Zona letting strangers in her car," Louise said to Gilda on Monday morning as they made their way to the shower.

"That's the problem with grown kids. They don't listen," Gilda said.

"Between Zona and Darling, my hair is going to be completely white under this blond," Louise complained.

"Darn dog. Where could he have gone?" wondered Gilda.

"I wish I knew," Louise said sadly. "You don't think he could have wandered as far away as the foothills, do you?" If he had, they'd never see him again.

"Let's hope not. If he has, a coyote probably got him."

There was a horrible thought. Louise blinked back sudden tears.

"Don't give up," said Gilda. "Remember the movie about the two dogs and the cat who crossed the Canadian wilderness to get home?"

"Yes, my granddaughter already reminded me of it." But movies were not real life.

"That could be Darling. And at least he doesn't have to cross a wilderness."

Louise tried to feel encouraged and failed. "It is what it is, as they say. I'll have to resign myself to losing him."

But later that afternoon, it looked like she wouldn't have to resign herself to such a sad fate after all. Louise was trying to concentrate on committing murder on the high seas and Gilda was crocheting when they heard whining and scratching on the front door.

"Darling!" Louise exclaimed.

"Trying to ruin your door," muttered Gilda as she set aside her crocheting.

She opened the front door and in bounded a dusty Darling. He raced to where Louise was struggling to get off the couch, tail wagging, and dropped a bone on the hardwood floor right at her feet. A bone, long and slender like a femur. Crusted with dirt, and something rusty that looked like—eeew—blood.

"What on earth?" began Louise as Darling put his front paws on her, ready to show her some love.

"Oh, dear God," gasped Gilda. "I think that's . . ."

"A human bone," Louise finished with her and they stared at each other in horror.

18

"WE HAVE TO BE WRONG," SAID LOUISE. "Where would Darling find a human bone?" Darling lay down and began to gnaw on the bone and Louise let out a shriek. "No, Darling!"

"Evidence," said Gilda, and snatched it up, using her handkerchief. "We need to preserve it." She marched off toward the kitchen.

"Don't put that on the counter," Louise called after her. If she did, Louise would never use her kitchen counter again.

A few moments later Gilda was back.

"Where is it?" Louise asked.

"In the fridge."

"Oooh." Louise felt suddenly faint.

"Don't worry. I wrapped it in plastic wrap."

Now Louise was sure she'd never use her refrigerator again.

"Didn't you say the woman next door has gone missing?" Gilda asked.

All those mystery and thriller writers were right. A chill really could run down your spine.

"Oh, no," Louise weakly protested. Of course, she'd entertained the grisly idea that Alec James had bumped off his girlfriend, but being presented with possible evidence was, well, it was so very real. "I did suspect, but seeing possible proof right here before our eyes, it's . . . horrifying."

"Happens every day somewhere," said Gilda.

"I knew he was getting rid of more than just her things,"

Louise said. Her voice was trembling, right along with her hands.

"You have to do something."

"What?"

"Call the police, of course. You can't find a human bone and not report it."

"But I don't know where Darling found it. If he was off in the woods somewhere . . ."

"Who knows where all he's been. But he's a digger, right? If he found it next door, there'll be a hole on your neighbor's property."

"We need to check it out," Louise said with a decisive nod.

"I'll go look," Gilda said.

"I'm coming with you," Louise declared.

Five minutes later she and Gilda were inspecting a hole in a corner of their neighbor's front yard. Darling the digger, who was shut in the house, had struck again, uprooting a strawberry tree in the process.

"There are no other bones," said Gilda, sounding disappointed.

"That doesn't mean anything. Remember the Raymond Burr character in *Rear Window*—what was his name?—Mr. Thorwald! That man had butchered his wife and buried her all over," said Louise. "No, wait. He buried her body in the river and put her head in a hat box. Was that it? Well, anyway, he cut her up. And we have a bone and here's the hole."

"Good point," said Gilda. "For all we know, the rest of her could be in the man's freezer. Like the man in LA."

They were about to go back to the house when Alec James drove up and pulled into his driveway. Louise's stomach dove for her toes.

"He can't take us both down here in broad daylight," Gilda assured her, and Louise swallowed her terror and raised her chin.

He got out of his truck and started toward them at a casual stroll. "Is there something you're looking for, ladies?"

"No. My dog found it," Louise said.

"And what was that?"

"A bone," she said.

"A bloody bone," Gilda put in.

"From that hole," Louise added, pointing to it.

His brows pulled together and he frowned. "A bone," he repeated.

"A human bone," said Louise.

His eyes got big. "You're kidding, right? You think your dog buried a human bone on my property."

"No, I think my dog dug up a human bone on your property," said Louise. "What do you make of that?" she added, and watched for his response.

"I think that sounds a little far-fetched," he said.

"Not necessarily," Gilda said boldly.

Martin happened to be driving past. He stopped his car and let down his window. "Am I missing a party?" he called.

"It's not a party," Louise replied. "Darling is back, and he's found a human bone. Here," she added, pointing to the incriminating hole.

That was all it took to get Martin out of his car.

"I find that very odd. Don't you, Mr. James?" Louise said to her neighbor as Martin hurried over. They had a witness now. Alec James wouldn't dare touch her. "I'm just wondering how a human bone came to be buried in *your* yard," she challenged, and raised both eyebrows.

Alec James stared at her, at first not comprehending, then he gaped. "Wait a minute. You think . . . ?"

She let her raised eyebrows speak for her.

"Oh, yeah, right. I'd murder someone and bury them in my flowerbed."

"Evidence doesn't lie," said Gilda.

"This is nuts. They think I'm burying body parts in my front yard," he said to Martin as he joined them. "Because if I was going to cut someone up and bury that person, I'd bury part of them in my front yard where everyone could see me," he finished in disgust.

"Nobody would see you at night," Louise informed him. Well, except her when she was observing him from her bedroom window. When had he found the time to do it? It must have been very late at night.

And this was only one bone. Where was the rest of the woman? She remembered the scene from *Rear Window*, with creepy Mr. Thorwald going back and forth from his apartment on a dark and stormy night, methodically getting rid of the grisly evidence. She shuddered and inched closer to Martin.

"Hiding in plain sight, like in *The Purloined Letter*," said Gilda.

Alec James began to laugh, and Louise's fear was replaced by irritation. "Oh, you laugh now," she said. "We'll see who has the last laugh when I call the police."

"Let's look at the bone first, shall we?" Martin suggested. "Where is it?"

"In my refrigerator," Louise said. Eeew.

"Ready for soup," cracked Alec James and Louise glared at him.

They trooped over to her house. Darling wanted to welcome everyone, trying first to jump on Alec James, but he walked right into the poor dog, forcing him down to all fours and making him veer away. What kind of man mowed over a dog! The kind with no heart and no conscience.

They all gathered around the kitchen table, waiting for Gilda to produce the bone. "Lay down some newspaper first," Louise instructed her. The bone was a gruesome sight and seeing that token of death made Louise shudder. Or maybe it was the fact that she was standing so close to a murderer.

Alec James took one look at it after Gilda put it on display and laughed again. "So that's the human I buried?"

"There's no flesh on it," Louise admitted, "but that's because something gnawed it off." *Please don't let it have been Darling.*

"Lou, that's a deer bone," Martin said mildly.

"A deer bone!" Louise exclaimed. "Where would Darling get a deer bone?"

"I'm guessing the foothills. I was walking a trail just last week and saw a cougar. It probably took down this deer," Martin said. "You can be glad it didn't get Darling."

"You can't know for sure this isn't human," Gilda insisted.

"I can," said Alec James. "I've done my share of hunting. It's easy to mistake a deer bone for a human one though," he added. Trying to be magnanimous or trying to fool them?

"So you say," said Gilda.

"So we both say," Martin said, and frowned at her.

"Who do you think I murdered and buried in my front yard, anyway?" Alec James demanded.

"You had a woman living with you and we heard the fights," Louise said. "And now all that yelling and screaming have mysteriously stopped and she's gone." She hadn't wanted to do this without police present, but he'd forced her hand.

"Lou, I think you should dial it down," Martin cautioned. "This is a serious accusation."

"I know what I heard," she said.

"Yeah, but you don't know the half of what you heard," snapped Alec James.

"I'm calling the cops," Gilda said, and stepped away, pulling her cell phone out of her sweater pocket.

Alec James glared at Louise. "Yes, I had someone there and thank God she's gone. But I didn't kill the woman. I'm too busy running my business to kill anyone. And I sure as hell don't have the energy to cut somebody up in pieces and bury her in my yard. Good God, that's sick. Why would you jump to such a crazy conclusion? You don't even know me."

"I heard the screams. We know you were being violent, and both my daughter and I heard her say you're a monster," Louise said as Gilda shared their address with the police.

Alec James let out a hiss. "Yeah, well, she says a lot of things. But I have never hit a woman in my life."

So he said.

Gilda had ended the call and jumped back into the conversation. "Then where is she now?" she demanded.

"Staying with someone who's almost as nutty as she is. And who the devil are you?"

"This is Gilda, my caregiver," Louise said stiffly. "Physical care," she added in case he thought she had a bunch of dead brain cells rattling around in her skull. "And I saw you getting rid of that woman's things late at night." *Mr. Thorwald the Second.*

He threw up his hands. "Unbelievable!"

"I'm sorry," Martin said to him. "She's writing a mystery."

"Martin!" Louise protested. Whose side was he on?

"Well, she's got the imagination for it," snapped Alec James. He gave a snort, then muttered, "Should have bought that place in San Dimas."

"Yes, you should have," Louise agreed.

They all heard the knock on the door.

"That will be the police," Louise said to Alec James.

"Good. We can give them the bone," said Gilda.

"Then they can search the foothills for the rest of the body," said Alec James. "I'm sure they've got nothing better to do than look for missing deer bones."

"I'll get it," said Gilda and hurried to the front door.

A moment later she was followed into the kitchen by two burly men in uniform, who introduced themselves as Officer Mead and Officer Trumble. Officer Mead looked to be in his fifties, and strands of white were burying themselves in his full head of dark hair. He was built like a tank. His partner was young, probably in his thirties, and one glance was enough to tell Louise that he worked out at the gym on a regular basis. They'd have no problem taking down Alec James.

She still wished she'd bought a Taser. She'd seen a cute pink one on Amazon.

"I understand you found a bone," said Officer Mead.

"My dog found it," said Louise. "We're sure it's human." And as soon as he confirmed it, she was going to accompany him right on over to that hole next door.

Officer Mead examined it, then exchanged a look with his partner. Was it a troubled look? Louise braced herself for the horrible confrontation about to ensue and moved closer to Martin.

"I can understand your concern, ma'am," said Officer Mead. "But not to worry. This bone isn't human."

"Not human!" Louise echoed.

"Are you sure?" Gilda demanded. "Don't you need to bring in a detective?"

Officer Mead smiled politely at her. "No. I've done a lot of hunting. So has my partner here. We know a deer bone when we see one."

"Deer bone," Louise repeated. How was that possible?

"They can be mistaken for human," said young Officer Trumble.

"It's not . . . He's not?" Louise suddenly didn't feel so well. Her whole face was on fire.

"Thank you for coming, officers. I thought that was what it was," Martin said.

"It's always wise to call us," said Officer Mead. "That's what we're here for."

The officers left and Louise lowered her shaky self onto a

kitchen chair. Gilda sat down hard on one next to her. Alec James remained standing, frowning and shaking his head.

"But then how did it get there?" Louise wondered. The minute the words were out of her mouth she knew, and the flame burned hotter.

Her neighbor made a face. "I'll give you two guesses."

"It couldn't have been Darling," she insisted. "He wasn't gone for that long."

"Well, it wasn't me," snapped Alec James.

"We might have jumped to conclusions," Louise began.

Both his eyebrows shot up. "Might have?"

"But we were concerned," she said. "You certainly can't blame us, with all the shouting always going on at your house."

It appeared that he could. He let out an exasperated breath and strode out of the kitchen.

Martin gave Louise a pat on the shoulder before he called to Alec James and went after him. They could hear him saying, "She's been under a strain lately." He might as well have added, "She's crazy."

It was sweet of him to try to smooth things over, but no amount of smoothing could explain away this mess.

"I guess we did jump to conclusions," she said to Gilda. It was so embarrassing. She'd never be able to look the man in the eye again.

"Maybe, but better safe than sorry," Gilda replied. "I mean, what if something was going on next door? You'd feel even worse if that had been the case and you hadn't done anything. Just like the neighbors of the freezer killer. And really, you still don't know the whole story of what went on next door. All you have is that man's word. And who knows if that's worth anything."

"You're right," said Louise.

"No, she's not," Zona said after she came home and learned

what had happened. "I told you how hard it is these days to get away with murder. How could you accuse our neighbor of it, especially with things already strained between us? You can be glad Martin smoothed those troubled waters. Honestly, Mom, what were you thinking?"

Louise's face began to burn. "I wasn't. I got so caught up in . . ." What had she gotten caught up in?

"In imagining things that weren't true," Zona supplied. "You overheard a couple of really bad fights and jumped to the worst possible conclusion."

Who did that? Crazy people, that was who. Was she losing it?

"Am I slipping mentally?" she fretted.

"What?"

"Maybe dementia is setting in. Or Lewy Body. Except I thought that happened primarily to men."

"Mom!" Zona protested. She sounded panicked.

"People can get childish in their old age, start to lose it. I think I'm losing it," Louise said in a small voice.

"No, you're not," Zona said firmly. "You're just operating under the influence of Hitchcock. And Gilda. I think you two should take a break from your true crime shows for a while."

Louise bit her lip and nodded.

"Or harness that creativity and work on your novel."

"I know who the murderer is going to look like," Louise muttered.

It resurrected Zona's sense of humor and she laughed. "If it makes you feel any better, remember, I've been suspecting him of things I have no evidence of, too," she said. "Bottom line, we don't know him well enough to pass judgment. Although, I've got to admit, being around him makes me edgy."

"Now we're probably the ones who make him edgy."

Zona chuckled at that. "At least we know he's not a murderer." She shook her head and smiled. "That had to be some scene. Mr. Hitchcock would have loved it."

What a mortifying scene it had turned out to be. "I'm sure the officers will keep everyone down at the police station entertained telling about it," Louise said with a frown.

"What happened to the bone?"

"Martin took it away."

"Thank God," said Zona.

"And Gilda scrubbed down both the fridge and the table three times before she left. Still, I may never eat at that table again. And my poor fridge. Serves us right, I guess. I'm sure Martin thinks I'm insane," Louise added. She wished she'd listened to him. Then at least the police wouldn't have gotten involved.

"Well, you are making his life interesting."

Louise frowned. "The neighborhood crazy lady." She couldn't even justify her behavior by adding, "But it's possible. He could have murdered his girlfriend." And cut her up in pieces and buried a stray femur in his front yard. Remembering how insistent she'd been and what a fool she'd looked like put a sizzle on her face.

Zona heaved a sigh. "I really hate to have to do it, but I think I'd better take over a peace offering. I'll bake some cookies."

"He'll probably think they're poisoned."

"Then he can have a turn calling the police," Zona cracked.

Louise didn't think her daughter was at all funny.

After they'd finished eating dinner, Zona baked a batch of frosted oatmeal cookies.

"These are bound to sweeten the man up," Louise said as she sampled one.

"I hope so," said Zona. "Or at least dissuade him from suing us."

"Suing us!" Louise squeaked.

Zona shrugged. "I don't know for sure if he can or not, but you did accuse him of committing a crime."

"Oooh," said Louise. She was going to be sick. Faint. Maybe both.

"Don't worry. I'll patch things up," Zona promised.

She was on her way out the door when Martin stopped in to check on Louise. "It's the least we can do," she told him before she left.

"I feel like a fool," Louise said as the door shut behind her daughter. She'd thought nothing would top her embarrassment over falling at the sail-away party on the cruise ship, but this dwarfed it completely.

"It was an honest mistake," Martin said. "You heard the officer. It's easy to mistake a deer bone for a human one."

"Buried in your neighbor's yard," Louise added miserably. "I made a terrible mess of things. What if he sues us?"

"He won't. And Zona's cookies will go a long way toward smoothing things over," Martin assured her.

"You know what's really awful, Martin? I still think something wasn't right over there."

Martin looked wary.

"We really did overhear some very scary fighting," she said. "And that man . . . he isn't nice. I've never seen him smile." He probably wasn't smiling now.

"How much have you seen him?" Martin argued. "And under what circumstances?"

"Never good," she admitted. "But he does seem to have a short fuse on his temper."

"Louise, you can hardly blame him."

"Well, what was I to think with that bone?"

"That Darling had found a bone and dug it up," Martin said reasonably. "Who knows what other dog might have buried it and how long it had been there."

"What a mess," Louise said miserably.

Martin gave her an encouraging smile. "Maybe someday you'll all laugh about this."

"I don't intend to have anything to do with him," Louise said firmly. "Once Zona delivers those cookies, we're even."

As if cookies balanced calling the police on the man. Maybe she should have suggested Zona tell Alec James her mother had dementia. It would have made a good excuse.

ZONA'S ENCOUNTERS WITH Alec James had only been marginally better than her mother's since the business with Darling had started, but at least she hadn't accused him of murder. Still, he'd shown them his ugly side, so other than offering up an edible apology she didn't plan to invest any further energy in being neighborly. No more communication whatsoever with the man next door after this.

After what had happened earlier, he'd probably be fine with that. Good grief, could the situation be any more awful?

Her heart started pounding as she made her way next door, and it picked up its pace when she rang the doorbell. By the time he answered, wearing a pec-hugging black T-shirt and board shorts, it was at a full gallop, not stopping to explain whether the rapid pace was due to nerves or something more primitive. He was built like an action movie star with that fit body and granite jaw.

The look he gave her could only be described as leery.

She held out the container of cookies. "I come in peace."

"More cookies?" He didn't reach for it.

So much for that clever remark. "They're oatmeal. I promise they're not laced with rat poison."

A corner of his mouth did lift at that, and he took them, then leaned against the door frame. "They got raisins in them?"

She nodded. "And cinnamon."

"Those are my favorite," he said. "Thanks."

"I kind of figured we owe you."

He did smile at that. "Is your mom . . . I mean, is she all there?"

"She's now wondering that herself."

He shook his head, looked heavenward. "Is she done spying on me?"

"She's so mortified she'll probably never look your way again." Zona was tempted to add that he could hardly blame her mother for thinking the worst about him after what they'd heard coming from his house, but it was best to keep her mouth firmly zipped. It was hardly the time to point an accusing finger his way when there were so many pointing in the direction of her house.

"She's got it in her head that I'm the devil."

"Are you? I'm sorry, but it hasn't exactly been quiet over at your house," Zona added. So much for keeping her mouth zipped.

"If you'd known who I had over there, you'd understand. Anyway, she's gone now. But not dead," he added, making Zona feel foolish by association.

She blushed.

"By the way, when are you taking her dog to obedience school?" he asked.

Oh, yes, the other thorn in his side. "It's on my to-do list," Zona lied. They were going to have to get Darling signed up soon.

"Dogs need to be trained from a young age. That saying about old dogs and new tricks is true. And I'm not mansplaining. It's just a fact."

"I know. We'll keep him off your yard from now on," Zona promised. "I'm not letting him out unsupervised and I'll try to get him signed up for some training. It's just hard with everything going on."

"Bring him over here one night and I'll help you whip him into shape. I'd offer to come over there, but your mom probably doesn't want a killer on her property."

Zona's cheeks burned. "I really am sorry about that. She's

been watching all these true crime shows. And then there was that man in LA who—"

He cut her off. "I know. I watch the news." He took a deep breath. "Look, we all got off to a bad start. I've trained a couple of dogs. I'll help you train yours. We can work out front. That way the whole neighborhood can keep an eye on me."

Okay, he could stop rubbing it in anytime. She frowned.

"Sorry," he said. "I mean it though. I'll help you with your dog. Just to prove I'm not a dog-hater."

"Good to know." The scenes they'd overheard had been awful. "How do you feel about people?"

He frowned. "What do you mean?" Understanding dawned. He rolled his eyes and shook his head. "Oh, yeah. The shouting, right? We keep coming back to that."

She didn't say anything. Just waited for him to elaborate.

"She's a spoiled drama queen and manipulative. I finally had enough and kicked her out."

"But didn't kick her."

He scowled. "Or hit her. What's with women these days? Do they really believe every man out there is garbage?"

"Of course not," Zona said, trying to keep her voice sympathetic. "Sometimes you hear things." Why on earth was she nosing around in this man's life, antagonizing him? If she got him mad enough, maybe he would sue them.

"Okay," he said wearily. "What exactly did you hear? It must have been real good for your mom to decide I cut Angela up into pieces."

Zona bit her lip. *Nothing. Say you heard nothing.*

"Come on, out with it. I really want to know."

Zona took a deep breath. "The woman said, 'You're hurting me.'" Actually, she hadn't simply said it. She'd cried out.

He looked like he'd just drunk vinegar. "Yeah, that's her favorite when I'm grabbing her by the arm."

"Why were you grabbing her by the arm?" Now Zona sounded like a detective interviewing a suspect. Good grief. *Law & Order, Special Snoop Unit*. This was not going to go over well. She swallowed hard.

"She was totally out of control. I was trying to get her back in the house and deal with her issues in private before the whole neighborhood heard and decided I was beating on her." He made a face. "I guess they did." He studied Zona. "Maybe they still do?"

She took a step back. "Everyone's got problems," she said, not even sure what that was supposed to mean.

"There's problems and there's problems. And there's reasons when people get mad."

And reasons why they grabbed other people by the arm?

He held up the container. "Thanks for these."

That signaled the end of a conversation that had seesawed back and forth between normal and creepy. "You're welcome," Zona said. She left his front porch and heard the door shut behind her and realized she felt relieved.

"How did it go?" Louise asked as soon as Zona was in the house. "You were over there a long time. What did you talk about? Is he going to sue us?"

Zona settled on a chair in the living room and tucked a leg under her. "I'm sure he thinks we're both cuckoo birds, but I doubt he's going to sue us. Still, it was awkward. Honestly, I can't figure that man out."

"What do you mean?" Louise asked.

Zona shared the gist of her conversation with Alec James. Louise was doubtful on hearing his claim to be a dog lover and more horrified than impressed by his offer to help Zona train Darling.

"I think that's downright sporting of him, all things considered," said Martin.

"That man is too cold to be a dog lover," Louise insisted.

"And do you buy his explanation about that argument we overheard?" she asked Zona.

"I don't know," Zona said. "Maybe it happened just like he said. We'll never know."

Louise frowned. "One thing I do know. I made a fool of myself."

"It was an honest mistake," said Martin.

Zona doubted he believed that, but it was kind of him to say.

"But I still think something was not right over there," Louise declared.

Something's not right over here, either, thought Zona.

And the something was her. There was no way she should have been attracted to that man.

"But we're not having anything to do with him from now on," she said firmly. The less she saw of Alec James the better, and that included turning herself into a watcher.

"IT SOUNDS LIKE you don't know the whole story of what went on over there," her friend Gracie said when Zona took her to lunch the next day. (At Taco Bell, which fit Zona's budget.)

"I don't think I want to." Zona shook her head. "The man unnerves me."

"But free dog training."

"Nothing is free. Everything comes with a price," said Zona, the newly minted cynic.

And she suspected that if she got to know Alec James any better she'd wind up paying for it. Her best bet was to stay away.

Gambling metaphor. Aack!

19

ZONA HADN'T SEEN MUCH OF BREE since her last visit. She'd texted when they'd found Darling but had omitted what Darling had brought home. Bree didn't need to hear about her grandmother's encounter with the neighbor or the fact that Zona had baked him cookies, even if the cookie baking had been nothing more than a gesture to smooth over troubled waters.

Bree had texted back and added a smiley emoticon, which Zona took as a good sign. By the end of summer, Zona would have a nice-sized check to give her daughter, which would allow her to start school in the new year and, hopefully, that would produce real smiles.

She clung to the hope that someday, they'd all find their way to a happier place, with their current challenges far behind them. Meanwhile she had enough to do working her day job, selling secondhand treasures online, and cooking for her mother and herself, and making sure there were always treats on hand for when visitors stopped by.

"It's too bad she broke up with that nice boy," Louise said after Bree's latest visit with her. "I think she regrets it but doesn't want to admit it."

"She wants love to come with a guarantee," said Zona. Good luck with that.

"We both know nothing in life comes with a guarantee," pointed out Louise.

"I know. But sometimes it's better not to take a risk."

"You sound like your daughter," Louise accused.

"Well, it's past time I got in touch with my inner Bree," said Zona.

She made the mistake of saying as much when Louise's friends came over to play Mahjong.

"You shouldn't give up," said Susan, who was breaking in her third man. "You never know when the perfect man might come into your life."

"There is no such thing," Zona said.

"True, but there can be someone perfect for you," Susan said.

Zona pushed the words out of her mind when she returned from walking Darling that same evening and found Alec James pulling his truck into his driveway.

"Ready for some dog training?" he called as he got out.

"No time," she called back. Meanwhile, Darling was straining at the leash, anxious to say hi to his neighbor.

"You can always make time for what you really want to do," Alec James argued.

He leaned against the truck, one ankle casually crossed over the other, arms folded across his chest, which made his biceps look massive. It was a great hot-guy calendar pose. The only thing missing was a tool belt.

"You afraid something might happen to you?" he taunted.

Not in the way he was insinuating. Between the sudden neighborly gestures and that smile he was showing off, Alec James was an emotional threat. She reminded herself that they were going to have nothing more to do with him. She also reminded herself that her daughter would have a panic attack if she did.

"What is that, a double-dog dare?" she shot back, ignoring the reminder.

"Good pun."

Darling did need to learn manners and with Louise busy with her friends there was nothing waiting for Zona but *Know Yourself, Know Your Money*, the latest book by finance guru Angel Ram. Well, and *The Psychology of Dangerous People*. She made a snap decision to forget about dangerous people and get to know herself later, and let Darling pull her over to where Alec James stood.

Darling immediately wanted to jump on him and he stopped it by walking forward, forcing Darling down and back.

"What's that called, the bulldozer move?" Zona said. It smacked of bullying to her. Alec James displaying his true colors.

He had an equally smart-mouth answer. "It's called the keep your dirty paws off me move."

"Seems kind of mean to me," she said.

"Does he look upset?" Alec James countered, pointing to Darling's wagging tail. Before she could answer, he continued. "It's no meaner than putting up a knee to keep distance." He bent to give Darling an ear rub, which got Darling's tail wagging like a furry metronome. "People often either stay put or back up, and both moves invite the dog to jump. This teaches the dog who's in charge." He cocked an eyebrow at Zona. "That doesn't count as mansplaining, does it?"

He obviously didn't expect an answer, as he turned his attention back to Darling. He pushed on the dog's rump, forcing it down, and said, "Sit." Then gave him another rub. "Good boy." To Zona he said, "You have to reinforce the good behavior with lots of praise, just like with kids."

It was hard to picture Alec James with kids. Unless they were running away from him.

He stood back up and Darling, delighted with all the attention, got excited and tried again to jump on him. He repeated the move and once more Darling backed down. "Do this enough and he'll get the idea." He once again made Darling sit and gave him more praise, and Darling showed his gratitude by trying to lick his hand. "Yeah, you're gonna learn to be a good dog," he said to Darling, all the gruffness gone from his voice.

This was a different Alec James than the angry neighbor who had showed up on Zona's doorstep with Darling in tow. Or the man the woman next door had called a monster. Once again, Zona found herself struggling to reconcile the two versions of Alec James.

"So, you're a dog whisperer," she said. It came out half tease, half taunt.

"I told you. I've had dogs."

"Why don't you have one now?"

"Not ready. My dog died a couple years ago. It felt like losing family. In fact, he was better family than most of my family."

There was a telling statement. She wanted to ask more, but he didn't give her time. He was back working with Darling.

Half an hour later, after bringing Zona into the process and seeing some success, he said, "That's probably enough for one session."

"Thanks," she said. "Now, if we can just keep him from jumping the gate, maybe I can let him out in the backyard."

"Did you put up the fence barrier?"

That he'd offered to help with. The good side of Alec James.

"I did, but like I said, he jumped over the gate. That's how he got out on the Fourth."

"You may have to put up a double gate. I'd offer to help, but I don't think you'd take me up on it."

He was being so nice, so . . . normal. She could not figure this man out.

"Martin will do it. He likes to help Mom," she said.

"He seems like an okay guy," Alec James observed.

"He is."

"Most men are, when given a chance."

That was subtle. Against her better judgment, she found herself saying, "How about something to drink?"

She thought he'd turn her down. Half wished he would because she was already regretting her offer. What was she thinking?

"What have you got?" he asked.

"No beer."

The lack of beer didn't appear to discourage him. He cocked an eyebrow, gave her a half smile. Even a half smile on this man had a lot of wattage, and it turned on the jitters in her.

"You think I'm a beer drinker?"

"You look like you could be."

"What makes you think that, the truck?"

"The T-shirt," she said, pointing to his black shirt that claimed he drank beer, fixed stuff, and knew things.

He nodded, still giving her that half smile. "I like a beer once in a while, but I'm good with anything."

"Lemonade?"

"Hard?"

"I can make it that way."

He nodded. "Sounds good."

"Meet me on my porch?" she suggested. No way was she inviting him in the house for her mother's friends to speculate over. She shouldn't even be inviting him on the porch for herself to speculate over. What a stupid idea this had been.

"Keeping me away from your mom, huh?" he said.

She couldn't tell if he was kidding or not, but she decided to act as if he was. "Just trying to protect you. Plus it's better to keep you outside where all the neighbors can make sure you're behaving," she added, throwing his earlier taunt back at him.

"Oh, yeah, that. Okay, ditch the dog and I'll be over in a few."

By the time she'd mixed vodka and lemonade in two tall glasses, assured her mother she was simply thanking their neighbor for the free dog training lesson, and stepped back outside, he was sprawled on the cement porch of their rambler, his legs stretched out over the two steps leading to it, and he had a large bag of corn chips open next to him.

She sat down opposite him and handed over his glass. The jitters were really going at it and she wished she'd paid for the free dog training session with only a thank-you. The last thing she needed was to sit on her front steps with this man.

He took a drink and nodded approvingly. "Good stuff." Then he tipped the bag toward her.

It was such a . . . friendly gesture. So innocuous. So not like the fierce stranger on the other side of the fence. So . . . misleading? What was she doing sitting there with this man? It was weird and she shouldn't have been. Maybe she had self-destructive tendencies.

She shook her head. "No, thanks. So, what's with the shirt? Do you really know stuff?"

"Gag gift from my crew for my birthday," he said and popped a chip in his mouth. He washed it down with another drink of her lemonade, then said, "So, how long has your mom lived here?"

"Years. I grew up here. I spent a lot of time at your house when I was a kid. My best friend lived there."

"The perfect childhood, huh? Lucky you." He took another chip out of the bag and popped it in his mouth.

"What about you?" she asked. Had his childhood been less than idyllic? If so, it would explain the anger issues.

He shrugged. "Long story."

Okay. So much for sharing.

She wasn't sure what to say next, so she settled for "Thanks for your help with Darling."

"Work with him and he'll turn into a good dog." He cocked his head and shared half a smile. "See? I can be nice. When I'm not hiding bloody bones in my yard."

Her face caught fire and she frowned. "Are you ever going to get over that?"

"Maybe someday. When it stops making you blush," he added, his voice teasing. "You look cute when you blush."

The fire burned brighter before a chill came over her. Maybe he'd get over her mom's goof, but she doubted she'd forget all the screaming and yelling she'd heard coming from his place.

"So, I guess your houseguest is gone for good," she said.

His expression soured. "Gone but not forgotten."

"People say that at funerals." Crap! Where had that come from?

Wherever it had come from, he didn't like it. "Not you, too."

"That was just a . . ." What was it?

"Freudian slip?" He frowned and set down his glass. "Like mother like daughter, I guess. Thanks for the drink." He stood up in one fluid movement and then was off walking across her lawn toward his house.

"You forgot your chips," she called after him, a great substitute for "I'm sorry." Good grief. She really was almost as good at antagonizing the man as her mother.

"Keep 'em," he called back, then marched into his house and shut the door behind him.

She gulped down the last of her drink, then picked up the bag of chips and dug one out, chomping viciously down on it. She didn't have anything to feel bad about. She wasn't the one scaring the life out of people. And she was glad she'd gotten him off her porch.

Now, if she could find a way to get him out of her mind. But he lingered there, reenacting different encounters, different scenes. The many faces of Alec James. They all made her nervous, and they all fascinated her.

Not good.

Of all the neighborhoods in all the world he had to move in to hers?

20

IT WAS OFFICIAL. ZONA HAD HER security clearance and was a HopIn driver.

Gilda had agreed to hang out with Louise on weekend nights when Bree or Louise's friends couldn't be around.

"Honestly, I don't need babysitting. I can manage an evening alone," Louise had protested.

"I just don't like the idea of you home alone, trying to get around with that big cast," Zona had said.

"I've been doing fine," Louise had reminded her.

It was true, she was. Louise had gotten creative and started slinging a canvas grocery bag around her neck where she carried a small thermos, her phone, and whatever book she happened to be reading, along with her barely used writing supplies. (After the great bloody bone incident, Louise's interest in becoming a mystery writer had dwindled.) Still, Zona felt better knowing someone was with her mother.

Gilda had been agreeable to putting in extra hours as long as she wasn't expected to spend the night. "And don't stay out all night," she'd added, making Zona think of the curfews of her youth.

"Don't worry, I'll be home by one," Zona had promised.

"Make it midnight," Gilda had commanded, and Zona had decided that was fine with her. After midnight she was more likely to end up chauffeuring drunks and that didn't appeal to her.

Her first Friday night was turning out to be a busy one. So far, she'd picked up one exhausted woman at the Ontario airport who was returning from a business conference, then returned to the same airport with a retired couple who were off to New York, their jumping-off place for a cross-Atlantic cruise. Then it was two women going to a bachelorette party followed by another pickup at the airport, a retired couple returning from visiting family. The couple had been chatty and friendly to the point of nosiness. She was happy to see that they weren't the norm. The last thing she wanted was people asking her why she'd decided to turn herself into a chauffeur.

By eleven she'd had enough of weaving in and out of traffic and was ready to call it a night when one last request came in from a club in Los Angeles, wanting a ride to Azusa. Her last drop-off had been Irwindale and this rider wanted to go to Azusa, so perfect. She took it.

She pulled up in front of the club to find two women her daughter's age, both dressed in stylish jeans, shirts, and jackets. Zona recognized that one indigo jacket, and the girl in it. Oh, no. There was her daughter. An angry, make-a-scene version. She blinked in shock as she pulled her car up.

The other woman opened the door and practically shoved Bree in with the concerned parting words of a bestie, "You owe me a monster apology when you sober up."

This was accompanied by a few other choice words, many of which were the notorious F bomb, and to Zona's horror, her daughter dropped a few bombs of her own. Zona had been raised to never "speak like a trash mouth," and she'd raised her daughter the same way. Who was this angry, drunken woman in her car?

"Get me out of here," Bree muttered.

"Gladly," said Zona as she pulled away. "Good heavens, Bree, what is wrong with you?"

There was a long moment of silence in the back seat. It was followed by an incredulous, "Mom? What the—?"

Zona cut her off. "Don't you dare say it. You were raised better."

"I wasn't raised. I was tortured!"

And to think Zona could have passed on picking up this last passenger.

"I hate my life," Bree wailed.

"You're one to talk. You're out getting trashed while I'm driving all night to make money," Zona shot back.

But life never remained static and it didn't have to stay bad. Zona was determined hers wouldn't. If her daughter was sober and sensible, she'd share that insight, but since Bree was neither, there was no point.

They were almost to the freeway entrance when Bree said, "Stop. I'm gonna puke."

All over Zona's freshly cleaned car. *No, no, no!*

She almost got the car pulled over and turned off in time, but round one hit the floor.

"This is all your fault," Bree said between heaves on the street as Zona held her hair out of the way.

"Yes, the minute I learned I was pregnant I started thinking about ways I could ruin your life."

Once they were back in the car, her daughter got quiet. Finally, she said in a small voice, "I don't want to go home and be all alone."

With her bitterness and fear, that was where her life was heading. "You can stay at Gram's."

"I don't want to wear Gram's jammies."

"Well, you're not wearing mine," said Zona, and turned the key in the ignition.

The car refused to start. Great. Just great. She had a barfy, angry daughter in the back seat and her car was rebelling. How she wished she had a new car with a push start. Of course, if she'd been able to afford a new car, Zona wouldn't have been driving people—including her angry daughter—all over Southern California. With a growl, she tried again. Nothing.

"We're gonna be stuck here all night," Bree predicted miserably.

"One of us is going to be stuck in the trunk if she doesn't shut up," Zona snapped.

"I hate my life," Bree wailed again. In case her mother hadn't heard her the first time. "And I hate Fen for dumping me."

Zona ignored her. "Please start," she begged her car.

It took pity on her and came back to life.

"Thank God," she breathed and got them on the freeway.

Half an hour later she was hauling her daughter from a very smelly car and escorting her up the walk to Louise's house. Thankfully, her mother had gone to bed and didn't have to witness her granddaughter's less than shining moment. She'd have to explain in the morning why Bree was sleeping over, but hearing about this after the fact would be better than Louise having to be stuck in the moment along with Zona.

Gilda had been in her favorite chair, crocheting. She stood at the sight of Zona and Bree. "I guess I'll be going."

"Thanks, I'll pay you tomorrow night," Zona promised.

She left Gilda to let herself out, ignored Darling, who was having a relapse and wanted to jump on her, and moved Bree upstairs to the bathroom. She made her daughter drink a glass of water, then stripped her down and stuck her in the shower. She found an old sleep tee, then took away Bree's messed-up shirt and pants and left her to find her way to bed.

Back downstairs, she started the laundry, then got Darling's leash on him and took him out for a final walk, trying to shake off her motherly cocktail of anger and guilt as she went. She couldn't. It had sewn itself deep into the fabric of her being.

Next, she had to deal with cleaning her car. She wanted

nothing more than to fall into bed, but no way was she going to let the mess sit overnight. A quick online search on her phone assured her that white vinegar and baking soda would work wonders. She could only hope. After she'd finished, she left a bowl of white vinegar on the car floor and hoped for the best.

The next morning, she filled Louise in on her miserable first night of work over coffee and English muffins. Going light on some of the details of her daughter's misbehavior.

"And my car barely started," she finished. "I thought we were going to be stuck."

"Oh, no."

"The last thing I need is for that to die on me when I'm driving someone. It's all I can afford, and I have to keep it going."

"I bet Martin could tell you what's wrong with it. I think he's handy with cars," said Louise.

"I hate to bother Martin," said Zona.

"He doesn't mind being bothered," Louise said easily. "He likes feeling useful."

"He *is* useful," Zona said. "And he's a nice man."

Louise nodded. "He's a dear friend."

"You ought to give him a chance," Zona said. It was a waste of breath, but she couldn't help herself. "You could whip him into shape, get him a gym membership. I bet if he got more fit you'd get more excited about him."

"Honestly, Zona. How superficial do you think I am?" Louise demanded.

"What else is keeping you from getting serious? You are looking."

Louise shrugged. "I think I need someone with a . . . stronger personality."

Zona thought of their neighbor. There was a strong personality, and it wasn't a good thing.

"A gentle man beats a beast any day," she said.

"That is true," Louise agreed. "I certainly don't want a beast. But I would like a man who is a little more . . . take-charge."

"Alpha male," Zona said, mildly disgusted. "They're great in a novel, not so much in real life."

"Maybe," said Louise. "Anyway, I'll call Martin and see if he can come over."

"I may have to use your car tonight," said Zona. She'd have to go online and quickly get the license on file.

"That's fine. So," said Louise, "other than a fussy car and an unhappy daughter, how was the rest of your first night as a HopIn driver?"

Zona sighed. "Piece of cake. Too bad it had to end with my daughter telling me how I've ruined her life," Zona said and glared at the dark brew in her cup. "She's right, of course. I have."

"You have not," Louise said firmly. "You need to stop this self-flagellation. Maybe she won't make the same mistakes you have, but she'll make her share. Count on it."

"She hates Fen for dumping her. Although I don't blame him."

"Thanks, Mom," said Bree from the kitchen doorway, startling Zona and making her feel a little ill herself.

Bree was still in Zona's sleep tee, so Zona went to the laundry room and fetched her clothes. It made a handy escape.

She returned to hear her mother saying, "You can't keep blaming your guy for pulling away. He's protecting his heart, just like you want to protect yours."

Bree yanked on her jeans with quick, sharp movements, as if she were pulling on armor, getting ready for battle. "No, he's giving himself permission to find someone else." She frowned and pulled on her blouse and jacket.

Zona said nothing as she set a mug of coffee on the table for her, along with a bottle of classic caramel coffee syrup.

"Why do you keep blaming him when you're not interested?" Louise argued. "He's looking ahead to the future and wants a family."

Bree plopped onto a chair and glared at her coffee mug. "No way am I going to be another Mom," she said, delivering a fresh knife prick to Zona's heart.

Louise stepped in before Zona could say anything. "All right, now. That is enough piling guilt on your mother's shoulders. She thought she was choosing well when she married, but Gary changed. His actions aren't her fault. She took a chance and trusted."

"Twice," sneered Bree.

"One of those chances I took gave me you," said Zona, unable to keep her mouth shut any longer.

"Yeah, well, I didn't ask to be born," Bree retorted.

"You didn't ask to be loved either, but you are, even though right now you're making it hard," Zona shot back.

"And you're making choices that could turn out just as badly," said Louise. Bree opened her mouth to speak, and Louise silenced her with a pointing finger. "And don't you dare start squawking about the evil patriarchy and how bad men are and how they can't be trusted. There are women out there who are just as bad. People are people. Some are selfish and some are kind. Some have been raised with principles and some haven't. Some walk in light, others walk in darkness, and it has nothing to do with what sex they are. You don't have to rush into any kind of commitment, but you'd better knock that chip off your shoulder before it makes you lopsided."

Bree's eyes filled with tears and her mouth trembled. "My head hurts. Can I go home now?"

"Yes. That would be a good idea," Zona said irritably.

She opted to take Bree home in her mother's car, not wanting to chance a problem with hers until she could get someone to look at it. She'd checked when she first got up and it still wasn't smelling too good inside. It would need a second cleaning to get rid of eau de barf.

"Why are we taking Gram's car?" Bree asked as Zona unlocked the door, her voice cold.

"Why do you think?" Zona replied.

Yes, it came out as snappish, but that was the only way it could come out considering how snappish she was feeling. It was hard being judged by her daughter, and even if she deserved it she was getting tired of it. She was working as hard as she could to fix things.

Bree said nothing to that, just climbed in and clammed up.

Zona had only seen the apartment when she first helped Bree move in, but she remembered where it was. Which was a good thing considering their current lack of communication.

Bree didn't get out once the car was stopped. "Thanks for washing my clothes," she said, looking down at her knees.

"You're welcome." Zona wanted to reach over and put an arm around her embarrassed and unhappy girl and kiss the top of her head, but the distance between them felt more than a couple of feet.

To her surprise, Bree closed it. "I'm sorry I was mean."

They were the sweetest words Zona had heard in a long time, and they produced a teary smile.

Bree leaned over and kissed Zona's cheek. "Thanks for being there for me. I love you, even if you did screw up."

Zona didn't know whether to laugh or cry or defend herself.

"I'm a screw-up, too," Bree added softly.

"And I love you. I always will," Zona told her.

Bree nodded, then was out the door and hurrying to her apartment.

Zona let down the window and called her daughter's name.

Bree turned.

"If you need a ride tonight, don't call HopIn."

Bree smiled, gave her a thumbs-up, and kept going.

BREE'S ROOMMATE WASN'T exactly happy to see her. Gaylyn was seated at their small kitchen table with her friend and their third roommate Monique, Gaylyn eating two-day-old pizza for breakfast and Monique, the skinniest woman on the planet, sipping her latest fad diet drink. Both looked at her in disgust.

"You know you made a complete joke out of yourself last night. And me, too, 'cause I was with you," Gaylyn scolded.

Bree hadn't started the night with plans to make a joke out of anyone, not until they'd gone in the club and she'd caught sight of Fen, seated at a table with a bunch of his friends. Seated between two girls. He'd looked her way, caught sight of her, and the smile had dropped from his face. He'd said something to his buddies, then left. For a second she'd thought he was coming over to see her, but he wasn't. Instead, he'd made for the exit. Things had gone downhill after that.

"Dumping your drink on that poor guy," added Monique, shaking her head. "So classless. And such a waste of booze."

"He only wanted you to dance with him," Gaylyn put in.

"He was with someone. Didn't you see?" Bree demanded. *The evidence is undeniable. Defendant is not guilty.*

"He was with a whole group of people," Monique informed her. "And guess what. It turned out that girl was his cousin."

"Oh." *The defendant is guilty as charged.*

"If you'd just stopped there. But, no, you had to climb up on the table and scream that every man in the room was scum and every woman who was with one was brain dead," Gaylyn continued.

Bree had a hazy memory of that. She also had a hazy memory of suggesting what those men could do to themselves.

"You looked like a complete crazy," Gaylyn continued.

"Oh, and you've never gone crazy?" Bree retorted.

"Like that? What do you think?"

"I'm sorry," Bree said, and fell onto the third chair at the table. "I guess I'm having a hard time over Fen leaving."

"You didn't want him so what do you care?" Gaylyn argued.

Bree had no answer for that.

"If you ever do something like that again, I'm canceling your girlfriend card, and you can go live with your grandma and your mom," Gaylyn finished.

At that, Bree burst into tears.

"Hey, okay, I'm not mad anymore," Gaylyn hurried to say.

She shoved the pizza box Bree's direction to prove it. The sight of it made Bree's stomach turn over. She shoved it back and went to the refrigerator to pull out a can of La Croix.

"And I was kind of worried," Gaylyn added. "That driver was supposed to bring you home. Whose address was that where you ended up?"

Bree settled back in her chair and popped open the can, tried to ignore the heat on her face. "That driver was my mom, and she took me to my Gram's." Who got picked up from a club by her mother? So lame.

Both roommates gaped at her.

"Your mom's a HopIn driver?" Gaylyn sounded both shocked and disgusted. Hardly surprising, since her mom owned a clothing boutique. "I thought she had a normal job."

The heat on Bree's face turned into an inferno. "This is her second job. She's doing side hustles to make extra money for my nursing school."

"Wow. My mom wouldn't do that," said Monique.

"I puked in her car," Bree said.

She might have been able to convince herself that she'd dreamed that if not for the fact that her mother had washed her clothes. Ugh.

"Gross-o," said Gaylyn.

"What about your dad? Isn't he paying for your college?" asked Monique.

"Her dad's a crook. He raided the savings account. That's why they're divorced," Gaylyn explained, spilling the tea.

Bree wished she could crawl under the table. "That's my stepdad." *No real relation.* Except her real dad wasn't much better. "My dad's giving me some money." A lot less than some if they were going to get technical.

"What a tool," said Monique. "So amazing that your mom is working extra for you. She sounds awesome."

"She is," Bree said.

Except when it came to picking men. Had Bree inherited her mother's love disaster gene?

She thought again of Fen. If only they could simply stay friends forever. But then they'd be stuck in limbo.

Except now what was she stuck in? Suckage.

Suckage was better than wreckage. She needed to remember that.

She also needed to do something to make up for her bad behavior of the night before. "I gotta go," she said.

A few moments later, she'd grabbed her purse, which Gaylyn had brought home for her, and her car keys and was on her way to Walmart.

21

ZONA HOVERED OVER THE CAR ENGINE next to Martin as he examined spark plugs and wires. Greasy car guts had never interested her. With her success as a rideshare driver on the line, that had changed.

"It started a little rough the other day," she shared. She shouldn't have ignored that. "Then last night it didn't want to start at all. What do you think is wrong?" she prompted.

"Well," he said slowly, "I'm no expert on newer cars."

Hers hardly qualified as new.

"But I'd say you need a new air filter."

Relief spread over her. "That's all?"

"I can't be sure. You probably should take it to the dealership."

She groaned inwardly. The last thing she wanted to spend money on was car repairs, especially if the fix was an easy one Martin could manage.

"But you could change the air filter, right?"

"Sure," he said.

"This afternoon?"

"I don't have any big plans."

"Oh, Martin, it would be great if you could."

He smiled at her. "I'm happy to help."

She smiled back. "You always are. You're such a great neighbor," she said, and his smile widened. "I don't know what we'd do without you."

His smile lost weight. "Oh, you'd get along fine."

Zona knew he hadn't meant her. "I don't think my mom realizes how lucky she is to have you as a friend."

Zona wished he could have more than just friendship with her mother. He certainly deserved to be happy.

But then people didn't always get what they deserved, she thought, bitterness trying to creep in.

She pushed it away. *You've got a place to stay*, she reminded herself as she went in the house to borrow her mother's car fob. *You're employed and healthy, your mom is recovering just fine from her break, and your daughter is . . .* Well, she was working, and she was safe. But she sure wasn't doing well emotionally.

If only Zona could find a way to help Bree get past the past. But first she had to be able to. The path still wasn't clear to her. Probably because her current situation was continually reminding her of what she'd been through.

Who said what doesn't kill you makes you stronger? Some sick masochist who didn't get the lure of being an emotional cream puff. She'd have liked nothing better than to spend her Saturday night flopped on the couch with her mother, watching movies, or snuggling under the covers with a good novel (not a romance!). Instead, she would be in her car, pretending that she liked driving around nosy strangers. Or barfy daughters.

Oh, well. Cream puffs got eaten. Bring on the emotional weightlifting.

"It sounds like an easy fix," Louise said when Zona shared Martin's diagnosis.

"I hope so," said Zona. "Do you mind missing out on garage sales this morning?"

"I have enough stuff. Feel free to stop at a couple on your way to the car parts store though, and if you find any pink Depression glass, snag it for me."

"Will do," Zona promised.

She didn't find any Depression glass, but she did score a vintage leather Betsey Johnson purse. A quick search on her phone showed her a similar one that had sold for fifty dollars and the garage sale seller only wanted twenty. She also found a Pokémon elite trainer box of cards. This turned out to be an even better deal. Ten dollars and it looked like she'd be able to sell it for fifty. Score!

It was a good thing she had scored, because once she got to the auto parts store, she experienced sticker shock. That much for a stupid air filter for her car? Holy moly! She left the store wearing a frown.

But what she saw when she pulled back into her mom's driveway instantly dissolved it. Bree was half in, half out of her car. A bucket of sudsy water sat on the parking strip.

She got out and walked over. "What's this?"

Bree kept scouring away at carpet on the floor. "I owe you."

Not as much as I owe you, Zona thought. "Thanks."

Bree straightened, opened the front passenger door, and pulled out a small gift bag, then handed it over. "Happy birthday early."

Zona's birthday wasn't until November. "You are getting an early start," she joked. She looked inside and found a collection of tree-shaped air fresheners nestled inside the colored tissue paper. "Just what I always wanted," she cracked.

"Just what you need," Bree said. She dropped her scrub brush in the bucket and took off the rubber gloves she'd been wearing. "It's not your fault Gary messed you over and I shouldn't be blaming you."

The words were such balm to her wounded spirit, Zona wanted to cry. She kept the tears at bay, slipped an arm around her daughter's shoulders, and hugged her. "Thanks. And thanks for this."

"I owed you after puking everywhere."

"I didn't mean about that," Zona said.

Her daughter nodded, didn't look her in the eye. "I know," she said, and bent to pick up the bucket.

They started toward the front walk just as Alec James was coming down his. Zona was careful not to look his way. They hadn't indulged in any neighborly chats since their awkward conversation on the front porch.

She could hardly blame him. He'd probably had more than enough of her mother and her. Which was for the best.

Under everything she still felt a sense of unease, and every time they started to patch up their neighborly relations, something went awry and tore at the patch. There was so much they didn't know about the man. Other than the fact that he hadn't buried someone's bones in his yard.

Who was that woman who'd been with him? Why had she left? Alec James was a man who walked in shadow. And Zona was determined to stay on the sunny side of the street.

But darn, that smile of his, when he chose to show it, drew her, even though he made her feel edgy. He was like some kind of emotional vampire, opening his cape and beckoning her to come on over and snuggle up next to him. It was hard to ignore the pull of that power.

She shook off the vision of herself pressed against him with him going for her neck. There was nothing sexy about a man sucking you dry. She'd been there, done that.

Bree picked up on her averted gaze. "Good idea, Mom. Don't even look."

"Good advice," said Zona.

"It's not that I don't want you to be happy," Bree added. "It's just that I don't want us both to be miserable."

Her daughter's reference to the future was so inaccurate. Bree was still miserable. Her well-laid plans had been knocked over like so many building blocks and her trust had been flattened. Bree was still on Zona's health insurance. Maybe she should broach the idea of therapy again. Bree had shot her down when she'd mentioned it a year earlier. Considering their latest tense interaction, the time probably wasn't right.

Still, she couldn't resist. "You know, if you need to talk to a professional," she began.

Bree cut her off. "I'm okay." She opened the door, striding quickly inside. End of conversation.

Zona sighed inwardly and followed her in. Her daughter shouldn't have to feel the way she did. She shouldn't have had to postpone starting her nursing program. And Zona shouldn't have had to move in with her mother. Why was it that life never went the way you planned?

Oh, well. What could you do but make new plans? Like start collecting side hustles.

She handed over the air filter to Martin, who took it and went out to make her car all better. "I hope that's all it needs," she said to her mother.

"I'm sure it is. Martin knows what he's doing," Louise said confidently. She turned to Bree. "How's the car smelling?"

Bree's cheeks turned a little rosy. The question was an unpleasant reminder of why she'd been cleaning the car in the first place.

"Better," she said.

"Good," Louise approved. She smiled at her granddaughter. "You're a good kiddo."

Bree gave a snort. "Sometimes."

"And we love you all the time," said Louise, which birthed a baby smile on Bree's face.

She nodded and went to the kitchen to dump the water from her pail.

"She is a good kid," Louise said to Zona.

Zona nodded. "Good but unhappy."

"She'll get over it. She's young."

Just because you were young it didn't mean you got over things. Zona still remembered getting tormented in middle school by a mean girl who taunted her over her flat chest.

"Nobody's gonna want you," Cindy Mathews had taunted.

Well, she'd gone and proved Cindy wrong. She got boobs and she got married young.

And got cheated on and got desperate and then got messed over again. And now look at her. She'd never admit it to her mother, hated to admit it to herself, but she was almost as cynical and untrusting as her daughter. Maybe she needed therapy.

Or just chocolate. She'd stock up before she started work. It would be good to have an emergency supply in the car.

Both Bree and Martin stayed for lunch and Zona made them a shrimp pasta salad.

"How's your book coming, Gram?" Bree asked.

Louise's cheeks turned pink. "I'm taking a break."

"How come?"

"I'm waiting for the muse to return," Louise said. "And I've been busy."

"Busy doing what?" Bree persisted.

Reenacting old Hitchcock movies, thought Zona, but she kept her mouth shut.

So did Martin.

"I've had a lot of company," said Louise. "I'll get back to it when inspiration strikes again."

If you asked Zona, inspiration had already struck enough.

AN HOUR BEFORE Zona left for her side hustle, Louise, who was at the dining room table working a puzzle, announced, "She's back."

Zona set a glass of iced tea in front of her. "Who's back?"

"The woman next door."

"We are done spying on the neighbor," Zona said, and peered out the window.

Sure enough. The woman was back, out of her car and walking to the front door.

But maybe not to stay. "She doesn't appear to have any luggage with her," said Zona.

"Well, I don't think she had any clothes left behind," said Louise. "Not after what I saw. Why would she come back?"

"Svengallow?"

"Who?"

"That man from the old movies you told me about."

"Svengali," Louise corrected. "Yes, our neighbor is definitely one of those. He's got some sort of hold on her."

"Women are stupid when it comes to men," said Zona. Herself included.

Why was the redhead back? Zona sat down at the table in a seat facing the window, and randomly picked up a puzzle piece.

"I hope she doesn't stay," said Louise.

"At least she's not dead."

"Yet. That man has suppressed violence. Oh, my gosh. Look."

Louise didn't have to tell Zona to look. She already was. The front door of Alec James's house burst open and ejected the redhead. It was obvious that she was crying as she ran to her car.

There it was again, the ugly side of Alec James.

"Don't you be giving him any more lemonade," Louise cautioned as the PT Cruiser backed out of the driveway at top speed. "Or cookies. And no more dog training. We want nothing to do with that man."

They certainly didn't.

Louise's friend Susan was coming over for dinner and cards, and the doorbell rang, announcing her arrival. Zona opened the door and let her in. Darling was on hand to greet her but settled for plopping down and thumping his tail on the floor when Zona stepped in front of him and commanded him to sit. Alec James would have been proud of both of them.

Svengali James.

"I brought appetizers," Susan said.

"Those look great," said Zona, eyeballing the plate of stuffed mushrooms.

"We'll save you a couple," Susan said as she walked to the table, Darling trotting along beside her.

"Don't make promises you can't keep," Louise said. "These look great. Let me try one." Susan held out the plate and Louise plucked a mushroom from it and took a bite. "Oooh, yum." Darling moved next to her, looking longingly at what was left in her hand. "No, these are not for you. Zona, will you get him a treat?"

"So, what's new with the neighbor?" Susan was asking when Zona returned. She'd picked up a puzzle piece and was searching for its spot in the half-formed picture of a dog.

"The woman who was with him returned," Louise informed her. "But she didn't stay. We think he hit her."

What was this *we* stuff? "Mom," Zona scolded. If they weren't careful, they were going to be back to Louise checking the man's yard for fresh bones.

Seeing what was in Zona's hand, Darling forgot his lessons and jumped on her. "Down," she commanded, and walked him back onto all fours, then made him sit before giving him his treat.

"I said we *think*."

"*You* think," Zona corrected her. "And you need to stop thinking."

Louise ignored the scold and bit into another mushroom. Then closed her eyes and groaned. "So good."

"Okay, I'm getting one now. Mom's right. There won't be any left by the time I get back," Zona said and sampled a mushroom. It was delicious, and she half wished she could stay home and play cards and eat curried chicken salad and stuffed mushrooms. "These are great," she told Susan.

"Stay and help us eat them," Louise urged. "You could use a break."

"I could use money more. You two have fun. I'll be back by midnight."

"Don't hurry on my account," said Susan. "I'm staying until I win at Hands and Buns. Which means I could be here until dawn."

Zona chuckled as she went to get her purse and keys. When it came to games, Susan was competitive.

She was also a loyal friend. She would stand guard over Louise for Zona, even if Zona was out all night. Of course, so would Carol. And Martin. And even Gilda.

It was probably a good thing Susan had invited herself over for fun though. If Zona had brought Gilda over, she'd have seen the latest goings-on next door and egged Louise on in jumping to conclusions.

Except was it jumping to see a woman running crying from a house, obviously upset, and suspect some sort of cruelty was behind it?

His truck was still parked in his driveway when Zona got into her car. What had gone on over there? None of her business, that was what.

Her car still smelled faintly of eau de barf, but it wasn't as bad as it had been. Keeping the windows down as much as possible would help. The night was warm. Maybe some of her passengers would enjoy fresh air.

And then again, maybe not. "Can you roll up your window?" asked a fifty-something woman with a carefully crafted hairstyle.

"Of course," Zona murmured and hoped the woman's olfactory glands weren't working.

They were. "What's that smell?"

Zona could see the wrinkled nose and downturned mouth in her rearview mirror.

She decided feigning ignorance was her best bet. "Do you smell something?"

The woman frowned at her. "Never mind. Let the window back down or I'm going to be sick."

The last thing Zona needed was a repeat of that.

"You really should do something about the smell," the woman said to her before getting out of the car.

Zona had a strong suspicion there would be no tip coming from that passenger.

She wasn't sure how many more passengers she wanted to pick up. The car still appeared to be running rough in spite of its new air filter. She'd go home and switch cars.

She decided to first take one more fare at the Ontario airport, since she was already close. The passenger was headed to Azusa, which would be almost to home for her anyway.

Her passenger was easy to spot as she pulled up to the passenger load area. He was checking his phone and the cars pulling up. He wore jeans, boots, and a fringed brown suede jacket. A messenger bag was slung across his chest and he had a small carry-on suitcase. A California cowboy. He wasn't very tall and he wasn't very big, but he was cute in a boy-next-door sort of way, with curly brown hair. Had to be single or there would have been someone meeting him.

"Well, hello there," he said happily when she let down the window to confirm that he was her passenger.

Great. A Mr. Friendly. He'd talk her ear off all the way to his destination.

He tossed his luggage in the back seat, then climbed into the front passenger seat. There were no rules against it, but unless it was a party of three, people almost always took the back seat as a sort of courtesy. Zona wished she'd seen that coming. Too late though. There he was.

"This is a nice surprise," he said. "A hot HopIn driver."

Ugh. This man obviously considered himself a player and the last thing she needed was him up in front next to her, practicing his moves. She wished she wasn't stuck with him all the way to Azusa. She managed a polite smile but said nothing.

"So, you live around here?"

"Not really," she said.

"But sort of? You must live somewhere nearby. Hey, maybe you live in Azusa, like me. What's your name?"

"Sorry, that's classified information," she said.

"Ha, ha. If you told me, you'd have to kill me, right?"

"That's it," she said.

"So, you're probably really a spy and this is your cover. You like working undercover?"

If this smarmy double entendre kept up, there would be more barfing in her car. "You must be a comic."

"I've been told I'm pretty funny," he said. "Seriously, what's a pretty woman like you doing working as a HopIn driver?"

"Earning money, like all the rest of the world," she said.

Her stony tone of voice should have been a clue. Mr. California Cowboy wasn't good at picking up clues. "Maybe we were meant to meet. You know, like in one of those chick movies."

"Or maybe you just needed a ride home from the airport."

"A pretty woman like you shouldn't have to be driving strange men around."

Like you?

"Why don't you have a sugar daddy taking care of you?"

"Not into sugar daddies," she said, then added, "Not into men." That ought to shut him up.

"Oh, come on now. You're not into women. I can tell."

She frowned at him. "I think this conversation needs to end."

"Just trying to be friendly," he grumbled, and settled into a pout.

Good. Maybe he'd pout all the way to his destination.

He didn't. They were almost to the freeway exit when he tried again. "I'm really a nice guy."

Good for you. She probably wasn't going to get a big tip from this man, but there was no sense reducing bad tip to no tip, so she kept her smart remark to herself.

Instead, she said, "I'm sure you have more than one woman in your life who's crazy about you." *Flattery and diplomacy, good job, Zona.*

"Yeah, but I haven't met *the one.* You know?"

There was no *the one.* She'd found that out the hard way.

"But maybe I have. Right here, tonight."

"Sorry, not interested."

"I know how to show a woman a good time."

"I bet there's somebody waiting right now for you to call her."

"There's not. Honest."

They got off the freeway and started down Grand Avenue. Another ten minutes and she'd be rid of him.

"No, really. There's no one," he said.

They stopped at a signal. He stretched out his arm and rested his hand on the top of her seat. She could feel her blood pressure rising. If this little Twinkie put his hand on her shoulder, he was going to lose it.

"I think you'd better keep your hand on your side of the car," she said sternly.

"Hey, just stretching," he said with a frown, and pulled it back.

The signal turned green and she put her foot on the gas to move the car forward. The car said, *No. Not going anywhere.*

Oh, no. No, no, no. She pushed again.

Still not moving, said the car.

"What's going on with your car?" demanded her passenger.

"Crap," muttered Zona, and tried again.

You are out of luck, said the car.

22

"**IS THIS THING OUT OF GAS?**" demanded the California cowboy.

"No, it's not." Zona swore under her breath and tried again to get the car moving.

Once more, it let her down. A car came up behind her and honked. She put on her hazard lights, let down the window, and waved him past.

The California cowboy gave a snort. "Don't you drivers get your cars checked out before you start doing this?"

That set her face on fire. "My car's been working fine," she informed him.

Up until the night before. She should have stayed home and played cards with her mom and Susan.

She pulled her phone from the dashboard and put in a call to the dispatcher. "Car trouble. I need a relief driver," she said, and gave her location. "Someone will be coming to take you the rest of the way in just a couple of minutes," she said to Cowboy.

His look of irritation vanished, replaced by a grin. "I guess we'll just have to get to know each other better while we're waiting."

"Oh, I don't think so," she said as she unlocked the car hood. She got out to open it—a good excuse to get away from that friendly hand reaching toward her again.

By the time she'd lifted the hood, he was right there next

to her, putting a hand on her shoulder and pretending to look at the motor along with her. "Let's see if we can figure this out."

"I've got it handled," she said, and stepped away.

"I know a few things about cars. I can help you," he insisted. "This has got to be a sure sign that we were meant to meet."

"I don't think so."

"Aww, come on now. It's fate. You'd better let me stay here with you. You don't want to be here all by yourself."

With cars whizzing by. It was hardly an isolated spot. "I'll be fine. I've got Triple A."

"They could take all night to come," he said.

There was a cheery thought.

He tried to close the distance between them, but she held up her hand. "I'm not having a good night. You really don't want to mess with me."

He blinked in surprise. "Whoa. PMS."

Yep. Pissed at Male Stupidity. She gave him the same glare that used to make Gary shake in his Vans.

A black SUV flashed its lights as it passed them, then parked a few feet ahead of them in the nearby parking lot of a strip mall. Her relief driver, thank God. She had a grateful smile on her face, ready to greet him as he got out, until she recognized that light brown hair and the slightly crooked nose, the stylish glasses, and the perfect smile.

"Gary?"

Her ex looked equally surprised to see her. "Zona?"

"Zona. So that's your name," said the cowboy. "I guess all you rideshare drivers know each other. You two dating?"

Both Zona and Gary ignored the question.

"Have you got luggage?" Gary asked him.

"Yeah, it's on the back seat." Gary went to fetch the luggage, and the cowboy turned to Zona. "Hey, we got off on the wrong foot somewhere. I really am a nice guy. I'm Carl."

"Safe travels, Carl. Gary will take you the rest of the way," she said, sounding properly professional.

"I really would like to see you sometime," Carl said.

Yes, she wanted to hang out with Carl from the Planet Clueless. "I don't think so." She pointed to the SUV. How had Gary managed to get such a nice car? "Your ride's waiting."

"Oh, come on. How about a phone number?" He pulled his phone out, ready to share.

Gary was with them now. "You ready to go?" he asked the cowboy.

"As soon as I get this nice lady's phone number," Carl said, smiling at Zona.

"You're not going to, so feel free to leave," said Zona.

"She's not kidding," Gary added.

Cowboy Carl's brows did the irritation dip, but he recovered and shrugged. "Okay, your loss," he said, and sauntered to where Gary had parked.

"What are you doing?" she demanded as her passenger walked away.

"Same thing as you, trying to make money," said Gary. "I took a second job on top of my one at Macy's." He looked at her sadly. "I'm sorry you're having to do this, Zona."

"Yeah, well, me, too." Her voice was frosty.

He looked around in concern. "Are you going to be all right here by yourself?"

"Yes, I'll be fine. And a lot happier by myself than standing here with you."

He pressed his lips together and nodded. Then he walked off. How *had* he managed to get a nicer car than hers? Oh, who cared?

She was standing by the side of her car calling for help

when a truck appeared and pulled up behind her. Oh, good grief. Really?

Alec James got out and joined her. "What's the trouble?"

"My car died and now it won't start."

"Let me try," he said, and got in.

Man to the rescue, she thought, and was pleased to see that it didn't start for him, either.

He got out and walked to the hood and Zona followed him.

Gary reappeared. "Zona, I'm going to stay with you until a tow truck comes," he said, giving Alec James the big dog look.

Yes, that was what Zona needed, her ex who'd screwed her over deciding he now wanted to be her knight in shining armor. Except Gary's armor was rusted and useless.

"Oh, Gary, go away," she said irritably. "I know this man."

Gary's eyes narrowed. "You do?"

Alec James simply stood there, saying nothing. Looking ten times buffer than Gary, his collection of muscles stuffed into his jeans and T-shirt and windbreaker.

"You're dating? Already?" Gary looked at her as if she'd somehow betrayed him.

"No, I'm not. Not that it's any of your business."

"Then who is this man?" Gary demanded.

"The lady just said it's none of your business," said Alec in a low-voiced growl.

"He's my neighbor."

"Hey, are we gonna get going or what?" called Cowboy Carl from Gary's SUV.

Gary managed one more suspicious once-over for Alec James, then said, "Okay, Zona. Be careful."

"Somebody should have told me that when I first met you," she retorted.

His wounded look was almost enough to make her regret her words. Almost.

"So I guess that's an ex?" said Alec James as Gary walked away.

"Ex-husband," said Zona. She grabbed her phone from the car and began to search for the number of her towing insurance company.

"Put your phone away. I've got a tow dolly," he said. "I'll get you home."

She didn't want to be indebted to Alec James. Things were already awkward enough between them.

He sensed her hesitation. "Don't worry. I'm not going to knock you unconscious and steal your beater."

She frowned at him. "I never said you were."

"You say a lot with those pretty, big eyes of yours," he informed her, and turned back to his truck to get the equipment he needed.

"And it's not a beater," she muttered as he walked away.

Fifteen minutes later she was in the cab of his truck with her car following along behind them, a mixture of gratitude and unease rolling around in her stomach. "Thanks for the help," she said. She had to be polite.

"Just being a good neighbor." He didn't smile and he didn't look at her.

"A reluctant good neighbor," she suggested.

He shrugged. "Is this the first time your car's crapped out on you?"

"No, it happened last night, too. Martin replaced the air filter."

"Guess it wasn't that."

"Guess not."

"It could be your fuel pump."

Here was cheery news. She frowned.

"I could be wrong. Cars aren't really my thing."

"Maybe they're not Martin's, either," she mused.

"I've got a friend who's a mechanic. He takes on side jobs at home. Want me to call him? We can tow your car right to his place. Don't worry. It's not at the end of a canyon."

Okay, these jabs were making her uncomfortable. "I believe you."

"There's a switch," he said. He used his hands-free and put in a call. Zona could hear voices and music in the background as a man answered, "Hey, dude. You sorry you left early?"

"Nope. Had enough of you clowns. You want some more work?"

"Sure," said the voice.

"Okay, then, get your butt home. I'll meet you there. Got a woman in need."

"Oh, no. Not Angela."

"Nope," Alec James said, and ended the call.

It was hard to refrain from asking who Angela was, but Zona managed. Instead, she said, "I appreciate this." Although she should have stuck with her original plan to call Triple A. She didn't need to be riding around with Alec James. At night. Just the two of them cozied up in his truck. "You didn't have to stop," she added.

"It looked like you had some trouble."

"Story of my life."

"I can identify with that," he said.

Alec James had trouble? He *was* trouble.

The silence felt awkward as they drove to his friend's house, but Zona was having a hard time figuring out how to break it so she gave up trying.

They got to the house before his friend. It was a seventies-style rambler with Alpine trim along the roof that made the house look like it had gotten lost on its way to the mountains. Beyond the large gate at the end of the driveway, she saw a two-car garage.

Alec James shut off the motor and turned to Zona. "That

ex of yours have something to do with why you're driving fools around at night?"

"You could say that. He lost all our money gambling, raided my daughter's college savings." Okay, this was too much sharing. A simple yes would have sufficed.

Alec James let out a low whistle. "Fun times."

"I'm trying to fix the mess he made." *So don't judge me.*

As if she cared whether or not Alec James judged her.

He nodded, looking surprisingly empathetic. "That sucks. Sometimes all it takes is one messed-up person to turn your life upside down."

"Try two." Lovely. Now, she sounded like a bitter loser. Probably because she was.

"So, second time in the fire for you, huh?"

"What can I say? I'm a bad judge of character."

"Yeah, maybe you are," he agreed.

She scowled at him.

"What?" he said defensively. "You misjudged me."

She cocked an eyebrow at him. "Did I?" *Great idea, Zona, get the man angry.* "Sorry."

He frowned at her. "Okay, so what do you think I am? Not a murderer. We've cleared that up, right?"

"Not a murderer," she agreed.

A truck pulled up behind them, and a short, stocky man with a shaved head got out and sauntered over to Alec James's side of the cab. "I guess this is the patient," he joked.

"It is," Alec confirmed. "Zona, this is Jasper."

"The car genius," Jasper said, and grinned at Zona. Then to Alec James, "Let's get this baby backed into the garage." He opened the gate, pulled in his truck, and then opened the second garage. It didn't take long for Jasper to guide Alec James as he backed Zona's car into the driveway and then the garage.

"It might take me a couple of days to get this done," Jasper said to Zona after she shared the car's symptoms with him. "I hope you're not in a hurry."

"I can manage," she said. It was a good thing her mom didn't need her car.

"Okay, then."

She watched in horror as Alec pulled a money clip out of his jeans pocket.

Alec? He was Alec now?

"I can pay," she said, and hurried back to his truck to get her purse.

By the time she'd turned around, it was a done deal. Jasper was heading for his front door and Alec was walking down the driveway.

Zona ran across the stone front yard. "Wait! I need to pay you." She had ten dollars in her purse. She could use it as a down payment and get the rest from her bank's ATM.

Jasper smiled, waved her away. "We're good. No worries."

"No, I want to," she insisted.

"Take it up with the man," he said. "And good luck with that. He won't take your money."

"Oh, yes, he will," she said, as much to herself as to Jasper.

Back in the truck cab, she demanded, "How much did you give him? I'll pay you back tomorrow."

He shrugged. "Not much. Don't worry about it."

"I've got money," she protested.

"And it sounds like you've got better things to do with it than pay for car repairs."

"Seriously, how much did you give him?"

"Just enough to cover parts. He's a friend. He owes me. I helped him replace the floor in his bathroom."

"Parts are expensive. I'm not going to let someone pay my bills," she said.

"Okay, you can pay me back."

"Great. How much?"

"Buy me a burger and fries and large shake at In-N-Out."

The last thing she wanted to do was go out to eat with Alec James. Alec James. She'd seen firsthand how relationships with him went. This was probably how he'd lured the redhead into his web. This was how he worked. Do a good deed here and there. Help with dog training, pick up a stranded woman. Who had been perfectly capable of getting herself home. She would be a fool to go out with this man.

"We can take separate cars in case you're worried I'll drive you off into the woods somewhere and chop you up into little pieces," he said. "Of course, I could do that right now," he added matter-of-factly, and she shivered. He glanced her way and his brows lowered. Did he sense her sudden unease? "It's just burgers, Zona, and I'm trying to give you a break."

"That's nice of you, but I don't need a break. Let me pay you," she said. Thank God they were finally on their street. She was more than ready to get out of his truck.

"Why do I get this feeling that, in spite of giving me cookies and drinks, you're actually scared of me?"

Her eyes widened. "You're kidding, right?" Okay, she shouldn't have said that. It sounded accusatory. "Why would you think that?"

"You blow hot and cold."

Like you.

Understanding dawned. "Oh, wait. All the yelling, right?"

"Look, we saw your girlfriend come back and then leave crying yesterday. Whatever was going on with you is clearly not over," she began.

"Girlfriend? I don't have a girlfriend."

"Then who was that woman staying with you?"

"Angela? She's my own personal nightmare."

"She said you were a monster." Not the wisest thing to

share. "It's none of my business. We didn't call the cops and now you've helped me and we're even."

"But you did call the cops," he said.

"My mom did that, and I apologized."

"But you believed her, didn't you?" he said, his voice low.

This conversation was getting awkward and creepy. He turned into his driveway and Zona put her hand on the door handle, ready to jump out. "Let's put that behind us."

He put the truck in Park and she opened the door, but he laid a heavy hand on her arm, stopping her. "Wait."

23

ZONA'S HEART RATE SHOT UP. "I need you to let go of my arm."

He did. "I need you to give me a minute here. Please," he added.

There was no anger in his voice. On the contrary, he sounded almost humble. It caught her off guard.

"Okay, a minute," she said and shut the door.

"Angela, the woman who's been staying with me, the one your mom thought I bumped off, she isn't my girlfriend."

Not anymore, obviously.

"She's my stepsister."

Zona's jaw dropped. "Your stepsister."

"And she's been making nothing but problems for me. She keeps coming back into my life like a virus."

Here was a nice way to talk about a relative. "You have no idea how lucky you are to have a sibling. My brother died when he was a baby."

Alec's expression softened. "I'm sorry." His features returned to stone. "This is different. Angela has done some really bad things. There's a reason I'm trying to cut her out of my life."

"She came back. It looks like she wants to be in it."

He shook his head. "I can't let her. She's created relationship problems in the past and now, this time she not only got ahold of one of my credit cards and ran it up, she also took one out in my name and went on a spending spree. Then she got mad at me for ruining her life by spoiling her fun. If you heard shouting, it was me yelling at her. And all that yelling she was doing was because I'd found the card and cut it up, threatened to report her for criminal fraud. She didn't like that. Called me a monster."

"Are you?" Zona asked softly. He sounded more like a man who had been pushed to the limits of his patience.

"I am if you ask Angela. She's great at making anyone who crosses her look like a villain. And yes, I yelled at her on more than one occasion. The tantrums, the spending, the thieving. And then, to top it all off she drops my phone in the pool." He shook his head.

"And pushed you in," Zona added.

His eyes narrowed. "How'd you know?"

I was watching through the fence would not be a good answer. "I heard."

"She caught me off guard. The woman's a spoiled little user and she makes me nuts. She finally messed me over one too many times and that's why I kicked her out."

"Kind of sad," Zona mused. She'd have loved to have had a sibling of any kind. Even though she'd been young when her little brother died, she'd felt the loss of him. Still did sometimes. "I'd love to have had a sister."

"You wouldn't want this one. She's been a problem since she was a teenager."

"Where is she now?"

"Staying with some fool she met in a bar. She'll use him up and then move on. But not back to my place. I took all her crap to her and told her I'm done enabling her. If she needs a place to crash, she can go crash with her sister in Montana."

So that was what he was doing the night Louise had seen him hauling all those things to his truck, making sure Angela didn't have an excuse to come back.

"Sounds like she has issues," Zona said.

He let out a long breath. "She creates them for everyone around her. I've run out of patience with her, and I'm tired of being used."

"I can identify with that," Zona said. "People will always use you if you let them. Why did you let her use you in the first place?" It was a judgmental question, and she was certainly in no position to judge. "Sorry, that was tacky."

"Nah. It's a question I've asked myself more than once. Our parents are dead. Her older sister got married and moved away and then I was the only one left." He gave a grunt of disgust. "Dad loved the girls, especially Angela. And after my stepmom died, they were all he had left of her. Ariel wasn't too bad, but Angela was another story. He refused to see she had problems and kept making excuses for her and indulging her. She's never had to grow up and accept responsibility for her behavior. She's always a victim. Whatever is going wrong it's always someone else's fault."

"And yet, there she was, in your life."

"When Dad died, he saddled me with her. Deathbed promise and all."

"As in watch over little Angela?"

"Something like that. But little Angela is out of control, and, like I said, I'm done."

No wonder he'd been yelling, and no wonder he'd had that angry air about him. It had started about the time the red PT Cruiser had showed up. And then along had come Zona and her mom, adding to his misery.

"I never hit her," he said, "no matter what you might have heard."

"So you told me."

"Not sure you believe me. Look, I was a jerk at times. Angela was driving me nuts and . . ." He let out another long breath. "That's no excuse for how I've been acting. I've been sour as a Meyer lemon ever since she showed up on my doorstep. I thought I was rid of her, figured she wouldn't want to be here in the burbs, figured she'd stay in LA where the action is."

"Why did she show up on your doorstep?"

"Because her latest boyfriend dumped her. She played on my sympathy. Again. So I took her in. Again. But then I discovered the whole credit card thing." He shook his head and let out a long breath. "I'd been busy with moving, sorting stuff out. She'd come over one day to *help* me," he said, using air quotes. "I didn't realize she'd been snooping and helping herself to my information and my plastic. After I saw the bills she'd racked up, I have to admit, I wanted to throttle her. But I do have some self-control."

"She was just back again. We saw her." *Watching from the window like the nosy neighbors we are.*

"It was a short visit. She wanted to move back in and I said no. So, how about it? Can we start over?" he asked, his expression earnest. "I don't need your mother searching my yard for dead bodies anymore."

Neither did Zona. They'd had quite enough neighborhood drama.

"Okay. Hi, I'm Zona Hartman," she said, and held out her hand.

"Hi, I'm Alec James. Nice to meet you."

He took her hand in his large one and there went the live wire. She felt the jolt clear up to her chest.

"So, how about that burger? Lunch tomorrow? Our personal détente."

Having lunch with this man could prove risky to her emotional health. "Just a lunch. Nothing more?"

"I'm not asking you to the prom, Zona. You did say you wanted to pay me back, didn't you?"

Money was safer.

But it was only burgers. And she did owe him for rescuing

her. "Okay, lunch tomorrow. The In-N-Out on Lone Hill. Meet you there at one."

"I'll leave my hatchet at home," he cracked.

"OH, MY," LOUISE said weakly when Zona shared her conversation with Alec about his stepsister the next morning.

"It looks like we jumped to conclusions about him," said Zona.

"Me, you mean."

"Me, too. I haven't exactly given him the benefit of the doubt."

"Well, who could blame us? Things sounded scary over there."

"I know. They did."

"So you believe him?" Louise still sounded doubtful.

"Why shouldn't I?"

"People lie."

"True. But what a weird lie to make up. It's too far-fetched not to be true." And maybe Zona wanted it to be true. Maybe she wanted Alec to be a nice, honest guy. "Plus, he did me a favor with the car."

"I'll write him a check for whatever it costs to repair and then you'll be even."

"We've already taken care of that," said Zona, and hoped her mother wouldn't ask her how.

"How?" Louise asked.

"I'm buying him lunch."

Louise's brows dipped into a disapproving V. "You're going out with the man?"

"Not really going out," Zona hedged.

"Don't you be rushing into anything," cautioned Louise, the internet man hunter.

"Especially not with the man you wanted me to check out when he first moved in."

"We've already checked him out."

"Let's not go over that again," Zona said.

"I know, I know. I jumped to conclusions. But he definitely comes with his own set of problems, and you don't need any more problems in your life."

"I'm not going to date him. This is a onetime goodwill gesture. That's all."

"Good. Then I'm coming with you," Louise said firmly.

"What? Mom, I'm forty-two. I don't need a chaperone."

"If it's a goodwill gesture, I should be the one to make it," Louise insisted.

Oh, boy.

IF ALEC WAS surprised to see both Zona and her mother walking up to join him at an outside table at In-N-Out, he hid it well.

"I came along to help Zona thank you," Louise said. No smile attached. "I'm sure you don't mind."

"Why should I mind?" he asked. "What would you ladies like?"

"You're not paying," Zona told him. "I'm thanking you."

"You're not paying, either," Louise told her. "I'm assuming you'd like a burger and fries?" she said to Alec.

He didn't look pleased at being indebted to Louise. "I'll pay."

"No, you need to let me pay," said Zona.

"Okay, we'll all pay for our own," Louise said, and marched off inside the building.

"Nice of your mom to come along," he said to Zona as they followed her.

She frowned at him. "Are you being sarcastic?"

"No. I'm teasing."

"She's . . ." Oh, boy. How to explain this?

"Making sure I don't have a psychotic break and kidnap you?"

Zona shrugged and held up both hands. "I did explain about your stepsister, but you're still a bit of a mystery."

"And she's Jessica Fletcher."

Zona's cheeks began to burn. "My mom did love that show. We watched it when I was a kid."

"I bet you did."

"Come on, you said yourself you were a jerk. You didn't exactly make a good impression that last time you brought Darling to the door."

"And at the next block party we'll all have a good laugh about it?"

"Maybe. Mom's writing a mystery, by the way."

"Heaven help us," he said as they reached the counter.

He managed to end up paying for their lunch, and Louise spent most of it giving him the third degree, wanting to know about his family life growing up. What had his mother been like? Zona had been dealt a raw deal by her ex-husbands. Did Alec have an ex?

With that one, Zona's cheeks turned from burn to three-alarm fire. "Mom!"

"Yes, I do, and she's alive and well," he said, which brought the pink to Louise's face.

She crumpled her hamburger wrapper and walked over to a nearby trash can.

"She really is Jessica Fletcher," he said under his breath. "Are you Nancy Drew?"

"No. And you know who Nancy Drew is?"

"Stepsisters. Remember? But even Nancy would give me a pass."

She shook her head. "I'm sorry. Once you've jumped to conclusions, it's hard to get away from them."

"It's okay," he said. "Eventually you'll both see I'm not so bad. How's the dog doing, by the way? Is he ready for some more obedience training?"

"He might be," said Zona, and smiled. Alec wasn't a murderer or an abuser. Maybe he was going to turn out to be a good neighbor after all.

If she and her mother didn't drive him out of the neighborhood.

"SO, HE'S ACTUALLY NICE," Zona said when she and Gracie met for coffee on Zona's lunch break later that week, and went on to tell her friend about how Alec had come to the rescue with car repairs.

"Your mom has to be so disappointed," Gracie joked.

"She'll have to go back to getting her thrills watching *Deathline*," said Zona.

"And how about you? How are you going to get your thrills?" Gracie asked.

"Not with the neighbor," Zona said, as much to herself as her friend. She tried not to think about that zing she'd gotten when Alec shook her hand in his truck cab. "We're just being neighborly."

"It could turn into more," Gracie suggested.

"No. No more. I've struck out twice and that's enough."

"Never say never."

"Unless you mean it. I'm resolved."

"Hot guys have a way of melting resolve."

"Not mine. He's got baggage."

"Does he have an ex?"

"Yes, but it's the stepsister who's the problem."

"Maybe that's why he's got an ex."

And maybe that was why Zona wasn't going to be getting any more neighborly with him.

EXCEPT DOG TRAINING didn't count as getting neighborly.

"So, what is the deal with your ex?" she asked him that night when they were working with Darling.

"The short version? She couldn't stand my family."

"Angela?"

"Yeah. Ariel's not so bad. She got her life together and is doing okay."

"Did you have kids together, you and your ex?" Zona asked.

He shook his head. "Couldn't. Maybe that's just as well. Things get complicated when you split and you've got kids. Right, buddy?" he asked, and gave Darling's ears a rub. Darling agreed by trying to lick his hand. "Kind of wish we had, but oh, well."

"Be glad you didn't. You don't have to deal with the anger," Zona said.

"Your kid's angry?"

"Her dad is barely in her life and her stepdad raided her college savings."

"So, angry."

"She hates men and she's never getting married. Thanks to me."

"You're not the one who screwed up. Why do you take the blame?"

"I don't take it. She gives it to me. She thinks I should have been psychic."

"People are unpredictable," he said.

"Including you?"

His only answer was a half smile and a huff, then he returned his attention to Darling. "Okay . . . Darling." He shook his head. "Sorry you got such a wussy name."

"It's a cute name, and my mother picked it."

"As if I couldn't guess. No man would be so mean to a

male dog. You need to learn to stay," he finished, addressing Darling.

Darling wasn't the only one who needed to learn that lesson. Zona needed to stay, too. Right where she was, single and safe.

They finished with Darling and Alec went back to his own house. But not before he suggested Zona go hiking with him on the weekend. "Give Darling some exercise."

"After his last escape, I don't see my mother letting him out of her sight."

"Okay. Will she let you out of her sight? I promise not to—" he began.

"If you say cut me up in little pieces, I'll smack you," she said, and he laughed.

A laugh. A genuine laugh out of Alec James. She stared at him in surprise.

His brows shot down. "What?"

"You laughed."

He looked thoughtful. "What do you know. I did. Haven't done that in a while." Then he smiled. "I guess it was time."

"Maybe it was," she said.

THE REST OF the week hurried by. Zona received her car back, good as new. Darling had another obedience lesson, and Zona made some good tips driving people around on Friday night. Saturday morning, she found several treasures hitting garage sales with Louise and Martin, and Sunday morning she put on her hiking boots and prepared to hike the Bonnie Cove West and East Trail Loop with Alec. It was a moderate hike, with some nice views of Glendora and a few challenging inclines.

Good for her health, she convinced herself.

"Hiking in the wilderness. Alone with that man we barely know. Except we know he's got a temper," Louise had said when Zona had shared her plans.

"And he bought us hamburgers. Nothing bad is going to happen. And besides, you're the one who nominated him as a love candidate in the first place," Zona reminded her.

"I wish you'd quit bringing that up. I changed my mind."

"And now we know he's not a murderer."

"We also know he comes complete with a crazy family. And an ex."

"I come with two. I'm ahead of him by one. This will not turn into anything, trust me. I've been burned enough," Zona had assured her.

But she was finding that easy to forget as she and Alec made their way up the trail. The sun warmed her back and her face, but it was Alec who was warming her heart. He'd had coffee waiting in his truck for her and he'd packed snacks and water for them both. He was a completely different man than the angry version who they'd heard on the other side of the fence. Was this the real Alec?

We hope so, said her starved hormones. He did look good in his jeans and T-shirt and hiking boots. And when they finished the hike and sat down at the picnic table at the trailhead to finish off their water bottles, the hint of his cologne mixed with the musky smell of overheated male upped her heart rate higher than it had been when they'd hiked up the incline. He was sitting close enough to her that she could feel the warmth from his body and she found herself wishing he'd kiss her.

Then she scolded herself for it. *Won't turn into anything serious, remember?* She didn't need to be kissing him. Shouldn't even be with him. Was her protective wall of caution crumbling? Not good.

We need to stop this right now, she informed her hormones.

They weren't listening.

"What are you thinking?"

His words jerked her back into the moment and her heart began to pick up its pace again. "What?"

"Just wondering what was going on inside your head."

"Honestly? I was wondering what on earth I'm doing here with you."

"Enjoying a nice day?"

"You know what I mean."

He nodded. "Taking a chance. Look, Zona, I'm not going to pressure you to sleep with me if that's what you're worried about."

"Well, darn. Just joking," she added.

We're not, chorused her hormones.

"Not that I wouldn't want to," he said, and his words coupled with his smile struck her heart like an electric charge. "You're a beautiful woman. But we're hanging out, that's all. Starting new diplomatic relations." He smiled at her. That smile looked delicious. "Now that we're not hissing and growling at each other, I kind of like being with you."

And she was liking being with him. And that was scary.

"I don't want to do relationships anymore," she said. She didn't want to cry, to feel unloved or unsafe or angry. Her exes had taken her there. She had no intention of making a return trip.

"We all do relationships," he said. "We just do some better than others."

She looked at those hazel eyes of his. He had nice eyes. And a nice mouth. Nice chin. He had nice everything. No, make that great everything. Why was he alone?

"Why don't you have a girlfriend?" she asked.

He shrugged. "Been too busy with work. And Angela," he added with a frown. "I've been divorced four years, but dating hasn't really worked out. Makes it hard to have a relationship when you have family drama in your life all the time."

"Hard on a marriage, too?" she suggested.

He nodded. "My wife got tired of the drama. She told me I needed to cut the cord. I didn't."

"Couldn't," Zona supplied. "Your stepsisters were family."

"It was toxic. I should have listened to my wife," he finished wistfully. "Anyway, water under the bridge. I'm ready to move on," he added, hitting her with that smile again.

It was magnetic.

"I'm sure not," she said, determined to resist the pull.

Don't fall for this man. You hardly know him and you don't want to know his family.

So very true. She assured her common sense that she was not going to fall.

But she had tripped. Not good.

24

THE FOLLOWING EVENING FOUND ZONA AND Alec out on the sidewalk in front of his house, working again with Darling.

"You have to be firm," he said when Darling decided he preferred to bound over to her instead of staying. He demonstrated again, making the dog sit. Then he held out his hand like a stop sign and said, "Stay." He waited a moment before giving Darling a treat. He repeated the process again and took a step back and then reinforced the command once more.

"He likes you better," Zona said.

"No, he just knows who the big dog is. You've got to be firm."

"Firm," Zona said. "You hear that, Darling? I'm the big dog."

"Not the big pushover," Alec joked.

It was a civilized, neighborly interaction. An observer would have thought the two of them had been pals forever, both smiling at each other. It looked for sure like they could be lifetime pals.

Then Zona caught sight of the familiar red PT Cruiser coming down the street.

Alec saw it, too, and his eyes narrowed and his smile compressed into a thin, angry line. The car slowed, he shook his head, and it sped up and hurried on down the street.

It had barely turned the corner before Bree pulled up. Zona could feel her daughter's disapproving frown before she even saw it.

"I guess it's time to go in," Zona said.

He nodded, gave Darling a rub behind the ears, and then turned toward his own house.

Bree was barely out of her car before she started her third degree. "What's going on, Mom?"

"Our neighbor is helping me train Darling. He needs it."

Bree narrowed her eyes and Zona suddenly felt like a teenager lying to her mother. She turned toward the house. "Come on, Darling."

"Just dog training?" Bree persisted, following them both in.

"Just dog training," Zona said. "And the price is right. It's free," she added, figuring that ended the conversation.

Louise was in the living room, streaming a Hallmark movie.

"How come you're not watching your crime show?" Bree asked and bent to kiss her cheek before plopping on the couch next to her.

"I'm taking a break," Louise said. "Your mother's orders," she added, and frowned at Zona. "How was the dog training?"

"Darling is making great strides," Zona reported.

"So is our neighbor," said Louise. "Hamburgers, hiking, dog training."

"You *are* hanging out with him," Bree accused. "Mom, what are you thinking?"

"I'm thinking that it's nice to know our neighbor isn't a murderer," Zona said, shooting a meaningful look at Louise.

"Murderer?" Bree repeated.

"Ask your Gram about that," Zona said.

"Never mind. It was a slight misunderstanding."

"What kind of misunderstanding?" Bree wanted to know.

"Darling dug up a bone on his property and Gram thought he'd chopped up his girlfriend and buried her in the flowerbed. Called the cops and everything," Zona tattled. There, two could play the tattletale game.

"OMG. Truth?" Bree looked positively gleeful.

"It was an honest mistake, and I don't want to talk about it anymore," Louise said stiffly.

"So I'm mending fences, that's all," said Zona. "There's nothing going on."

"Yet," said Bree. "You're gonna fall for him, I know it. I swear, I'm the only one in this family with a working brain."

"Our brains work fine, and that's enough of that, young lady," Louise scolded.

"Sorry," Bree muttered.

"And never mind us," said Zona. "What's going on with you?"

"Nothing," Bree said with a shrug. "My life sucks. At least my savings is growing."

Zona had planned on inviting her daughter over for Sunday dinner and presenting her with a check for her first semester of school. Louise had one for her also. But there was no time like the present.

"We have something for you. What do you think, Mom? Should we give it to her now?"

"No time like the present," said Louise.

Excited to see her girl's reaction, Zona hurried upstairs to where the two checks and the card were lying on her dresser. She and Louise had both signed it the day before when Zona brought it home. She stuffed the checks in the card and returned.

"Here," she said, handing it over.

Bree looked at her, puzzled. "It's not my birthday."

"Happy birthday early," Zona said.

Bree opened the card, took out the checks, looked at them

both, and then began to cry. Zona sat down next to her on the couch and Bree threw her arms around her and continued to sob.

"This will get you started. We've got your first year covered," Zona promised.

Bree kissed her, then hugged her grandma. "Thanks, you guys. I . . ." She bit her lip and studied her knees, swiped tears from her cheeks.

"Our girl at a loss for words, there's a switch," Louise joked.

"I don't deserve you being this nice to me."

"Of course you do," said Zona.

"Oh, my gosh, I can finally start!" Bree squealed and hugged them both again.

"I promised way back I'd make it up to you for what Gary did and I meant it," Zona told her.

Bree's eyes narrowed to slits. "I hate him."

That made two of them. "He's history. We're moving on," Zona said.

Bree's expression regained its intensity. "Mom, don't move on with that man. Don't move on with any man. I don't want to see you hurt."

"I don't want to see me hurt, either. And I don't want you to have to deal with the fallout. Don't worry," said Zona. She was going to keep things purely platonic with Alec. She had to, for both her sake and her daughter's.

The appearance of the red PT Cruiser had been a sign. She needed to step away.

It would be hard to step away. Alec's contact info had found its way into her phone. And, worse, he was in her mind and knocking on the door of her heart.

You still don't really know the man, she reminded herself. Which made right then and there the perfect time to pull back. She ignored the text that came in from him when she was at work the next day. *Ignore the problem and it will go away.*

Another came in a couple hours later. You ghosting me?

Yes.

But it wasn't that easy to ghost someone who lived right next door. She and Louise had finished dinner when he knocked on the front door.

"Okay, what's up?" he asked as she stepped out onto the porch, shutting the door behind her.

"We can't keep hanging out."

He shoved his hands in his jeans pockets. "Yeah? Why?"

As if on cue, the red PT Cruiser crawled past. Zona nodded at it.

Alec swore under his breath, turned, and started across the lawn. The car sped away.

"That's why," she said when he returned.

"I'm getting a restraining order," he said.

"Good luck making it stick."

His jaw took on a stubborn set. "I'll make it stick."

"Look, I like you." There was an understatement.

"I like you, too," he said. "I like being with you. I want to spend more time with you."

"Let's settle for being neighbors."

"Good neighbors."

"Good neighbors," she agreed. Here came Martin, up the street to visit her mom.

"Like Martin and your mom," he said.

She half laughed. "They're inseparable."

"Like Martin and your mom," he repeated. Then, before her frown could turn into words, he continued, "Let's not let the losers in our lives stop us from having a good time together."

"I don't want to have a good time." Okay, that sounded stupid.

He took a step closer. She could feel his body heat. Or maybe she just felt her own body warming up. "What do you want, Zona? Tell me."

"I want to be happy. And I want to feel safe. I don't want any more relationship trauma in my life. Can you promise me that?"

"I don't have a crystal ball. I can't guarantee things would work out between us, but I can guarantee I'm not like your exes. I'm not out to hurt you. I'm into you and I like being with you. A lot. I want the same things you do. I'm tired of chaos and drama. I'm tired of being pissed all the time. I want to enjoy life, and I want some peace. You do, too, so let's see where this goes."

He was so persuasive. She wanted to believe him.

"Hang in there a little longer with me," he urged. "If things get scary, then I'll back off and we'll wave at each other from opposite sides of the property line."

She let out a tired breath. It would be so nice to enjoy a relationship with no drama, no hurt. But she was beginning to think her daughter was right. Maybe there was no such thing.

"I think we may have started something good. Let's not let the people around us ruin our lives," he said. "I'm sick of that happening."

So was she. Darn it all, didn't she have the right to some happiness, some calm waters? Could she and Alec make that happen?

He nodded in the direction of his truck. "Let's go get a drink."

The porch they were standing on suddenly felt like a high dive over a shallow swimming pool. To jump or not to jump?

She jumped. "Let's go. But as friends. Just hanging out."

"Just hanging out," he agreed.

"Tell Mom I'm going out for a while," she said to Martin, letting him in the house, then she walked with Alec to his truck and got in. She'd jumped. She hoped the water would be good.

It sure felt like it as they sat down at a table at Kalaveras, a colorful Mexican eatery in Covina. The painted skull on the outside of the building was simply for atmosphere, not a subtle warning, she assured herself. It was only drinks.

And conversation. And a shared laugh over something funny he showed her on social media. And more conversation, talking about their respective pasts and how they were leaving them behind. And his hand brushing over hers and making her thirsty for more than another frozen mango margarita.

She wanted laughter. She wanted hot kisses and a honeymoon style ever after. She wanted that happy ending she used to enjoy reading about when she believed in the books she'd read once upon a time. She wanted to live out a fantasy and leave reality behind.

But she would settle for a nice, easy friendship, something manageable like what her mom and Martin had. Something platonic would be safe and good medicine for her heart.

If only her body didn't crave more.

Back at Alec's house, once they were out of his truck she found herself leaning up against it, him next to her. "I could fall for you," she blurted. Could fall? She already was and almost down for the count.

"Funny, I was thinking the same thing."

"But I don't want to."

"That I wasn't thinking," he said.

He was looking at her lips. They suddenly felt very dry, and she had to run her tongue over them.

"Is that an invitation?" he asked. His smile was as tender as his voice.

His cologne danced up her nose and whispered, *I taste as good as I smell.*

A kiss. Just one little kiss . . . would be like eating one salted caramel. She'd want more. She wouldn't be able to stop.

"Zona." It came out like a caress.

He moved closer and the heat between them bloomed. *Salted caramels are good. So are kisses.*

Don't do it!

Too late. Those big strong arms of his had already slipped around her. His lips touched hers and lightning struck. She felt the bolt all through her body and it felt great. Her hands slipped up his back and held on. He was so solid, like a human wall. A wall of protection?

Or would that wall fall on her and crush her? What on earth was she doing?

She pulled away. She was stupid drunk on him. "I am out of my mind."

"That kiss about drove me out of mine," he said. There was that smile again. It gave her an emotional aftershock.

"My daughter doesn't want me to see you."

"Her, too, huh? And here I thought I only had to win over your mom."

"Bree doesn't want me to get hurt again. And she's tired of dealing with the emotional fallout when everything crumbles."

"It's not your daughter. You don't trust yourself, do you?" he said.

"You're right. I don't. And I still don't know you well enough to trust you."

He ran a hand along her arm, bringing every nerve to life. "Yet. Let's work on fixing that. I get that you don't want to be burned. I don't either, so we'll take it slow."

As in no more lightning bolt kisses. There was a sad thought. But it was a smart one. Once things got physical, she'd be tethered. She'd never want to leave.

Maybe she already didn't.

"What do you say?"

She hesitated. What did she say?

"I know what I should say."

"What do you want to say?" He didn't give her time to answer. "How about I pick you up from work tomorrow and take you to lunch? You have to eat."

Yes, she did. "All right," she said. It was only lunch.

Louise and Martin were camped out at the dining room table playing cards when Zona came back in the house. The drapes were pulled to the side, and the window framed a perfect view of Alec's truck.

Zona and Alec had been standing on the passenger side of the cab, but how visible had they been? What had Louise seen? Zona felt like a teenager again, worried that she was about to be busted for sneaking into the house after curfew.

Louise laid down a collection of cards. "Gin," she announced. Then turned her attention to Zona and demanded, "Where did you go?"

Martin was pretending to consider his cards, but the slight flush on his cheeks was a sure sign that he was feeling uncomfortable.

Sure enough. He laid down his cards and said, "That's it. You got me. I'd better get home." Without another word, he hurried to the door, Darling escorting him.

Zona retreated to the kitchen under the pretense of getting a drink of water. "Just out for drinks."

She barely had the water in her glass before she heard the clump, clump of Louise's crutches. "With Alec?"

"Yes, with Alec."

Louise settled at the kitchen table. "Bree's not the only one who worries about you."

"I know."

"I do want you to be happy."

"I know that, too."

"But I want you to be happy with someone . . . solid. Like Martin."

"He's too old for me," Zona joked.

Louise pointed a finger at her. "Don't be smart."

"Come on, Mom. Maybe you should take your own advice."

"Maybe I should, but . . ."

"Yeah, I know. You want someone more exciting. Alec is exciting," she added.

"He's unstable."

"No, that's his stepsister. I think we have to let go of our earlier opinions of him. Wouldn't you yell a lot if someone had done to you what she did to him?"

"Yes, I would. If that's the real story. The thing about narcissists is that they do a great job of hiding who they really are and they're great at gaslighting. You don't know which is the real Alec, the nice one you're seeing now or the angry controlling one we saw earlier."

"True," Zona admitted. "That's why we're taking things slow."

"I saw how slow you were taking things."

Busted. "That was a one-off."

"Oh, I know how those work," Louise scoffed. "Be careful, Zona. There is so much you don't know about this man."

"I know. I won't get fooled again. I promise."

And that promise was to both her mother and herself.

LOUISE WAS CONCERNED. She wanted her daughter to enjoy the second half of her life, wanted her to find someone wonderful to spend it with. But she wasn't convinced that Alec James was that someone. He came with baggage, and Zona already had enough baggage of her own. But what to do?

"You can't do anything," Gilda said the next day as she helped Louise out of the shower. "She's an adult. All you can do is be ready to pick up the pieces when everything falls apart."

Those were hardly encouraging words.

Bree wasn't any happier. She stopped by to check in on Louise that evening only to find her mother and Alec James on the front sidewalk, working with Darling.

"Gram, you've got to do something," Bree said, her eyes flashing.

"What exactly do you want me to do? Your mother is a grown woman."

Bree let out an angry huff and went to the kitchen in search of lemonade. Zona and Darling were back in the house. Darling trotted over to Louise for an ear scratch and Zona and Louise exchanged looks. A scene was about to happen.

Sure enough. Bree came back out of the kitchen. "Mom, what the heck?"

"Now what?" Zona responded.

"You know what. You're doing it again. You're falling for a guy."

"I am not," Zona insisted.

Louise knew it was a lie, and she knew that, deep down, her daughter knew it, too.

Bree plopped onto a chair and set her glass on a side table. "Crap, Mom. How bad do you need a man at your age?"

Zona gave her daughter a warning look.

A warning wasn't enough, so Louise jumped in. "Your mother's still a young woman," she said sternly.

"She needs to chill," Bree said.

"You don't need to talk about me like I'm not here," Zona informed her.

Bree's disrespectful attitude was getting old. "And you do need to quit giving advice to the people who raised you," Louise said, pointing a finger at her. "You haven't lived long enough to earn your DIO degree."

"What's that?" Bree scoffed.

"A Dish It Out Degree. You won't be qualified for another twenty years."

"So, I'm supposed to just sit by and watch Mom make another mistake and get hurt?"

"Maybe you need to worry a little less about my life and take care of your own," Zona said shortly.

Bree scowled and threw up her hands. "I give up." She walked her half-empty glass back to the kitchen and then walked out the door.

Zona sighed. "What do you think really happened after Cinderella married the prince?"

"She had a couple of kids. He got bored and took a mistress," Louise joked.

"I guess, when it comes right down to it most princes are frogs," said Zona.

"Keep that in mind," Louise cautioned.

"I'm being careful."

"I hope so," Louise said. "But sometimes longing can put a blindfold on you."

"You're right," Zona said.

"I think that's what both Bree and I worry about. I know I jumped to conclusions about Alec James. Over-the-top ones. But that doesn't mean my concerns now aren't justified. Be careful."

"I will," Zona said, and that was the end of the conversation.

Louise could only hope her daughter would be as careful as she promised to be. Sadly, it wasn't a very strong hope.

ZONA HAD MEANT what she said. She was enjoying hanging out with Alec, and that kiss they'd shared had taken up residence at the back of her mind, playing like a movie trailer. Maybe someday, if he did prove to be safe, if his stepsister really did vanish from his life, they'd have a chance together.

But contrary to what her daughter thought, Zona's brain wasn't dead. She was going to be careful. And they were going to take things slow.

Meeting Alec for burgers on her lunch break was slow. Training Darling out in the front yard was slow. Going out for drinks was slow. Wanting to snuggle back in his arms was . . . not slow.

No, no, she was okay. She hadn't acted on that desire. She was in charge of her lusty hormones, not the other way around.

She could picture herself and Alec continuing to hang out a couple of times a week as summer moved along, maybe going to the beach on a Saturday afternoon. Her taking him cookies at whatever job site he was working at.

Maybe, just maybe.

She came home from work to learn that Louise was planning a game afternoon the following day for her gang, which had grown to include Gilda.

Cooking was not in Gilda's job description. Neither was running errands, so that left the grocery run to Zona, who found herself wishing her mother had texted her at work rather than waiting until she got home, ready to eat leftover spaghetti before turning into a HopIn driver for the evening.

"I don't suppose you'd make your black bean brownies, would you?" Louise asked as she handed over her debit card.

"No problem," said Zona. When you were living rent free with your mother, you pitched in whenever and wherever needed. And she was happy to. She'd work a longer shift the next night.

So, off she went, to get the needed ingredients. She didn't notice until she pulled into the parking lot of Vons and saw the familiar car pull in after her that she'd been followed. Okay, it was a coincidence, right? Angela had no reason to follow her.

A feeling of unease crept over her, but she shrugged it off. Maybe the woman was staying nearby somewhere and, like Zona, was doing a quick grocery run.

Was there really such a thing as coincidence?

The PT Cruiser drove through the parking lot and exited

back onto the street. Zona frowned. What was that all about? Was Alec's stepsister trying to rattle Zona? If so, why?

Forget about it, she told herself and went into the store.

But ten minutes later she was inspecting avocados when someone ran into her grocery cart, pushing into her hip. What the heck?

There stood Angela, behind an empty cart, wearing a smile that looked downright sinister.

25

THE WOMAN DIDN'T WASTE TIME ON an excuse me or hello. "You need to know something about my brother."

Okay, this was weird. Zona braced herself for whatever Angela was about to share. "What do I need to know?"

"He's not as nice as he seems."

Zona raised an eyebrow. "Oh?"

"He's really good at pretending to care, but he doesn't. He's cruel and violent." She said it so vehemently. Had Alec lied about how he'd treated his stepsister? No, he couldn't have.

"Did he hit you?" Zona asked.

You're hurting me. Angela's words returned and blazed across her mind in giant neon letters. Someone was lying. The possibility that it was Alec made bile rise in Zona's throat.

No, it wasn't possible. He'd told her so much about his family. He couldn't have been lying.

Angela lowered her gaze. Her lower lip began to tremble. "I can't talk about it," she whispered.

Zona struggled to match the Alec James she was coming to know with the picture Angela was painting. "If he was so awful to you, why did you keep coming back?"

"I had no place else to go."

And yet she'd found someplace after Alec had turned her out. And why was she still driving by his house?

"He's the only family I've got. I need him."

Zona frowned. Here was a true false note. "I hear you have a sister in Montana."

Angela shook her head, looked sorrowful. "I can't talk about my sister. She's sick. She's under, uh, care."

Alec hadn't mentioned anything about Ariel being in need of medical supervision. In fact, he'd said she was doing fine.

"You don't know what he's like," Angela insisted. She was so urgent, so sincere.

And she was right about that. Zona had only known Alec for a few weeks. This woman had known him for a lifetime.

"Oh, believe me, he'll be nice to you for a while, then, once he's got you all tied up emotionally, he'll turn on you. Like an adder. He's divorced, you know. That should tell you all you need to know about him."

As if that made him a bad person. As if that made anyone a bad person. Zona's doubt melted into irritation.

"So am I," she said.

Angela was temporarily at a loss for words. But she recovered quickly. "Whatever happened with your husband is nothing like what will happen if you stay with Alec. He's not stable."

Which was what he'd said about Angela. "If he's so dangerous, why do you keep driving down our street? Why are you following me?"

"I'm trying to warn you!" Angela shrieked.

A woman with a small child who was standing nearby picking out lettuce quickly moved away.

Zona was ready to move away, too. "Thanks for the warning," she said, and backed her cart up.

Angela pulled up alongside Zona, her sorrowful expression gone. "I mean it. Stay away from Alec or you'll be sorry."

Zona refused to be intimidated. "Whatever is going on between you and Alec is between you two. Leave me out of it and quit following me."

Angela's eyes narrowed to slits. She stood her ground, glaring at Zona. The mask had slipped.

Okay, enough of this woman. "Move out of my way or I'll call the manager," Zona ordered her.

Angela moved, but her glare remained fixed on Zona, and Zona could feel the heat of it on her back as she walked away.

She threw the rest of her groceries into her cart and stomped to the checkout line. The last thing she'd needed after a long day of work was to get drawn into Alec's drama. Bree was right. She didn't need to be hanging out with this man.

This man who made her skin tingle just thinking about him, who'd rescued her when her car broke down and she was stranded, who Darling was coming to love more than either her mother or her.

Who came with baggage way too heavy for Zona to lift.

They had to stop seeing each other.

Once in the parking lot, she discovered that she had a flat front tire. Slashed. It wasn't hard to figure out who'd done it. Of course, there was no sign of the PT Cruiser in the parking lot. Lucky for Angela because after this act of war Zona was ready to rumble.

"Better hope I don't see your car on my street again," she muttered. She stowed her groceries, then got out her spare tire and got to work. By the time she had it on, she was grimy and sweaty and in need of chocolate. She marched back into the store, where she washed up in the restroom and then bought two packages of Dove dark chocolates.

Gilda was gone when she returned home and Martin had taken her place, bringing pizza. He was camped in the living room with Louise, the TV tuned to an episode of a new detective series they'd discovered.

"Join us and have some pizza," Louise called as Zona made her way to the kitchen.

"No, thanks, I've got stuff to do," Zona called back. Like

devour half a bag of chocolates while she baked for her mother's party and wished horrible fates on the evil Angela. *May all her hair fall out. May she get an incurable case of adult acne.* Too mild. *May she get to star in her own reality show. Prison Babes.* That thought brought a bitter smile to Zona's lips. Yes, let Angela learn how to make license plates or whatever it was women did in prison. Alec should have pressed charges.

Bree was right. Men weren't worth the trouble, even ones that seemed to be good.

She'd finished making tea sandwiches for Louise's party and had pulled out a batch of black bean brownies when a text came in from Alec. Dog training?

No, she texted back. We need to talk.

K. Come on over.

"Is everything okay?" Louise called as Zona headed for the door.

"Everything's fine," Zona answered. It wasn't her happiest tone of voice and her mother probably saw right through it. They'd be having a mother-daughter shrink session at some point, but for the moment Zona kept moving. It was time to end the madness she'd started with Alec.

She was about to walk next door when she spotted the PT Cruiser, parked a little way down the street. She stepped back inside the house.

"That was fast," Louise observed.

"I forgot something," Zona lied. She ducked into the kitchen and called Alec. "Your sister is parked down the street. I'm not coming over."

"Shit," he said.

"She followed me into the grocery store and warned me away from you."

This time he swore. "What exactly did she say?"

"That you're the only family she has. Oh, except for her sister, who is under medical care."

"She's a liar."

"She also told me you're not stable and to stay away, and to make sure I got the message she slashed one of my tires. If I could prove it, I'd call the cops."

There was a long silence before he said, "I'm sorry, Zona. I'll make this right."

The anger leaked out of her, replaced by sadness that this had happened just when she was getting to know Alec and like him. Once again, Cupid had stuck it to her.

"We need to go back to being nothing more than neighbors," she said.

"Do you really want that? I don't. I want to see where this goes. Don't you?"

"I can already tell where it's going," she said.

"Don't give up. Give me a chance to fix this."

"You can't."

"Oh, yes, I can," he growled. "I'll be over in a few."

True to his word, ten minutes later Alec was ringing the doorbell.

Zona led him through the house and out onto the back patio, ignoring her mother's suspicious look and leery, "Hello, Alec."

"This really isn't going to work," she said once they were seated at the patio table.

"Yes, it is," he said. "I talked to her. She's been served that restraining order and I threatened to call the cops on her if she breaks it. She'll stay away now."

"From you maybe, but not from me."

He reached across the table and covered her hand with his big one. It felt comforting, reassuring. She wished she felt reassured.

"I'm sorry. I didn't mean to bring this into your life."

"But you did. Alec, I've had two men turn my world upside down. I'm not up for a third time."

"I promise she'll be gone from now on."

"How are you going to make that happen?"

"I already did. I also told her if she doesn't leave us alone, I'm going to have her arrested for credit card fraud. She knows I mean it this time."

But did he? Probably not. If he meant business, he'd have already turned her in.

"Let's not call it quits before we've barely gotten started," he urged.

"That's the best time to call it quits, before we get any more involved."

"Too late for me," he said. "I'm too into being with you."

She felt the same way, but this was looking like such a high-risk relationship. Inner alarms were going off. Danger, danger. Step away.

"Don't."

"What?" She reined in her wandering thoughts.

"Don't let my crazy stepsister drive you away."

"She's like the dragon at the castle door," said Zona.

"Let's not let her win. Let's take the castle."

"Even if we take the castle, we might find we don't belong there," she said.

"Or we might find we do," he said softly. "Don't give up."

He traced a finger along her chin, leaving a trail of warm tingles. Her eyelids dropped. Almost against her will, she leaned slightly forward. She didn't see the kiss coming, but she felt it, felt the nearness of his mouth. Felt both his hands on the sides of her face, rough but warm. By the time their lips touched, she was already half melted.

She should have kept her resolve and kept her hands to herself, but she didn't. Resolve was highly overrated.

"Come here," he said against her lips, and she shifted from

her chair to his lap, tangling her hands in his hair as their kisses turned white-hot.

"What am I doing?" she said when she came to her senses and pulled away.

"Slaying dragons," he said, and ran his hands up her back and kissed her again.

Zona the dragon slayer finally had to make room for Zona the commonsense woman, and they both left Alec's lap. With great regret.

"Okay, enough of that. I am not going to rush into anything," she informed Alec.

"Okay, no rushing. Let's hang out on Saturday."

Darn it all, why should she have to give up being with Alec? Wasn't she entitled to some happiness after everything she'd been through?

"After my garage sales, and no more of . . . this," she said. Because her brain drained of caution and common sense when he kissed her.

"For a while," he clarified.

"A long while," she said. They'd be hanging out. Like her mother and Martin.

Except there was one very great difference between what was going on with Zona and Alec and what was going on with her mother and Martin. Where Louise was happily keeping Martin in the friends corner, Zona was sure she was not going to be able to succeed at doing that with Alec. There was too much heat between them.

Which meant someone was going to get burned.

"You're right," said Louise, after Martin had left and it was the two of them, sitting on the couch. "You won't be able to keep this platonic. And who could blame you? He's a good-looking man. You're a healthy young woman. It's only natural that you're attracted to each other. But this stepsister of his . . ." Louise shook her head. "She's trouble."

"He says she won't be back."

Louise dismissed that with a disgusted snort. "Of course she will. It's never that easy getting rid of a toxic person. My goodness, think of *Fatal Attraction*. The woman refused to drown and instead came up out of the bathtub with a knife. It's like that in every movie. The good guy thinks he's taken out the bad guy and he hasn't." She held up a staying hand. "And don't say that this isn't the movies. Real life is just as messy and less predictable."

"So I just give up on him?"

"He's got a crazy stepsister who doesn't want you around. Pull the plug."

Zona sighed heavily. Her mother was right. She needed to pull the plug before she drowned. But how did you pull the plug when you didn't want to, when you were keeping your hands behind your back?

26

A WEEK HAD PASSED, AND THE PT Cruiser had not shown up. Angela had not made another surprise attack in the grocery store and Zona's tires were still intact. Alec had paid to replace the one Angela had slashed, and Zona had thanked him by taking him enchiladas, which she'd stayed to help him eat. Everything was working out.

They sat by the pool, enjoying both the enchiladas and the margaritas he'd made to go with them. The early evening was still hot but not unbearably so, since Zona was in shorts, and the sunshine felt good on her shoulders. So did being with this relaxed, happier version of Alec that she'd been coming to know.

"I could get used to this," he said, and smiled at her before forking in another bite.

"Getting meals delivered?" she teased.

"Yeah, that's good, too. But I was thinking more about the company."

She smiled and took a sip of her drink. Crossed one leg over the other and let it swing, admiring her self-administered pedi.

"Do that enough and I'm gonna forget about food," he said, pointing to her bare leg.

"Taking it slow," she reminded him.

"Slow and steady wins the race. That's what my old man used to say." His easy smile turned wistful.

"You miss him."

Alec nodded. "Yeah. He was a great guy. He worked his whole life as a welder. Eventually wound up with lung cancer. He and Mom were savers, and he sent me to college hoping I'd come out and get a high-paying white-collar job. Wanted me to be a lawyer."

"What did you want?"

"Not that. I started working construction the summer after my freshman year. Bagged the whole lawyer thing and decided to get a business degree instead."

"He had to be proud in the end that you built your own business," said Zona.

"Yeah, he was. He got it in his head that I'd build him and Myrna their dream house, but she died before I could."

"That was your stepmom, right? What did she die of?"

"Aneurysm. It broke Dad's heart."

"What happened to your mom?"

"Breast cancer. Lost her when I was eight. Dad made it until I hit middle school and my brother was in grade school, then he got lonely and went looking."

"Wait. What? You have a brother?"

"He's a purser on a cruise ship. We hang out whenever he's in LA."

"So he's not involved with . . ."

"The girls?" Alec gave a bitter chuckle. "No, he was smart. Pulled away and stayed away. Poor Dad. If the cancer hadn't killed him, the stress the steps laid on him would have. Especially Angela. She was out of control even as a kid. But Dad loved Myrna, maybe even more than he loved Mom, so he gave what was left of his heart to the steps."

"That's so . . . tragic," Zona mused.

"Tragic is the mess Dad left me with. The girls were in their teens when their mom died and out of school when Dad packed it in. Ariel got it together, but Angela never did. Obviously. I did what I could for her, footed the bill for her traffic tickets, paid overdue rent, got her out of a bad relationship, you name it, I did it. But now I'm done. She's sucked me dry. Sorry, Dad." Alec downed the last of his drink. "I need another one of these. Want one?"

"No, thanks," she said. One drink was enough. Just being with Alec went to her head. She didn't need to add more alcohol to the equation.

He went back inside the house and left her still trying to digest the sad family saga he'd shared. It was a messy, tragic one, and the responsibility he'd shouldered had left its mark on him. Cost him his marriage.

"What would you do differently if you could go back in time?" she asked when he returned.

"I'd have taken my wife and moved far away. You know what they say on planes, put your own oxygen mask on first. I never did."

"Maybe that makes you noble," Zona suggested.

"No, it leaves me suffocating." He dug into the last of his enchiladas. "There's a difference between being useful and letting yourself be used. I think I've finally figured that out."

"Why does life have to be so hard?" Zona mused.

"Dunno. Probably the bigger question is why do we make it even harder?"

"I'm done with that," she said firmly.

"Me, too. I am ready to have some fun. Baseball games, backyard barbecues, Super Bowl parties. Maybe even learn to dance. How does that sound?"

She smiled. "You had me at dance."

No, he had her at the way he was looking at her. It goosed up her heart rate and her body heat climbed another six degrees. He had the kind of body a woman couldn't help wanting to claim, and even more attractive, the heart beating inside it appeared to be supersized. Was he someone she could safely move forward with or would he land her in another smelly mess?

She bit down on her lip and studied the pool. The turquoise water looked so calm and inviting. Rather like the future Alec was painting.

But people drowned in pools.

"You make starting over sound so easy," she said. "It's not."

"I know it's not. But it beats staying stuck in one place."

"What if the place you're stuck in is safe?" Zona argued.

"A padded cell is safe."

She laughed at that. "Oh, now, there's an interesting metaphor."

"Okay, the womb is safe."

"Very poetic," she said.

"Yeah, that's me. Like it or not, at some point you get pushed out. From then on, what happens is up to you. You can't hide forever, Zona."

She frowned at him. "I'm not hiding. I'm rebuilding. And I'm doing it very carefully, making sure this time that I've got a solid foundation. How's that for a metaphor?"

"Pretty impressive," he said with a nod. "Building is a lot of work, and a lot of doing. You can't squat on a foundation forever because you're worried the walls will fall in on you if you put them up."

The walls had fallen in on her twice before. "I'm afraid." The words crept out on a whisper.

He reached over and laid that big, solid hand of his on top of hers. "I know you are."

"I don't know you, not really."

She'd seen his temper. What else could set it off besides his out of control stepsister? Was he solid and trustworthy or was he truly a Jekyll and Hyde? People were so good at hiding their true selves.

"You keep saying that, but I hope you're starting to." He studied her a moment. "What's got you worried? Be honest."

"I've seen an angry side to you. What brings it out besides your stepsister?"

He thought a moment. "Being lied to, being used, lazy workers. Cheaters." He half smiled. "Seeing the Dodgers lose."

"Dogs pooping on your lawn," she added.

"Yeah, that."

"You yell a lot."

"I yell a lot at Angela," he corrected.

"Did you yell at your wife?"

"Once. When she got rid of my favorite jeans. I apologized later," he quickly added.

That seemed like a small offense. Zona frowned. "Were there times you didn't yell at her when you wanted to?"

"When she wrecked the car. I was just relieved she wasn't hurt. Oh, yeah, and when we were first married, she sucked at budgets, always overspent. That made me crazy, but I never yelled. Nagged a lot, but never yelled."

"I yell," Zona confessed.

"Yeah? What makes you yell?"

She could almost see a reflection of her exes' faces on the surface of the water. "Cheating and lying. I yelled at my first husband because he thought it was okay to cheat on me. I yelled at Gary because his gambling ruined our lives."

"I'd have done more than yell," said Alec.

"I managed to forgive Luke. God only knows how. But Gary . . ." Her eyes narrowed at the memory of what he'd done, and her fists clenched. "I can't forgive him. He stole from me. And from Bree. That was the worst. He made a mess of our lives and I'm still cleaning it up."

Alec nodded. "I feel the same way about Angela. Only difference is I caught her before she could totally screw me over."

"I felt . . . violated," Zona confessed.

"But you're moving on," he pointed out.

"On my own. How do I dare do that with someone?"

He took a deep breath. "Therapy? Hire a hit man?"

"Don't tempt me."

"Look, I don't exactly know how we get those two out of our heads, but we can't let them keep hanging on to us. I say we leave 'em in the dust. We break the rearview mirror, rev the engine, and go for it."

"You know, for a builder you do have a way with words," she said.

"I have a way with my hands, too," he said. He gave her a full smile and, once more, her body temperature shot up.

Maybe she was ready to rev her engine.

"AS LONG AS you're taking it slow, you'll be fine," Gracie assured her when they met for coffee.

But the more time Zona spent with Alec the more tempted she was to forget going slow and race forward. Until she envisioned that horrible moment when she'd discovered the savings for Bree's college fund had been drained, the moment when the truth came out and she learned that Gary had taken them to a very high cliff and pulled them all off it. After that it wasn't hard at all to put on the brakes.

GARY SHOWED UP at Louise's house on a Thursday right after Zona had gotten home from work, an unwelcome ghost from the past. She was about to put together a shrimp salad for Louise and Gilda, and Martin, who had been invited to hang around for dinner and a movie, then planned to work a shift for HopIn. Gilda had been anxious to indulge her sweet tooth and had gone to fetch something for dessert and Martin hadn't yet arrived, so it was just Zona and Louise in the house when the knock on the door came.

Assuming it was Martin, Zona opened the door with a

smile on her face. The smile got gobbled by a glare the second she saw Gary standing there. The smile he'd been trying for collapsed.

"What are you doing here?" Her words came out like shards of ice.

"Can I come in for a minute?"

"No."

He took in a deep breath, resigned to the stony welcome he was receiving. "Okay. I won't stay long."

"You won't stay at all. Why are you here, Gary?"

He cleared his throat, pulled a check out of his slacks pocket. "I have something for Bree." He held it out to Zona.

She took it. It was for seven hundred dollars. Surprise and anger cycloned through her. It was so little compared to what he'd taken. If he was looking for gratitude, he was going to be disappointed.

He spoke before she could say anything. "I know it's not much. But I wanted to prove to her, to both of you, that I'm going to make things right."

"Why didn't you give it to her?" Silly question. Bree had blocked him from her phone. She wouldn't welcome him at work any more than she'd take a call from him.

"Frankly, I figured if I showed up at Starbucks, she'd throw hot coffee on me and end up getting fired."

"If she did, I wouldn't blame her," Zona said.

He nodded, dropped his gaze. "I wouldn't, either. I've joined Gamblers Anonymous, Zona."

If only he'd done that before he'd taken a wrecking ball to their lives.

"I'm sorry for the hurt I caused you and Bree. We had a good thing, and I screwed it up."

"Yeah, you did," she said.

Louise chose that moment to come swinging down the

hall, ready to greet Martin. She stopped at the sight of Gary standing at her front door. "Gary," she said in disgust.

"Hi, Louise. How are you?" he ventured.

"On crutches, that's how I am," she said, her words clipped. "Why are you here?"

"I'm working on changing my life for the better. I brought a check for Bree," he added, probably fearing Zona wouldn't share that info.

"Good. I'm glad to see you're trying to make up for your past mistakes."

Mistakes. Was that what you called what he'd done? "Gary was just leaving," Zona said, and started to shut the door.

"Zona, wait," he begged.

"What?" She kept her hold on the door, ready to slam it.

Louise hovered behind her. Darling came running up and Zona stepped outside to finish their conversation.

"I need you to know how sorry I am, and I'm hoping you can, somehow, forgive me for what I did. I honestly didn't mean to hurt you," Gary said, sounding so sincere.

"But you did."

"I was going to replace the money."

She didn't bother to ask how. "But you didn't."

"It's a sickness."

"And you let it grow until it killed everything we had, Gary. How am I supposed to get past that?" *Break the rearview mirror, rev the engine.*

"Maybe you can't. I don't blame you." He pointed to the check in her hand. "But I'm going to spend the rest of my life making up for everything, I promise."

It was a beginning. He had good intentions, but who knew if he'd follow through on them. It was a lot of money to pay back.

She held up the check. "I'll give this to Bree." She didn't add a thank-you. It wasn't a gift.

Louise was seated at the dining table, on a chair nearest the door, when Zona stepped back in. "Okay, what was all that about?" she asked.

"He wanted me to hug him and tell him what a good boy he is," Zona said, and showed Louise the check.

"It's something, and something is better than nothing."

"Which is what he left us with."

"He's trying to make amends," Louise pointed out.

"Too little, too late."

"Was this a onetime deal?"

"No, he says there'll be more," Zona said. "He's joined Gamblers Anonymous."

"Good for him."

"Yeah, good for him. Why couldn't he have done that before ruining our lives?" Zona demanded.

"Because he couldn't see that he was ruining your lives," Louise suggested.

"Oh, he could see," Zona said bitterly.

"Sometimes people have to hit rock bottom before they can really take stock of where they are. It looks like that's what happened with Gary. At least he's working on making things right. Maybe you could work on forgiving him just a little."

"He devastated me, Mom. And now here he is with his little check, hoping I'll give him absolution. It's like somebody stabbing you multiple times and then visiting you in the hospital with flowers."

"We all get stabbed by someone sooner or later."

Those were not the words Zona wanted to hear. "You know, it wasn't so long ago that you were wishing all kinds of bad things on him."

"You're right," Louise admitted. "I hated him for what he'd done to you, and I wasn't happy to see him at the door just now. But this is a new Gary, trying to make things right. Maybe it's time to forgive him."

Zona gave a disgusted huff. "How am I supposed to do that?"

Louise shrugged. "Don't give him any more headspace. Quit looking back. After all, you can't change the past. Be thankful he's at least trying to improve your future. Just don't depend on him for it."

Break the rearview mirror. Rev the engine. Run over Gary's foot as you drive away.

"I'll think about it," Zona said.

Maybe it was time to get Gary out of her head. She didn't need him in there, messing with her decision-making gears.

Zona texted Bree that there was a check waiting for her at Gram's and got busy getting dinner ready. She doubted seeing a small check from her former stepdad would soften Bree's heart toward him any more than it had hers. Either way they'd take the money.

Gilda arrived with cupcakes from Crust & Crumble, with Martin on her heels bringing wine and a DVD.

"What are you guys watching tonight?" Zona asked him.

He held it up. *"Invitation to a Murder."*

"Charming," she said. "Just make sure Mom doesn't accept the invitation."

He chuckled. "Your poor mother. She's never going to live down her mistaken assumptions about Alec James."

"Afraid not," Zona agreed.

Louise had arrived to greet him and in time to overhear their conversation. "I wasn't all wrong. There was trouble over there."

"Well, there's not now, so you can put away the crazy," Zona told her.

Louise scowled. "I have never been crazy. Mistaken maybe. But not crazy. Or senile," she added.

Zona was glad to see Louise had gotten rid of that worry. And no, her mother wasn't crazy. Just a little . . . overimaginative.

She left them to their murder and went off to do a shift in her car.

It felt like a sick coincidence when the next evening she was at the Ontario airport, dropping off a traveler, and saw Gary pull up in front of the rideshare pickup curb to meet someone. She unloaded her passenger, then drove past him, keeping her eyes looking straight ahead. She could almost feel him knocking at the back of her mind, asking to come in and stir up her anger.

Sorry, no headspace available.

27

ZONA'S FRIDAY NIGHT AS A RIDESHARE driver turned out to be uneventful. But it did give her a ringside seat into relationships, both troubled and happy. She dropped off a trio of girlfriends, perfumed and giggly and ready for a fun night out.

"We're going gunting," one explained.

Guy hunting. That was a distant memory for Zona, but she could still almost recapture the excitement of going out with friends, looking forward to dancing and flirting and laughing the night away.

The mother in her couldn't help cautioning, "You all be careful."

"Oh, we are," said one of them as she shut her designer purse. "We've got each other's backs. We're the three muskrats."

"Musketeers, Mimi," one of her friends corrected. "Sheesh."

"Sorry," Mimi said, sounding far from it.

"We've got you, anyway," said her other friend, obviously the peacemaker. "Thanks," she chirped as they slid out of the car.

"Have fun," Zona said.

They hadn't heard. They were already in party mode, chattering excitedly.

Zona couldn't help feeling a tiny bit jealous. It was great to be young, with no worries, no problems.

Although youth was no guarantee of a carefree life. Her own daughter was a shining example of that.

Another ride request came on her app and she accepted it. Where the girls had been happy and bubbly, this thirty-something couple were tense and silent. Angry vibes got into the car along with them and swirled up to where Zona sat behind the wheel.

She couldn't help taking a spying peek in her rearview mirror. Both had their lips pressed into angry lines. His jaw was clenched as he faced the window, determined not to look the woman's direction.

"You better have this figured out before we get to your mom's," the woman hissed.

He said nothing. Just clamped his molars down harder.

Zona pulled up in front of a modest house in City of Hope and they both got out opposite sides of the car. He shut his door, she slammed hers.

"Have a good night," Zona muttered as she drove away.

If it weren't for men like Martin, Zona would be tempted to believe her daughter's claim that all men were jerks. *And Alec*, she added. He was looking more and more like the kind of solid man a woman could count on. A heart healer and not a heartbreaker. She was so ready to be healed.

He'd taken her for an early dinner before she started work, and the kiss they'd shared had gone a long way toward cauterizing her emotional wounds. Snugged up against that hard, muscled body, she'd felt like she was in a fortress. And yet she feared to get her hopes up.

Her next ride was another couple, this one middle-aged. The woman talked all the way to the restaurant that was their destination. The husband, like the man before him, said nothing, preferring to look out the window rather than engage with his wife.

Zona wondered if what she'd witnessed between those couples was a normal occurrence or if she'd caught them in a moment where they simply weren't at their best. She'd have liked to think it was the latter but suspected it was the former. She could almost hear her daughter saying, "See? This is why you don't want to get involved with anyone ever again."

But then she picked up the sweet older couple. He was wearing a suit, and she had a gardenia corsage on the dressy jacket over her cocktail dress that filled the car with fragrance. He had only a few strands of hair left on his head, and she looked like a walking bed pillow. Both of them were beaming, and the minute they got in the car they held hands. They were adorable.

Their destination, The Penthouse in the Huntley Hotel in Santa Monica. Gary had taken Zona there once. The view from the eighteenth floor had been breathtaking, with the Pacific Ocean stretching out forever, and the food had been delicious. The whole evening had been romantic.

"It's our fifty-second anniversary," the woman informed Zona.

"Wow, congratulations," Zona replied.

"Last year we took the family on a cruise," her husband said. "This year we're doing something just the two of us."

"You've picked a great restaurant," Zona said.

"A great restaurant for a great woman," said the husband.

The warmth in his voice left Zona wishing she'd found a man like him on her first try.

"So, what's your secret to a long and happy marriage?" she asked.

"Simple," replied the husband. "Always love the other person more than you love yourself."

"Simple but not easy." It hadn't been for her husbands.

"Oh, he didn't say it's easy," put in the wife. "Every relationship takes work. But if you care about the person, you'll be willing to roll up your sleeves and do it. Are you married?" she asked.

"I'm divorced," Zona said. It felt like a shameful thing to

admit to this couple who had worked hard at creating a happy marriage.

"I am sorry," said the woman. "I hope you'll find someone who's willing to do the work with you. It's worth it."

"Sure is," said her husband.

They arrived at the hotel. "Have a lovely time," Zona said as the man came around the car to help his wife out.

"Oh, we will," said the woman. "And you have a lovely life."

A lovely life. What would that look like? Baseball games, backyard barbecues, Super Bowl parties. Dance lessons.

Well, who knew? Maybe.

SATURDAY MORNING IT was time for Zona to focus on her other side hustle. Even though she and Martin and her mom had left early, the garage sale scene was in full swing.

Zona was quick to scoop up a mid-century modern starburst clock. People loved those and she was sure she'd get a lot more for it than the twenty-five dollars the seller was asking. She also found a vintage Lorus watch featuring Mickey Mouse. Score.

Two more garage sales proved to be worth their time also. Zona found a purse and a Fitz and Floyd cookie jar shaped like an ice cream truck. Louise was happy with her sequined top and the same Betty Crocker children's cookbook she'd had as a child.

"You going to make some of those recipes?" Zona teased as they waited for Martin to move the car from where he'd had to park it a block down the street.

"I just might," Louise said. "Or I might save it and make something with a great-grandchild someday."

"I hope you're not holding your breath on that one. Bree's sworn off men. Remember?"

"The young vow all kinds of things," Louise said, still confident in a happily-ever-after for Bree.

"I'd rather see her single than miserable," Zona said.

"Who says she has to be miserable?" Louise argued. "I wasn't with your father."

"Men were different back then."

"Men have always been men. You just have to know how to separate the wheat from the chaff."

"Someone ought to teach a course in that," Zona muttered as Martin pulled up.

After their last stop, they went home via In-N-Out. They chatted and laughed and Louise complimented Martin on the half dozen Nancy Drew books he'd found.

"Little Hildy is going to love them. You're a good grandpa," she said, and he beamed.

They were so cute together. Zona was going to have to have another talk with her mother about paying attention to the perfect man who was right under her nose.

She forgot all about that plan when they got home. Louise was concentrating on swinging herself up the front walk and Martin was next to her. Neither was paying attention to what sat in the driveway, but Zona saw it as she walked past. An ugly slash ran all along the driver side of her car.

She hurried inside the house, set down her purchases, and then went back out. Walking around the car she saw the passenger side had been vandalized as well. It had clearly been keyed.

Something cold stole over Zona and grabbed her heart. There was only one logical suspect.

When had she done this? It had to have been a quick job, done while they were out hitting garage sales.

This woman didn't hesitate to destroy property. What else wouldn't she hesitate to do? A fresh chill stole over Zona. What would follow this malicious act if Zona continued to see Alec? What or who would be the next target? Maybe Darling. Maybe Mom. For sure, Zona.

"I'll see you tomorrow," Martin said to Louise and started down the front walk. Then he stopped and stared at Zona's car. "When did this happen?"

"Probably when we were out. Don't tell Mom. She'll just worry."

"You need to report that," he said.

"I'm going to, right now," she assured him.

So much for being rid of Alec's stepsister. So much for the happy interlude they'd been enjoying.

Underneath that calm, the Loch Ness Monster was thrashing around, ready to surface and devour her.

What turned people so toxic, and was there ever a way you could pull the toxin out? In the case of this woman, that would be impossible.

She pulled her phone from her jeans pocket, took pictures, then went online and filed a police report. Even though she couldn't prove who the vandal was, the crime still needed to be reported. And she'd need the report for her insurance company.

Back in the house, she casually asked Louise if she could borrow her car for the evening. "Mine's low on gas."

A flimsy excuse, but Louise didn't hesitate to say yes. "I'm not going anywhere," she said.

It was hard to concentrate on cleaning and putting her latest finds up on eBay. She'd look at her computer screen and see her damaged car. Then she'd see red. Angela had better stay hidden, because if she didn't, Zona was going to take her down.

ZONA WAS IN the kitchen, working on a chicken stir-fry when Gilda arrived for Louise patrol. Zona could hear her in the living room, talking to her mother. A moment later she heard the clomp clomp of Louise's crutches.

"Why didn't you tell me your car had been keyed?" Louise demanded.

So, Gilda had seen. Thank you, Gilda.

"Not much you could do about it. Not much I can do right now, either," said Zona.

"So, you're not out of gas," Louise accused.

"That, too," Zona lied.

"People who destroy property ought to have it done to theirs as punishment," said loose lips Gilda, who'd followed Louise into the kitchen.

"You know who it is, don't you?" Louise said to Zona.

"I'm pretty sure it's Alec's stepsister," Zona said. "But I can't prove anything."

"You should report it to the police," said Gilda.

"I've filed a report."

Louise's eyes narrowed. "That woman is dangerous! You need to quit hanging out with Alec James."

Gilda was all ears. "The neighbor? We knew he was trouble all along, didn't we?"

"Look, you two. I can handle this," Zona said, and gave the sliced bell peppers, carrots, and onions in her mother's electric wok an angry shove.

"I bet that's what the woman in LA said right before she got cut up and stuck in the freezer," Gilda said.

"I'm going over there," Louise announced.

Okay, enough was enough. "You are not. I'll handle this myself. Gilda, take over," she said, walking away from her dinner in progress. "I've got to get ready to go to work."

"Me! I don't know how to make stir-fry," Gilda protested.

"It's easy. You stir it," Zona said, her irritation with Gilda bleeding through. "If you get stuck, Mom can help you She's an expert when it comes to knowing what people should do." Silence fell in the kitchen as Zona stormed out.

She brushed her teeth, put on some jeans and a top, and then hurried downstairs. She could smell sesame oil and frying onions as she grabbed Louise's car keys from the bowl on the small table by the door.

Her mom wasn't any good at stir-fry. She always overcooked everything, but she and Gilda would have to cope because Zona had no intention of returning to the kitchen and being served a lecture. She didn't need it. She already knew what she had to do.

She had to get to work, so it would have to wait until Sunday. Dealing with this required a face-to-face conversation.

BREE STOPPED BY her grandmother's house to pick up the check Gary had left for her and found Gram and Gilda seated at the kitchen table with a plate of cookies and two glasses of milk, playing cards.

"The check from Gary is on the buffet," Gram said. "Want to stay and play?"

This was what Bree's Saturday nights had come to, cards with her grandma. But, oh, well, she liked hanging out with Gram.

"We'll start over," said Gilda, scooping up the cards.

"Handy for you, since you were losing," Gram teased.

Bree went to the buffet and picked up the check and frowned at it. *Big frickin' deal, Gary.*

"He probably felt real proud of himself for coming up with that money," she said to Gram as she went to pour herself a glass of milk. He probably hoped she'd feel grateful. She didn't.

He'd stolen from her. The fact that he'd done it legally didn't change how wrong it had been, and it didn't change her feelings toward him.

"It's something," Gram said.

"Loser," Gilda muttered.

Somewhere along the way Gilda had become like a member of the family. It seemed she knew all their dirt. But so what? The more people who knew what a rat Gary was the better.

"Compared to what he owes me, it's nothing," Bree said. "It's you and Mom who came through for me. You guys are the true heroes."

"Take the money anyway," Gilda advised.

"Oh, I will, believe me. I hope if he keeps paying Mom can ease up." Gary had done the crime and Mom was doing the time. Not fair at all.

"She wants to do it for you."

"She has no life," Bree said. It was sad, and it was all Gary's fault.

"She has one with our neighbor," Gram said with a frown.

Bree mirrored it. She wanted her mom to have a fun life and do stuff, just not with a man.

"There's something off there," Gilda said with a knowing nod.

"I don't like what comes with him," Gram said, and proceeded to tell Bree about the vandalism the woman had done to Mom's car.

"You're kidding me." Bree felt stupid for having missed seeing it. Then she felt angry.

With a woman like that coming after her, Mom had to be out of her mind to want to be with Alec James. At least Gary was able to admit he had a gambling addiction. Mom had a love addiction and refused to see it.

"I've tried to warn her, but she won't listen," Gram said.

"Then we'll have to make her," Bree said. "We'll do an intervention."

"An intervention," Gram repeated.

"Yeah, both of us at the same time. Kind of like what you and Mom like to do to me," Bree added.

"I don't know," Gram said, shaking her head.

"Well, I do. Come on, Gram. That woman is obviously crazy. And she's jealous. Who knows what she could do to Mom?"

"Your mother's not going to like this," Gram predicted.

"Nobody likes it." But you had to do what you had to do. "I'll come over tomorrow."

"I don't think she's ready for an intervention," Gilda cautioned. "Your mom already has a bee in her britches from your grandmother trying to talk to her today."

"We can't just sit by and do nothing," Bree argued.

"You're right there. Glad I won't be around to see it though," said Gilda.

ZONA'S PASSENGERS WERE all cheery and happy, out for a night of fun or off to the airport and chattering all the way. One woman, trying to be friendly, asked Zona how she liked her job.

Normally Zona would have replied that she enjoyed meeting so many nice people because, for the most part, her passengers had been nice. This night she was in no mood for chitchat.

"It helps pay the bills," she said shortly.

"That's a good thing, right?" the woman persisted.

Zona merely nodded and the woman got the message and settled back against the seat. There would be no tip coming from this passenger, but Zona didn't care.

She packed it in at half past eleven and pulled up to her mother's house. She could see the light from the TV glowing behind the sheers pulled across the window, and the shadow of two heads. Heaven only knew what those two were watching.

She was pulling into the driveway when she caught sight of the PT Cruiser sneaking up from around the corner. Oh, no. Not tonight.

She grabbed her phone, pushed open the car door, and raced down the sidewalk, phone pointed at the car like a gun.

Angela saw her coming and floored it.

"I know it was you!" Zona hollered, aiming her phone. "You'll pay for this!"

The car disappeared around the corner and Zona stopped her running, adrenaline racing through her veins. She checked the photo. A little blurry, due to the lack of light, but it would do.

If she collected enough pictures of Angela misbehaving, maybe she could get a stalking order of protection.

Although soon Angela wouldn't be an issue because Zona and Alec wouldn't be an item.

Still buzzing with adrenaline, Zona went back to her mother's car and put it in the garage. Darling heard her enter the house and went racing to greet her, barking all the way.

"Good grief, you scared us," said Louise as Zona entered the living room.

"If you'd stop watching murder and mayhem, you wouldn't scare so easily," Zona retorted irritably. "Gilda, I'm going to take Darling for a walk and then you can go home."

Gilda nodded. She didn't quite look Zona in the eye. Feeling guilty for her contribution to the family squabble earlier. Well, good. She should feel guilty.

Zona leashed Darling up and they headed down the sidewalk, toward the corner where Angela had disappeared. There was no sign of her car when they rounded the block. Very wise.

28

BY THE TIME ZONA RETURNED, GILDA had on her sweater and her purse was slung over her shoulder. "Good night," she said, still not looking Zona in the eye, then slipped out the front door.

Zona took off Darling's leash and he trotted over to Louise while Zona started for the stairs.

"I don't know why you're so mad at me," Louise called.

Zona stopped on the first stair. "Maybe because I already know what I need to do, and I don't need you telling me."

"Sorry." Louise didn't sound even remotely sorry.

Zona kept walking.

"But I'm worried about you," Louise called after her.

Okay, this conversation was not over. Her mother would pick it up in the morning if they didn't settle things then. Zona turned back and joined Louise on the couch.

"You know I'm right," Louise said softly. "That woman will continue to make your life miserable, and you can't have the man unless you take the woman also."

"I know, Mom. I'm going to cut things off tomorrow."

"Thank God," said Louise.

Zona was feeling far from thankful, but she kissed her mother's cheek, told her she loved her.

"I love you, too," said Louise. "By the way, Bree's coming over for lunch tomorrow," she added. "Maybe you can make that crab quiche you were talking about making."

"I can do that."

Zona would have looked forward to seeing her daughter, but knowing what loomed ahead for the next day took the shine off the prospect of a visit.

If only Alec hadn't moved in next door. She'd have still been miserable, but at least she wouldn't have had false hope piled on top of the misery.

LOUISE WAITED UNTIL Zona was in her bedroom before she called Martin. It was late and he'd probably gone to bed, but she needed to talk to him.

Sure enough, he answered with a sleepy hello.

"Martin, I'm sorry to call you so late."

"No problem. What do you need?"

"I need you to come over for lunch tomorrow. Bree wants to do an intervention with Zona about her seeing Alec and I'm not at all sure this is a good idea. I need backup."

There was a long silence. "Martin?"

"I'll be there," he promised.

"Thank you," she said, relieved.

"But you're right. It's not a good idea," he added.

Maybe not, but they had to do something. No matter what Zona said, it was obvious she'd become attached to their neighbor and by morning her resolve could very well have weakened.

SUNDAYS HAD ALWAYS been easy and pleasant days when Zona was growing up. This Sunday didn't feel either easy or pleasant. Zona went through the motions, creating the quiche her mother had requested. She'd also picked up asparagus when she made her store run, and frozen lemonade, which she'd doctored with some of the lavender from Louise's flowerbed.

Martin was a surprise addition and was the first to arrive, bringing French bread and a box of chocolates. Zona sent him to the living room.

He and Louise chatted out there as Zona put the finishing touches on their lunch. Meanwhile, Zona's stomach tied itself in knots as she thought about what she had to do.

The knots got tighter when Bree arrived. She'd barely kissed Zona hello before saying, "Come out to the dining room. We need to talk."

Zona put the quiche on the counter to set and followed her daughter out of the kitchen. "What's wrong?"

"This is an intervention," Bree said and plopped onto a chair. "Gram, get out here."

Louise was taking her time getting her crutches, Martin hovering next to her.

Zona's brows pulled together. "What?"

"You're about to ruin your life again. You can't see that man," Bree said.

First her mother and now her daughter. "I'm handling it," Zona said, her words clipped.

"No, you're not. You're getting in deeper," Bree insisted, her voice rising. "And what happened to your car, Mom? Don't bother to answer. Gram told me."

Louise slowly made her way to the table. "I'm sorry, Zona. She's been out to get your mother ever since she started seeing Alec," she told Bree.

"What are you thinking, Mom?" Bree demanded. "We need to talk about how you're ruining your life."

Martin was edging toward the door. "I should go."

"No, you shouldn't," Zona told him. "Lunch is ready, and Bree can dish it up. You three go ahead and eat. I need to go take care of something."

"Mom! We're not done," Bree called after her as Zona marched to the front door.

"Yes, we are!" Zona slammed the door shut behind her and launched herself down the walk. She could see the PT Cruiser lurking at the end of the street. She raised a hand and gave Angela the one-fingered salute. Very unladylike, her mother would say. Well, Zona wasn't in the mood to be ladylike, and the obscene gesture felt good.

Up Alec's front walk she went and banged on the front door. He opened it with a smile, but the smile vanished at the sight of the expression on her face.

"We need to talk," she said.

"Whoa, I guess," he said, as she marched past him into the house.

"IS SHE GOING over there?" Bree demanded.

"Let's eat on the patio," Louise suggested. Zona had been determined to handle her problem herself, but it couldn't hurt to have some listening ears on the other side of the fence. She shoved her cell phone in her sweater pocket and started for the back door. "Bring the quiche and the dishes, you two. And the asparagus."

"Maybe we should eat inside," Martin suggested, but Louise kept on going.

"I WAS ABOUT to call you," Alec said.

She got right to it. "Your stepsister keyed my car."

"What? Here, sit down, let's talk."

Zona kept pacing. "I didn't sign up for this, Alec."

"Okay, calm down. Go on out by the pool. I'll make us something to drink."

Zona was pacing in front of the pool when he joined her, carrying two margaritas. "I guess we could use this," he said, handing one to her.

She set it on the patio table. "Alec, I can't do this anymore."

His brows lowered. "What? Us? Not this again."

"Yes, this again. The good news is we hadn't gotten too far into a relationship."

Only far enough that she'd hoped the third time would be the charm.

He set his drink down and led her to a chair and sat down opposite her. "I'll pay to have your car refinished."

"It's more than the car, and we both know it," she said miserably.

"I'll take care of it."

Zona threw up her hands. "You can't keep taking care of everything she does. She obviously sees me as a threat and she's not going to stop doing this crazy stuff until she drives me away. Who knows what she'll do next or who she'll do it to?"

"She'll do nothing. I'll get her out of our lives for good."

Zona shook her head. "You're not going to be able to succeed and I can't deal with another messed-up relationship. Right now she's parked down the street."

"I won't let her do anything."

"She already has!"

He caught Zona's hands and held them. "Zona, don't give up on us. You're the best thing that's happened to me in a long time. I want to be the same for you," he added softly.

"Isn't that sweet."

Both Zona and Alec turned at the sound of the sneering voice. There stood Angela at the edge of the patio, glaring at them. She wore a crop top and booty shorts, and her red hair was caught up in a sloppy bun. Just your average girl-next-door type, complete with crazed expression.

"This is the real reason why you couldn't be bothered to help a family member in need, why you wanted me out of your place. It was because of this gold-digging piece of trash."

"Need?" Alec roared. "In need of a new cell phone, clothes, on top of that car I got you. You're a leech, Angela. You always have been, and I'm done with you sucking me dry."

"I needed help!" she cried, her voice rising. "And every time I had to beg you. What would Daddy say?"

He glared and pointed a finger at her. "Don't you dare bring my father into this."

"He was my father, too!" she cried, moving closer toward them. "And he'd hate what you've done to me. A restraining order against your own sister? You're a monster."

Zona couldn't keep quiet any longer. "No, you're the monster. You vandalized my car. Twice. And guess what. I've made a police report, and I've got a picture of you stalking me."

"A picture of me in my car?" scoffed Angela. "Big deal. And *someone* vandalized your car, but who knows who that was. And who knows what might happen next. Maybe your stupid dog will die."

As if he'd understood the threat, Darling began barking from the other side of the fence.

Zona jumped out of her chair, took a threatening step in Angela's direction, and pointed a finger at her. "Just try it and see what happens to you."

Angela wasn't threatened. Instead, she let out a growl and ran at Zona, closing the distance between them, and gave Zona a hard push, sending her into the pool with a screech.

"OKAY, WE'RE CALLING the police," Louise said, pulling out her cell phone.

"They'll never get here in time," said Bree. She shot out of her chair and raced around the side of the house toward the fence gate, Darling following after her.

"Martin, do something!" Louise cried. Of course, Martin the milk toast wouldn't do anything even though both Louise's daughter and now her granddaughter were in danger. And her dog.

She was reaching for her crutches when, to her surprise, Martin transformed into Super Martin and ran off after Bree and Darling. Who knew Martin was capable of running so fast?

Well, Louise wasn't going to sit all by herself, unable to see what was happening next door. She put in a call to 911, then grabbed her crutches and got going.

ZONA HAD SPENT her adult life getting taken advantage of, first by a cheater, then by a gambler, and now this little beast had just pushed her in a pool. This wasn't over. She found her footing and started for the side of the pool. Angela was history.

Alec was leaning over the edge, his hand extended to help Zona out. "Take my hand."

Behind him, Angela picked up a nearby deck chair and swung it.

"Alec, look out!" Zona cried.

Too late. He wasn't able to completely dodge the chair, and the impact sent him into the pool as well. The chair went sailing off to the side.

With a roar, Zona pushed herself up out of the pool. Angela let out a squeal and bolted toward the gate.

Bree had come in and was posed in front of it like a goalie, but Angela never made it that far. Zona was super fueled with anger seeing this woman who was dead set on ruining the lives of everyone around her charge toward her daughter. She reached the woman first, caught her by the hair, and yanked her toward the pool.

"You're hurting me!" Angela cried and tried to pull away.

"You haven't begun to see hurt yet," Zona snarled. She took Angela by the shoulders and hurled her like a giant discus toward the pool.

BREE HAD COME through the backyard gate in time to see the red-haired woman try to break their neighbor's back with a plastic deck chair, then watch her mother surface from the pool right after he landed in it.

Mom looked like some sort of angry sea goddess, rising out of the water. Before Bree could get to the woman, Mom had her by the hair. She threw the redhead into the pool and jumped in after her. The two were under for only a second before they popped back up. Mom with a fresh fistful of the woman's hair, and the redhead screeching swear words at her and shoving her hand in Mom's face.

Mom had been through enough. No one was going to mess with her from now on if Bree had anything to say about it. She raced for the pool and cannonballed in, colliding with Alec James, who was also trying to get to Mom.

"Get out of the way," he commanded.

She snapped back something Gram would wash her mouth out for, but so what? This was her mom. And he was part of the problem.

Just as Bree lunged for the home invader to push her under, what felt like a baby whale landed practically on top of her. Martin? Next in was Darling, entering with an excited bark, scrambling over Martin's shoulders and dunking him in an effort to reach Mom.

It was getting crowded in the pool as they all thrashed around, grabbing for each other, and someone's elbow caught Bree in the eye, making her yelp. Mom.

"Bree, are you okay?" Mom cried, turning to her, and the red-haired pool monster pushed her under.

Bree swore and took a swing at the woman, catching Martin in the jaw, making him grunt.

"Bree, we've got this," he said tersely, as Mom fell against him and knocked him back and under the water.

Gram appeared, waving one of her crutches and yelling, "Hurt my daughter and I'll sue you!"

Bree was still trying to get a hand in as the two men worked to separate Mom and her attacker when two policemen arrived on the scene. "It's about time you got here," Gram said to them.

The one, an older hefty dude, just shook his head. "Okay. Everybody out of the pool."

29

EVERYONE CROWDED AROUND THE OFFICERS, ONE giant, dripping amoeba, talking at once, while Darling shook himself dry, then ran around the edges, forgetting his training and trying to jump on everyone.

"Darling, sit," Alec commanded when Darling tried for attention by jumping on the older policeman. Darling sat with a whine.

"Officer Mead, arrest that woman," Louise said to Darling's new friend, not bothering to specify which woman.

"She assaulted me," insisted Angela, pointing to Zona.

"No, you assaulted me," said Zona.

"I have a restraining order against this woman," said Alec, pointing to Angela, "and she's obviously broken it."

"And she hit him with a chair," added Zona.

Officer Mead held up a hand. "Okay, one at a time." He turned his attention to Alec. "You say you have a restraining order."

"He didn't mean it," Angela protested, and her lower lip began to wobble. She pulled her sodden hair out of her eyes and squeezed out a tear.

Zona took in the tat on her arm, a cute little fairy. Ha! It should have been a demon.

"I did mean it," Alec said calmly. "And she also assaulted both myself and my neighbor here. She pushed Zona in the pool, and she whacked me with that chair."

"Would you like to press charges?" Officer Mead asked both Zona and Alec.

Zona had had enough. Of everything.

She shook her head, but Alec said an emphatic, "Yes."

"What about her? She assaulted me," Angela cried, pointing to Zona.

"She went after my mom first. I saw it," said Bree, narrowing her eyes at Angela.

"Officer, I want to press charges on assault, and on identity theft," Alec continued. "This woman used my name without my permission to get a credit card and then went on a spending spree."

Angela gaped at him. Then she went from gaping to red-faced fury. "You bastard! You would do this to your own sister?"

"Only by marriage," he said. "I'm sorry, Angela, but someone should have reined you in long ago. It's time. You're out of control."

"I hate you," she screamed, and rushed at him, hand raised.

"Whoa, that will be enough of that," said Officer Mead, catching her by the arm.

"This is all your fault, you bitch," Angela informed Zona.

"That's enough, young lady," Officer Mead said to her. "Okay. Folks, we'll take your statements and then you can all go home."

The younger officer cuffed Angela, who had gone from sobbing to wailing, and led her off to wait in the patrol car while Officer Mead did cleanup duty, taking everyone's statements.

Zona, Martin, Louise, and Bree all gave theirs. Once done with them, the officer sent them on their way, remaining to talk further with Alec. And that closed the book on the almost love story of Zona Hartman and Alec James.

"Mom, you were a beast," said Bree, full of admiration as

they all dripped their way across Alec's front lawn toward Louise's house.

"I'm done being a victim," said Zona. The adrenaline was still coursing through her veins and she was ready to karate chop through an entire tower of cement blocks.

"Good for you," said Louise.

"You should have seen her, Gram," said Bree. "It was totally dope. Awesome. Like women's wrestling. Mom, the way you took down that woman, you could be a WOW."

Zona smiled. Yes, that had been satisfying. "Thanks, daughter." She saw the skin around Bree's eye was turning red. It looked like it would soon be blooming into a black eye. "I'm so sorry about your eye."

"It's no big deal," Bree said. Then added, "I'm sorry about . . . everything."

"That's life," Zona said stoically. "But you can't keep a good woman down, right? Not even in a pool."

"You got that right," said Bree.

Zona lowered her voice so Louise and Martin, who were walking a couple of steps ahead of them, couldn't hear. "And, by the way, you can be glad your Gram didn't hear some of those choice words you said in the pool."

Bree grinned. "Heat of the moment." She, too, lowered her voice. "It looks like Martin got some superhero points with Gram."

Louise had an arm linked through his and was smiling up at him. Her words drifted back to them. "You were so brave."

"Brave? He almost drowned us," Bree whispered, and Zona laughed.

"It's all good," she said, but then sobered at the knowledge that what had looked like such a promising beginning with Alec was at an end. And what an ugly end it had been. It wasn't all good, not even close.

Bree picked up on her changed mood. "This kills things

with the neighbor, right? Unless you want his sister to come after you with a piece of broken mirror."

"Stepsister," Zona corrected.

"Maleficent," Bree said. "You don't need a man to be happy, Mom. You're good enough on your own."

"I know," said Zona. Bree was right, she didn't. But she wasn't happy.

Martin went home to change into dry clothes. Bree decided it was time to go home and she, too, left, holding a package of frozen peas to her face.

"We still have food left. We may as well finish it," Louise said to Zona. "Except it's been sitting in the sun."

Yes, let's have a picnic, Zona thought sourly. "I'm tossing the quiche. How about peanut butter and jelly sandwiches?"

"That sounds perfect."

"Let me just dry off first," said Zona, and went upstairs to shed her wet clothes.

Once she was dry, she cleaned up the leftovers from the interrupted lunch and made her mother a sandwich.

"You're not having one?" Louise asked, when Zona joined her at the dining room table.

Thinking about what had happened and what would no longer be happening had stolen Zona's appetite. "I'm not hungry," she said.

She looked out the window at the house next door. The cop car was gone, and Alec's truck was still in the driveway. What was he doing? Probably patching up his back. Had Angela broken a rib?

Louise laid a comforting hand on Zona's arm. "I'm sorry, sweetie."

"He's not a bad man," said Zona.

Louise nodded. "But we've both seen what he comes with."

Zona sighed deeply. If she truly loved Alec, would it matter who his family was? In novels it wouldn't. The couple always overcame any obstacles so they could be together.

But that was novels. Zona's love life had to be a shared love one because she had a very scarred daughter to consider. It wasn't fair to Bree to bring more chaos into her life.

It wasn't fair that Zona had to make that choice, either. It wasn't fair that it had taken her two love losses to find Alec. But life wasn't fair. She wanted to cry. She was going to cry. She deserved to cry.

"Maybe it's all for the best that this happened," said Louise.

What a stupid saying that was. Zona vowed then and there never to use it on anyone.

"I'm going to go upstairs and lie down for a while, Mom. Will you be okay?"

Louise's eyes were filled with sympathy. "Of course, dear."

Zona went upstairs to her bedroom, shut the door, then flopped on the bed, buried her face in her pillow, and howled.

But self-pity was a waste of time and crying was giving her a headache. She gave up, got up, washed her face, and went back downstairs, determined to be a new woman. No more rushing into love, no more needing a man to prop herself up emotionally. Her daughter was right. She was strong enough on her own.

And she wasn't going to think about how much she'd been enjoying being with Alec. Or how his kisses had been fire. He was fire.

Fire was dangerous. She owed it to both her daughter and herself to level out her life. No more crazy ups and downs. Just a nice straight line.

Like what appeared on the heart monitor when you died.

She frowned. She'd been doing fine on her own before she got involved with Alec. She'd be fine without him. Eventually. As long as she didn't think about him.

Her cell phone rang. Alec.

"She'll go to jail, Zona."

"For what, a couple of months?" Zona scoffed.

"A couple of years at least. More time once assault is tacked on."

"But then she'll be out, and she'll be back."

"I've already talked to her sister. After she gets out, Ariel will take her to live with her in Montana. She'll be far out of the picture."

"She won't stay that way," Zona predicted.

"She will. She's only stuck around here because she thought she could keep leeching off me. She knows she can't now."

He made everything sound so easy. His stepsister would end up in an orange jumpsuit in front of a judge. She'd get hauled away and they'd live happily ever after. Happily-ever-afters were for fairy tales.

"Alec, I'm sorry. I really do want to be with you, but with everything that just happened I can't. It's not fair to my daughter. I've put her through enough."

"What about fair to yourself?" His voice was soft, reasonable.

"I guess I lose."

"I guess we both do."

She had nothing to say to that. There was nothing to say.

"Think about it, Zona. Please. Don't make a rash decision. Can you do that much for me? For us? We've started something good. Let's not let anyone take that away from us."

She could almost see Bree's angry face, hear her demanding, "What are you thinking, Mom?"

It's all for the best.

"Alec, I'm sorry," she said. Then she ended the call. And that officially ended what they'd started.

"AND TO THINK I missed it all," said Gilda the next day as she helped Louise steady herself in the shower.

"It was something," said Louise.

"It doesn't look good for your daughter and him."

"It's all for the best," said Louise.

"Does she think so?"

Louise sighed. "I doubt it."

"Well, let's hope she gets over him."

If a woman was truly in love, did she ever get over the man?

"And Martin," Gilda went on. "I bet you never thought he'd go all macho like that."

Now, there was a memory to bring a smile to Louise's face. "He jumped right into the fray without hesitating. It's a side of him I've never seen before."

"All men like a good brawl," said Gilda.

"But he didn't go over for a brawl. He went to help Zona and Bree."

"Well, gotta say, he's a cut above your average man," Gilda said, holding out a towel. "Has he got money?"

Louise grabbed it. "As if that matters."

"Money always matters," Gilda said.

"I'm sure he's got enough. Anyway, so do I." She may not have been rich, but she would never have to worry about being a bag lady, either.

"Well, then? What are you waiting for? He's been hanging around like a loyal old hound dog ever since I came to work for you."

"Long before that," said Louise.

"So maybe you quit dragging your feet and give him a little whoopsie-doopsy."

"Whoopsie-doopsy?"

"Boink, boink."

Louise laughed.

"At least kiss the poor slob and give him some hope," said Gilda.

Kissing Martin. Hmm. "He's still not what I had in mind,"

Louise said, thinking of the Texan stud from the cruise. What was his name, anyway?

"What, you want Kevin Costner?"

"My husband was a Kevin Costner," said Louise. "Martin's more of a . . . teddy bear."

"Teddy bears are cuddly. Myself, I've always liked a big man. Had the hots for John Goodman until he lost all that weight. Anyway, I think Martin's got potential."

"Well, he definitely impressed me yesterday," said Louise.

"So, get him in a lip lock and see how he impresses you," Gilda advised.

"Maybe I will," said Louise. She'd always rather liked John Goodman, too.

Louise wasn't getting much opportunity to see if she would like kissing a teddy bear. Martin was popping in regularly, as always, but by day Louise had Gilda, her faithful companion, hanging around and Bree dropping in on her to bug her about the book she'd lost all interest in writing, and Zona underfoot in the evenings, looking morose.

Finally, on Friday, with Gilda egging her on, she called Martin. "I'd like to get out of the house tonight and Gilda's busy," she said.

Gilda sat next to her, smirking.

"Do you fancy going out for a drive?"

"Sure. Where would you like to go?"

"Oh, I thought we could grab a bite to eat at Luca Bella and then maybe drive up to the city, Mulholland Drive."

"Mulholland Drive," he repeated slowly.

"It's historic," said Louise, and Gilda rolled her eyes. "And offers beautiful views of LA." More eye rolling. "I'm sure we can find a place to park and enjoy the view."

"Oh, brother," said Gilda in disgust.

"Louise, whatever you want," he said, sounding like a teen who'd just found a date for the prom.

"Not that I want to jump into anything," Louise added. "But, well, we should talk."

"And other things," Gilda whispered.

"I'll see if I can get us in at the restaurant," Martin said, and ended the call.

"Enjoy the view," Gilda repeated with a snort. "Honestly, Louise, looking at the view? Talking? When were you born, the eighteen hundreds?"

"I'm hedging my bets," Louise said primly.

"Then you should have just had him come over here. At least that way you could have sent him home. If things don't work out, you'll be stuck riding back with him."

"I didn't consider that," Louise said. It would be a long ride if things didn't go according to plan.

"Oh, well. At least you'll get dinner out of the deal," Gilda said blithely.

LOUISE DID, INDEED, get dinner out of the deal. But she found herself too nervous to eat. What had she been thinking? Martin was her friend. Kissing him would feel like kissing her brother.

"Louise, I'm wondering why all of a sudden you're proposing dinners out and parking on Mulholland Drive."

"Well, why not?" she said.

He leaned on the table and considered her. "What's this about? Really?"

She squirmed in her seat, fiddled with her wineglass. "I don't know, Martin. Maybe I'm coming to see you in a new light."

"All because I jumped into a pool like an idiot?"

She smiled at the memory of him helping Alec separate Zona from Alec's demented stepsister. "All because you were willing to do something. I never realized what a man of action you are."

"I'm not, really. I'm a peaceable man, a logical man. I'm not Arnold Schwarzenegger or Sylvester Stallone, and I have no intention of becoming an old gym rat, trying to look like them." She started to pout and he held up a hand to stop her from saying anything. "That's not to say that if you asked me to go on a diet and do some push-ups that I won't do it to please you. But in the end, I'm not . . . exciting or glamorous. I am who I am."

"And I'm coming to realize how much I appreciate who you are," she said. "I'm not suggesting we jump into bed."

"Although I wouldn't object to that," he said, a sly smile on his face. He reached across the table and ran his fingers up her hand. "You're a smart woman, Louise. I know I don't have to tell you how crazy I am about you, but let me. You're the first thing I think of when I get up in the morning and the last thing I think of before I go to sleep. I lived most of my life not knowing you, but I don't think I could live the rest of it without you. Even if this night doesn't work out the way I hope it will, I want you to know I'll always be there for you. As long as I have breath in my body, I'll be yours to command."

Louise blinked back sudden tears. Her own husband, whom she'd loved dearly, had never offered her such a speech. Martin, her kindhearted buddy, not only had a heart of gold, he had the soul of a poet.

"Oh, Martin, you amaze me," she said.

He smiled. "Let's take a drive and see if I can amaze you some more."

They did and he did.

It was funny, how much stronger Martin's arms were when they were around her than she'd realized. And good heavens, he knew just what to do with that smiley mouth of his.

"Martin," she said breathlessly, "you are . . ."

"Something?" he supplied. "My wife always said I was a good kisser."

"Your wife was right," she said, and went back for more.

The Man Next Door

ZONA GOT HOME from her shift as a HopIn driver before Louise. It looked like the date her mother had planned for Martin and herself had gone well. Either that or they'd gone off the road somewhere and were lying in a ditch.

Lovely thought, Zona, she scolded herself. She was now an Eeyore, determined to see the worst possible scenario for everything and anything.

Hardly surprising because life was just one big bundle of worst possible scenarios.

Darling was delighted to see her, and although he remembered his manners and didn't jump on her, there was much tail-wagging and excited barking.

"I know. You need to go for a walk," she said. "Let's get your leash."

The night was beautiful, the sky filled with glittering stars. A night for lovers. She looked wistfully at the house next door. Alec's truck sat in the driveway, but the porch light was off and no glimmer of light shined out from behind the living room curtains. What was he doing in there? Was he in bed? Was he thinking about her as much as she'd been thinking about him?

Didn't matter. Darling was ready to trot on over and say hi. She gave his leash a little tug. "No, Darling. We're not going that way," she said, and started them in the opposite direction.

30

ZONA USED UP THE LAST OF August avoiding Alec. He respected her decision, to both her relief and dismay, and didn't try to contact her. The red PT Cruiser was no longer anywhere to be seen. Alec's truck stayed parked in his driveway most evenings, except for the occasional weekday night. When he was probably out with his buddies, who were probably commiserating with him and telling him how unworthy Zona was of him. She'd left him. Just like his wife.

She finally ran into him at Vons, when she turned into the frozen pizza aisle, looking for an easy meal. He stopped his cart and stared at her like a thirsty man looking at a mirage.

Then he gave her a sad smile and nodded. "Zona." It came out wrapped in yearning.

"Alec," she said and could hear the same yearning in her own voice. "Well, now that we've proved we know each other's names." It was a lame joke. She stood there with her cart of lettuce and cheese and avocados, her brain as frozen as the pizza in the glass case beside her.

"I miss you," he said. "I hate where we are."

She bit her lip, nodded. So did she. "What's happening with your sister?"

"Jail," he said. "After she's served her sentence, she'll get shipped off to Montana. I'm going to try to get her some help. Therapy maybe. But she won't be coming back to California."

Zona nodded. "I'm glad you're rid of her." She wanted to say more. She couldn't seem to get the words out.

He pulled his cart up level with hers. "I know it's going to sound nuts, but I'm in love with you."

"We haven't known each other long enough," she protested, not wanting to admit to either him or herself that she felt the same way.

"You're wrong. It doesn't take that long to fall in love. It takes a lifetime to grow it, I get that. Even though we're through I keep hoping we could have a lifetime."

"Maybe we could have had that, if we'd met earlier. If . . ."

"If two other men hadn't messed you up so bad. I hate men who hurt women. They bruise you and then leave you broken."

He reached over and laid a hand on her arm and she felt the electric charge all the way to her heart. She bit down harder on her lip, didn't look at him. She couldn't.

He removed his hand. "I'm selling my house."

That did make her look at him. "What?" She couldn't be with him, didn't want to be with him, except she didn't want to see him go.

"Putting it on the market in a few days. I can't stay there, knowing you're next door, remembering what we almost had. Don't really need a house, anyway. I just bought that one because it was a steal. I'll flip it and move on." The look in his eyes burned into her heart. "I wish you were moving on with me."

"I wish I could. I really do. Where will you go?" she asked.

"Got a friend with a condo for rent in Azusa. I'm going to live there for a year while I figure out what to do next. Azusa's not that far if you change your mind," he said softly.

"Oh, Alec. Why did you have to move in next door?" she said miserably. This time it was her laying her hand on his arm.

"To torture you?" he joked and tried to smile again. It was

a lame joke, too, and he dropped the smile and the comic act. "Ah, Zona." He put a hand to her cheek.

An older woman pulled up next to them. "Do you two mind doing that somewhere else? Some of us would like to get a pizza."

"Sure. We're done anyway," said Alec. He gave Zona a kiss, just long enough to make her want more, wish they could have more, then he wheeled his cart away.

The woman gave a snort of disgust. "You kids these days. Can't live your lives without drama."

As if Zona had chosen all the drama she'd been living. She started to laugh. "Oh, my gosh. If you only knew." The laughing got crazier, then turned to sobs, and the woman grabbed her pizza and bolted. No words of comfort or encouragement. Not the motherly type, obviously.

Zona called Gracie on her way to the checkout stand. "I just saw Alec."

"Oh, dear," said Gracie.

"He's moving," Zona said, and started crying again.

"Where?"

"Azusa."

"Okay, he's not moving to another country."

"He might as well be. Did you know he's selling his house?"

"It just came through on the multiple listings."

"I don't know what to do."

"Zon, I'm not sure there's anything you can do," Gracie said gently. "Where are you now?"

"Vons."

"Drop off your groceries and meet me at the Metro. I'll buy you a drink and give you my unsolicited advice."

"The drink sounds good," Zona said. "Is it okay if I cry?"

"Of course. Why wouldn't it be?"

"Well, because I just scared a woman half to death in the frozen foods aisle."

"You won't scare anyone. The staff will probably all give you a hug."

"I just wish they could give me my life back," said Zona.

"Which part of it?"

Good question. She'd had plenty of sucky years. "The part where I had hope," Zona said. "Take me back in time to when I was eighteen." No, not that far. Just to when she was happy with Alec.

"Can't do that. But I'll take you to Metro," said Gracie.

An hour later they were seated at an outside table at the Metro Restobar with an order of truffle fries between them. Mojitos and moaning.

"I hate my life. Again," said Zona and glared at her glass.

Gracie pointed to it. "Half empty or half full?"

Zona downed the last of her drink. "Totally empty, thank you." She scowled. "I'm a cliché. Drowning my sorrows."

"You're only half a cliché. You're not eating a quart of ice cream."

"Give me time. I'll get there. Why did he have to move in next door?" Gracie had no answer and Zona continued. "Why did he have to turn out to be nice?"

"Because you needed nice?" Gracie suggested. "Maybe you still do."

Zona picked up a fry and bit down on it. "It would never work. His stepsister won't be behind bars forever. She's supposed to end up in Montana but who knows."

"Who knows if we won't have the big quake next week and all our houses fall down on us," said Gracie. "Who knows if the Second Coming won't happen tomorrow? Who knows if you will even live to see tomorrow?"

"Gee, thanks," Zona said with a frown.

"Nobody knows the future, Zona. You can't spend the rest of your life being afraid of it. What if you've already had your share of bad things happen and it's all good things waiting for you now? Do you want to miss out on that?"

Did she?

"Life's a gamble."

"Aack. No gambling metaphors!"

"It's true though. There are long shots and there are sure things. Even though I didn't get to meet him, from everything that's been happening, from everything you've told me, Alec looks more like a sure thing."

"I can't," Zona said. "Bree will have a fit."

"Bree isn't the one who's going to end up alone and unhappy. It's your life."

"But she's a big part of it, and I've messed her up big-time with all my love fails."

"Then maybe it's time she saw you having a love win. If Alec is as solid as he sounds."

Zona took a deep breath. "I think he is."

"Well, then? What are you waiting for, a cosmic sign? A thunderbolt?"

"Maybe," said Zona.

She returned home to find her mom and Martin happily cuddled on the couch, overdosing on *Deathline*. At least someone's love life was looking healthy.

"Join us," her mother invited.

Happy as Zona was for her mother she didn't think she could take a supersized serving of ooey-gooey in her present state of mind. "I have some eBay stuff to do," she lied, and went to her bedroom. Her Angel Ram finance book was waiting.

She opened to her next chapter: Security Versus Risk.

"Sounds like my love life," she grumbled.

Life is full of risk. We take a risk just crossing the street. But we take that risk because we know it's a low risk. We have traffic laws to keep us safe, we have a traffic signal telling us when to walk. With money, as with all aspects of life, you put your safeguards in place and then, when the signal says walk, you step out and walk.

Good advice. For money. When it came to love, Zona definitely needed a signal that told her she could put her foot out. And it needed to be a big, flashing walk signal, a sign from heaven.

Of course, nothing came. She didn't find any treasure with some cosmic meaning when she hit the garage sales the next day. No ceramic heart, no little wall hanging with Follow Your Heart painted on it. No HopIn passengers that night had any profound remarks to share about love. Oh, well.

LOUISE AND MARTIN had gone for a drive Sunday evening and it wasn't until Zona was on her way to bed that Louise finally clomped in the door.

"You two are sure becoming cozy," Zona observed. At least someone in the family was enjoying life.

"We are," said Louise. "There's so much more to Martin than I ever realized. Funny, isn't it, how blind you can be."

Was that some kind of sign? Probably not. "I'm going to bed," Zona said. She sounded grumpy but so what? Grumpy was an improvement over miserable.

SHE WOKE UP that night to a strange bright flash outside her bedroom window. What on earth? She shot out of bed and looked out the window. There it was again. Lightning flashing, illuminating the house next door. A few seconds later a rumble of thunder followed.

But no rain came. A dry thunderstorm. The sky rumbled

at her one more time and she saw a flash in the distance. This was creepy. This was . . . a sign?

"Did you hear the thunder last night?" she asked Louise as she served her an early cup of coffee before Gilda's arrival.

"Thunder?" Her mother looked puzzled.

"You didn't hear it?"

Louise shook her head.

"I thought I heard thunder. And I saw lightning."

Louise looked out the window at the clear, blue sky. "Everything looks dry as usual," she said. "Did you hear anything, Darling?" she asked.

Darling barked a happy, *Who cares?*

Okay, had Zona only dreamed that? Maybe she had.

But what if she hadn't?

She didn't look Louise's way as she pulled her premade lunch from the fridge. "Mom, what if I made a mistake with Alec?" Stupid to ask. She already knew what her mom thought about him.

Louise didn't say anything for a very long moment. Then she asked, "Do you think you did?"

"Do *you* think I did? I mean, you weren't sure all along."

"You going to listen to a woman who thought he was an axe murderer? What do I know?"

"When you're not on Jessica Fletcher overload? A lot. Seriously, I don't want to get burned a third time. But I already feel burned. I want him and yet . . ."

"You're afraid." Louise sighed heavily. "I don't know what to say, Zona. I'm afraid for you. Each time your heart got broken, mine broke for you. You know I want you to find someone who will be good to you. Good for you. But I don't want to see you hurt, and we both know this man has . . . baggage."

"I have baggage. And I'm already hurt, Mom."

"I know you are, sweetie. But . . ." She cut herself off.

"Life's short. I guess neither of us wants to spend it in limbo. But I want you to be very sure."

"I thought I'd had a sign."

"A sign?"

Zona shook her head. "Never mind." There was no more time for a shrink session. She was going to be late for work.

"Well, you'll sort it out. Speaking of sorting things out," Louise began.

"It looks like you and Martin have been doing some sorting out."

"You could say that," Louise said.

"I'm glad, Mom. I want to hear more, but right now I've got to get going. I'm going to be late for work."

Louise looked a little disappointed.

"I expect a full report when I get home," Zona said. "Gilda should be here any minute." She kissed her mother on the cheek. "I'll see you later. And thanks, Mom, for listening. I love you."

"Love you more," said Louise.

It was good to be loved. By your mother, your daughter, your friends.

What about by a certain man? Did she dare take the risk?

"I DON'T KNOW," said Gilda when Louise shared her concerns over Zona. "Everybody's got somebody crazy in their family."

"But this woman . . ." Louise shook her head.

Gilda blew off her concerns with a shrug. "This woman is nothing. Did I ever tell you about my cousin? He got into drugs and went all paranoid. Shot a friend in the stomach and went to jail for years. He's out now, but he's a hermit. Nobody sees him."

"Somehow, I don't see this girl becoming a hermit once she gets out."

"No, but after all this she'll see the well's run dry. She'll move on, find some other family member to mooch off of and make miserable. That's what users do."

"Maybe you're right," said Louise.

"I still think he's kind of a jerk though. Even if he did teach Darling to sit," Gilda added. "He wasn't very nice about the whole bone thing. The man has no sense of humor."

THE FOR-SALE SIGN was up in Alec's yard when Zona got home. She didn't bother to pull her car into the driveway. She kept on going right to the grocery store. There she purchased an entire half gallon of cookies and cream ice cream. There was nothing wrong with clichés.

She came home to find her mom and Gilda busily planning Louise's cast-off celebration. "We can have it the weekend after Labor Day," Louise said.

"Isn't your cast coming off before that?" asked Zona as she stowed away the ice cream.

"It is, but Martin and I are taking a little trip to San Francisco to celebrate," Louise said, looking smug.

"Pretty soon I'll be out of a job," said Gilda.

"But not out of a friendship," Louise assured her. "You will come to the wedding, right?"

Zona dropped onto the nearest chair. "Wedding? What? When?"

"Where," added Louise with a wink. "I wanted to tell you this morning, but there wasn't time."

Because she'd been too busy counseling her self-absorbed daughter. "You should have told me to shut up."

"Okay, shut up," Louise joked. "We're getting married right here in our backyard. I'm thinking early October. I love fall."

"Well, that's fast," said Zona. "Oh, wait. You've been stalling that poor man forever. It's about time. I'm happy for you, Mom."

"Happy ending. One down, two to go," Louise said to her.

Zona sighed. "I think Bree's a lost cause."

"Maybe you're not," said Louise. "Maybe you'll get that sign you're looking for."

BREE WAS SUMMONED for dinner so Louise could make her big announcement. She did it over Zona's black bean brownies and the ice cream Zona had bought.

"Wow, Gram, that's awesome."

"I want you and your mother to be my bridesmaids," said Louise. "I found these really pretty dresses we can get in orange."

"Orange?" Bree looked horrified.

"Okay, we'll find other color options," said Louise.

"If you want us to wear orange, we'll wear orange," Zona promised and shot Bree the famous Mother Look. *Do it or die, kid.*

Bree shrugged and helped herself to another brownie. "Where are you guys going to live?"

"I'm going to move in to Martin's house," said Louise.

Selling her childhood home. The idea hit Zona like a gut punch. Of course, it would be the smart thing to do, but she suddenly felt like a shipwreck victim who'd just lost her grip on the last piece of the wreckage. She was Jack in *Titanic*, turning blue in icy waters.

"You're going to sell the house." The words came out dull and heavy as lead. Zona went to the freezer for more ice cream. A quarter gone already. She shouldn't have shared.

"No, it's going to go to you," said Louise. "If you want it."

The ice cream fell to the floor with a thud. "Mom!"

Bree and Darling raced for the ice cream. Bree barely beat him to it.

Ice cream forgotten, Zona stumbled back to her chair. "This house is worth a lot. You can't just give it away."

"To my only daughter who will inherit it after I croak? Why on earth not? You need it now, not after I've finally packed it in when I'm a hundred," Louise said with a grin. "Martin's going to help me figure out how best to do that." She sobered. "Unless you don't want it?"

A house. Free and clear. And not just any house. Her house, the house she'd grown up in, had slumber parties in. The very symbol of love and comfort. Zona sat in her chair, staring at her mother, trying to wrap her mind around the amazing news.

"I think she's in shock. Quick, give her that ice cream," Louise said to Bree.

"Oh, Mom," Zona said. She swiped at the tears racing down her cheeks and hugged her mother. "I don't know what to say."

"Say you want it."

Zona fell back onto her chair and smiled at her mother, who was looking a little blurry thanks to Zona's teary vision. "Of course I do!" she replied, half laughing, half crying. She took the ice cream from her daughter. "If you need a place to stay, you can move in here," she said to Bree.

"It's okay. I like adulting."

"Just as well. I'm thinking there might come a point when you want to move in someone else and want this place all to yourself," Louise said.

Zona bit down on her lip and hugged the container of ice cream. And thought again about that lightning she wasn't sure she'd seen.

"Gram," Bree scolded.

"Bree, dear, there's going to come a time when your mother will move forward and find someone," Louise said.

Bree looked suspiciously at Zona. "Not that someone. Mom, his stepsister."

"Will be locked away," said Zona.

Bree's brows lowered. "But not forever," she said in a voice of doom.

"Let's not put our lives on hold for some nebulous day in the future when something might happen," Louise said. "You need to let your mother make her own decisions. She's taken enough hits. She's wise enough now to know what bullets to dodge."

Am I? Zona asked herself. Where was that darned sign when you needed it?

"Now, you two, finish that ice cream and let's talk about my wedding," said Louise.

Bree snatched the ice cream back from Zona, sat down, and dug into it. "You two are driving me cray-cray." But after that she didn't say anything more. Instead, she weighed in on the wedding plans, starting with finding a dress she liked. "That shade of brown looks good on the model so it will look good on us," she said, turning her phone so Zona could see.

Zona was still in shock and could only nod and smile and say, "Sure." A wedding in the backyard. Of her house. Wow. Cupid wasn't coming through with any firm confirmation, but this kind gift from her mother was certainly an assurance that her financial future was going to be secure.

Martin showed up half an hour later and was given a brownie and apologies that the ice cream was all gone.

He patted his middle. "That's okay. I'm watching what I eat. Want to take off a few pounds before October," he added, and winked at Louise.

"Congrats, Martin," Bree said, and hugged him. "Welcome to our reality show family."

"Glad to be part of it," he told her. He bent and kissed Louise. "How's my darling?"

Darling barked and wagged his tail, making everyone laugh.

"We're both great," Louise said, reaching up a hand to take his. "Sit down and we'll tell you all about our wedding plans."

"Can I at least get you something to drink?" Zona offered. "Lemonade, an Arnold Palmer?"

"Just water," he said. He took the chair next to Louise and kissed her again, then said, "And kisses. That's all I need," making Louise giggle.

"You two are enough to put us in a diabetic coma," Bree teased.

"Good thing you're going to become a nurse. You can save us if that happens," said Louise.

Bree smiled. "I still can't believe I'm finally going to get to start school."

"And finish it," Louise told her. "Martin and I are going to give you the rest of the money you need so you and your mother can quit worrying. And driving strangers all over town," she added, looking at Zona.

Now it was Bree gaping in shock.

"Oh, not in one chunk. We'll dole it out as you need it," Louise said. "Merry Christmas early."

"Gram, you don't have that much money," Bree protested.

"I do," said Martin. "Always been a saver. I can spare enough to help my new granddaughter get through nursing school."

Bree looked from one to the other. "I can't take your money, you guys. You need it for your old age."

"Between the two of us, we have enough for our old age," Louise assured her. "And if we run out, Martin will get a job as a greeter at Walmart," she added, and winked at him.

Bree was still looking dubious.

"We'll be fine," Martin assured her. "Not every millionaire drives a BMW or lives in a mansion."

"Wow," Bree said. Then she jumped up with a squeal and ran to hug both Louise and Martin. "I'll pay for all my books and living expenses," she promised.

"And provide free nursing care," Louise said, hugging her back.

"Absolutely," Bree said.

"I still can't believe it," she said to Zona as Zona walked her to her car later. "Did you know about the tuition thing?"

Zona shook her head. "I had no idea. I didn't even know about the wedding until I got home from work. And I sure didn't know about the house. Your grandmother is one big bundle of surprises today."

Bree's happy expression got overtaken by one of concern. "Mom. Are you wanting to get together with Alec?"

Without a cosmic sign, no. Sadly, depressingly, no. "Don't worry. I won't. No matter what your Gram says."

"But do you want to?" Bree persisted.

Wanting had nothing to do with it. "I'm not going to do anything to hurt you," said Zona. Much as she missed him, much as she wished things could be different. She sighed inwardly.

"That's not what I asked. I know you were into him."

"I was, but I can't drag you through any more turmoil."

Bree took in a deep breath. "I hate to see you go through any more crap, Mom."

Zona nodded. It was settled. She had a house. She'd learn to love living in it alone.

They stood together a moment in silence. Bree was the first to break it. "But I don't have to worry about him getting my college money. And it won't be my car getting keyed if his sister comes back."

A little seed of hope sprouted. "Stepsister," Zona corrected.

"Creepsister," said Bree with an eye roll. "I don't want to see you get hurt again, but you already are, aren't you?" Zona started on a half-hearted protest that she wasn't, but Bree stopped her. "I can see it. You act like you're fine, but your smile is off. Sometimes you look like the first victim in the zombie apocalypse. I hate that for you."

"Don't worry about me," said Zona. "You just live your own life and be happy."

Bree's mouth corkscrewed. "I haven't been happy all summer."

"I noticed," Zona teased.

"I hate men! Look what they do to us."

"Yeah, they make us miserable. Except for the good ones. Your Gram's found a good one."

"Maybe you have, too. Maybe you should give it a try."

Zona had to have misheard. She stared at her daughter.

"I mean, what if Gram's right? I don't want it to be my fault if you're alone all your life and end up a crazy cat lady."

"I like cats."

"You like Alec James, too. And at least we know he's not an abuser or a murderer. And he did fix your car."

"Are you sure?"

Bree bit her lip. "Not really. But I don't want to be stuck with the blame if you get any more depressed. He doesn't gamble, does he?"

"I don't think that's his thing."

Bree nodded. "Well, then, go for it."

There it was, the sign. The signal. *Walk*. More like run.

"Just don't marry him for about fifty years."

Zona laughed. "Fifty?"

"Okay, ten. At least wait a couple. Let me get through nursing school, okay?"

"Okay."

"And be careful. And tell him if he hurts you I'll come after him with a needle full of something very bad."

Zona laughed again. They hugged and Bree drove off.

And Zona looked at the empty house next door and, for the first time, didn't want to cry.

31

"**DID YOUR DAUGHTER GIVE HER PERMISSION** for you to have a life?" Louise asked when Zona rejoined her and Martin. "As if I can't guess from that grin on your face."

"She did."

"Good," Louise said with a nod. "It looks like things are finally working out for the Hartman women."

"But are you sure about this generosity? Are both of you sure?"

"We are," Martin answered.

"As far as the house goes, I can't think of anything nicer than it staying in the family. It's been hard to see you struggling for so long. I'm glad I can finally do something," Louise said.

"Finally? You've been there all along. Helping me pick up the pieces when things ended with Luke, then taking me in after everything with Gary imploded. Mom, I don't know how I would have managed without you."

"Just fine, that's how. You're a strong woman. Now, I suggest you get busy and track down the love of your life. I think I want to go over to my future home and talk about redecorating," she said, smiling at Martin.

"Heaven help you, Martin," Zona said.

"Heaven already did," he said, and squeezed Louise's hand.

They left and Zona got busy on her laptop. Was it too late for her to find the kind of happiness her mother had found?

She hoped not. She did a search and found the location of the office for Better Builders. It was a good name for a company. It was . . . a sign.

ZONA TOOK OFF from work the second it was time for her lunch break, driving to the strip mall in Azusa where Better Builders had its office. It was small. On one wall of the cramped reception area hung a copy of the famous black-and-white picture of workers sitting on a beam on a skyscraper in progress in New York, eating their lunches. Another held a charcoal drawing of a house, maybe one Alec had built. By a door that probably led to Alec's office was a rough-hewn reception desk complete with receptionist, a lean thirty-something man with a coif, wearing jeans and a pale green shirt with micro polka dots and a sage-green tie. The sleeves of his shirt were rolled up, which made him look both hardworking and ready for a magazine shoot.

He looked up from his laptop and gave her a professional smile. "May I help you?"

"I hope so. I need to find Alec." She knew it wouldn't be in his office. His truck was nowhere in the parking lot.

"He's not here. He's at one of our sites. May I give him a message? Or would you like to wait?"

"I can't." Okay, she sounded desperate, and he looked suddenly wary. She let out a frustrated breath. "It's . . . personal."

Now he looked protective. He must have known about Angela.

"I'd be happy to give him a message," said the man.

"I need to tell him myself." And now she sounded more desperate and probably crazy. "Okay, I know I sound a little, um, well, it's just that." *Spit it out already.* "I broke up with him and it was stupid."

The man nodded knowingly. "Ah, that explains so much. He's been a bear. Wouldn't say why."

"I'm why," Zona admitted. "I need to fix this."

"You've got that right," the man said. He grabbed a Post-it note and wrote on it. "It's not far. Up in Rowland Heights."

Zona took it. "Thanks."

"No, thank *you*. Maybe he'll become human again."

He always had been human. Just wounded.

"By the way, my name's Joe. I'm betting I'll see more of you in the future."

"I don't bet," Zona said with a smile. "So this better be a sure thing."

She hurried to her car and headed for the high-end part of Covina. It came with expensive homes, gorgeous views, and a golf course. Whatever Alec was working on there, it probably was amazing.

Sure enough, she wound up at a half-complete mansion that promised at least four bedrooms and had a driveway large enough for a couple of stretch limos. Workers in hard hats wearing dusty jeans, T-shirts, and sweat hammered on walls or ran noisy saws or walked around carrying long planks of wood over their shoulders. And there in front of it all stood Alec, a set of blueprints in his hand, talking to another man and pointing to who knew what.

He hadn't seen her drive up. Would he be able to hear what she wanted him to hear above all the noise? There was only one way to find out.

She took advantage of a lull in the sawing, cranked up her car's sound system, and started the song playing. ABBA began singing "Take a Chance on Me." She picked her way past debris as fast as she could to get to him in time for him to hear the heart of the message.

He did. He turned in confusion. Then he saw her and his eyes opened wide. He shoved the blueprints against the other man's chest and closed the distance between them, hauled her to him, and kissed her like a desperate actor auditioning for a part.

The kiss ended to wolf whistles and applause. "Get back to work, you clowns," he called, and led her away toward her car, ABBA still serenading them. "Please tell me that song means what I think it does and I didn't just make a fool of myself."

She smiled. "It does. I've been so afraid to take a chance, but I don't think being with you is a gamble. I think it's a sure thing. I'm sorry I've been so afraid. I'm sorry it took me so long to get brave. I'm—"

"I'm sorry you're making this speech so long," he said, cutting her off, and pulled her back to him and kissed her again. "Oh, man, I've missed you," he said against her mouth.

"I've missed you, too," she said.

He smiled down at her. "Have you had lunch?"

"This is lunch," she said. "I have to get back to work."

"Dinner then. I'll pick you up at six." His brows pulled down. "Your mom okay with this?"

"Yes, she is. Except, I need to ask you one important thing. Please be honest."

"Always. What?"

"You don't gamble, do you?"

He laughed. "I don't even play Mega Millions. I took math. I know the odds. And trust me, when it comes to us, they're in our favor."

Best gambling metaphor ever.

ALEC NOT ONLY took Zona out to dinner that night. He also included Louise and Martin and Bree. Bree grilled him mercilessly about past women, what his plans were to keep his stepsister out of his life, then poked around, looking for bad habits.

"I swear when I'm mad, and I yell."

"So we heard," Louise murmured.

"That's it? There's got to be more," Bree pushed.

"I bite my nails."

"And you're not very patient," pointed out Louise, which

made Zona blush. Her mother had been one of the ones who'd tried his patience.

"You do have a temper, Alec. Admit it," Louise said.

"You're right. What can I say? I got stuff I need to work on."

"Don't we all?" said Zona.

He smiled at her. "We'll work on stuff together."

WORK HAD NEVER been so fun, squeezing in a couple of hikes with Darling as chaperone (Louise finally consenting to let him out of her sight), visits to favorite restaurants, bowling with Alec's buddies. And a night of virtual bowling at Gracie's house with her boys. And hot kisses.

Alec kept the for-sale sign on his front yard, deciding that even though he liked living right next to Zona he didn't like the house. "Right now I'm fine where I am, only a few minutes away from you. If I decide to get another house, I'd rather start fresh somewhere else," he'd said. "With someone special," he'd added, taking her hand and making her heart turn over.

"How do you feel about the house next door?" she'd asked, and told him about her mother's gift. "No bad vibes there, I promise."

His comment that he wanted to be anywhere she wanted to be was exactly what she hoped to hear. "We can spy on the new neighbors together," he'd cracked, making her laugh.

Meanwhile, the lack of proximity didn't keep him away. Oh, yes, life was good.

Alec was on hand at Louise's cast-off party, making margaritas for one and all while Martin manned the barbecue.

"So what do you think?" Zona asked Bree as they dug into seconds of Louise's fruit salad.

"He may work out," Bree said. "But no rushing, right?"

"Right," Zona agreed.

"One wedding in a year is enough," Bree added.

AND WHAT A wedding it was. Alec and his buddies set up the multitude of chairs in the backyard, and Louise's pals Susan and Carol helped decorate, adorning the rows with red and orange bows and a multitude of silk flowers. The stage where the couple would say their vows was adorned with pumpkins and vases of fall flower arrangements. Gilda insisted on paying for Louise's bridal bouquet, and Zona and Bree spent the entire weekend before baking the requested pumpkin cupcakes.

Louise looked ready for a fashion shoot in her cream-colored cocktail dress and Martin, who had lost twenty pounds, looked properly svelte in his new suit. Zona and Bree both walked down the aisle with her. The two granddaughters she'd inherited acted as flower girls and Darling was the ring bearer. Thanks to Alec, he was very well-behaved. He sat between Martin and Louise like a good boy during the ceremony, hardly begged at all during the reception, and didn't jump on anyone.

Toasts were made, well-wishes were given, and so were plenty of gift cards. "Where are you taking your bride for your honeymoon?" asked one of their neighbors.

"We're going on a cruise," Martin said, smiling at Louise. "To Hawaii."

THE WEDDING WAS one big lovefest. Gram was so happy she should have been in a Hallmark movie. Apocalypse Zombie Mom was gone, and her smiles reached her eyes again. Alec was smiling, too, and looking at Mom like she was found treasure. Well, she was, and he'd better remember it.

Bree was glad both her mom and her Gram were so happy. But watching them, and all the other people at the party, she felt . . . apart from it all. There but not present.

She knew why. Fen wasn't there with her. She didn't want

to, but she missed him. Who was he with now? Had to be with someone. A guy like Fen wouldn't stay alone forever.

Alone. She kept telling herself that alone was good. Alone was safe.

You never realized how much alone sucked until you were alone in a group of happy people.

Did she want to be safe or did she want to be happy?

The question continued to bounce around in her brain.

"Your Gram sure is happy," said a voice at her elbow. Gilda.

"Yeah, I'm glad. She deserves it."

Gilda nodded. "Yep, she does. You know, I had men interested in me."

Gilda was a box with legs. Inside that box was a know-it-all . . . not so bad once you got to know her. Still, it was hard to imagine Gilda as a heartbreaker.

"How come you're alone then?" Bree asked.

"Hey, at this age men only want a nurse or a purse."

"Not Martin," pointed out Bree.

"Yeah, Louise got lucky," Gilda said with a smile. "He's okay. Every once in a while, you stumble on one who is. They're rare though, about as easy to find as a diamond on the beach. Still, there's a few out there, I suspect. I haven't seen one in years."

Bree had. Fen was a good guy. School had started for him again. Was he home for the weekend? His birthday was the next day.

She looked to where a few cupcakes remained, chewed on her lip, considering.

"Go ahead, take another cupcake before they're gone," said Gilda. "Cupcakes are like those rare men. You have to get one while you can 'cause they go fast. In fact, I think I'll get another right now. Cupcake, that is."

Bree followed her to the cupcake table and grabbed one. Then she went to where her Gram stood, holding hands with

Martin, and visiting with his daughter. "I'm going to take off, Gram," she said.

"Oh, but you have to stay and catch the bouquet," Gram protested.

"Don't worry. I don't need it," Bree said. She hugged her grandmother and her new grandfather, said goodbye to her new cousins, then went to say goodbye to her mom.

"You're leaving already?"

"I need to go see someone."

Mom looked at the cupcake in her hand and raised an eyebrow.

"See you later," Bree said, and kissed her.

Fifteen minutes later she was standing in front of Fen's house. It was already decorated for Halloween, with a collection of Pinterest-worthy carved pumpkins on both sides of the front porch. A fall wreath hung on the front door.

Several cars were parked out front, including his Jeep. Probably an early birthday party was in progress. His whole family would be there. The family who knew her and knew she'd broken up with him twice. This had been a stupid idea.

She sat in her car, staring first at the house, then the cupcake. *They go fast.*

Maybe Fen was gone now, already hooked up with another woman. There was only one way to find out. She took a deep breath, got out of her car and walked up to the front door. By the time she rang the doorbell, her heart had almost banged its way out of her chest.

His mother opened the door and blinked in surprise at the sight of her. She smiled. It looked forced. "Hello, Bree."

"Hi, Mrs. Clarke. I was wondering if Fen's home." She held up the cupcake. A lone stupid cupcake. She was an idiot. "I know it's his birthday tomorrow."

"Yes, it is. We're just having a little family gathering while his brother's in town."

And here was Bree, dressed for prom in her stupid bridesmaid dress. What drug was she on that she hadn't thought to change?

"Come in," said Mrs. Clarke, and stepped aside so Bree could enter. She didn't sound all that welcoming, but at least she hadn't shut the door in Bree's face.

Bree followed her down the hall and into the Clarkes' supersized great room. Leather furniture, stone fireplace, which was more for decoration than use. Balloons dancing over a chair in the corner and a pile of opened presents lying beside it. The small remains of a birthday cake sat on a long table, along with an array of mostly empty appetizers plates. Some paper plates and napkins lay along the granite kitchen counter. People were seated, talking and laughing, and kids ran in and out of the sliding glass door. Salsa music was blasting. It all reminded Bree of the many times she'd been at this house for parties as a teenager.

And there, coming in from the back patio, was Fen, wearing jeans and a shirt, backlit by evening sun, looking like a Greek god. He stopped at the sight of her and stood there, forever, just looking at her, and she squeezed the cupcake so hard its frosted top blew off and fell to the floor. *Shit!*

"Sorry," she said to his mom, and bent to pick it up.

But then he was right there with her, kneeling on the floor. She scooped up the top and put it back on. "I brought you a cupcake for your birthday," she said. "Three-second rule?"

He half smiled. "Since when do you bake?"

"I'm learning. It's from my Gram's wedding. She got married today."

"Yeah? I guess that explains the dress." He took the mangled cupcake from her. "Thanks. I'm surprised you remembered my birthday. Figured you'd forgotten all about me."

"Had you forgotten all about me?" she asked.

One of his little nephews raced up to him. "Can I have that?" he asked.

"Sorry, buddy. It's mine," Fen said.

"You going to eat it?" Bree asked.

"No, but maybe I'll keep it as a souvenir." He stood up. So did she. "Why are you here, Bree?"

"Because . . . because."

"Spit it out. You can do it."

"I miss you."

"I miss you, too."

"Can we . . . talk?"

"We are talking."

He wasn't making this easy.

His mother had gotten momentarily distracted, but she was back. "It looks like you're on your way to a party," she said. Surprisingly, she didn't add, "Don't let us keep you."

"My Gram got married today," Bree said.

"How nice for her." That was it. No invitation to stay and have something to eat.

"Could I talk to Fen for a minute?" Bree asked her.

Mrs. Clarke didn't look happy about the idea. Who could blame her? But she nodded.

Fen led the way back to the front door and they stepped onto the porch, shutting out the noise. He leaned against the door and folded his hands across his chest. "Bree, I'm not sure what you want from me."

"I want a second chance. Please tell me you're not with someone."

"Why?"

Of all the answers he could have given her, this wasn't the one she'd expected. "What do you mean?"

"Why? I want to know why you want to be with me when you know I want more than you want to give."

"Because I can't stand being without you," she cried. "I've been wrecked all summer."

"Yeah, well, I haven't exactly been happy."

"It didn't stop you from going out," she said.

"Didn't stop you, either. Look, I'm trying to move on. You left me shattered, Bree. I've been working all summer to try to get over that. I don't think I can take it if you do it again."

"I don't want to do it. I want to get past being so messed up. I want what's in there," she said, motioning to the door. "And I want it with you. Please give me another chance. And don't let me blow it."

"Aww, Bree," he said, and pulled her up against him so hard she almost got whiplash.

It wasn't a gentle kiss. It was filled with a determination and power and all that stupid stuff she'd read about when she was young and thought that true love existed. Maybe it did. Maybe it could.

He broke off and ran a hand through her hair, loosening the silk flowers pinned in it. "Do you know why I couldn't move when I first saw you tonight?"

She shook her head, held her breath.

"Because I thought I was hallucinating. When I stood in front of that birthday cake and Mom said, 'Make a wish,' I wished you were here. Wished we were back together. I knew it would never come true though. And then, there you were. If I hadn't just now kissed you, I'd still think I was seeing things."

She stared at his shoulder, couldn't bring herself to look him in the eye. "I'm still afraid."

"But you're here. What brought you here?"

Hope. "Gram got married, to her neighbor. They've been friends for years and then she just decided. My mom's trying again, too. They're both so happy." She did venture looking up, looking for understanding in his eyes, for encouragement. "I want that, too. I don't want to be angry and bitter and alone."

"I don't want you to be. I swear, Bree. You can trust me. You can trust us."

Could she? What if this was one big mistake? Her lower lip began to tremble, and tears made a stinging attack on her eyes.

"We'll get you through this. I'll be there for you," he promised. Then he kissed her again. This time slowly, softly, as if he was afraid he'd break her.

She could get broken. It was still possible. "We have to take this slow," she said.

"We will."

"I mean really slow, slower than a dying slug."

"Maybe a little faster than that. I'd like to have kids before I'm fifty," he joked. Then sobered. "We're going to be okay, Bree. Better than okay. We're going to be great." He opened the door. "Come on back inside. Let's celebrate with the family for a while. Then we'll go someplace, just the two of us, and celebrate. Slowly," he added. "Like two dying slugs."

She laughed and followed him inside.

THE PARTY WAS OVER, the guests gone and the cleanup done, and Zona and Alec sat on the couch of what would be their future home, him rubbing her feet. She'd swapped out her dress for jeans and he'd shed his tie and loosened his shirt. A hint of his woodsy cologne still hung around and so did the smile he'd been wearing all day.

"You know, you're downright nice to be around when you're happy," she teased.

"I intend to be nice the rest of my days. And happy. How about you?"

"What do you think?"

"I think we should be next," he said.

Zona's brows drew together. "Next?"

"You know, cupcakes and champagne. Maybe Louise will loan us Darling for a ring bearer."

Oh, no. Zona sat up, pulling her leg off his lap. "I can't. It's too soon."

"I didn't mean tomorrow," he said, looking hurt.

"That's good because I promised Bree."

He frowned. "Promised her what, exactly?"

"That I wouldn't do anything until she'd graduated from nursing school."

"How long is that?"

"It's a two-year program." Two years did sound like a long time. Zona frowned, also.

"Okay, so no getting married for a while."

"We need time anyway," she said.

He nodded, looked thoughtful. "Did she say anything about . . . diamonds? Or sleepovers?" he added with a sly smile.

"Well, no," Zona said, and smiled back.

"Then maybe I can wait for the cupcakes and champagne. You're worth waiting for and I'm never letting you go."

Maybe there was something to those romance novels after all, she thought as he drew her to him for a kiss.

Except no words could describe the joy, the happiness, and the promise of that kiss.

The Woman Next Door

THE NEW NEIGHBOR MOVED IN NEXT door to Zona right before Thanksgiving. Belinda Burns was middle-aged, pleasantly plump, and pretty. She was recently widowed, new to the area.

"I've lost two husbands," she shared with Louise and Zona as they sat in Zona's living room, eating sugar cookies and drinking tea.

"I'm so sorry," said Louise. "Do you mind me asking what happened?"

"My first husband died at fifty-four. He had a heart attack."

"I'm so sorry," Zona said.

"What about your second husband?" asked Louise.

Zona suddenly felt uneasy.

"I'm afraid he died quite tragically. It was our second anniversary, and we were on a cruise."

"Oh, no. What happened?" said Louise. She leaned forward, all ears.

Oh, good Lord. Zona raised two eyebrows, sending Louise a message. *Cut it out.*

Louise refused to look her way.

"Food poisoning, I'm afraid," said Belinda.

"Food poisoning," Louise echoed. "How awful."

It was time to change the subject. "How about another cookie?" Zona said, reaching for the plate.

"Oh, no. They were delicious, but I should be going," said their guest. "I still have so much to unpack."

"I bet she does," said Louise when Zona returned from seeing her to the door. "Stocks, bonds, all kinds of things she probably inherited after two husbands conveniently died. Did you see the size of those rocks on her hands?"

"Mom!"

"You have to admit, it's all very suspicious," said Louise.

Zona sighed. Oh, boy. Here they went again.

★ ★ ★ ★ ★

Acknowledgments

A book may get written alone but thank God it doesn't get finished alone. Which is a very good thing for me! I am so grateful to April Osborn, my editor, for all the hard work she put in on this one. April, you are a genius. And to my agent, Paige Wheeler, who is always working hard on my behalf and has a fine eye for fixing a story. You're the best! I so appreciate the team at MIRA and the wonderful art department, who gave me this great cover. It didn't only make me smile when I first saw it. It made me laugh. Thank you!

I'm also indebted to Cheron Wittman, PA-C, and Karl Hilsenberg, PA-C, for trying their best to explain to me the gory details of broken legs. Anything I got wrong is certainly not their fault. I sure hope to never have to find out firsthand what that's like! I also want to give a shout-out to the women who shared the stories of their own financial challenges with me. My hope for you is that like Zona, you, too, can work your way to healing and a better life.